OF THORNS AND WINGS
THE DRAGON AND THE DEVOURING TREE
PART 2

HAPPILY EVER AFTER DARK

DARVA GREEN

CONTENT NOTE

This is a fractured Sleeping Beauty/ Robin Hood retelling that incorporates a lot of dark fairytale elements. It contains content intended for readers 18 & up and some potentially upsetting themes and topics.

Content notes include: graphic sex, captivity, burnings, domestic abuse (not between the main characters) implied SA, confinement, murder, violence, grief, perceived loss of a bonded animal companion, parental loss, graphic injuries, alcohol consumption, death of children (off page, mentioned)

Please take care <3

PROLOGUE
CANDIDE. LOLLISHIRE'S COUNTRYSIDE.
EIGHT YEARS AGO.

Wisps of smoke curl into the lavender sky, the scent harkening back to a more violent twilight.

We can never escape the fear we felt the night of that fateful May Day feast. It follows us no matter how far we run from the King's City.

I catch the tick in Diana's jaw and wonder if she's thinking about the same thing.

"I told her to be back by sundown." She lifts the muddy hem of her dress as we stomp up the hill. "She knows better than to stay out this late."

Anxiety has rubbed her nerves raw, turning her mood prickly. I know how she's feeling. There's nothing more troubling than having a piece of your heart grow outside of your body and develop a will of its own.

A stubborn will at that.

"And you know better than to expect her to listen these days." I sigh. "She's probably made a new friend. I'm sure she's fine."

Grace hurries behind us, her fair cheeks flushed from the

1

exertion. "She's right, Diana. We were just as wild at her age. Remember that time we snuck out to—" She sucks in a breath as she crests the hill. "*Oh.* Look."

Villagers are gathering around the bonfire blazing in the meadow below, their hands clasped as they form a circle. Rosemary stands away from the crowd, embers sparking behind her wild golden strands as she dances to a mandolin's reel. She's wearing the pendant I gifted her this morning, the amethyst sparkling near the hollow of her throat.

I touch the empty space between my collarbones, where it rested for years after my mother gave it to me on my sixteenth birthday. "See, she's fine."

"We should let her have some privacy," Diana concedes. "It is her birthday, after all."

But we stand rooted on the hill, watching our Rosemary throw her head back, laughing as another girl pulls her toward the ring. She clutches her linen skirt and saunters barefoot through the wildflowers, their yellow petals skimming past her hips.

"Oh, to be like that again," I say wistfully. "So happy and carefree."

When we found her in the forest, we thought it would be easy to keep our promise to the Goddess. We never expected our feral girl child to fall so in love with life and the world and everything in it.

Grace threads her fingers through mine. "I'd give anything to buy her more time."

Diana and I nod our quiet agreement. So would we.

I

ROSEMARY

Time blurs in a haze of sleep.

I live somewhere between the nightmare of my reality and an oasis of pleasant memories, unsure if I'm awake or dreaming as I toe the edge of a dark wood. The forest has been overtaken by invasive ivy. Decayed trunks are wrapped in thick barbed chords that writhe unnaturally. Translucent fingers claw at the tangled heap, ripping small spaces for glowing eyes to stare at me.

"Zelladine. You were supposed to set the forest free." A hundred ethereal voices form an accusing chorus. *"Now you'll be like us. Trapped for all eternity."*

I step back from the vines slithering near my feet. "I'm sorry. I never meant for this to happen."

"Rosemary." Deep within the bramble, a woman calls for me, her black velvet voice soft and familiar. I want to respond, but my thoughts are thick and oily; they slide around in my head incoherently. All I know is that I'm somewhere I shouldn't be.

"Rot with us, Zelladine."

"Block them out," she commands. "There's only you and me."

I throw my hands out in front of me, searching through the weeds. A single word forms in my head and crystallizes on the tip of my tongue. "Carabosse."

"Yes, I'm here."

The wall of thorns weaves tighter, closing up any space between the trees. *"You're not going anywhere, Zelladine."*

"Don't listen to them. You're doing so well, love. Keep going," Carabosse coaxes, but I'm trapped.

Prickly tendrils snag on my hem and ghostly hands snatch at my ankles. Fear pins me in place, rendering me immobile as bindweed climbs up to my waist. It doesn't matter how hard I try to reach her. I never can. "Help me, please."

"I will," she vows. "I'm coming."

I tip my head back to take one last breath before the ivy covers my eyes and climbs into my mouth, pulling me down to the soil to rot into the floor of the Hartwood.

Shadows seep into my organic shroud, and Carabosse whispers directly into my ear as if she's here with me. "Remember a time when you were safe and happy."

Soft magic cocoons me, its warmth tingling from my chest to my extremities.

A branch snaps overhead, waking me from a strange dream. I'm not sure why I decided to take a nap at the edge of this creepy forest, but I need to head back before my godmothers get worried. They always make a fuss when I wander too far from the wagon.

I skip toward the sound of Candide's singing and see her at the clothesline, the cinnamon halo of flyaways around her head visible between the linens blowing in the breeze.

"Sweet Milly was a bonny thing. She knew how to make a fiddle sing."

She sticks a clothespin between her teeth, humming around the wood as she pulls a quilt from the basket. I cover my mouth to keep from giggling.

She hasn't noticed me yet. I tiptoe around the line and hide behind our damp shifts, waiting for the right time to jump out and say *boo.*

"I see her face when the smoke fills the air, a twinkle in her eyes and pink ribbons in her hair," she croons, fastening the blanket. *"Me and her sister go down to the river, pickin' pretty flowers to remember. We set 'em on down by the stone with her name and sing that old song she used to play. Ooo, dolly lolly dilly, what a blessing to be alive in spring. To fill my arms with lavender and..."* Her hands drop from the line, then reappear around my waist as she lunges for me. *"Rosemary!"*

I'm hauled up into the air, squealing and twirling beneath a bright blue sky. The sunshine is warm on my face, and I know I'm always safe with Candide, but I can't shake the feeling that someone is watching.

Beyond the clothesline, a woman cloaked in darkness leans against a tree. Shadows swim beneath the hood hanging over her face. I can't see who she is, but I'm not afraid of her. I know she won't hurt me.

"I promise I'll find you," she says. "Wait for me."

Washing day with Candide is over almost as soon as it begins. I blink and I'm flat on my back, shuttering my eyes against the harsh light filtering in through the gauzy cloth above me.

Washing day was a dream. Only a dream.

I try to fall asleep and escape into it again. Sometimes, if I try hard enough, I can.

The scent of lavender soap fills my nostrils, and for a moment, I think I've succeeded in burrowing into the warmth of my godmother's neck, but I can hear a woman speaking quietly. Her chattering pulls me back to my surroundings.

I force myself to become aware of them, using all of my senses to root myself in my reality.

There is a soft mattress beneath me and lofty green blankets around me. I'm lying in a four-poster bed, locked away in the castle. I'm in the King's City, and I've been here for two weeks. Maybe three. Possibly more. It's hard to keep track of the details.

There are two maids on each side of the bed, their features obscured by the canopy. Their faces are mere beige blurs above their brown gowns, mostly concealed by the lace-brimmed bonnets they're wearing.

Every day, they work in pairs to wash me, dress me, serve me three meals, and administer an elixir that puts me into a sleep so deep that not even Carabosse can find me.

She's looking for me. I know she is. She must be beside herself.

Wait for me. I'm trying.

I made a deal with King Stefan, an arrangement to help him restore our dying kingdom—my cooperation in exchange for the hatchlings' safety and a promise that no one would harm me. It didn't seem like I had much of a choice when I was riding in a carriage alone with him, so I agreed.

I left Sarteal thinking I'd be able to reach my wife in my dreams. I was wrong.

The maid continues gossiping as she draws the canopy open, and I pretend to be asleep. It's easier this way. I don't have to awkwardly avoid eye contact as she washes my face and brushes my hair.

"I know Her Majesty can be...*difficult* at times, but do you believe the rumors are true?" she asks her companion.

I've come to recognize her voice well enough to know her

name is Marwenna. She usually works with an older maid named Marge during her rotations. I wait for her to answer, but Marwenna's question is met with silence.

I hear her wring out a washrag, and she continues, "I can't blame her if they are. A third wife without an heir of her own? She must feel threatened by the King's fascination with this woman."

A wet cloth is pressed to my forehead. I keep my eyes closed as water trickles down to my lashes. There's no need for Queen Roberta to feel threatened by me. The King only visits my chamber with tomes of old spells. I am *not* his mistress.

But I can't tell the maids that. They wouldn't understand. I can't even fully comprehend why I'm here.

"We're not supposed to be gossiping in this room," the other woman whispers. She isn't Marge or any of the other maids that usually come in here. I peer through my lashes at a petite woman with a pale, wan complexion. Her gown is too big for her small frame. There's something familiar about her large brown eyes beneath the shadows of her bonnet.

I know her from somewhere, but I can't quite place her.

Cowed by the other maid's stern response, Marwenna shakes my arm to wake me up. "It's time to eat and get dressed for your appointment with the King."

I don't fight or complain as they lace me into a fine golden gown. I've learned that there are two guards posted outside my door at all times. If I cause too much trouble, they'll intervene.

Once I'm dressed and primped in a way that won't earn the King's disdain, they lead me to a small round table beside the window and set my food tray down.

I ignore my plate of cold toast and lean toward the sunlight coming through the golden grid drilled over the window's frame.

The Hartwood lies beyond the castle walls, humming like it

used to before I pricked my finger on the Tree Mother's spinning wheel. My head is still foggy from the elixir. If the forest speaks to me, I cannot hear it.

"Your Majesty."

I take a bite of toast as the maids bow for the King. He stands in the doorway, his crown sitting straight on his faded auburn hair. His green jacket is decorated with a gold brocade pattern of leaves. It matches my gown perfectly.

I loathe his attention to detail. I'm always dressed as if I'm castle property.

"You may wait outside until I call you in," he says, dismissing the maids without so much as a glance in their direction. Shutting the door behind him, he strides to the opposite side of the table and drops a dusty tome beside my food tray.

"The farmers outside of the capital are complaining about the harvest already," he says, walking to the window. He stares through the screen of the grid with his hands clasped behind his back. "People will starve if you don't do something about it."

The small bit of toast I've swallowed turns to lead in my belly. He's never explained why the fate of our harvest is my responsibility. He's only told me that I was born to a forest maiden and that I fell into an enchanted sleep in the Hartwood, only to be awoken the night my godmothers found me.

That's when all of his troubles started.

"I might be able to do something once I have more information, Your Majesty," I say, pushing my plate away. "Perhaps if I speak to my godmothers, they could explain how I'm linked to the kingdom's well-being."

"And allow four witches to collaborate against me?" he scoffs. "I don't think so. Turn to the page I've bookmarked."

I pull the tome closer to me, a premonition creeping up my

back as I run my hand over the cover. The script embossed in its worn aubergine leather is written in an archaic language. It hints at the type of dark magic that makes me think of death-less, ageless witches, and hags who can shift their bodies at will.

This text is probably filled with curses and enchantments that disrupt the natural balance of chaos and order. Of good and evil.

I touch the spine, not wanting to crack it. "I'll read it once you give me an update on my hatchlings."

Whenever I catch half an hour of clarity between my long sleeping sessions, I find myself thinking of them. I have to remind myself they're ok.

King Stefan is cruel, but he understands the significance of raising two dragons. That's why he proposed our deal. He'd be a fool to hurt them.

"I will update you once you do as you're told," he barks.

I flip the pages open to see what spell he's chosen for me to attempt today. It will fail like they always do. I don't know what he's expecting from me when I'm too numb to feel my magic.

There are only a few notes scrawled beneath drawings of symbols on the paper. "What are these?"

"Binding sigils," he says. I feel the blood draining from my face as I skim through the pages of marks meant to be carved or burned into one's skin. I land on a half-moon shape, like the scar on Carabosse's forearm, and read the words beneath it. *A bond only to be broken by death.*

"A bond would make it easier for power to be transferred between us, but you'd have to take the mark willingly."

"No." I close the book. He can threaten me and keep me here, but I won't let him own me. "I'll never agree to that."

"There are mages who can perform binding rituals without

your consent. Why do you insist on making things difficult for yourself?" He tuts. "I believe you'll live the long life of a demi mortal, a secret to be passed down through my family. Poor flower, it would've been easier for everybody if you'd only stayed sleeping." He turns his face slightly. "But now you're awake, and we must find a way to revive the kingdom."

"I'm barely awake."

His shoulders drop back. "And whose fault is that? I wouldn't have to dose you to keep our secret safe if you'd left with my guards when you made it through the Hartwood instead of going off with the wraith. I can't risk her finding you here."

Tears burn in my eyes, hot and angry. I stare straight ahead, letting them water until everything is blurry. I won't cry in front of him.

Wait for me. "She will find me, and she'll make you pay for this."

The corner of his mouth dips down for a second and tugs back up into a cold smirk. "Why would she do that? You do know she's aware of your plan to abandon her to join the rebellion, don't you? She's the laughingstock of Sarteal because her little bride tricked her and ran away. She wants you to be found and punished."

He thinks I was leaving without her knowledge when he captured me. That means Carabosse is still pushing our story and working behind her Queen's back. She's still helping Robin and the rebels even though she hasn't heard from me in weeks.

I'm her mate. That revelation stands out from the murky memories I have of the night I left Sarteal. She won't give up on me or the plans we made.

I won't either.

"Don't worry," King Stefan says, mistaking my awe for fear. "I will keep you safe from the wraith. And maybe someday, when she's moved on from your betrayal, I'll allow you to spend more time awake. You could have books and art for entertainment. Walks in the garden, if you behave. I'll raise Prince Edward and Prince Richard to show you respect when it is their turn to share your gifts. This can be an agreeable arrangement for all of us," he says, proudly, as if he believes it's some noble deed to keep me here as a royal houseplant. "You can show your commitment to helping the kingdom by considering the binding sigils and removing the curse you placed on me."

"Curse?" I think back to the day his guards had me sprawled out on his dining room floor and the words I spat at him with the taste of blood in my mouth. *You will choke on the shadows of your dark soul, Stefan, and when death comes for you, you will fear it.*

I'm glad my words still torment him. There isn't a boot cracking against my ribs, but I hate him even more now than I did back then. It makes me feel good to have something to hold over him.

Powerful, even.

I press my shoulders against the high back of my chair. "I'll never remove that curse, Your Majesty. You'll wear it beneath that crown on your head until you're dead."

His nostrils flare with an involuntary spasm, and my bravery wanes.

This is it, I think. This is where he breaks his promise not to hurt me.

But he doesn't move any closer. He never does. He always keeps at least four feet between us.

"Very well, then," he says, the ruby on his crown catching the sun. "You won't be earning any privileges this month. I have a busy schedule, so I won't be stopping by any time soon." I'm hit with a wave of panic and relief as he turns to leave. I hate these meetings, but it's the only way I get to hear anything about the world outside this room. "Oh. I almost forgot to update you on your hatchlings."

I try not to look too eager, but I am. I want to know how they're growing and if they're using their wings.

"My beautiful queen has been so upset about these visits to your chamber that she threw a fit over it," he says. "I'm sorry to inform you that she had the dragons cooked up and served to me on a silver platter."

There's no sympathy in his apology. His tone is so chipper that I'm sure he must be telling me that the fair has rolled into the city, or that I'll be having sweets with my dinner this evening. Not that something happened to my hatchlings.

The gruesome thought sinks through the cloud covering my brain. Something happened to my hatchlings.

Those hot tears finally run down my face before I can fully process what he's saying. "No. We made a deal. They're safe."

He swirls a finger around a leaf carved into the molding on the doorframe. "It is a pity to lose two dragons. But my wife is a thoroughbred princess. What she wants, she gets. Even *I* cannot control that woman when she's jealous."

I stand up too fast, and the room spins. I brace my hands on the table. Surely I would have felt a terrible ripping pain the moment Sun and Moon were torn from me. I've spent most of my time here numb or asleep, but we were bound. I should have felt *something*.

"Get her back to sleep," he says to the maids on his way out and glances back at me. "You're never getting out of here. Your life will be easier if you cooperate."

I will never cooperate with him. Never.

The maids approach me and I fling my plate, shattering it against the wall. "Stay away from me."

"Do you need help in there?" asks one of the guards, sticking his head in the room.

I don't care. I'll fight him too. I push away from the table, but my emotions aren't enough to bolster my knees. The floor rises up to meet me.

"I have this under control," the petite maid says, waving the guards and Marwenna away. Marwenna is more than happy for the chance to escape.

I push up on my knees, exhausted already. "I'm getting out of here. My dragons can't be gone. I'll find them."

"I'm sure you will," the maid says, taking the kettle from the table. "Let's make you your tea."

She holds my gaze, her fingers curling around the bottle of sleeping elixir. The gesture reminds me of another time, another place.

I've seen those small, pale hands before, wrapped around black feathers. She was in the King's dining room that day he sent me into the Hartwood, clutching a mangled bird with broken wings.

I heard him call her name. I try in vain to pluck it from my memory, but it's lost to me.

It doesn't matter. I've lost everything. My life. My wife. My Sun and Moon. The chance to set my godmothers free.

Maybe I am ready for a cup of tea that will put me to sleep. When I wake up I can convince myself this was all a terrible dream.

The maid presses a finger to her lips, her eyes widening in a warning, large and unblinking. Then she points to the door and mouths the words, *"They're listening."*

"Come on, it's time to lie down," she says, and I crawl toward the bed, stretching out on the mattress. This could be a game to get me to settle down, but I'm curious.

She stops at the nightstand and angles the sleeping elixir

over the washbasin, pouring it into the sudsy water. Pocketing the empty bottle, she hands me the teacup and leans in close to whisper in my ear. "A songbird has called your name, so be ready to run with me tomorrow evening. It's time to wake up, sleeping beauty."

2

CARABOSSE

I cannot reach my mate.

Every time I see Rosemary in my dreams, the darkness thickens into a wall between us. All I can do is tuck her away in her happier memories.

The shadows I wield so easily have become my enemy. They follow me into the waking hours and press on my shoulders, making everything feel heavy.

Knuckles rap against the chamber door, but I'm not ready to start my day. I'm too busy fretting over Rosemary. It's been a month since she left, and I haven't received a single update on her whereabouts or well-being. Not a word in our dreams or a damn crow from her rebellion leader.

Where is my wife? And who *the fuck* is keeping her from me?

A dark voice swirls through my head. *"You should have never let her leave."*

"It was the safest option," I grunt, tugging on my hair. "I had to get her out of Sarteal."

"She'd have been safer with you if only you'd—"

"I know." She'd have been safer with me if only I'd never let my Queen carve her mark on me. If I'd have done one thing differently. "But what's done is done."

And I'll do my best to help Rosemary secure her freedom and safety. Lollishire's rebellion will succeed and she'll gain the protection of Robin's army.

I'll make sure of it.

I worm my index finger beneath my tunic and dragon scale vest, feeling the spray roses she put in my hair the last night we saw each other. Their pink petals are still fluffy and pink, never wilting despite the weeks that have passed. They puff back up no matter how many times I turn them over in my hands.

Like Rosemary, they're special, resilient.

Touching them helps me to feel grounded again.

"Commander." There's another knock on the door, louder this time. "The Queen's meeting has already begun."

I spear the dragon pin through the cowl of my black cloak and rest my hand on my chest, feeling the mate bond thrumming within. "I'll be there in a moment."

Wind whips through the archways sliced into the stone passage running between the mountains. I toss my hair out of my face as I stride to the Queen's conference room at a controlled pace, fighting the urge to call on Snovida and hurl myself out of the Vellessentian Palace. This is the last place I want to be right now.

I enter the chamber, and seven Sartealean nobles swivel their heads toward me. Mal had them flown in on dragon back this morning to discuss the growing threat from the east. They all squirm in their seats.

Perhaps they haven't recovered from traveling. None of them are accustomed to flying.

Mal sits at the far end of the black limestone table, her violet eyes narrowing.

I bow my head. "My Queen."

"Commander." She taps a lacquered nail along her scepter. "How nice of you to join us."

"I apologize for my tardiness. The late-night flight took a toll on me."

Her mask is set, expressionless. "That's quite alright. We were discussing our plans to work around Dardaran's blockade. Please sit."

Dim grey light streams through the high rectangular cutouts striping the exterior wall. It doesn't penetrate the cloud of gloom hovering over me.

Chairs scrape across the stone as our guests inch away from the inky tendrils of shadows trailing behind my boots. That green tinge of unease on their faces has nothing to do with heights or dragons.

They're all afraid of me.

Fuck it. I let my shadows roll freely. This plan will work better if I act like the fae monster they're expecting.

A vicious attack dog for the Queen.

"Lady Myrren, I believe you were about to ask a question," Mal says, once I've settled in my seat.

The noblewoman is sitting a few feet to my right, her copper spirals pulled back into a tight knot at the nape of her neck. Orphaned by the Queen's War, she's had to shoulder this responsibility since she was seven.

"Yes, Your Highness." She clears her throat, the faintest lines between her eyes creasing her golden brown skin. "As you know, my territory lacks the arable land to support our community, leaving us dependent on aid from the crown. We're facing the worst of Dardaran's violence, and we're growing weary of the unreliable shipments from the pirates. Do you have a long-term solution in mind to keep a steady supply of goods running to the Midlands?"

"We do," Mal says. "My right-hand woman can share more information about our arrangement with Lollishire."

The back of my neck burns from the attention. "We've made a deal that will allow us to import a share of Lollishire's harvest quarterly."

"A share of their crops in exchange for what?" Lord Derwin asks, stroking his short grey beard.

I choose my next words carefully. "Military support to end the conflict in their kingdom."

As far as Mal knows, I'm set to fly my dragon into the woodland kingdom to burn out the rebellion. I can't let her discover my true intentions until I turn on the King and sway the odds in favor of Robin's rebel army.

"Sartealeans do not want to go to war with their neighboring kingdom," he says, gesturing to the people beside him. He excludes Mal and I from the circle he draws around them, as if we haven't been here since we were teenagers. "That's why we signed a treaty of neutrality that states we will stay out of each other's affairs."

"The Queen and I don't need you to recite the terms of the treaty to us. We were there when it was drafted." I lean back and cross my ankle over my thigh. "But the world has changed since then, and it is still our duty to protect the Dragon Valley. From food scarcity as well as our enemies. We must adapt in order for Sarteal to thrive again."

His throat bobs above the Sartealean emblem pinned on his cloak–a symbol of his devotion to Vellesse. Despite his religious leanings, the prick has never accepted the outcome of the Vellesentere. He's too stubborn to kneel for a woman from Faerie.

"The return of Vellesse's flame was supposed to restore glory to our kingdom, but it's been over twenty years since the tournament, and I have yet to see anything glorious happen," he says. "Our history texts say that wild dragons used to fly freely across the continent, seeking worthy riders to live in the Dragon Valley. Bards sang of an otherworldly green light emanating from the pit, casting its glow over the land around it."

Lord Derwin is walking on thin ice. I can practically hear it shattering beneath him as he throws his chair back. "I will always honor my Goddess and the dragons, but I can't help but question this fae's right to call herself a Queen. Why would she ask us to go against our customs to import crops from Lollishire when she could use Vellesse's flame and force the royalists to bow down to her?"

Mal shoots a look my way, and a prickling sensation crawls along the semicircle branded on my forearm.

Smoky whorls unfurl from her slinky gown as she rises, a bright green fire sparking along the edges of the darkness. The flames split into two lines and run along the floor, blazing toward Lord Derwin. They come to a halt on each side of his feet and reverse directions, encircling him.

Emerald light dances across the nobles' stunned faces.

Mal takes her time strutting past the table, making a show of it. The Starlight Court no longer exists, but its grandeur lives on in the last Starlight princess. She's always known how to captivate her audience.

"There are valid reasons to question my claim to the throne, but refusing to burn my people isn't one of them. Choosing to be a merciful Queen doesn't make me weak," she says, tapping her scepter along the ground to punctuate each step. A cold smile curves her lips as she stops before the ring of fire. "Vellesse chose me for a reason. As you can see, I'm more than capable of wielding her flame to protect the Dragon Valley. "

Lord Derwin licks the sweat beading along his upper lip and puffs his chest. "I feel no heat."

The circle unravels into a deadly serpent made of flames, slithering closer to its prey. Gasps and shocked protests mix with the sound of the sizzling fire.

Mal's pointed ears twitch beneath her crown of silver braids. "Do you still doubt me?"

"Your kind is known for their trickery. I don't trust you or your henchwoman," he says. "Does anyone actually believe her wife made it out of Sarteal with two dragons?"

I resist the urge to press my hand to my chest and stare straight ahead, trying to appear cold and uncaring. Everyone is looking at me, their judgment flashing in my periphery.

"Because I have a nagging suspicion that she—"

Fire twists around his legs and climbs up his neck, choking off the accusation. His mouth flaps open and shut to say something, but only gurgling sounds come out as smoke rises from his singed skin. He's incinerated in a matter of seconds, his final words dying along with him.

The flames go out, breaking into a dozen dark wisps of smoke that retreat under the table.

"Would anyone else like to challenge my status as the victor of the Vellessentere?" Mal turns away from the smoldering heap of Lord Derwin's ashes, sliding her eyes across the table slowly, offering each of her guests a chance to speak.

"Nobody?" she asks. "Good. Let's try to stay focused on the current events troubling our kingdom."

The meeting lasts for hours, the conversation carrying on despite the flecks of ash that stir on the breeze and settle on our ledgers.

Once everyone has left, I loosen a breath and bow to the Queen. "That took longer than expected. I'll have to leave now if I want to make it back to camp before I meet with King Stefan."

"Stop." Mal spins her scepter, the flames dancing within its orb as she steps into one of the large cutouts overlooking the ancient city below. "Don't leave yet."

I'm ready to take to the sky again. It's the only place where I can find some relief from my anxiety.

Curling my fists at my side, I forgo making an excuse and lean against the other side of the opening. The faster we get this over with, the faster I can leave.

"Lord Derwin spoke of old Sartealean legends," she says, the sunlight turning her silver lashes invisible. "Can you picture this place as some majestic city?"

I peer out into the Dragon Valley. The mountain range stretches as far as I can see. Two wild dragons chase each other around a peak in the distance and dive back down again, vanishing in a blanket of mist. It's nothing like the Starlight Court, but it has its own magic.

When we first arrived here, Mal collected as many books as she could get her hands on to learn about Sartelalean culture and history. I used to complain that we were wasting too many coins on the texts she made us read until it felt like our eyeballs might pop out, but I secretly liked the stories about the golden era of dragons. I'd pass the time while scavenging by imagining how things were back then—the sky painted with winged creatures carrying their riders to and from the burrows built into the mountains.

"I can," I admit. There aren't many sights that compare to the beauty of the sun rising over the Dragon Valley. I still daydream about the place it could be.

Mal stares at the range for a few moments, then shakes her head. She's never shared that vision with me.

"I didn't mean for that to happen. It will make me look

petty," she says, flicking a hand toward Lord Derwin's remains. I wince and brace myself for an outburst of self-destructive anger, but her face softens with rare empathy as she looks at me. "But he shouldn't have spoken about your bride's betrayal like that. It was rude and unnecessary."

I tamp down on the low growl rumbling in my chest. It comes out in a short grunt that she interprets as an agreement.

She steps closer and places her hand on my shoulder, sending my shadows skittering in both directions. "I hate how that dark cloud has been hanging over your head since that little rat left. When I find her, I'll make sure she pays for hurting you."

Mal would have to step over my dead body to lay a finger on Rosemary, but I need her to believe I'm a scorned lover until she's safe.

Gods. Please let her be safe.

I clench my teeth so hard I fear my jaw might crack, hoping my face doesn't give my inner thoughts away.

"We'll get through this humiliation together." Mal runs her hand down my arm, giving it a squeeze. "I want things to go back to how they were before I took the throne, back when I had you and you had me. You and Thea are all I have left of Faerie, *nyxsisium.*"

A year ago I would have given anything to hear her say those words to me, to call me nyxsisium—*the sister of my soul*—again.

But it's too late now. I've already broken my vow to put her above all else.

"Commander." Nylah's brusque greeting interrupts our conversation. Mal and I look toward the door where the lieutenant is standing rigidly, her eyes darting between us and the ledge before bowing her head, seemingly realizing her mistake in addressing me before the Queen. "We're supposed to be leaving for Claw Ridge. I was just checking in."

When I look back at Mal, her lips are pressed into a neutral pout, her mask fixed as if she never let it slip.

"That's right," she says. "You'll only have a few hours to drop supplies before meeting with the King. You'd better get going."

She drops her hand away and leaves the chamber, her silver silk gown trailing in her wake. I exit in the opposite direction, heading to the landing room to meet Snovida. Nylah stays on my heels, jogging to keep up.

I know she wants to say something to me, but I'm not in the mood to talk to anybody.

Clouds float past the dome, obscuring the jagged rocks below. I run my thumb along the handle of my new knife, itching to check the blade out of habit. I wonder if the inscription on my father's knife still lights up now that Rosemary has it.

Does she know I'm losing my fucking mind thinking about how I'm going to find her?

"Tear the world apart for her," the voice says, creeping out of the darkest crevices of my psyche. *"That's what I would do for my love."*

"Boss." Nylah joins me beneath the wide archway I've chosen instead of making her way to her own jumping station. "I need to talk to you."

I pull my gloves on, ready to mount Snovida as soon as she flies by. "Can it wait?"

Her tousled hair falls over one eye as she checks that no one else has entered the space. "It's important. A man came to me claiming he knows where to find Rosemary."

"Let me guess," I grouse, fastening my bracers. "He wants a reward for this tip just like everyone else who has come forward with some information about my runaway bride so I can have her punished for her treachery."

My throat tightens. I know how most people see me, but it stings that Nylah thinks I'd want to hurt Rosemary.

"I've known you since the day Nova and I climbed down into the pit, looking for a chance at a decent life," she says, folding her arms over her chest. We both glance over the ledge where Nova's bones lie far beneath us. "It's never once crossed my mind that you'd want to *punish* your wife, but I can feel that something is amiss, even if you refuse to tell me what it is."

I don't want to drag Nylah any further into this ordeal, but her concern seems genuine, and I need all the help I can get. "What makes you think this man is any different from the rest of them?"

"He wanted me to relay a message to you. He said a little bird told him you should work together to find Rosemary." She lifts a shoulder. "Do you know what that means?"

"Yes." It's dangerous to get my hopes up too soon, but my heart lifts in my chest despite my best efforts as Vencel and Snovida snake around the palace. "Take me to see him."

3

CARABOSSE

We land at the edge of Tresoran.

Dismounting from Snovida, I channel a message through our bond, warning her to avoid being seen from the palace. Mal can't leave on a whim without a dragon, but she's always watching.

Nylah and I walk into the city with our hoods pulled low over our faces. Down here the sun bakes the streets, and the late-afternoon crowd only intensifies the heat. I dodge strangers weaving across the square, and step over a fly-infested pile of discarded vegetables.

A young woman palms an orange from a market stall and slips past me, her eyes meeting the shadows beneath my hood as she rolls the fruit into the pocket of her dress.

"The wraith," she murmurs, sprinting off before I can reassure her that I don't go around hunting people down for petty acts of theft.

A few more people stop to stare at me, then hustle in the opposite direction. My height and my dark aura are attracting too much attention. This is why I prefer working at night, when my shadows help me to blend into my surroundings.

Nylah leads me down an empty alley, sticking close to the siding of a stone building. I rarely visit this part of Tresoran, but I've been here before. I walked this path a few years ago with Nova. She brought me to this same back entrance to show me her friend's establishment.

"Did you seriously bring him to *The Dragon's Den*?" I ask as the lieutenant loops her fingers through the knocker's brass ring.

"Yep. Tied him up and everything." She flashes a grin. "Thought you'd approve since Margery is an old friend."

"It seems like something your sister would've done." I shouldn't be surprised that they'd have similar ideas, but they were always polar opposites. "It's brilliant."

Margery was exploited by the same man who scooped Nylah and Nova off the streets in one of the southern cities. Now she runs Sarteal's most exclusive pleasure house, catering to wealthy folks looking to explore their kinks consensually. Her business thrives on discretion, and she loves Nylah like a sister. She won't report our actions to the Queen.

A maid answers the door, and Nylah exchanges a password for two masks. Our faces are covered as we step into a candlelit tavern. Patrons order drinks from the barmaid and take them to the tables below a large stage where the dancers are preparing for tonight's performance. Their costumes are made of flimsy leather straps that barely cover their nipples. Swaths of sequined fabric tied around their thumbs flutter behind them like scaly wings as they race across the stage to drop dragon masks over their faces.

I have to avert my eyes from the acts of depravity happening in plain sight as Nylah guides me into the back corridors of the club. A curvy blonde woman touches my shoulder, stopping me in my tracks.

She tugs on the letter strap attached to the collar around her neck and places it in my hand. "Would you like to go for a walk?"

"No thanks," I stammer, dropping the leash immediately.

"Are you alright?" Nylah laughs.

I'm grateful for the mask, or else she'd rib me mercilessly for my flushed cheeks. I'm not a prude by any means, but there's only one woman who does it for me. Stepping foot inside *The Dragon's Den* feels like a transgression when she's missing. "Mhmm."

I join her at the top of a stairwell, and an aroma of fermented fruit rises on a draft of cool air. Ducking beneath the wrought iron lamps hanging from the low ceiling, my eyes adjust to the dim lighting of a wine cellar as I clear the last step, and I see a pair of legs sticking out from between two barrels.

"There he is," Nylah says, jerking her thumb toward the man tied to a support beam. I take in the man's long limbs carved with lean muscles that ripple beneath his black breeches. Fox-like eyes stare at me through the auburn strands falling over his forehead.

My breath halts for a beat. I know him.

The last time I saw him he was clean-shaven and practically drooling over Rosemary, but I still recognize him with a scraggly beard covering his chin. I unknot the white fabric tied over his mouth. "What in the underworld are you doing here, Alex?"

Lollishire's eldest prince takes a few breaths before he speaks. "Robin sent a message that I could trust your lieutenant, but the bird lady must've been mistaken because she threw me on her dragon and tied me up in this musty sex dungeon."

"That's not what I mean." I crouch down and draw my knife. "What are you doing here in Sarteal?"

"You know, I'm not really into—*ah*." His eyes widen as I press the tip of the blade to his neck. "Whoah. Ok. Let's calm down. I came here to save Rose."

Blood drains from my extremities. "From who?"

"You," he says. "I left as soon as I heard she was alive and under your protection."

"Are you serious?" My shadows lash out, grasping the stiff collar of his red cape. "You watched as your father had her beaten and fed to the Hartwood and you want me to believe you traveled all the way here to save her from *me*?" I tug him upright until his spine is ramrod straight and the ropes are digging into his chest. "Did you really think you could take her from me?"

"No, but I thought I could buy her some time to get away." His chin quivers, but he holds it high. "You're right that I messed up that day, and I've regretted it ever since. I don't want to die a cowardly prince. When I found out she survived the forest, I thought I had a chance to prove myself."

"You thought I was holding her against her will," I state, going numb as his words sink in.

"I did until Robin explained your mutual feelings." He frowns at the dark claws digging into his skin. "No offense, but you don't exactly have a reputation for kindness."

I let the shadows fall and tilt my blade away from his neck. There are a thousand questions swimming through my mind, but one floats to the surface, my top priority. "I'm obviously not keeping her here with me, so where is she?"

"With my father. In the King's City."

I can't hear anything. A wave of dark thoughts crashes through my mind, roaring with terrible possibilities. "What's he doing to her?"

"I'd reckon he's keeping her locked away." He studies my face, then adds, "Safely. He won't hurt her. Not when he believes she's the key to wielding true power over the kingdom."

"What is that supposed to mean?" I ask through gritted teeth.

He glances at Nylah. "Do you mind if we switch to the common language? My tutor wasn't as thorough as yours."

"Cut to the chase already." I switch languages with ease without mentioning that I've never had a tutor. Only a stack of textbooks and Mal's nagging.

"A long time ago, a forest maiden fell in love with a human man," he starts. "She died giving birth to a child and was reborn from the soil without her memories. All of the maidens were bewildered by her hybrid offspring, a small girl who didn't quite belong to the forest. They did their best to raise the child they called Zelladine, shielding her from the dangers of the outside world until someone brought an offering under false pretenses."

"Was the girl's father the trickster prince?" I grip the blade handle, my palms sweating as I piece together the story of the slain forest maidens. "Is he the one who poisoned them?"

"No, her father was consumed by the forest before she was born. The Tree Mother punished him for trespassing when she found out what he'd done," he clarifies. "The man who tricked the maidens was a mage who dabbled in forbidden practices like necromancy and soul harvesting. When he entered the Hartwood, he had a plan to poison its deities and steal the magic flowing through the forest. The maidens and the

Goddess all drank from the same spiked chalice, and they fell into a cursed sleep."

"I already know this story."

"Not all of it. They fell into a cursed sleep," he repeats. "All of them except for Zelladine. By time the mage noticed the girl was unaffected, she was being drawn up into the forest's canopy. The Tree Mother used the last vestiges of her energy to plant her magic inside her chest, and then she summoned Vellesse. The Goddess of the underworld heard her lover's dying wish and placed the girl under a sleeping spell to keep her safe before retreating from the realm to grieve."

"What does this have to do with Rosemary?" I ask, but I fear I know the answer already.

"When the forest maidens died, the dragons disappeared and the devouring trees stopped fruiting. He attempted to retrieve the girl by burning a large portion of the forest, but the Hartwood became a vicious, vengeful thing, determined to protect the child." He leans his head back. "Then a little over twenty years ago, on the night of the May Day feast, a withering fruit fell to the ground, and the dragons awakened. It was the same night my father sent the Devouring Tree Coven to the pyre. The same night Rosemary's godmothers ran to the forest and escaped the fire."

This story has too many interconnected threads. I can't convince myself they're all a coincidence. "How do you know all of this?"

He shrugs. "A priestess of the Woodland Temple prophesied that there'd come a day when the girl would awaken and set the forest free. She wrote about it in the *Grimoire of the Devouring Tree*, but my ancestor ransacked the temple and had those pages erased from history."

I remember Rosemary reading through the grimoire that

day in the temple. I watched with rapt attention as her fingers danced over the weathered pages, searching for something that was missing. "Why would he do that?"

"Because he could pretend he held the Goddess' gifts as long as the girl stayed sleeping. People were afraid of the Hartwood's eerie melody and snapping trees, so he promised to protect them. He built a boundary to protect the city he built and convinced them the burnings were necessary to stop the forest from overtaking everything. Several generations passed, and people stopped asking questions. They were too afraid of getting hauled away for the burnings by then. The facade worked until the devouring trees started fruiting again."

He shifts in his binds and slumps against the beam. "Since then, the kingdom has been slowly dying without the Goddess' gifts flowing through the Hartwood. My father orders bigger pyres every year, swearing the ritual will bring a bountiful harvest, but it's all a distraction. He's been obsessed with finding the lost daughter of the forest for as long as I can remember."

"How could he possibly find someone who'd been sleeping for centuries?"

"By hunting for girls who matched our ancestor's description of a golden-haired nymph. If they were the right age, he'd feed them to the forest to see if they would survive it."

"Like Rosemary did."

I shudder to think of her facing her death like the other girls who came before her. She could've died for nothing like the rest of them. She could've been anyone, a woman born without gifts or a Goddess' blessing. My heart wouldn't have known the difference. Losing her before I knew her would've wrecked me all the same. I would have mourned the absence of our mate bond just as keenly if she'd been ordinary.

Prince Alex nods. "Yes, and now he has a coven of witches at his fingertips to help him steal her gifts."

A line from our wedding vows drifts across my mind. *It was always meant to be a tale of the dragon and the devouring tree.*

I flip my knife into its sheath, lightheaded from a realization I'm not ready to dissect yet. "I have to leave."

"Where are you going?"

"To kill the King," I say, striding to the steps.

"You can't do that."

"I most certainly can. Just because he's keeping her alive doesn't mean there aren't other ways he could be hurting her." Nausea rolls through me. I wish I could reach Lollishire's capital instantly.

"He won't touch her," he says. "He's terrified of witches. My mother and Rose, especially. She cursed him before her punishment, and he spiraled over it for hours. He'd never let her get close enough to let it happen again."

She cursed him to his face? She never told me that. Pride flares beneath my anxiety. I'm going to get her back and strangle Stefan for this. "He should be afraid of me."

"He is, but he's been fortifying his castle against the fae since your Queen won the Vellessentere." His voice grows louder, traveling up the stairwell. "His guards have been trained to target your weaknesses, and the ceiling is vaulted with iron curtains. If you go storming in there, you'll give him exactly what he wants. He'll have a reason to kill you, and Rose will be his. Even if you succeed, you'll ruin your chance to help the rebellion. Robin is asking, no, *begging* you to approach the castle with caution and meet with her instead."

I freeze mid-step, setting my impulses aside to think rationally. I'd rather solve this problem with my shadows and my fists, but if he's prepared for me...if I fail Rosemary...she'll be stuck as that fraud's prisoner for the rest of her life.

However long that may be.

Nylah arches an eyebrow as I spin around. I wave for her to come back down with me.

"If what you're saying is true, then how do I know you're not trying to capture her for your own use?" I move around the barrels, twirling my blade as I question him. "Why should I trust a man who spends his days deep in his cups and wastes his gold on frivolous things?"

"Because I watched my mother burn when I was seven," he says, his voice lowering as if he's telling me a secret. "I've always wanted to avenge her and put an end to my family's horrid legacy, but I've never had the chance to be that person. Not with my father watching me. He could've easily disposed of me after having two more heirs with his second queen." He closes his eyes as the ceiling rattles with dancers' footsteps and the vibration of violin strings. "There's safety in being a scandalous disappointment, of course, but it also has its perks. No one ever notices how closely I'm watching them with a drink in my hand. I've observed lots of things over the years."

"What kind of things have you observed, princey?"

"My father's plans. His fears, weaknesses, and alliances. I've gone carousing with enough of his friends to know which ones are most likely to turn on him. Robin might berate me for abandoning the rebellion to wander around your kingdom, but I'm not *quite* the fool she thinks I am." He looks me over from head to toe. "And I'm guessing you're not as awful as everyone says you are, but I have to wonder why your Queen is so determined to make the world see you as a villain."

His body tenses as I slash the ropes around his hands. "We're not here to talk about me. If you want to help, tell me everything I need to know about your father and the rebellion. First things first, who is Robin?"

"I have no idea, but she intends to make me her groom and

rule with me." He guffaws a laugh, his somber expression brightening. "With my luck, she's probably some old hag covered in feathers and bird shit. Anyway, there are a few things she wants you to know before your meeting," he says, reciting what she wrote to him in her letters.

I tap a finger on my knee as I go over the information with him, making sure I've memorized every detail. "And I'll know how to find her when I hear the words *orange spiced tea*?"

"That's the secret phrase she told me. Don't ask me what it's supposed to mean." He pulls out a vintage red and blows the dust off of it. "Now, how am I going to get back to my kingdom?"

I take the bottle and place it back on the shelf. "I suggest you go back the same way you came."

"That's far too dangerous. Robin needs my pretty face for her campaign." He tosses his hair and grins, reverting back to his role as the jackass prince.

I don't give a damn about him or Robin, whoever she is, but Rosemary's long-term happiness depends on this rebellion.

Unfortunately, he's a part of it.

"I'll get you back to the Wildlands," I concede. "But you'll have to take the ferry to Heartshire. My dragon can't be seen in rebel territory without raising the King's suspicions."

Scrubbing a hand over my face, I try to think of a way to make that happen. Everything is ten times more difficult when I'm required to travel with Thea.

I curl my fingers around the bridge of my nose, staring over my knuckles at Nylah. I'm thankful that her knowledge of the common language is limited. The less she knows, the safer she is.

"Let me help you with whatever's happening," she offers, unprompted.

Am I that obvious? "I can't bring you into this."

"If you haven't noticed, I'm already in it." She throws her arms out, gesturing toward Alex. "Something is wrong. Vencel senses it from Snovida, and I can feel it from him."

"We promised not to let the bond between our dragons complicate things," I remind her. "We can't always parse out what they're feeling."

"Will you stop acting like a twat about this? I'm not a fool," she says, calling me out like she used to during our years in the pit, before the dragons took the sky and we had to start being mindful of public appearances. "I saw how you and Rosemary were around each other. Back in Claw Ridge, she searched for you like she was seeking refuge. She wasn't some seductress trying screw you out of a couple eggs to take back to her rebellion. And the way you looked at her..."

White lines thread around her mouth as she searches for words. "I've never seen anything like it before. It wasn't a look of mortal longing. Your story about her up and leaving doesn't make any sense. I know you're trying to protect her from someone, and I think I know who it is."

There's no point in denying the obvious.

I knew I was being reckless, training Rosemary on the cliffs and letting her sleep in my tent. Maybe things would have gone differently if I'd kept my word to myself to keep my distance. I could have gotten her to that apothecary in time if I hadn't been so damn selfish.

But how could I have resisted my little witch's warm body between the sheets? She enchanted me and sank beneath my skin.

I had to let her in. "Why are you so adamant about getting involved in this?"

"Nova would've wanted me to," she answers. "You two cared for each other in your own way. She always worried that if something happened to her, there'd be no one to look after you."

"I've never needed anyone to look after me."

"Yeah, she said you'd say that," she says, sticking her tongue in her cheek. "Did you know I saw her an hour before her death?"

I shake my head.

"She wouldn't have jumped." She looks me straight in the eye. "We both know that."

It hits me that Nylah has her own suspicions about the Queen. "Are you looking for revenge?"

"No," she says. "I'm looking out for the dragons. Things aren't right around here. They haven't been since Mal's coronation."

"Why didn't you confront me sooner?"

"Because I understand you're not in control of all of this." Her eyes drop to my branded forearm. "We have to do something."

We shouldn't be having this conversation. I should put an end to it, but Nylah is far too clever for that. She'll find another way to bring it up again because she's on to something. "You understand that this counts as conspiring against the Queen, which is..."

"Treason," she says, finishing the sentence because I can't. "Yes, and I know the consequences just as well as you do. Let me help. Please."

"Alright." My stomach churns at Mal's words from earlier. I'm the worst kind of traitor, but I can't stand by my oath to her and protect Rosemary. It's one or the other. "Make up a reason to take Thea with you to Claw Ridge, and I'll take care of the prince."

Alex perks up. "I have plenty of stories to help pass the

time. Oh, I can tell you about this one time at the apothecary when Rose—"

I whirl around and he shuts his mouth. "Please stop talking, or I might shove you off my dragon."

I'm only containing my rage to help Rosemary and her rebellion, but it simmers beneath my skin as I mount Snovida, ready to ride until morning.

4

ROSEMARY

It takes a full day for the effects of the elixir to wear off completely, but I only nod off a few times when I can't fight my fatigue. I dread falling asleep. Even without the medicine clouding my brain, I can't find Carabosse in my abbreviated dreams.

I spend the night in my dark chamber stretching my limbs and making my muscles move. When the sun rises, I dab the tears away from my raw cheeks and pretend to sleep as the morning maids check on me. I get back to work as soon as they leave, bending and lunging to get myself ready.

Walking back and forth across the room leaves me winded. I mop my damp brow with the bedsheet and press my face into my pillow, letting out a cry of frustration.

If anyone expects me to run tonight, I'm screwed. But I walk another circuit around the room, preparing for my potential rescue. Too many emotions claw at my chest anytime I try to rest, so I keep moving.

My thoughts keep drifting back to Sun and Moon. The mark they left on my heart isn't the kind that fades with time.

They were gentle creatures who deserved to grow up and stretch their wings against the sky.

They were precious. And they were mine.

I can almost still feel them in my head, the ghost of our bond haunting me. Random images of grey rocks and tombstones flit behind my eyes, but I blink them away, not allowing myself to believe Sun and Moon are trying to send me messages. Giving in to that delusion will only make it harder to accept that I'll never see them again.

My throat clogs with thick emotion. I sprawl out on the floor, spent from my exercises. There's no way to stop my tears from flowing, so I muffle my sobs in my sleeves to prevent the guards from hearing me.

At some point, a pinkish coral light presses against my eyelids, pulling me from my silent weeping. Dehydrated from crying, I lift my head from my damp forearms to find the sun dipping toward the horizon.

The maid should be here soon.

I realize what she said yesterday could've been a delirious dream or even a cruel scheme, but I'm going to be ready for what's coming. I pick myself up and take a seat on the window cushion.

Hugging my knees, I press my forehead against the golden grid, spotting a portion of an emerald tower looming over the castle walls. I pull on the bars, letting them dig into my scalp as I angle my neck to get a better look. Long strands of green leaves twist and fold around the structure's circumference, occasionally revealing strips of cream stucco between.

I'm so close to the Ivy Keep.

If Robin has sent for me, then maybe she has a plan for my godmothers too. Maybe tonight we'll all run free.

Tears roll down my wrists and hit my shins. I know how silly I'm being.

For years, I've been trying to hold on to something to get through a helpless situation, but I've lost my grip. After losing Sun and Moon, my hope is withering.

There's a scratch at the window followed by a soft whispering, the sound muted by the thick window pane. A red vine pokes out from the green leaves bunched around the sill, its single tendril climbing the glass and curling in on itself. Fuchsia buds erupt along the furled frond, blooming into heart-shaped flowers that hang from the vine. White petals split through the pointed tips of their bottom ends, their hearts bleeding just like mine.

I don't want this heavy grief. I'd rather transmute it into something I can wield.

Robin can have her rebellion and the King. If—no, *when*—Carabosse comes for me, I'll demand to be the one who takes down the Queen. I draw her face in my mind, making her my enemy.

Threads of green trace their way up my forearm as my magic comes to life, and the vine transforms into a deep shade of rust. Sharp thorns rip through the stalk, as ugly as the rage inside me.

That's better.

The rush of dark, strange magic is oddly comforting. I'm so immersed in it that I hardly notice when the maids come in, pushing a cart into the chamber.

The maid from yesterday lifts a finger to her lips and lifts the stack of linens beside the washbasin. I leave my window seat, glancing apprehensively at her companion. She's not one of the regular maids. In fact, I'm certain I've never seen her before. Still, she smiles like we're old friends as I take the linens and unfold the maid's uniform hidden within.

She gestures for me to put it on.

Pulling my sleeping gown over my head, I step into the

plain brown dress and tug it over my ribs. The scratchy fabric is too tight around my breasts and arms, and the overly long bodice sags around my waist. It fits poorly, but both maids look up from the tray they're setting on the table and give a nod of approval. I suppose it will have to do.

The pale, wide-eyed maid finishes arranging the tea set and tucks my stray hairs into my cap. "You need to come with me."

"What about her?" I chew on my lower lip as the other maid climbs into the bed. She pulls her cap off, letting her blonde waves fall to her waist, then spreads her hair across the pillowcase.

My stomach sours. She's going to take my place to let me escape. No bribe could make that a fair trade. "I can't ask her to do this."

The maid notices my resistance and sits up, hiking her skirt up to show me a row of throwing knives strapped to her thigh. With a wink, she mouths the words *don't worry about me.* Then she lies back, pulls the covers to her chin, and pretends to be asleep.

At a glance, she really does pass for me. I hope her confidence in this plan is genuine, and that Robin hasn't done something awful to set me free—like holding charges over her head or blackmailing her family.

"We need to leave." The maid points her chin at the cart. "Keep your head down," she hisses as I take the spot beside her.

Marian. Her name comes back to me in a moment of clarity. I try to mimic how meek she looked that day in the King's dining room, staring at my feet as we push past the guards in the hallway. Marian mumbles a polite greeting. They don't seem to notice anything is off about me. We park the cart at the end of the hall, and I curl my hands by my sides, feeling exposed without the prop.

My adrenaline kicks in as I follow her through the castle. I'm putting all of my faith in this stranger without knowing her true intentions. Averting my eyes from the servants carrying feather dusters and brooms, I count each step across the dirty floor of the back corridor stretching out before me. Walking a few yards seems to take an eternity.

I hold my breath, my ribs burning with anxiety as we approach the guards posted at the servants' entrance.

My heart is pounding so hard, I'm surprised they can't hear it. The next five seconds pass in a blur. It doesn't hit me that we're outside until I feel the evening breeze.

I breathe the fresh air in, letting it carry the stale feeling of confinement from my skin as I note the thin sliver of a crescent moon hanging in the twilight sky.

Have I really been here for a whole moon cycle?

Carabosse, where are you?

A rope bridge swings above us as a guard carries a torch from a watch tower to light the sconces on the castle wall, and a flock of larks goes flying. The birdsong blends with the haunting sound of the forest.

"Will there be a carriage waiting?" I ask, tempted to hum along with the hypnotizing melody.

Marian jerks her chin toward the men patrolling the curtain wall. "Don't ask questions yet."

The Hartwood lives beyond the high tower at the back of the diamond-shaped bailey. Overlapping voices whisper through the rustling treetops, calling out to me, beckoning me to come closer.

Zelladine. Zelladine.

My eyelashes flutter, and I step away from Marian, staggering toward the Ivy Keep.

"No," she says, yanking me to the left. "This way."

My dread intensifies as we move right past the livery stable, and she brings me to a faded brick wall jutting out from the inner ward instead. I can't see past the thick vines woven through the gate, but she pushes it open and leads me into a garden. Night-blooming jasmine flowers open their petals shyly as we step over the untamed fescue.

A woman sits on a bench beneath a half-rotted trellis, a crimson gown spilling past her feet. She looks over the rim of her teacup, her eyes meeting mine. My heart skips as I note their unique shade—pale blue like a robin's egg.

Those eyes peered down at me a few months ago, wine-glazed and bored while I was being kicked around on a cold marble floor. They're dancing with mild amusement now.

Marian has brought me to Queen Roberta.

My sworn enemy sets her cup in the saucer and places it on the bench, folding her hands in her lap. "I'm so glad we can finally have this conversation in person."

Anger curdles in my gut as she sits there, a placid smile on her full lips. I want to wipe that look from her face. She's brought me here to taunt me. She wants to see the pain she's caused me.

I won't let her view my anguish for her entertainment.

Thorny roses wind their way up the trellis grids, and I encourage them, gnashing my teeth to give a command, the inhuman words coming naturally.

"Crush her."

Marian grabs my shoulders, attempting to break my gaze, but I've already given in to my rage. The vines twist around the bench, their thorns pricking the Queen's wrist.

"Ouch." She blows out a breath to quiet her reaction, slipping her fingers between the barbed bits, trying to loosen herself from my grip. "Damn it. Marian, please get her to stop."

"*Shh.* Listen to me." The maid shakes me so hard it rattles my teeth. "Stop it. She needs to speak to you."

But I'm not interested in having a conversation. The Queen lost the privilege of speaking to me when she killed my dragons.

Marian gives up on trying to get through to me.

"Aren't you going to do something?" she calls out, searching the dark hedges behind the Queen. The dense shadows between the overgrown shrubs make it hard to see who she's speaking to, but somebody is lurking behind the trellis.

"Since no one has told me what the devil is going on, I'm quite content to let my wife handle the situation as she sees fit." Carabosse steps out from the darkness, threads of it clinging to her body as if the night has been stitched into her black uniform. "Hello, darling."

5

CARABOSSE

Rosemary sways on her feet, her vines recoiling. They curl over the bench, their thorns poised to strike again. Beyond the castle walls, the trees groan and creak along to the forest's spectral singing. The tempo flares along with Rosemary's breathing.

When I saw her enter the garden, I concealed myself in the shadows to watch her from a distance. Queen Roberta assured me she was fine, but I wanted to assess her physical and mental condition without the distraction of our reunion.

After seeing her reaction, I'm not sure I believe a word that woman has told me.

My instincts kick in, and I reach for my wife, filled with fury. I'm shocked when our hands actually meet after weeks of searching for her in my dreams. Her heat seeps through my gloves, sending our mate bond into a wild frenzy thrumming between my ribs.

"I was promised you'd be unharmed." I run my thumb over the swollen skin beneath her eyes. "Why have you been crying?" The maid pulls Queen Roberta away from the bench, touching her fingers to her wrist. They come back stained with red droplets. "And why did you unleash your thorns like that?"

Rosemary sniffles, her eyes wide and fixed on mine, unblinking.

"Commander, if you don't mind my intrusion," Queen Roberta says, unfazed as her maid tends to the small tear in her sleeve. "We don't have a lot of time for this discussion."

But I do mind. My wife is here, and she looks fucking traumatized. I need to hear it from her own mouth that she's alright.

"You're going to have to wait." I throw a wall of shadows around us. With a growl, I slide my hands up to Rosemary's wrists and hold onto her before she can disappear again.

"Carabosse," she whispers.

She's here in one piece, I assure myself as I flip her palms open and push her sleeves back, inspecting her skin. I pat her ribs, working my way down to her waist.

"Carabosse." This time her voice cracks around my name.

"What's happened?" My head snaps up, and I search her face frantically. "Are you hurt?" The wall of shadows crackles with dark energy. "Your Queen asked me to hold myself back until she's said her piece, but if anyone has harmed you, they will die by my hand. Slowly. Painfully."

"I'm not hurt. Not physically. But I need you to—" She pushes at my hands where they're squeezing her hips. I tighten my grip, searching for bruises. *"Ugh.* Hold me for a second."

She flings herself forward, pressing against me like a battle-worn rider meeting the solid ground when she thought she never would again. I run my hand up her back and twine my fingers in her soft hair, bringing her closer. I've been so focused on looking for signs of abuse that I've overlooked what she really needs from me.

"Forgive me." I nuzzle the top of her head, inhaling her warm scent. My heart rate slows. The tight knot between my shoulders unravels as I exhale. "I'm still not used to being someone's soft place to land."

"There's nothing to forgive. I'm the one who messed everything up. You trusted me with the hatchlings and now they're —" She rolls a shoulder up to wipe her nose and makes an awful noise in her throat that creaks right through me. "I'm so sorry."

"What are you talking about?" I lift her chin gently, and she drags her gaze upward as if it pains her to look me in the eye.

"The Queen, she killed them."

I drop the shadows and face Queen Roberta. "You didn't tell her? How much does she know about this plan of yours?"

"Nothing," Roberta answers, folding her hands over the tight bodice of her corset to hide her injury. "The King has been keeping her drugged out of her mind. We couldn't risk her spilling our secrets in her sleep. "

I was already upset that *I* was excluded from this plan, but to think they've kept Rosemary in the dark this whole time... that she's been suffering.

"Release them," I grit out, forgetting the rules of diplomacy. I don't care that she's a queen. "Now."

"You heard her, Marian," she says. "Let them out."

Rosemary's fingers dig into my back as she twists to watch Marian traipse through the weeds to the mausoleum. The crumbling structure is built into the corner of the garden where the exterior wall meets the main building of the castle. She pushes on the tomb's entrance, the stone slab scraping against the foundation.

As soon as there's a wide enough gap, claws scratch at the frame, and two creatures launch themselves out of the building in two orange and silver streaks.

"The King wanted to break them and tame them for his own use," Marian explains to Rosemary. "We had to convince him they were dead, or else he would've searched the grounds high and low when they went missing. We served up two lambs on a silver platter and let him believe the Queen killed them during a fit of jealousy."

The dragons claw at the dirt, their wings fluttering so excitedly they catch air for a few seconds and tumble to the ground again. Moon rights themself instantly and prances straight for their mother while Sun rolls over and scrambles to join them.

Rosemary doesn't run to them. She seems terrified to let me go. "Am I imagining this?"

"No." I rub her lower back, nudging her toward them. "They're real."

Folding at the waist, she presses her hand to her belly, sobbing.

Sun and Moon rush her, knocking her off balance. She sinks to her knees, taking them down with her in a pile of thumping tails and beating wings. She bumps her forehead against Moon's while Sun climbs onto her lap, nipping playfully at the ends of her hair to get her attention.

"*Oh,* I've missed you too," she says, her sniffles transforming into a fit of giggles as she embraces the dragons. "You've grown so much, my little loves." She kisses the tops of their heads. "We're going to get you out of here."

She glances back at me, and I look to the Queen. "I'm going to take the three of them somewhere safe, and I'll come back to do whatever you need me to."

Rosemary's forehead crinkles in confusion. "Why would you do anything for her?"

"I can't let you leave," Roberta says before I can explain anything. "Not yet."

"Excuse me?" I take one step forward to position my body in front of Rosemary. "It's not like you can stop me."

"You're right. I can't," she agrees. The torchlight barely touches this side of the castle. Shadows sink into the pits beneath her eyes and stretch along the hollows of her high cheekbones. "But where will you take your wife? I'm assuming she won't be welcome in Sarteal after this, and we both know how she'll be treated in this kingdom as long as *he* is ruling. You need me to succeed. "

Gods damn it. I've never had to question my own strength, but now I have one giant glaring weakness that everyone can see.

Prince Alex already called it out. And now I'm being humbled by Lollishire's queen.

Rosemary grabs ahold of my thigh to steady herself as she stands. "What is she talking about? What's happening?"

Two crows fly in through a hole in the garden wall. Squawking, they flit around the tree behind the Queen and settle on a flimsy branch. "This is the woman who calls herself Robin. She's the one who's been pulling the strings to overthrow the monarchy."

Rosemary's mouth hangs open. "That can't be true."

I had the same moment of disbelief a half an hour ago when Queen Roberta invited me to her garden, promising to show me the herbs used to make her secret recipe for *orange spiced tea*. I recognized the phrase Alex had told me and thought I might have misheard her.

How can she be the mastermind behind such an elaborate scheme when I've never heard a significant thing about her?

She's never earned the common folks' love like Stefan's first wife, Queen Rina, nor has she issued another heir for him. I only know basic facts about her, the kind advisors give us to study before diplomatic visits.

Descended from the original royal family, Roberta was the youngest of seven daughters born to Lollishire's oldest noble house. King Stefan selected one of her sisters to be his bride after his second wife died, but an illness swept through the household a few weeks before the wedding. Roberta was the only one who survived it.

She was never meant to marry him.

"It *is* true." The Queen straightens her neck to look down her nose at Rosemary. Half of her chestnut brown brown hair is braided beneath a diadem of golden twigs and leaves. The other half flows back on the breeze, exposing a patch of mottled skin beneath her ear, bruised from the suction of rough kissing. "I have every reason to hate the King, and in two nights, I'll finally be free of him. If you help me with one last thing, I promise to take you with me."

"Why should I trust you?" Rosemary asks. "You've betrayed me in the past."

"I'll eat crow and apologize for that." Roberta watches a bird pass by, its black feathers streaking against the deepening sky. "I viewed you as a threat when you started getting too close to Prince Alex, but I eventually came to see what an asset you could be."

Rosemary scoffs. "I'm so glad I could prove myself worthy."

Roberta waves a hand, ignoring her sarcasm. "Anyways, it's all water under the bridge now. I'll get straight to the point— you don't trust me, and I don't trust you, but we both want the same thing. We'll be stronger if we work together."

"Why do you suddenly need Rosemary's help?" I'm skeptical of the Queen's intentions. She can dress this up as teamwork, but I know that keeping my wife here works to her advantage. If I turn on her, she can cause collateral damage. "You were supposed to take her somewhere safe as a condition of our original agreement. She was never supposed to be here in the first place."

"No she wasn't. She was supposed to be tucked away in Heartshire, but my plan was derailed by her abduction," she says, wringing her hands. "I'm still not sure if there was a breech on your side of things, or if my husband intercepted a message, but now that she's here, my most trusted friends— my so-called *Merry Men*—have been tasked with getting her out in addition to freeing her three family members from the Ivy Keep. Our resources have been stretched to the limit, but there's something we need to handle before we leave." She points to Rosemary. "That's where you come in."

Rosemary crumples her skirt in her fist—a habit that I've missed. "If I help you, my godmothers will be set free?"

"Yes. They're considered essential to the rebellion since their knowledge of spell work will help us revive the kingdom." Queen Roberta toes her silver slipper into the dirt. "I have a loyal friend working as a guard in the Ivy Keep. He'll be responsible for getting them out."

Rosemary glances at me. "What do you think?"

I lift my hand, letting my shadows swim around us lazily. "This is your decision. Say the word and I'll take you somewhere far across the sea, but you'll still be hunted by your King. If I could, I'd bring you home with me, but I can't protect you from my Queen." It goes against my very nature to admit that aloud, but I can't deny it. She needs to be aware of the risks. "Even my power has its limits."

A ghost of a smile plays on her lips. "It's good to know your arrogance is still intact." Rising on her toes, she cups my face. "We all have limits, and I know you're pushing yours to do this."

She wraps her arms around my neck and pulls me in,

pressing her lips to mine. In the madness of worrying about her, I forgot about this. The way she feels against me. How perfectly our mouths fit together when the tips of our tongues meet. I'm breathing hard when we break apart, our noses still touching.

"Thank you for coming for me," she says as the dragons butt their heads against our calves. "Again."

"I told you I would." It will probably be the last time I can swoop in for a while, so I need this to go smoothly. I'll see that she's reunited with her family and hope that she'll be happy. I kiss her one more time, humming against her mouth. "Go with your gut on this, but don't forget your gifts. They need you too."

I let the shadows drop to my feet, and Rosemary turns to her rebellion leader.

"What exactly do you want me to do?" she asks. "I need to know the conditions before I can agree."

"Stefan has another guest visiting the castle this week, the Duke of Syldringham. The corn in the borderlands has made him very wealthy, but he oversees one of the most impoverished duchies," she laments. "For the past year, I've had farmers pilfering from him to help feed and clothe my army. In retaliation, he's planning to blow up one of his granaries and blame it on me. I need you to find out which one it is so we can save it."

I smooth my thumb and middle finger over my eyelids. "You're asking her to stay here to *spy* for you?"

"Yes. We have a harsh winter ahead, and folks are already fretting about the harvest. Nothing will kill a rebellion faster than hunger, especially if people believe I'm responsible for destroying a precious food source. "

Her gown swishes around her slippered feet as she walks to one of her trees, pushing a clump of leaves aside to pick a few peaches swelling on its thin branches. "The witches insist they can break the Hartwood's curse by spring. We must protect what we have until then." She carries the ripe fruit in her arms, dropping a couple in our hands. "Here, a small gift for my new friends."

Rosemary raises the peach to her mouth and bites right in. I swear she's going to drive me mad before the end of all this.

"How will we find out where he's planning to attack?" she asks, licking up the juices. I turn my fruit over in my hand, watching as her tongue trails along the fuzzy skin. The heat blooming in my lower belly doesn't feel appropriate in this situation.

I can't look away, though. Can't take my eyes off of her when our time is limited. I'll absorb every moment I can get.

"My handmaiden will fetch you again in the morning, and she'll show you where to look," the Queen says. "We have until sundown two nights from now to find this information. Everything is set in motion for our escape, and I have the timing down to a T. The King will lose his shit once he realizes the Sartealeans have turned on him. We need to be miles from the castle by then."

I pick that schedule apart in my head. "That'll put me miles away during the escape."

"Yes, your job will be to attend your meetings and make Stefan believe his plans are going swimmingly while we sabotage them."

"You can't expect me to leave Rosemary behind."

"I'm asking you anyway," she snips. "My husband will have eyes on you when you leave. He'll notice if you run off with one of the maids, and he might think to check on Rosemary. If he discovers the assassin I've placed in her bedchamber, she won't be able to fight her way out of the castle, and then I won't have the power to evacuate three women from the Ivy Keep."

She walks us through the scenario as if she's considered everything that could possibly go wrong already. "Every choice we make from here on out will have a ripple effect. So I'll ask you once before you commit—are you all in?"

"Yes," Rosemary says, standing tall despite the slight tremor of nerves running through her limbs. I bite my lips, determined not to undermine her courage. This is what she's been waiting for. This is her time to shine. "Let's bring it all down."

She lifts her peach pit out of the hatchlings' reach as Sun climbs on Moon's back and snaps their teeth. Moon rolls them off and jumps into a tussling stance, their tail wagging with pent-up energy. "Last year I would've given anything for this opportunity, but it's not just about my godmothers anymore. The dragons are going to need a place to stretch their wings safely."

"They would have plenty of space to fly in the Dragon Valley. If only you'd..."

If only, if only....That voice has been relentless lately. I exhale sharply through my nose to drive it away.

"That's it, then." Queen Roberta claps her hands. "It shouldn't take too long for us to reach safety on horseback now that I've taken all of the land west of Maletna."

The rebels have covered a lot of ground in the past month. That shaves a four-day trip down to one, but there's still a lot that could go wrong during that time.

The Queen smiles, looking a little too pleased with herself for my liking.

My shadows spill across the lawn. Marian spots them and moves closer to the trellis. The maid is a few inches shorter than Roberta, and looks as though she'd blow away in a strong breeze.

Still, she positions herself protectively over her Queen as I issue an ultimatum, "I'll give you until the nightfall on the next day to meet at an arranged location. If you're not there by then, I'll fly into the King's City. And if anything happens to my wife, you won't have to worry about winning your rebellion. You'll be the ruler of an ash kingdom."

A dark look settles on Roberta's face, sharpening her delicate features into something fierce. I'm not looking at a queen anymore, but the infamous Robin.

"I would expect no less from the wraith of Sarteal," she says. "But I'll do everything in my power to keep that from happening. I've dreamt of taking King's City with my army riding behind me for years. *I* will be the one who kills the King, and I will do it properly by earning the kingdom's trust before rallying. The people must choose me."

She shifts her eyes to the gate. "That's all the time we have for this evening. Stefan will be expecting us in a few minutes. Marian, please take the hatchlings back to the mausoleum."

The dragons wrap their tails around Rosemary's legs, refusing to budge for the maid. I understand their reluctance. Ten minutes together isn't nearly enough. My hand is still clasped tight around hers.

Roberta forces an open-mouthed smile, speaking through her teeth as she passes by me. "We have to leave."

I kiss Rosemary's knuckles and let her go. For a moment I think she might run behind me, but she bends down to help with the hatchlings instead.

"It's alright," she soothes them, guiding them back to their temporary shelter. "I'll be back soon, and you can send me as many messages as you want to."

Each step away from her lands with a blow that ricochets

through me. I trek back to the inner ward, reminding myself of the game we're playing as her voice fades in the distance.

My jaw is set by the time I face Stefan. He ushers us into the castle where we're greeted by the twang of a harpsichord. A woman perches on a stool near the bottom of the stairwell, plucking the instrument's strings. It's a pleasant yet obvious distraction from the constant wailing of the devouring trees.

The King strides beneath a curving balcony, the underbelly of the mezzanine decorated with ribbons of gold and green banners. "Tell me, Commander, what do you think of my Queen's garden?".

I bounce the uneaten peach in my hand. "It's lovely."

"It's a strange hobby for a woman of such fine breeding, but she insists on doing most of the work herself." He chuckles. "She's done a splendid job of making it look pretty."

Queen Roberta bows her head, peering up through her lashes. "You flatter me."

He strokes her cheek. "You're free to run along to my chambers. We won't bore you with any more of our political nonsense this evening."

"Thank you, Your Highness." She smiles demurely, giggling.

In another life, she could have performed in a grand theater. She has King Stefan wrapped around her finger. He has no idea he's just delivered a viper to his bed.

"Happy wife, happy life." He places his hands on his hips, pushing his cloak back. His smirk falters as her footsteps echo down the hallway. "By the way, I was sorry to hear about that fiasco with your bride. She'll regret her decision when we crush her beloved Robin's rebellion."

He taps a finger on his belt, drawing my eye to the weapon resting near his thigh—a knife sheathed in a leather holster, its polished black handle carved with remarkable fae crafts-manship.

Is he fucking kidding?

I'm standing four feet away and he's taunting me with my father's knife. It would take five seconds to grab it and plunge the blade into his throat. I imagine sticking the tip in and pushing it through the cartilage.

Where is that voice inside my head telling me to go for it?

"Don't be stupid. Can't you feel that?"

I shut my eyes and the back of my neck tightens. There's iron nearby.

I glance at the ceiling, dropping my eyes before he realizes I've seen the edge of a metallic net peeking out from beneath the tapestries.

Of course Stefan wouldn't take such a risk without the right precautions. Even now, with guards all around and the ability to block my magic, he's merely teasing himself with the threat of a confrontation.

I doubt he wants to provoke me outright.

It probably makes him feel powerful, thinking he's got me running his errands while my wife is locked up in one of his chambers. I bet he gets off on it.

I pat his shoulder like we're old pals, pretending I haven't caught on to his bullshit. "Queen Mal would never approve of using the Dragon Army for personal reasons, but I'll admit that I'll take pleasure in burning the ones who've wronged me."

He drops his hands, letting his cloak fall over my blade, just like I thought he would. "When people forget their place in this world, chaos ensues. We need to remind them where they stand from time to time."

"Oh. I agree, Your Majesty." His downfall will be sweet.

We walk down the corridor, my magic strengthening as we move away from the iron. I sense something behind me, a soft presence mingling with my shadows. Coughing into my fist, I turn my head over my shoulder and catch a glimpse of two maids scurrying in the opposite direction.

My shadows have found Rosemary.

I command my magic to follow her. I want to know exactly where she's going.

6

ROSEMARY

There's a slight tickle at the back of my heel, a kiss of magic that wraps along my ankle and trails behind me as I follow Marian back to my bedchamber.

I'd know that feeling anywhere, the way it mingles with my own energy. Carabosse has found me. That gives me enough strength to keep my feet moving toward captivity. Away from the three beings who mean the world to me.

It makes my heart ache to leave my little family. That's what we are now, I think. A ragtag group of creatures who've been thrown together by fate. My mind still hasn't fully caught up to the news that we're all here, and my chest is still sore from the hours I spent mourning the hatchlings.

Rubbing my sternum to ease the pain, I tell myself we'll be ok.

We just need to survive the next couple days and get to rebel territory. I tuck my chin low as we approach the guards and let Marian do the talking.

"Just here for the nightly check-in," she says, and they let us in.

Once the door is closed, the woman in my bed sits up and drops her feet on the floor in a fluid movement. With all of the commotion of the evening, I almost forgot she was in here.

I size her up once before I slip into my nightgown. How in the world is this graceful woman an assassin? The Queen sounded confident she could fight her way out of the castle, but she doesn't look particularly tough as she swings her hips to an imaginary tune, prowling across the room.

I crawl under the covers, deciding not to press the issue. My head is filled with enough worries, and she doesn't seem overly concerned about anything.

She waves as she leaves with Marian, and I hold my breath, straining my ears for any signs of violence. I'm convinced the guards will realize we've pulled one over on them at any moment.

But minutes pass, and nothing happens.

My chamber is quiet enough to hear my vine tapping at the window. I try to take comfort in the silence and get some rest, but now that I'm sitting still, the night's events are finally catching up to me.

I toss and turn on the mattress, questioning my reality.

Robin is the Queen. Nothing could have prepared me for learning her identity.

Over the years, I've come up with plenty of theories about the woman who kept me running around the apothecary. Not once did I imagine her as the Queen. Thinking of her lying beside the King while trying to overthrow the monarchy is so absurd, I'd laugh about it if it weren't for the tight band of pressure around my forehead.

I open my mouth wide to unlock my jaw. If I'm going to be stuck here for two more days, I can't afford a migraine. I need to clear my head.

After a few deep breaths, a series of images flashes behind

my eyelids. There are stone walls and snippets of scaly red fore-claws pawing at a marble statue as Moon watches Sun climb a tomb. Then there's my face, coupled with the dragon's happiness to see me.

I bite my thumb, blocking my bittersweet emotions from flooding our bond. Instead, I recall one of my happiest memories—the day we were picking flowers in the Wildlands when a summer storm rolled in. We raced back to the inn and sat on the covered porch, laughing and watching the rain, not caring at all that we were drenched.

I'm not confident in my ability to communicate with the hatchlings yet, but I try my best to channel that feeling over to them while deciphering the messages they send. Even after our time apart, I can tell the difference between Sun's excited reactions and Moon's pensive observations.

I do my best to respond accordingly.

Eventually, they either grow bored of me or drift off to sleep, and my mind goes blank again. I open my eyes to a darkened room, unnerved by the shadows beside my bed. One looms taller than the rest. I clench my fists around my blankets, noting the way it moves, like it's tilting its head. There aren't any dressers in here that should be making the shape of a human silhouette.

Someone is in here. *Watching* me.

Bolting upright, I smack the back of my skull against the headboard and rip the pillow out from under me, swinging at the canopy. The shadows break into a dozen dark ribbons on impact and slip through the gauze. They swim around my feet and glide over my legs, dragging silky tendrils of night over my body.

Carabosse's voice sounds from the shadows. "Rosemary?"

"Yes, I'm here," I whisper back to her. "You scared me."

"Sorry." The shadows move continuously, swirling in a dark cloud above me. "Are you really ok? Please be honest."

I consider her question for a few moments. I'm tired, stressed, confused, and terrified that none of this will work out the way I want it to, but it's the first time I've felt the slightest bit of hope in weeks.

"We're all alive. I guess that means I'm doing alright." I turn on my left side like I would if we were lying next to each other. "Are *you* ok?"

"I'm fine," she says flatly, her shadows spiking outward.

"Really? It kind of seems like you're not fine."

"Maybe I'm not," she says. "I've been going mad wondering where you might have been these past few weeks. I think I would've gone on a rampage if I couldn't feel you through—" The cloud stutters, then flows back into its circular rhythm as she catches herself.

I've heard the fae can feel their mates. A slow grin spreads across my face as I contemplate what that means. Does she carry me around like an extra weight in her limbs, or am I noise in the back of her head?

If she could see me, she'd realize I already know what she's been hiding from me. I'm about to tease her about it when I hear the guards laughing in the hallway. My smile fades. All of the questions I want to ask her suddenly feel too intimate for this place.

"I don't like this," Carabosse says, breaking the silence. "Not Robin, and certainly not the fact that she wants you in the castle until she leaves. We didn't agree to this."

"No, we didn't, but at least the end goal remains the same after we're done here." I draw my knees up toward my belly, and her shadows mold around my curves. "This is merely a bump in the road."

"Only you would consider a month of captivity a *bump in*

the road." She chuckles, and I curl my fingers beneath my chin, wishing I could see her.

"One of us has to remain optimistic in these trying times."

"Glad I can always count on you to see the bright side of things," she says. I close my eyes, imagining her wry smile. Her next words are spoken so softly, I nearly mistake them for a noise in the hallway. "I miss you."

"I miss you too."

"I wish I could handle this the way I want to. I'd love to kill Stefan and go on the run with you."

"I'd like that, but that's not in the cards for us, is it?"

"No, it's not." Her answer is definitive, her oath to her queen an ever-present barrier between us. She can't outrun that cursed mark on her arm. *Yet.* Someday I'll figure out a way to repay her for all she's done for me.

"You should get some rest," she says, filling the quiet around me. "We can speak more freely in our dreams."

My body won't relax. I'm too afraid to give up control of myself by losing consciousness. "Will you stay with me until I fall asleep? I dread floating into nothingness."

"Of course, darling. I won't let you float away." Her dark tendrils press against me, slithering over my body to wrap around my wrists and belly . The gentle compression lends a sense of gravity. Green threads loop around my fingertips and swirl up to my elbows. "You're safe anytime we're in the same place. If you call out for me, nothing will stop me from running to you."

I know she can't keep me safe forever, but I feel better when she's near. Dragging my hands over my skin, my magic awakens beneath her promise of protection.

I make a silent vow to never give it up again. I'd rather die fighting than feel powerless.

"What are you doing?" she asks as I run my fingers along

my inner thighs, stoking the thin green lines running from my knees to my pelvis. "Your energy has...shifted."

"You can sense that?"

"I always can," she says, her statement edged with a soft growl.

My face heats as I catch my fingers near the edge of my thin undergarments. Sex has been the furthest thing from my mind, but her gravelly voice is giving me ideas.

It's been weeks of stress and worry for her. Weeks of solitude and sleep for me. We both need a release. Neither of us know what tomorrow might bring.

Biting my lip, I lift my nightgown higher and slip my hand beneath the layer of my undergarments, brushing my curls. "How about this?"

Her breath shudders in my ear. *"Yes."*

I part myself, coaxing her shadows into the cleft between. "I've spent too much time asleep. Help me feel awake in my body."

"Rosemary." Another low growl, a warning. "We need to be careful here. The guards might be listening."

The guards think I'm lost to the effects of the sleeping elixir. They have no idea what's going on behind my closed door while they pass the time playing card games, occasionally making jokes about my situation.

That thought emboldens me. I palm my breast with my free hand, feeling its fullness.

Finding pleasure in a place like this is an act of defiance.

"Your antics have already been maddening enough this evening," Carabosse groans.

"How so?"

"You didn't even check that peach for poison. I was beside myself watching you eat it."

"You should have eaten yours too," I say, pinching my nipple into a stiff peak. "It was delicious."

I can still taste it, its flavor enhanced by the memory of Carabosse's kiss on my lips. It was the best thing I've had in weeks, perfectly juicy and sweet.

"I'm sure it was." She draws in a serrated breath. "That's what your scent reminds me of. Fresh peaches and honey."

I bring my hand lower, recalling the sweet inhuman scent of her skin beneath all the smoke and leather from dragon riding. "Then you should run your tongue along its seam and think of me."

Her shadows wind around my thighs and pull them apart, snaking down the bed to curl around the posts. I'm tied in place, splayed wide open in the dark. My pulse drops between my legs, pounding in a steady rhythm.

"I need you to stay quiet for me." A dark claw grips my chin, its pointed digit tracing over my lips. "Can you do that, little witch?"

"Yes."

"Then think of me watching while you touch yourself," she says, not only sensing the shift in my energy, but matching it as if she knows exactly what I need. I can feel her presence even though she's not physically in the room with me.

I picture her sitting on the window seat as I trace my fingers over my sensitive skin. Her forearms would be braced on her thighs, and she'd watch so patiently, her body unmoving, her breathing even.

But I know there'd be tension coiling beneath her trained stillness, her fingernails digging into her knees while thinking of all the things she'd like to be doing to me.

My belly quivers as I flutter over my mound, working one finger into my entrance. I draw it back up to rub a few wet circles around my clit. Keeping my rhythm light and easy, I block out any thoughts that don't involve Carabosse. I think of her muscles against my soft curves. Her onyx stare boring into my core.

The gentle pressure around my throat is the next best thing to feeling her on top of me; it pulls me back into my body. I'm buzzing all over with the knowledge that my wraith and her shadows will always find me.

My lips part as I hit the brink of my release, and her shadows tighten just enough to choke off the moan that threatens to break free. She holds on until the last wave passes.

"There you are, little witch," she says, releasing my neck. My legs are freed next, falling on the mattress. "Rest and I'll find you in your dreams."

I'm still afraid of what awaits me in my sleep, but my body is warm and heavy, and it takes me easily.

I drift past a shimmering lake, watching the moon rise over the violet mountains in the distance. A lonely cry echoes through the night, and I see a silver bird circling a peak, its long feathers peppering the sky with dusty starlight. I wonder if there are others like it in Faerie, or if the creature is stuck searching for something it lost in the Fade.

"What are you doing up there, darling?"

I tip my head back toward the palace behind me. Carabosse steps out onto a marble balcony, her cape flowing down her back as she leans against the railing. She looks up at me with a cocky grin, and I notice how my skirts are floating up above me.

I thrash my legs beneath the sheer pink layers flowing past my feet and give a pitiful squeak. "I'm falling."

"Yes, you are," she muses. "Very slowly, and in the wrong direction."

"It's not funny." I flap my arms like I'm swimming, attempting to propel myself downward. My legs bob right back up again.

Her grin widens, and she reaches out for me. "Let's get you down from there."

Reeling me in, she moves her hands beneath my shoulders as they pass over the railing. Lowering my face to mine, she kisses me, her mouth still curved in a smile. I wrap my arms around her neck, and she twirls me onto the balcony, setting me down on my feet.

"I told you I wouldn't let you float away," she says.

I hold onto her until I find a sense of gravity, and then I take my place beside her at the railing, studying the swoop of her long lashes and the way the moon casts pearly highlights on her cheekbones as she stares out at the mountains.

Her eerie beauty fills me with a pang of longing. I want to look at her face whenever I feel like it. It's not fair that we have to steal moments like these while we're sleeping.

She extends her pinky, brushing it against mine. "We don't have to talk about what went wrong that night if you'd rather enjoy the quiet."

"And miss the chance to yap your ears off?" I quip, swallowing the lump in my throat. This isn't an ideal situation, but it beats any other alternatives.

Carabosse chortles. "My nights have been quite boring without our conversations. Yap away."

"I left for the carriage like we planned, and Stefan was waiting for me," I say, recounting the details quickly to hide my shame. I wish there was more to the story, but I folded so easily. "He killed my escort, and I complied with his wishes in hopes of sparing the hatchlings." The night comes back to me in bits and pieces—the smell of blood and the dead body. "In retrospect, I should've brought a tree down on him, or summoned a vine to blow out a wheel. I could've used your knife. I didn't think of that at the time, though. He had my dragons and I—" Hanging my head, I confess, "I froze and hoped you'd find me."

I feel so damn pathetic.

"Don't ever blame yourself for that. You did what you thought was best in the moment, and you survived. Besides, you were right to believe I'd come looking for you." Her eyes are pitch black when I look up again. "I'd have flown here right away if King Stefan hadn't blocked us from meeting. He knows more about the fae than I thought. I had no idea he was aware of my dream walking abilities."

"Well, I knew you'd show up eventually," I say. "Although I'm a little surprised you didn't make a grand entrance by kicking the doors in."

"Trust me, I wanted to. But Prince Alex warned me how detrimental that would be to the rebellion."

I scrunch my nose in disbelief. *"Alex?"*

She tells me everything, from his half-baked rescue mission to the pages ripped from *The Grimoire of the Devouring Tree*. The new information fills in most of the blanks left by Stefan's revelation, but there are still a few pieces missing. My head spins as I think back to my time as a small child in the Hart-wood. I can't conjure a single memory.

"I don't know what to make of it," I mutter. "It would've been nice if someone had provided a text or a pamphlet if they wanted me to fulfill some prophecy. *Set the forest free.*" I push away from the railing to pace the balcony. "How am I supposed to stop a kingdom from dying? I'm not even sure who I am anymore. A daughter of a forest maiden. What does that make me—half woman, half tree?"

I feel weightless again. I point my toes, scrambling to touch the ground as I float. Carabosse hooks an arm around my waist and pulls me down.

"You're still the same tenacious witch I met at the edge of the forest. We'll figure out the rest," she says, keeping me grounded with the weight of her hands on my shoulders. "What I don't understand is how Stefan knew you'd be heading to that particular carriage, although I suppose he could've intercepted a message like Roberta suggested. Did anything stand out to you that night? Was anyone following you?"

"Not that I noticed." The hair on the back of my neck stands on end as I think of the way the plants whispered to me as I walked to the carriages. I shouldn't have ignored their warning, but it was too late to turn back.

And there was someone else there, now that I think about it. I haven't had much time to replay the events of that night with a clear head.

"Thea saw me leaving," I say, remembering her lavender eyes crinkling with worry. "But she encouraged me to escape before Queen Mal tried to harm me."

"Thea was there?" she breathes, putting an arm's length between us.

"Yes, she shared your concerns about your Queen. She also feared she'd try to keep you from getting too close to anybody. You don't think she had something to do with it, do you?"

A crease forms between her eyebrows, wordlessly confirming the truth I'm trying to deny. I've let the memory of that night sit buried beneath the fog of the elixir, not wanting to touch it.

"Thea has served Mal's family for centuries," she says. "The fae are loyal to their rulers. She's oathbound to her Queen."

"So are you."

"That's different." Rubbing her face, she turns away from me and props her forearms on the railing. "Did she say anything else to you?"

Only that I'm your mate. "Nothing that would have made me think she'd want to push me into an enclosed space with Stefan."

Her wide shoulders lift and drop back. "There's something you're not telling me."

I don't know why the words are all tangled in my throat. Up until Thea revealed her secret, I assumed Carabosse was keeping her word to deliver me to safety. I figured her feelings developed naturally as she got to know me.

A mate bond changes everything.

It's an otherworldly attraction I can't understand. Acknowledging it might shift our dynamic.

As if she senses my apprehension, she looks back at me, her expression softening. "What is it, Rosemary?"

I can't hold the truth back when she's looking at me like that. "She told me what *nyxstrystia* means."

My words hang in the air. Several seconds pass before Carabosse gives a nearly imperceptible shake of her head. "Why would she have done that?"

"Because I asked her about it." Her silence stretches on and on. It's the worst reaction I can imagine. I pick at the layers of my gown, embarrassed. She said that word more than once, but I want to brush it off. I feel too vulnerable. "Sorry, perhaps it was a misunderstanding. I might've misheard what you said when I woke up on that porch to you cleaning my face."

"You remembered that?"

"How could I forget it?" I was all out of sorts that day, but the image of her touching me so tenderly is permanently inked into my memory. My head was filled was horror stories about the wraith, and she wiped them all away with her actions. She carried me from my burning apothecary and treated me like I was worth something.

She saved me.

I think I'd like to be bound to her in every way. Yes. I want that, even if it's frightening.

But that possibility seems like it's shrinking with each passing second, my heart sinking as I await her explanation.

"It's not a misunderstanding." She sighs deeply and drops her head in her hands, working her fingers into her black waves.

"Is that such a bad thing?" I ask, my voice faint. I lift my hands. The edges of my body are turning transparent.

The double doors behind me swing open, and warm steam rolls across the balcony. Carabosse glances back, concern pinched into her features.

"Never mind that for now." White rings form around her irises as she speaks calmly. "You're waking up, and you need to stay aware of your surroundings. Please be safe moving around the castle."

"I will be." My promise dissolves into the fog pouring from my mouth, but I catch her last words before I'm yanked from the dream.

"My shadows will be with be with you until I leave."

7

ROSEMARY

Hot vapors sting my sinuses, and I snap my eyes open to Marian holding a cup of tea beneath my nose. The robust blend is enough to jolt my senses.

"Good morning," she says, sweetly and louder than necessary for the sake of the guards outside my door. "We'll clean you up and get you some breakfast. You can have some nice porridge if you promise not to fight today."

Rolling my eyes, I mumble a promise to behave, chug a few mouthfuls of tea, and force a few spoonfuls of the cold porridge down even though I'm feeling too jittery to eat. Marian stares me down until she's satisfied by the dent in the bowl and takes it from me.

"Can't have you passing out," she whispers, handing me my maid's uniform.

The blonde woman from last night–the pretty, alleged assassin—takes my place in the bed as I crawl out of it.

I jump into the gown, self-conscious of how the women are watching me.

They might be strangers, but their mistress has been

spying on me for years. I'm sure the *Merry Men* know plenty of invasive details about me—my habits and headaches, and how sick I get when I don't eat.

It's another thought to add to the chaos bouncing around inside my pounding head. The abrupt ending to my dream with Carabosse has left me feeling moody. I have more questions than answers after our meeting.

Thin rings of shadows circle my knuckles as I shake out my cap, the wisps stretching out and lingering against my fingertips before retreating to the dark corners of the room. Carabosse's magic is hiding where I can't see it, but I know she's here with me.

I take a breath and refocus. I promised I would be safe today, even if she couldn't hear me.

Today's mission requires my full attention.

I walk through the castle, following Marian down the back hallways designed to keep the servants hidden from the nobility. When we reach the ground floor, the kitchen opens around us, crammed with copper pans and cauldrons hanging from the ceiling. Two maids work side by side at the table in the center, kneading pale blobs of dough on the floured surface.

A stout woman with steel grey hair spares a glance at us as she stokes the flames on the roasting range. "What kind of errands does the Queen have ye runnin' this morning?"

"She's got tea in the garden, Ruth," Marian answers, her country accent thickening noticeably. "Gonna need that tray of sweets for the fine ladies."

"Aye." Ruth spins the chickens on the rotisserie spit, a sweat stain spreading across the back of her olive dress, its fabric a few shades darker than the sage uniforms the rest of the kitchen staff is wearing.

I realize she must be the head cook and try to shrink in my gown as she disappears into an alcove lined with shelves of cooling racks. She comes out a few moments later, carrying a white box filled with the finest pastries I've ever seen—miniature cakes and flaky shells filled with berries and cream.

"Help me set these up," Marian says to me, taking the box to a long counter running along the length of the back wall. She pulls a golden tray from the cupboards beneath it and places a few sweets in the middle, working outward toward the edges. I follow her pattern, filling in the spaces as she speaks with Ruth.

"The house staff will be changing the linens in the guests' chambers at ten o'clock on the dot," the cook says. "That'll give you three hours to find what you need."

Marian makes room for one more petit-four, completing the arrangement. "Perfect. I appreciate your knowledge of the housekeeping schedule."

"Anytime, my dear girl. You'd better get going before Marwenna and Marge come to fetch the King's breakfast." Ruth bumps her hip against hers. "You know how they love to wag their tongues."

They pass information covertly, chatting as if they're swapping gossip about the household staff. It occurs to me that Robin's rebellion isn't being won by warriors, but by the secrets carried on crows' wings and servants' tongues.

Shops, taverns, and kitchens all around the kingdom make up a patchwork warfront.

"Here." Ruth takes the last two pastries in the box and hands them to Marian and me. "These are too pretty to go to waste, and you two deserve a treat considering everything."

My anxiety subsides as I nibble the fried dough and taste the sweet cream inside. This woman isn't a threat. She must have been in the Queen's plan to cook the lambs.

"Thank you," I tell her, hoping she knows I appreciate her

for more than just the sweets. She smiles broadly, the mole near her lip sinking into the deep line on her ruddy cheek.

"Anything to help," she says, speaking so softly I can barely hear her above the clatter of dishes being washed in the scullery. "I was eleven when they took my aunt to the Ivy Keep. It's too late for her, but there are many families who are still waiting. Do this for all of us. Goddess protect you, ladies."

Marian lowers her chin. "May she keep you too, dear friend."

Ruth grabs my hand, gives it a quick squeeze, then spins around to pull a wooden spoon from the rack above her and waves it at the two maids entering the kitchen. "Don't get your underthings in a twist, Marwenna. I've got the King's plate coming."

We take that as our cue to leave, carrying our tray out into the inner bailey where the Hartwood's song is humming gently through the trees this morning. I tune it out, shifting my attention to my grip on the platter's handle. I struggle to pull it up to my hip as we enter the garden, cursing the fact that it'll take me weeks to regain my strength.

Queen Roberta is sitting at a table set beneath the peach tree. She takes a lump of sugar and passes the canister to the three women keeping her company, all of them dressed in crisp white day gowns embroidered with tiny rosebuds and daisies.

"Someone needs to put an end to this madness," a woman says, pouring a dot of cream into her cup. "Our summer home was robbed two weeks ago, and the thief stole all of the jewels I was planning to wear to next season's ball. The worst part is the note that horrendous Robin woman left, saying it would be used to aid the rebellion." She touches her perfectly coiffed blonde hair with her white satin glove. "Can you imagine some plain peasant wearing the diamond David bought me for our anniversary?"

"Such a large bauble would look tacky on anyone else's neck," Roberta says, deadpan over the rim of her teacup. Her teeth clink against the porcelain. "The horror."

"Perhaps she meant it would be sold," the woman beside her says, fiddling with her gold necklace. "I heard Lady Diselka complain that Robin stole from her husband's coffers and used the coins to buy food for people who couldn't even pay their rent this year." She blows on her tea. "It's unfair if you ask me."

The third woman giggles. "Don't worry, our King will put an end to this birdbrain nonsense. As we all know, my husband is working very closely with His Majesty to ensure Robin's name is ruined for good. The duke has assured me the conflict will be over within a week."

Two spirals of brown hair have been strategically pulled from her elaborate updo. They swing past her pearl earrings as she bounces in her seat, giddy for an opportunity to mention her husband's relationship with the King. Based off what she's mentioned, I think it's safe to assume she's the Duchess of Syldringham.

"We must trust the men on this one," she says.

"Indeed." Robin smirks and sets her cup down. "Ladies, look. Our pastries are finally here. Why don't we talk about something more interesting? What shall we serve at our parties to celebrate the peace?"

The women break out into a titter of laughter, bantering about cheese spreads and crystal bowls as Marian and I place the platter on the table.

The duchess looks up from her tea, narrowing her eyes at Marian. "Isn't that your handmaiden, my Queen? What is she doing out here?"

Roberta licks pink frosting from her fork without missing a beat. "Yes, that's her. The awful wretch ruined one of my favorite dresses in the wash last week, so I've demoted her to housekeeping duties."

"A month of hard work should prevent another error like that," the duchess replies, slicing a petit-four into thin slices before taking a bite. "It's so hard to find good servants these days. I swear that Robin woman has filled their heads with the silliest ideas."

Marian bows her head to Roberta. "Do you have any special requests for me, my Queen?"

"Go tend to the mausoleum." Roberta dismisses us with a flick of her wrist. "Don't come out until it's squeaky clean. Let us break our fast in peace."

"Yes, Your Majesty," we say I unison, and the noblewomen turn back to their dainty dishes, praising their Queen's creative punishment.

We stomp through the dewy grass with our damp hems sticking to our ankles, making sure the nobles are distracted with some salacious gossip before opening the building's stone entrance. The hatchlings flap their wings and race toward me despite my mental warning to stay back. Marian manages to close us in the dark tomb without anyone noticing.

My eyes adjust to the dark as I greet the dragons. Thin beams of light shine through the cracks in the roof, reflecting off the surfaces of the crypts. A statue of a woman is positioned with her hands folded in prayer over a row of the compartments. Wildflowers are carved into her waist-length hair, and a sweet smile rests on her lips.

"That's Queen Rina," Marian says. "The King had it removed from the square after she was put on the pyre, but he never got rid of it. Roberta pretends that it bothers her, but she's done her best to preserve her likeness over the years."

"Does she want people to love her the way they loved their common-born queen?" I study the marble face of the woman who inspired so many ballads and stories in the countryside, contemplating the familiar shape of her eyes. "Is that why she's doing this?"

"She's not in this for glory," Marian says. "Toppling this cursed monarchy is her first priority."

"But why?" She said she had her reasons to hate the King, but I'm curious to know what could have motivated her to put herself in such a high-risk situation.

"You're not the only one who wants to protect the people you love."

Who could she be protecting?

Her family is dead, and she never had a suitor before the King. People whispered that she was a sickly thing who spent all of her time reading and studying. No one ever saw her outside of Heartshire's castle. When King Stefan met her for the first time on their wedding day, he was reportedly stunned by her beauty.

A beautiful queen. That's all anyone ever says about her.

The rest is a mystery.

Marian frowns as I scritch between Sun and Moon's wings. "We didn't come here for a visit."

"Stay here and be good." I rub their necks as I give the command. "Tomorrow we get to leave."

Begrudgingly, I let go and step to the back of the mausoleum where Marian is standing next to a life-sized sculpture of a man built into the wall connected to the castle. "What *are* we doing here, exactly? I'm not sure how we're supposed to find out which granary the King is targeting in an old shed full of bones and paintings."

"Just be quiet and come help me."

She presses her hands against the sculpture, and I take a closer look at it. The man's figure protrudes from a flat oval stone decorated with trees. It reminds me of a sarcophagus lid.

"Please tell me this doesn't involve digging through dead bodies," I whisper.

"Shh." There's a *click* as Marian jams a hairpin into a small hole next to his knee, and the slab moves toward us slightly, breaking its seal against the wall. "The trickster prince had a passageway built into the castle," she explains, grasping the edge of the slab. I do the same, prying it open. "It hadn't been used for years when we discovered its entrance, but most of its branches are still safe to use."

We pull on the stone until we reveal a hole that comes up to my chest, its width narrower than my armspan. I gape as she ducks into it. "Most of them?"

"You'll be fine if you follow me. Thanks to the Duchess of Syldringham's loose lips, we know her husband keeps a detailed journal of all his plans. We just need to find it while he's out for a morning hunt with the King and get out of his chambers before the maids show up to clean, otherwise they'll report us for snooping."

I crouch into the tunnel behind her. "No big deal."

The passageway reeks of mildew.

Gagging, I waddle until it widens and I can stand at my full height. It's too dark to see anything, but I can hear Marian's skirts rustling in front of me. I rely on the sound of her footsteps as she leads me up a narrow staircase. I stumble up uneven risers and chipped edges, noting whenever we hit the plateau of a landing.

That's the second floor.

And the third.

Even with how weak I'm feeling, I have to slow down to keep from bumping into Marian. She exhales harshly with each step, her throat whistling as she clears the fourth floor and turns right, leading me straight into a solid wall. Catching the outline of her fingers moving across the surface, I work with her to find another opening.

"I think this is it," I say, discovering a hard lip beneath a layer of grit. It gives when I push on it.

"Careful." Marian wheezes, her stomach going concave in the meager light. "Check that the room is clear."

"Do we need to turn back?" I pat the empty spot on my hip where my satchel should be, apothecary remedies for soothing inflamed lungs springing into my mind.

"We can't." She shoos me away. "It's just the dust. I'll be fine in a second."

She backs up as I press on the seal. It's much easier to open than the one downstairs. I crack it open another half an inch, sticking my fingers through the gap to lift the edge of the tapestry covering it. I jump back with a gasp, startled by the full suit of armor propped up on a stand beside the opening. Swallowing a string of curses, I search my surroundings.

Two burgundy couches are positioned on opposite sides of the room, and there's a fireplace next to the door on the wall across from me. I have to crane my neck to see the entirety of the spacious room. It spans at least two stories, with a gilded staircase leading up to a railing that wraps around the upper level. There aren't any entrances up there as far as I can tell.

"No one else is here," I croak, stepping beneath the tapestry. Marian comes out behind me, her nose red and eyes watery.

She sticks her head out the door, doing a quick sweep of the hall. "This way."

Portraits of the trickster prince's descendants hang high on the walls. Deceased members of the ruling family seem to sneer down at us as we meddle in the castle they helped to build, working to tear it down from within.

A painting of King Stefan's sister is located near the end of the hall. Marian pulls me into the chamber underneath it.

"The duke left an awful mess for the maids," I comment, taking in the clothes strewn across the floor. Champagne glasses litter the nightstand. I wrinkle my nose at the cigar butts floating in their flat contents.

"That works better for us," Marian says, opening a dresser drawer. "He's less likely to notice something is amiss and blame the maids on duty."

"I guess that's true." I step over an open valise, lifting a pile of riding breeches to unbutton a pocket in the lining.

No luck.

We check the obvious places—his bags, the vanity, and the bookshelf. All we can find are scraps of parchment with random scribbles and notebooks detailing his quail-hunting victories.

I crawl along the perimeter of the bed frame, sifting through the junk beneath. "What if it's not in here?"

"It has to be." Marian turns his jacket pockets inside out. "Keep looking."

Her frantic searching incites my anxiety. I hop on the bed, gingerly pinching the sheets. Frilly red undergarments are balled up in the bedding.

"Duchess," I *tsk*, trying to lighten the mood for Marian. Her hands are shaking so hard she keeps dropping everything. "How scandalous."

She leans back and makes a face. "Those aren't hers. Noble couples never share a bed."

"Pardon me." I drop the blanket. "I didn't realize that was common knowledge."

A pillow squishes beneath my hand as I'm about to push myself off the bed, and I feel the hard edge of something beneath the downy feathers. Tossing the pillow aside, I uncover a leather-bound journal lying face down on the mattress and bring it to Marian.

I run my eyes over the passage describing plans to use hot pitch to destroy a granary in Puddlewood, a county ten miles west of the King's City. The handmaiden reaches over my shoulder and flips back a few pages before I've finished the last sentence scrawled at the bottom.

"You read fast," I remark. My godmothers always stressed the importance of literacy, but plenty of common folk from the country barely know their letters, let alone how to read. "Did the Queen provide a tutor?"

"Something like that." She runs a nail over a list detailing each mill, granary, and dairy farm in Syldringham's duchy, along with their profit margins. "The folks who owe the lowest rents will be left to starve, and the crown will provide him a pretty payment. How predictable." She snorts her disdain. "At least we found what we needed. That was too easy." Her lips pinch tight for a second, and then she shakes her head, moving for the door. "Let's put that back and get out of here."

She doesn't have to ask me twice. I shove it back into the right position. My hand is stuffed beneath the pillow when I hear a creak from outside the chamber.

Marian freezes in the doorframe. Her eyes are as wide as saucers as she turns to me and hisses, *"Someone is coming."*

Shit.

I'm on the other side of the room, and the bed is blocking my path to the doorway. I scramble around it, striding as quickly as I can without making any noise. Marian is already a few yards ahead of me by the time I make it to the hallway. Two distinct voices drift up from the main landing.

"It's always a treat," a man says. They're approaching the corner of the hallway. They'll see me once they make that turn.

"They've been a rare commodity since the Queen's War ended."

"Luckily I have an acquaintance who supplies them."

Marian throws a quick glance over her shoulder as panic bleats through me. It's the King.

"I'll write to him after tomorrow's ordeal is done and over with," he says. "He'll send you a shipment."

I picture my body being more agile than it is in its current state, my legs springing forward and landing softly, carrying me into the room with the secret exit. I enter as Marian is lifting the tapestry and slipping beneath it. Holding my breath, I twist the doorknob to close it silently. I'm almost there.

I take another step, the boards groaning beneath my feet.

I hear the men's footsteps outside the room and measure how many strides it will take to disappear into the passageway. There are too many.

I won't make it. The men are too close.

I dive under the stairwell as the door reopens and curl myself into a ball, peeking over my knees. I can see the King moving through the holes in the gilded step above me.

"Here they are," he says, pulling a wooden box out from under one of the couches. He opens it, and his friend lifts a cigar from the satin lining. "Sourced from—"

The light beneath the stairwell is swallowed by shadows as Carabosse strides into the room, uninvited.

"Pardon my intrusion, Your Majesty." She bows to the King. "I was touring the castle, and I overheard you two discussing tomorrow's plans." She stands up straight, her shadows whipping around her muscles, a stark contrast to the friendly smile she gives them as she touches the pointed tip of her ear. "I want to touch base about that before I fly out with my dragon."

I cover my mouth with my hand and bite into the flesh.

The men are too focused on her imposing physique and

blustering darkness to notice how her eyes darting around the room, or how her shoulder is twitching. They can't see how uncomfortable she is, but I can.

She's trying to bullshit with them, and she's *really bad* at it.

"Of course, come in, Commander. The Duke and I were going to speak to you later," the King says, holding the box open for her. She lifts a cigar and frowns before taking a match and settling into a couch across from them.

She goes over their agreed plans for tomorrow's attack, and the men respond stiffly, the conversation adopting a formal tone in the wraith's company. Carabosse plays up her arrogance, blowing smoke rings with her ankle crossed over her thigh, her shadows caressing me the entire time.

I know that even if I'm caught here, she'll defend me with her life. My wife is the embodiment of night, and she knows her power. I wish I could own mine the way she owns hers, wearing it like a second skin with confidence.

She never allows an opening for the men to dismiss her. She carries on with them until they both stand to leave and slips out behind them.

I wait for three minutes before crawling out from under the stairwell.

I touch the tapestry's fringe as the door opens, and fear shoots to my extremities.

"*Nyxtrystia,*" Carabosse says, the single word a warm balm that soothes my weariness. "Where do you think you're going?"

8

CARABOSSE

Rosemary turns around, grasping onto a suit of armor's plated shoulder, her dark eyes fanning open adoringly. With all of the mistakes I've made, I'm not sure I deserve a look like that, full of love and sweet as honey.

"The exit is right there," she says quietly, tilting her head toward the tapestry depicting the Woodland Temple. I heard the maid moving around behind it while I kept the men distracted by my presence. "I have to leave."

"Not yet. The King is on his way to the stables. I'll hear him if he comes back." I step toward her. My shadow peels away from my body, leaning against the door to keep it shut tight. "That was too close, Rosemary."

I touch her cheek, feathering my fingers down to the soft spot beneath her jaw where her pulse is jumping. She leans into my palm. "I know, but we found what we needed."

"Good." Tracking her around the castle drains my magic quickly, and I want to preserve it in case she needs me. "Hopefully Roberta will let you rest in your chamber until tomorrow."

"I can't say I get a lot of rest there either," she says, dark humor creeping into her reply. "The big bed is nice and all, but I'll be happy if I never have to spend another night in a castle after this."

"You won't." Her smirk falls, her attempt to laugh off her situation failing in the face of my stern promise. "I mean it. You'll get out of here and start practicing your magic immediately to prevent something like this from happening again."

"Never again," she says, backing up against the wall. The tapestry dips into the opening behind it, but I'm not ready for her to vanish. Not when there's a loose thread hanging between us. I've spent the whole morning wishing for a chance to tie it up and make things right again.

"What happened in our dream last night," I start, and she holds up a hand.

"Don't worry about it," she says. "Your stubborn determination to protect me makes a lot more sense now, and I know you had your reasons not to tell me. I'm sure discovering your mate was an apothecary you found in the forest had to have been disappointing." A flush spreads over the swell of her breasts and climbs up her neck. "At first at least. I like to think you grew to genuinely care for me...*love* me eventually."

Is she joking? I study her face, looking for the signs of her wry amusement that I've come to know so well. But there's only a trace of pain flickering in her gaze.

"*That's* what's been going through your head, little witch?" I press a hand to the stone wall above her shoulder. "How could you ever think I was disappointed?"

"Because you kept it a secret from me."

"And you're right that I had my reasons, but disappointment isn't one of them. I'll explain everything tonight in our dreams." This moment is reserved for my mate. I won't speak about Mallory. "My soul has longed for you since I was born. I have traveled across realms and kingdoms, never expecting to heal that ache. I never thought I'd find that missing piece. When I met you, I finally felt complete." Lifting her chin, I kiss her forehead. "Fate might have drawn us to each other, but I would've fallen for you anyway. I've admired you since the beginning. You enchanted me with your clever wit and strange magic. And I love how fiercely you love your family, even though you tend to aggravate my fae instincts with your stubbornness."

Her mouth tips up. "Who, me?"

"Yes, you," I sigh. "Tricky little witch."

She grips me tighter, rubbing her thumbs along my obliques. "Well, I hope you know you're part of my family now, so don't expect me to give you up so easily."

A storm of conflicting emotions swirls through my chest. I'm proud to have earned her affection honestly, but I can't bear the thought of leaving her lonely when I return to my Queen.

Nothing could have stopped me from loving her, but she was never supposed to fall for me.

"It would be easier to tame the wind or claim the moon than to expect that from you." I peck her on the tip of her nose and kiss her gently with a soft brushing of our mouths that leaves her lips parting sweetly. "Sorry to hold you up, but I had to make up for last night's reaction before I could let you run off."

I wait for her to pull away from me. She doesn't. Widening her stance, she pulls me closer instead, her hand running from my hip to my ribs. "I'm not ready to go yet."

She tips her face toward me, her body swaying subtly as she nips my ear. *Gods.* I want her to bite me all over, mark me up with her teeth.

"Aren't you afraid of getting caught here?" I ask.

"Not when I'm with you," she says, glancing at my shadow

standing guard at the door. She's right. There's nothing to be afraid of when she's with me. "Besides, I'm finding that spite is a strong antidote to fear. I want to cause as much damage as I can while the King thinks he has me locked away here. Isn't there something satisfying about that?"

"I suppose." I'm having so much trouble interacting with that man. Just thinking about it has me growling. "But killing him would be much more satisfying."

Rosemary smiles knowingly, as though she can see right through me. "I'm proud of you, holding yourself back for the sake of the rebellion."

I huff out a laugh.

Supporting Robin's rebellion is the right thing to do, as it serves the greater good.

But in my heart, I know I haven't chosen this side for purely noble reasons.

I grab the fabric of her skirt, lifting it an inch and dropping it again. "You know it's all for you."

"Yeah, I do," she says. "So touch me in this room where he thinks he's all-powerful. Help me cast a spell. Make me come apart while I envision these walls crumbling."

She runs her nails down my back, her eyelids dropping heavy as hot energy builds between us. I'm lightheaded from the musky scent of her arousal when she digs into my hips, pulling me flush against her body.

She presses her pelvis forward, and I push against her, slipping my thigh between her knees. She slides down on it.

I'm not thinking.

My thoughts are consumed by her slow, rocking movements. Her lips on my neck. Her hands on my back.

"There's not enough time to do everything I want to do with you," I say, in pain because I want endless hours with her more than anything.

She flicks her tongue along my pulse and smiles into the crook of my neck. "You could do some of those things."

I pick her up and lay her down on the velvet couch, pushing her cap back to let her golden tresses flow over the throw pillows.

She hikes her dress to her thighs, walking her heels up toward her ass as she slides her bloomers down to her knees. I move to the edge of the couch and tug them the rest of the way down, damn near dying at the sight of her bared to me. Her hand rests on her belly, her pinky skimming close to her curls and that tight, wet heat I want to sink my fingers into.

I have to stop for a second and take it all in, tracing her whole body in my mind's eye, noting the sun-kissed glow missing from her skin.

This isn't sex for the sake of it. This is survival, a reclamation.

I kneel, positioning my torso between her shins. "Fuck. You're so beautiful. I've missed looking at you."

I kiss the top of her mound and each side of her folds before bringing my mouth to the tight bud of her clit. "I've missed kissing you."

Humming, I drag her hips toward me and run my tongue along her pussy. "I've missed tasting you."

She claws at the velvet and bucks her hips. I push my hand down on her belly, flattening her back against the cushions to feel this moment in all of its intensity.

There isn't much time, but I'll make the most of it.

I dive down again, licking her thoroughly, feeling her opening for me. I kiss her clit and rise, settling back down onto my knees at the end of the couch. Grabbing one of her ankles, I lift one of her legs toward my shoulder and prop a pillow underneath her hips. I have perfect view like this. I can see just how wet and glossy she is.

Every inch of me is humming with deep longing. My own pulse is beating against my riding leathers, accelerating with the joy of giving Rosemary what she needs. I summon my shadows to swirl in my hand, forming a bulbed shaft. Pressing it against her slit, I watch as it sinks in, inch by inch.

Nothing feels better than the ache that sight sends through me.

I draw back and plunge back into her again, spurred on by the open-mouthed face she's making. I grip her soft thigh, nudging it back a little further as my shadows delve into her wet heat.

My little witch guards her heart so carefully, but she's so pliable, so trusting for me.

Only for me.

Each thrust heightens my desire to make her come. I need to feel her. I open her knee out to the side and dissolve the shadows, replacing them with my fingers.

"Envision what you want," I encourage her, rubbing tight circles around her clit with my thumb. Green threads crisscross past her knees, brightening with her mounting magic. "Cast your spells and make it happen."

"*Come apart, come undone. The lovers prevail when the war is won.*" She tosses her head back, her soft murmuring unhinged.

I fucking love it. My shadows do too.

They run along her body as she hits her climax, luxuriating in the rush of magic.

I watch the rise and fall of her ribs, waiting for her breathing to slow before I release her. She stands, her glow returning to her cheeks as she tugs her undergarments back on and kisses me. "I've got to get going."

Neither one of us can stay here much longer, but it's the last time we'll see each other in person before tomorrow's big event. Things could go very wrong, and we both know it.

"I'll see you tonight in our dreams," I say. Delaying the inevitable will only make the goodbye harder.

"See you then." She moves beneath the tapestry, her fingers curling around the stone edge of the opening. Her head reappears in the gap for a second. "By the way, when I cast spells of protection over my loved ones, you're always included."

Then she's gone.

A few moments later, I hear Marian's hissed whispering further down the stairwell. "I've been waiting down here this whole time. Was the romantic interlude really necessary?"

I smile despite the emptiness I feel from watching my mate leave again. I miss her already.

Smoothing my hair back, I reach for my blade, preparing to handle whoever's coming down the hall. I detected their footsteps about a minute ago but didn't want to rush Rosemary.

I stride out, relieved to find it's just a guard patrolling the wing. He opens his mouth when he sees me, and a dark tendril of magic tunnels into his nostril, moving into his mind before he can scream to alert somebody.

"You didn't see anyone here," I say, carefully plucking out the memory of me lurking in the cigar room. I try not to take too much else from him, or else the King will grow suspicious. "There's nothing to report to His Majesty."

"There's nothing to report," he repeats, blood trickling from his nose.

"Wipe your nose," I command, walking past him. He makes a garbled sound as I let him go and march up to the floor where I'm staying.

I stand on the balcony of the Celestial Palace, staring out into the distance as I wait for Rosemary. She was already asleep when I finished a final meeting with the King's military advisors this evening. It shouldn't take too long for her to get here.

I trace the map of stars, searching for her distinct energy, the pathway to her dreams. The atmosphere ripples as I connect with it, and she drifts down from the sky, landing right beside me this time. She watches the single silver sorrowgale do a flip over the river.

"You seem more at ease tonight," I say. Even the air feels lighter with her arrival.

Her hair flows back as she closes her eyes. "I think it's because I get to leave tomorrow. I'm so ready."

The same thought terrifies me. "It will be dangerous. You'll need to..."

Her chiffon sleeve slips off her shoulder as she looks at me, and I back off with my lecture to stop her excitement from waning. She's risked her life for Robin's rebellion for years. It's time for her to reap the benefits.

"I know," she says. "But all I can do is cling to my hope and stay ready. I might actually see my godmothers tomorrow. I still can't wrap my head around that." Her cheek twitches. "It's probably better if I don't think about it until it happens."

"Then come here," I say, stepping back and patting the railing. "I owe you a story."

"We could both use a distraction," she says, moving in front of me. I hold her close as we look out at the city.

"This is where I was born." Raising a hand, I curl my fingers, transforming the terrain. "But I want to show you where my life changed."

The dreamscape darkens, and amethyst boulders break off the mountains, splashing into the lake and turning into a black canyon. Sharp rocks drill through the crystalline slopes, forming jagged peaks. The lonely sorrowgale disappears with the stars. They wink out one by one until only threads of green light remain, glowing through the cracks of far-off caverns.

The Starlight Court is gone. A dark mist hangs over everything.

"This is where the Vellessentere took place," Rosemary says.

"I'm impressed that you recognize it." I only pointed it out to her once while we were flying. "During the trials, a few of the competitors discovered a way to speak to Vellesse by entering a sort of underworld lobby." I gesture to a thin green stream of light pouring out from a black hole in one of the mountains. "Mal and her mate ventured into it, hoping to seek guidance on how to win. We were starving at that point, and we were desperate." I don't mention the horrors we saw in the days leading up to our decision or the terrible price we paid for it. "She succeeded in summoning the Goddess, who shared her fate with her. Vellesse told Mal that my mate had died in the Fade and that we'd need to join forces to rule Sarteal. To make it a better place."

My past naivety both amazes and disgusts me. I'll never be that loyal fae guardian again. This realm has made me far less trusting.

Rosemary's nail scrapes along the sleeve of my tunic, making the shape of the scar underneath. "She lied to you."

"Yes, and I believed her. I believed every word she said to me for twenty years. I devoted my life to my Queen, knowing I'd never fill the emptiness inside of me." I play with her hair, twirling locks around my fingers mindlessly. "Then one night, I caught the scent of a little witch at her apothecary, and I started doubting everything. Things that didn't make sense started to add up for me."

"Like what?" she asks.

"There were several strange incidents." I shift my weight.

"The worst of them was when the only woman I'd ever been close with turned up dead outside of the Vellessentian Palace."

"Nylah's sister? Nova?" She speaks her name delicately, spinning in my arms. "I thought that was an accident."

"So did I."

Her lower lip folds between her teeth. "She would do all that just to keep you to herself as her right-hand woman? She'd kill your...sweetie?"

I flex my fingers. "I suspect there's another reason. The Goddess must have told her something that made her want to prevent us from meeting."

Rosemary is always thinking. I can see the wheels turning in her head already. "It dealt with your mate specifically."

"My life became entwined with Mal's when I took the blood oath." I turn my palm up on the railing, and she glances at my arm. My mark isn't visible, but we both know it's there. "She made sure I'd never be able to fully bond with anybody. If she goes, I go too."

Her brow furrows. "She tricked you."

I let out a rueful laugh and rub my eyes. I'm angry too.

When I heard Rosemary's revelation about Thea, I realized that Mal is already aware of what she is to me. She's known since before she left Sarteal. She's only been screwing with me and faking her sympathy. "I've been trying to protect you from her this whole time, but I can't keep up. I'm always one step behind."

"She can play her games, but she can't win every time." She reaches for my face. "We'll find a way out of this too."

I know there's no way out.

An echoing murmur kicks up beneath the wind whistling through the canyons. *"Could have had it all...Threw your chance away..."*

Rosemary drops her hands and shrinks against me. "Is there someone else here?"

My body goes rigid. "You can hear that?"

"Yes. It's unnerving." She cocks her head. "There's something off about it, as if it's not meant for human ears. What is it?"

"It's..." My mouth opens and closes on the word, and a burn prickles along my forearm. I can normally say it, but the blood oath stops me whenever I try to use it in the context of my Queen's biggest secret. "There are some things I can't tell you."

She looks confused, but she doesn't argue. "Then let's go somewhere else tonight and leave this all behind."

"That's a good idea." I wrap my arms around her, and she does the same to me. "Hold on tight."

We're swallowed in a swirl of shadow and starlight that blocks out everything. The new dreamscape comes into focus, and she lifts her skirt up to run across the marshy grass to the rock formations jutting out over the valley beneath.

"It's Claw Ridge," she exclaims, taking a seat on one of the rocks, dangling her legs over the ledge. "I think I like it better this way. "

There are no army tents. No watchtowers. A few wild dragons fly overhead, and the saltmeadow cordgrass sways in the breeze.

Things are just as they should be, if only in our dreams.

9

ROSEMARY

I drop the heavy bucket so hard it nearly tips over. Water sloshes over the side and trickles into the cracks of the cobblestones, running beneath my shoes. A circular wall extends out behind the scullery. It's filled with clotheslines and tools for washing.

"I'm assuming you know how to do this," Marian says, climbing down from a cart filled with dirty linens. She throws a pile down near my feet. "Or do you need me to show you?"

I load my arms with the staff's undergarments and dump them into the vat, pouring the freshly boiled water in. "I've got this."

She plunges her hands into the sudsy water and starts working next to me, huffing as she lathers a filthy shift with lye and scrubs it across the board. Sweat rings the collar of her uniform and darkens her underarms, her scent sour from nerves.

"At nightfall, there will be two jailer's carts waiting over there," she says, wringing out the shift and soaking it again.

"We'll climb into them and pick up horses for all of us once we've made it out of the city."

My eyes flit to the stables and over to the Ivy Keep, my breakfast revolting in my belly. "The jailer's cart?"

"One of our Merry Men works for the sheriff," she explains. Another maid carries a linen basket into the washing area, and Marian drops quiet, returning to her scrubbing.

I've never been fond of doing the laundry, but I try to lose myself in the repetitive movements. At least we get to spend the day out here. I don't think I could bear the wait inside. The sunshine touches the shade of the castle walls, and I angle my head toward it like a flower seeking its light.

"What a blessing to be alive in spring," I croon, passing my time with the folksongs I learned from Candide. It helps to center me when the scattered voices of the Hartwood are calling from all directions. *"To fill my arms with lavender and..."*

I flinch as glass shatters, my gaze swinging to the maid churning clothes beneath the shelf lined with washing supplies.

"Damn it." She flings her paddle aside, picking up pieces of the broken jar from a pile of white powder. "I'm going to have to ask someone to bring us more lye."

"No, it's fine, Anne-Marie. I'll get it," Marian volunteers. She snaps her fingers at me, then points to a basket of rinsed linens. "The new girl can hang these up."

I clip the clothes to the line near the wall's opening, hiding behind the wet fabric as I watch people cross the bailey.

I sense Carabosse before I see her. The guards and stable boys all snap to attention, shifting their paths to get out of someone's way.

Peering between two chemises, my worldview is compressed into a small frame. She strides into it briefly, filling it entirely with her presence. Power rolls off her body in dark waves. Her quads move and flex beneath her riding leathers, and she wears a gold pin at her throat, marking her as the Dragon Army's Commander.

My sense of security disappears as I watch her leave.

The castle's shadows seem to stretch toward me, threatening to draw me back in.

I shudder at the thought of being kept here forever and remember what I said to Carabosse. I won't let it happen.

Never again.

A sad song sweeps through the trees, calling for me. *"Zelladine. Zelladine. We're waiting."*

"Rosemary." Carabosse's voice cuts through the buzzing in my ears, floating on a thin shadow fondling my cheek.

I step around the line and move to the entrance of the washing station, spotting her beside the stable. She appears to be reading a parchment spread over her thighs, but I can see her lips moving discreetly.

"Pungo, not Puddlewood," she murmurs. "Syldringham's book was a plant. Tell your Queen."

My heart thumps against my ribs. The Queen has already sent her birds flying with a message to protect Puddlewood's granary. "I will."

She lifts her head, and our eyes meet. Hers narrow into black slits.

She's going to change her mind, I know it. She's going to say *screw the plan* and carry me out of here. Half of me wants her to, and the other half...I glance up at the Ivy Keep.

"Don't tempt me with that worried look on your face," she whispers, following my gaze. "You'd regret leaving without them."

It's true. Abandoning them when I have this chance would tear an irreparable hole in my heart. I'd never be able to fill it again.

"See you tomorrow," I say, pushing my anxiety down. I touch my fingers to my lips and blow her a kiss.

She splays her hand open, then makes a tight fist, catching it. "See you tomorrow."

I hope that's true.

For me, and for the rest of the King's City.

The groom leads a mare out of the stable, and she takes the reins. I break eye contact before she can see my tears, wiping them away with my pruny fingers as I look for Marian. The handmaiden is already back at the washing station.

"Where were you?" she asks, beating a soiled sheet.

I get close to her. "We need to see the Queen. It's an emergency."

"This had better be important."

"It is."

She blinks twice and calls to Anne-Marie. "We'll be right back. I forgot that Her Majesty requested something." Once we're out of earshot, she presses her shoulder into my arm. "Wait until we're in her chamber to speak," she advises. "We might cross paths with the King."

I take that warning to heart and keep my mouth shut, barely taking note of my surroundings as we enter the monarch's wing. Marian taps out four beats against the Queen's door, and we're met with a sing-song invitation. *"Come in."*

Roberta isn't sitting on the chaise below her window or lying on the high four-poster bed. A bawdy drinking song drifts from the small room attached to the chamber. Marian and I find her in there, soaking in a tub.

"Oh hello." She hiccups and sits up, bubbly water running down her bare breasts as she grabs the goblet on the stool beside her. Tipping it into her mouth, she sinks beneath the foamy layer again. "I'm so glad you stopped by, my dear friends."

"What the devil are you doing?" Marian uses her foot to roll an empty wine bottle out from under the tub. "We're supposed to be getting ready to leave."

"Not me. Stefan has invited me to dine with him tonight." Her wine-stained lips curve into a sardonic smile. "He says it's a special occasion. How lovely."

"Get it together," Marian sasses her, unfolding a towel. "Rose has something to tell you. She says it's an emergency."

I wait for the Queen to backhand her maid for speaking out of turn, but she grips the lip of the tub and shakily steps into the towel she's holding out for her. Pink strips of scarred flesh show between the wet ropes of hair hanging down her back, but Marian wraps her up, covering them quickly.

Roberta turns to me. "Well, spit it out, already."

I relay Carabosse's short message, and she scrunches her towel as she thinks about it.

"Pungo," she repeats to herself. "But why would they choose to attack that county? They only have a tiny granary. Next to the healing center." She sobers quickly, leaving a wet handprint on Marian's sleeve. "*Goddess*, no. We must warn them to evacuate, or else we'll lose the healers in that region. And the maids who were on duty in the duke's chamber will be punished for spying."

Marian bobs her head a few times. "There's still time to get a message out on raven wings. But what are we going to do about you?"

Roberta curls her hand around the stem of her goblet. "Nothing. Stefan will expect me to be at dinner."

"Tell him you're ill," Marian suggests, snatching the drink away. There's no space between them. Their chests touch when they breathe in. "Tell him you can't get out of bed."

100

"You know it won't matter."

"We can't leave without you."

"Yes, you can," the Queen says, cupping her face. "You've always been able to do this without me. If he wins, these past few years will have been for nothing. Remember the promise we made to each other. Win the fight. Stop the burnings."

"You're really trying to make me do this on my own, huh?" Marian asks, her tone suggesting the phrase has some inside meaning.

"You have to." The corner of the Queen's mouth twitches as she brings her lips to Marian's ear, whispering something I can't hear.

I pry my eyes away from them. The moment feels too intimate. My face is warm from watching.

That's who the Queen has been protecting. I hear her lips smack against her maid's cheek, and she pulls back, taking a silk robe from a brass stand.

"Don't do this to me," Marian pleads, but the Queen's blue eyes are set with a rehearsed iciness as she knots the sash at her waist.

"It's time for you two to leave," she says. "That's an order from your Queen."

There's no point in arguing. She's made her mind up already.

We shrink out of the chamber together.

Even knowing who Roberta is, and what she's done to me, it makes me sick to walk away, knowing she'll have to face the King alone. "I'm so sorry."

Marian ignores my condolences, watching her feet as we wind through the castle. Once we're back outside, she pulls me behind the clothesline and stops in front of me. "What's something poisonous that can be hidden in a dessert dish?"

"I—I don't know," I stammer.

"Yes, you do. You're the fucking dark rose of Briar Apothecary." Her stare hardens. "You've taken down plenty of men for the rebellion. You can take him down too." There's no mistaking what she's implying.

"We can't kill the King," I whisper-scream.

The vines twist around the Ivy Keep, their leaves flipping upward to show their pale underbellies. I want to get Roberta out of here too, but this will put us all in jeopardy. "The Queen said that has to be done properly."

"I don't give a damn," she says. "No one leaves without her. Not you. Not your godmothers. Not your hatchlings. Now tell me."

I work my jaw, thinking of what might be available in the pantry. Most household poisons would be too obvious. "Belladonna berries. They're usually ripe this time of year, with purplish-black fruits that swell like cherries beneath green leaves. Whoever you send should avoid handling them with their bare hands."

"I'll find them myself," she says. "Wait here and stay unnoticed."

I return to the laundry as she leaves me without another option.

My back is aching from stooping over the basin when she returns, motioning for me to follow her into the kitchen.

We're sucked into a crowd of men and women in sage uniforms, fitting between their buckets and trays. Ruth is stirring the cauldron hanging over the roasting range.

Her shoulders slump as soon as she notices us.

"I guess you heard the news?" she asks, resting the spoon on the handle. Marian nods and reaches into her pocket, producing a handkerchief. She peels it open to show the cook the belladonna berries.

Ruth presses her mouth into a thin line. I curl my toes in

my shoes, hoping the cook will tell her what a terrible idea this is.

"I think I'll whip up a nice berry cobbler for His Majesty," she says instead, pocketing the poison. "He did request a special menu for this evening, but I'll need some help with this particular recipe."

The look she gives me sends nausea roiling in my belly.

We're really going to do this. We're going to try to kill the King. I glance around, hoping to find some magical exit, but there's nowhere to run. Not without my godmothers or dragons.

I can do this, I tell myself.

I've already killed dozens of Robin's enemies, and Stefan is not above them. It's easier to think of him as just another tally to add to my list.

"It's easy to make," I say, grabbing an apron from the hook beside the stove. "The berries are surprisingly sweet."

Ruth gets started on the batter while I stir the belladonna into a mixture of blueberries, sugar, and lemon zest. In a separate bowl, I do the same thing but omit the poison. Marian cleans up the mess and diverts the rest of the kitchen staff as we prepare the dessert for the royal couple's special dinner.

Two pans are laid out on a wood top counter. I fill them both and top them with a cinnamon crumble blend, making two distinct patterns to mark the difference.

"Make sure he eats this one," I whisper to Ruth, touching one of the panhandles. Her crow's feet crinkle up in a sad smile. It's a wordless *good luck* and *goodbye* that I return to her before she takes the cobblers to the oven.

I catch Marian signaling to me from across the kitchen and hurry outside with her, rubbing my skirt together between my fingers. The coral sky feels too open and wide. I find myself hopelessly searching for the dark silhouette of Snovida, knowing full damn well the dragon is miles away by now. Carabosse will be preparing to turn on the King's men if she hasn't already.

"Zelladine." The voices of the forest jumble on top of one another. I can only pick a few words out from the incoherent mess. *"Heed. Rot. Free. The three. The three. The three."*

"Come along. We don't have time for you to keep daydreaming," Marian says. She carries a bucket from the washing station, using it as a prop as we move into the bailey. "Willow will be meeting us out here any minute now."

"Willow?"

She licks her teeth, looking past me. "There she is."

A maid comes into focus, gamboling down the back steps with a basket. She swings it by her hip, whistling as she joins us. The handle slips around her blood-splattered wrist. She winks at me and pulls her sleeve down to cover it.

It's the assassin from my bed chamber. I realize who she is as she flashes a devious grin, transforming into the woman I've seen depicted in several wanted portraits.

Willow Scarlet. The former troupe actress is infamous for luring wealthy men to seedy inns along the countryside to steal their coins and sometimes, their lives.

"I knew the guards on duty outside your room. Trust me when I say they had it coming," she says, pushing a knife handle lower beneath the scooped neck of her gown. "We have an hour or so before someone notices them. Let's get this thing rolling."

"There's been a slight change of plans," Marian says, giving a condensed explanation.

Willow raises her eyebrows. "That's unfortunate, but Little John is already here with the carts, and Tuck is waiting for us to give the signal to leave the Ivy Keep. There are more than a few lives depending on us tonight. We can't fuck this up, or all of this will be for nothing."

"We can still make it work," Marian insists, but Willow doesn't budge.

Finally, someone around here has some common sense.

The handmaiden continues her plea, her voice cracking. "Give me twenty minutes. If we can't handle it, we'll leave."

Her desperation is palpable.

I have felt what she's feeling—the agony of being unable to save someone she loves dearly. Sympathy creaks through me.

Willow must be affected by her distress too. I can tell the assassin is softening.

"Fine," she says. "Twenty minutes, that's it."

Marian is moving before Willow finishes her sentence.

Shit. Shit. Shit. I chant the word in my head.

We're really doing this.

Two padlocked carts are parked next to the stables. A tall, broad-shouldered man in a jailer's uniform is adjusting one of the horse's harnesses. His eyes stare a hole into Marian's cap as we walk past, and she holds two fingers out in a signal to him.

I was dragged into the rebellion a few years ago, but now I'm officially knee-deep in it.

Anxiety distorts my surroundings. The bailey looks like the painted backdrop in a dream. Guards peer down from the battlements. Every glance in our direction convinces me that someone has guessed our plan already.

My chest tightens as we enter the garden. I can't get stuck here again. I won't.

"Zelladine. Zelladine." The vines stop writhing around the Ivy Keep. They halt for a second and switch directions, their leaves pointing upward in quick succession, like pages in a book flipping open on a strong breeze.

Marian whips her head toward the tower. "Something is happening."

I stand still, a thousand invisible strings forming a web of energy. It all flows from the Hartwood and connects back to me.

"Not powerless. Pull the strings." The voices are becoming more distinct. I hear their message clearly as they throw my own words back at me. *"Never again. Never again. Never again."*

The strands vibrate above my fingertips. It would be too easy to pluck them and find out what will happen.

"Get her into the mausoleum," Marian says, frowning at the green threads racing up my wrist as I lift my hand.

Willow rounds back and tugs me into the building, the stone walls muffling the sounds of the forest. The world drops quiet again.

IO

ROSEMARY

The silence doesn't last long.

My hatchlings dart out from behind Queen Rina's statue and drop into a protective stance at my feet. Sun spits an ember at Willow, and Moon swipes a claw at Marian. They both defy my requests to stay back, batting their tails around defensively.

"How are we going to get those little beasts on the cart?" Willow asks. The women are looking at them like they're monsters. I'm flooded with a strong urge to stand up for them.

"They'll be fine." I crouch between them and wrap my arms around their torsos to calm their beating wings. "They're only being aggressive because I'm frightened." I hug their necks, promising to come back for them. They don't listen. Their sharp teeth nip at my ankles as they follow me to the secret passage.

"We'll have to block them from following us," Marian says.

I choke back a sob as I push their maws back from the gap and seal it. They claw at the other side of the stone, trying to get to me.

This is the last time I'll be leaving them without a proper guardian until they're ready to fly off on their own adventures. No one will make another decision for me about my dragons. The lichen growing on the ceiling groans, releasing a faint woody odor.

"Never again."

"The King and Queen will be in their private dining room," Marian says. "This path is unfinished, so watch your step."

Willow and I form a line behind her, clinging to each other's skirts. We open a hatch and climb down a musty set of steps beneath the castle. Tree roots dig into the soil around us as we traverse the underground passage. We must be close to the boundary of the forest. My foot goes straight through a step on our way back up to the main level. Willow reaches back for me as I right myself again.

We reach the opening to the dining room. It's covered by a tightly knit grid. Marian hangs back to catch her breath while Willow and I creep forward on our bellies, spying through the small square holes.

There's a marble floor right before us. Golden chandeliers hang from the ceiling between loops of green and gold banners. The King and Queen are seated next to each other at the table pushed toward the back of the room. I'm viewing them from the side, but the last time I was here, I was looking up at them. Crying. Bleeding. Waiting for someone to save me.

Willow crawls forward, pointing to the guards posted at the tall double doors. She holds up her fingers to count them—*one, two*—then she holds up a thumb. I assume that means she thinks she can handle them.

"You've hardly touched your duck," Stefan says, stuffing a forkful of meat into his mouth. "I thought it was your favorite dish. Is there something wrong with the way the cooks have prepared it?"

"No. It's delicious, but my stomach is uneasy tonight." Roberta pokes at her meal, moving her utensils to make it look like she's eating. She's as drunk as a skunk, but if I hadn't seen her chugging wine a few hours ago, I'd never be able to tell. "I'm not very hungry."

"Hmm," he hums, spearing a roasted potato. "Perhaps dessert will bring your appetite back. I know how you enjoy your sweets."

Marian joins us, breathing forcefully through her nose to control her wheezing as the two guards carry a silver tray to the table. They lift the lid, presenting two plates. Marian clamps a hand over her mouth to stifle a whimper.

Both of the dishes are empty.

Twin lines form between Roberta's eyebrows. "My King?"

"Oh yes." He wipes his mouth with a napkin. "I'm sorry about that. There was an issue in the kitchen. A scullery maid reported that two separate desserts were prepared to be served tonight. She thought that was strange. So did I. I had the entire staff questioned." He balls his napkin and throws it on the table. "The head cook ended up claiming responsibility for the whole thing, but they were all punished. She planned to poison me tonight, and none of them gave up any information. Traitors. The whole lot of them."

The Queen grabs her stomach.

"You look ill, my love," Stefan says. "You really didn't know anything about the cook's plan, did you?"

She blinks rapidly. "No."

"That's a relief. For a while, I worried you might have been in on the plan to kill me, and that would have ruined the entire evening." She looks away as he pinches one of the ringlets hanging from her damp crown of braids. "I've been planning this surprise for weeks. I don't want anything spoiling it."

Marian's fingers twine with mine, her hands trembling as

Willow inches closer to the grate. The King claps his hands, and the guards step out of the dining hall, reappearing with a cart between them. A blue cloth is draped over the large object stacked on top of it. The men strain as they wheel it toward the table.

Queen Roberta fidgets with the ruby heart resting between her collarbones. "What is it?"

"It's a special art piece I had commissioned for you. It was made by the best welder in the city." He drapes an arm over the back of her chair and gestures to the guards. "Gentlemen, show my wife, please. The excitement is killing me."

The guards obey, pulling the cloth away to reveal rounded iron bars twisting into multiple arches. Hinges are welded into its side, positioned a couple feet away from a latch with a keyhole in it.

Marian's nails dig into my skin.

It's a giant birdcage.

"Speechless, I see," Stefan says, removing his arm from Roberta's shoulder to watch her profile. She stares at the creation with her mouth open. "After working so hard to have this made, I was hoping you'd say something."

His cruel intentions lie beneath a mask of arrogance. He folds his hands on the table, his knuckles going white as he waits for her to plead her case.

Roberta grabs the wine bottle and turns it upside down to fill her goblet.

Glug.Glug Glug.

She slumps back, closes her eyes, and takes a drink. Running her nail along the rim, she raises a toast and says, "Congratulations for finally catching up with me."

"You don't deny it, then?" He pushes his chair back, his lip curling. "You *are* Robin."

"It took you this long to figure it out, you fool." She bursts out laughing. "No wonder it was so easy to turn your kingdom against you."

A vein bulges over the King's temple.

"Enjoy your dinner and drinks tonight, princess. It will be the end of your pampering," he says, jabbing a finger at the cage. "That is where you'll be spending the rest of your days until you issue a true Heartshire heir for me."

Roberta sputters out her drink, laughing.

King Stefan's nostrils flare as he works to contain his contempt. "Do you still think this is funny?"

"Oh. I do."

"You won't be laughing when I build the most magnificent pyre our kingdom has ever seen."

Roberta sets her goblet down. Her tongue flicks out to catch the droplet of wine at the corner of her mouth. "If I burn, it'll still be worth it. Every bit. The rebellion will outlive me. You can't stop it."

"I can." He smirks, and the Hartwood's tune vibrates through the castle walls. "I've already sent the wraith of Sarteal to deliver a crushing blow to your army. And once I've bound her wife to me, the Tree Mother's power will be mine to wield. Everyone in my kingdom will submit to me."

Roberta rolls her eyes and takes another drink. "Sure they will, Your Majesty."

He stands up and pulls her chair back, nearly knocking her out of her seat. "I'm not enjoying your company tonight. Why don't we end dinner early?"

Roberta's body is still swinging forward when he yanks her hand and pulls her to her feet. Her heels click against the marble as he walks her toward the birdcage.

Marian sits up, and Willow lifts her skirt, taking a dart from her garter and sticking it between her teeth.

A convulsion runs down my body.

The forest roars, howling words that beat at the stained glass windows. *"Rotten. Pull the strings."*

I'm not in the passageway anymore, but buried beneath the soil of the Hartwood. My sisters are calling out to me, their messages vibrating along the threads that bind us together. Their emotions rot the forest and I can feel them all—their centuries of anger and grief. Rage is quicksand in my belly, pulling me down into its pit until I'm two eyes glowing in the sludge, focusing on the cream bricks of the castle walls outside the canopy of leaves.

I hate what it stands for. I loathe the royal family's greed.

"Crush it. Pull the strings. Set the forest free."

I want to. Those strands of power are so enticing.

Marian's hand presses over my mouth, sealing it shut to stop my snarling. I snap back to the present moment.

Roberta is resisting the King's efforts to throw her in the cage, but he won't allow his guards to aid him.

"Stay back," he orders. "The princess belongs to me."

Willow crouches with her knife tip tilted toward the grate.

"We can't reach her," she whispers as the Queen struggles loudly. "Not with the King fully conscious. We have to leave."

Marian doesn't respond. Her stillness is a protest in and of itself.

She's not going to move, and I understand why. I wouldn't leave my love here either.

"Remember what's at stake," Willow says, turning her head toward the stairwell. Her eyes widen at the sparks flaring through the darkness.

Mreep. There's a flurry of claws scraping along the steps. I rock forward on my knees as Sun and Moon launch themselves toward me. *Mreep.*

"Shh." I catch the dragons, keeping them away from the

grate. They paw at me with wet foreclaws; the poor things have scratched themselves bloody to get to me.

They're making too much noise, but I can't soothe them when my own heart is beating frantically.

"What was that?" King Stefan asks, his grip tight around Roberta's elbows.

I stop breathing as he looks in our direction.

A force hits the castle, the impact causing him to flinch, and he casts his eyes upward.

The chandeliers swing, their jeweled strands knocking together. Dust rains down from the ceiling as a bone-chilling screech shakes the walls, reverberating into our tight hiding space.

"Don't you know what that is?" Roberta arches her back, laughing maniacally. "The wraith has come to claim her bride."

II

CARABOSSE

The Hartwood rampages as night falls on the castle.

A venomous song rises from the dark bramble below. I don't have to speak the inhuman language to understand its lyrics. Something has gone wrong. The plants have been calling to me from far outside the Hartwood's boundaries.

The dreadful sound began hours ago, before I left the King's soldiers in a cloud of smoke behind me. I turned around as soon as I could. By the time Robin's birds found me, I was already coming back for Rosemary.

The devouring trees thrash and lean toward the castle.

"Higher," I command Snovida, avoiding the vines whipping violently at the sky. They grab ahold of the Ivy Keep, their green stalks undulating along its surface like they're chewing. Fissures spiderweb across the tower's stones. They splinter as we dive down toward the fortress.

Flying my dragon directly into the King's City is a violation of our treaty. Still, I'm not about to land miles away and trot my way in on a godsdamned horse when I have this awful gut-rotting feeling.

Guards race on the ground, shouting their confusion. "Attack from Sarteal! Stand at the ready."

Torchlight glints off the javelin heads notched in the crenels of the battlements, aiming for Snovida. The King has equipped his soldiers with weapons intended to harm dragons.

This is not a welcoming party.

A tower door lowers to a parapet, its planks smacking the stone walkway as an armored fireteam rolls out a scorpion. They load it with a crossbow and crank the string.

"Griffe, Snovida," I mutter.

She shrieks and swipes at the arms of the scorpion, her claws slashing through the soldiers operating them. She swings her tail, throwing a guard from the wall.

Their armored body hits the ground with a sickening *crack*.

"Vellesse's horns." I curse as I dismount in the bailey. Those aren't green flags rolled out on the walls; they're bodies, strung up by ropes around their necks. I shield myself with my shadows as the day surrenders to night completely, scoping out the area.

Swords and baskets are dropped in the dirt as people abandon their duties, their eyes locked on the line of menacing trees. Servants and soldiers flock to the gates. I can't tell if they're fleeing the forest or Snovida.

"We're under attack," a guard calls and blows his horn.

"What's happening in the Hartwood?" a maid asks, her voice shrill.

"It doesn't matter," the guard says. "There is a *dragon*. Everybody grab a weapon. Stand your ground."

I communicate with Snovida, indicating that she should fly

off and stay safe until I've retrieved my mate. She snorts at a man brandishing a broadsword and takes off, knocking him over with the gust from her wings.

I dissolve my shadows, and I'm rushed by a squad of soldiers. The tall woman leading them hurls a knife that pierces my tunic. I dislodge it from my dragon scale vest with a growl, and the crowd splits up, scattering in different directions.

The man with the horn lifts it to his lips, and I push him against the closest building before he can summon help. "Where is King Stefan?"

"I can't tell you," he says, his chin quivering.

I don't have time to wear him down. I reach into his mind instead.

"Tell me where your King is," I say, my order echoing through his head.

"He's in his dining room." He shoves against my forearms, but it has no effect. "He's with his Queen."

That's all I need to know. I let him go, still breathing.

"You could take them all down," the voice says, rattling through my head. *"There'll be no one to stop you on your way out."*

I block the noise.

There's no need for excess bloodshed. Most of the guards see the shadows swirling around me and step aside immediately, leaving my path to the castle stairs clear.

There's a frenzy in the foyer as guards march down from the mezzanine, calling for everyone to evacuate the building.

"Move to the southeast side of the fortress. There could be more dragons coming," they shout, a team splitting off as they're ordered to protect the King.

I follow them quietly, hiding in the shadows of an alcove,

listening to the pattern of their footsteps before revealing myself to them.

Two of them turn tail. Three try to stop me.

I raise a hand and curl my fist, snapping their bones without thinking twice. I've been flying for hours with that panicked song humming in my ears. My thoughts are dark and foreboding.

Your wife is in danger. Come quickly.

XOXO,

Robin

That is the message Robin sent me. I must find Rosemary.

Two more guards attack as I approach the dining room. I draw a blade, twisting it into the weak spot in one man's armor, just below his ribcage. The other man collapses with my shadows wrapped tight around his neck.

I throw the double doors open, my boots tracking blood and mud on the white marble. The King is standing behind a table, set for two people.

My ears prick up at Roberta's breathy snickering. She's huddled in the corner of the room, hiding behind an iron cage. Her hair has come loose from its braids, and her dress is disheveled.

What in the underworld has happened here this evening?

"Commander," King Stefan greets me, his face paling. "I thought you were returning to Sarteal after your mission."

I hold a piece of parchment between my fingers. "I received a concerning message regarding my wife. Where is she?"

A shiver runs through me, a marriage of energy.

Rosemary is close by. I can feel her.

He has the audacity to feign confusion. "I don't know what you mean."

"My wife," I repeat. "Where is she? Don't play games with me."

I'm so tired of moving pieces along a board, calculating each decision with a strategy. This is not how things were done in Faerie. If someone stole a bride away, they would have done it proudly.

"Your wife," he laughs nervously. "She ran off with the rebel—"

I step closer, and he holds a hand up for his men to stay back.

"If there's one thing you need to know about me, Stefan, it's that I really fucking hate liars."

His face drops, and he lifts his other hand, removing it from his sword hilt. "Alright, you caught me. I have your bride, but what good is she to you? She left you. Willingly. I saw her leaving the masquerade that night."

"Yes, because we came up with a plan to help Robin's rebellion," I tell him, finally showing my hand. "That part went quite well, actually."

Roberta leans against the iron bars, laughing as blood rushes back into the King's face.

"You didn't," he says.

"I did. The rebels gained a foothold in Trasselton because of it."

His throat bobs beneath his parted collar as his hand reaches back to the lever behind him. He pulls it down, and there's a metallic ringing in my ears as an iron net falls down from the ceiling, cutting off my magic and my connection to Rosemary. I can't feel her.

"Take the Commander to the holding cell," the King orders. "We'll bring her out again when it's time for the binding ceremony. Seize her wife and bring her to me."

Binding ceremony? Darkness swells inside of me.

"*Go deeper,*" the voice whispers. "*So deep they won't be able to stop you.*"

I dig in as they leave to fetch Rosemary. I have to get to her before they do.

Boots stomp on the floor. The guards that have just left come running back in. "Your Majesty. We can't seize her wife. She's missing. The men posted outside her chamber have been slain."

Thank the gods, she's out of her chamber so she can't be taken. Hopefully she'll stay hidden until I can find her.

Mustering my strength, I rise to my feet. The net is heavy, its chains singeing every bit of my exposed skin. My face burns as I lift it slowly, the metal clinking on the marble. It will take me too long to remove it.

The guard is already coming to drag me to the holding cell.

Thwip.

His eyebrows shoot up, and he grabs his throat, only noticing the slim weapon sticking out of his neck as he's falling back. A wall grate to my left swings on its hinges, and two maids barrel out of the cutout behind it.

One of the women has a blow dart in one hand and a knife in the other. She runs to the cage to protect the Queen.

The other woman runs straight for me.

Rosemary. Her mouth twists into an odd smile as she pulls the chains off of me. My magic flows back into my body.

What is she doing here and why was she hiding in the wall? This is another deviation from the Queen's plan. Somebody botched it. The rebels called me here to fix their mistake. I could wring their necks for putting her life at risk.

I angle my body in front of my mate's, glad that I gave into my fae instincts and came right away. There'll be no more

119

careful planning or tiptoeing around the conflict. I face the King with a promise in my eyes. He'll die tonight.

"Think this through, Commander." Stefan draws his sword. "My death would spark a chain of catastrophic events. Sarteal would suffer the consequences."

"Fuck the consequences. We're doing this my way now," I growl. "Did you think I would let you get away with stealing my wife?"

"I had to do it," he says, lifting his elbow to stay on guard. "You don't understand how important she is to my kingdom."

My shadows spill out, ripping my father's blade from his belt. I catch it and spin the handle, balancing it with the tip out. "You don't understand how important she is to *me*. Did you know she's my mate?"

"I–I didn't," he stammers.

"You couldn't have kept her locked away here forever. You're a fool, Stefan. I would've felt her. I would've smelled her."

"Guards," he screams, realizing his error. If he's educated on the fae, then he knows he's made a fatal mistake by taking one's mate. "Defend your King!"

No one comes rushing to help him. Most of them have run away.

He tries to save face, sliding back behind the table to protect himself, pretending to be calm again. "This is a dramatic overreaction. Are you willing to start a realm-wide war over one woman? Because that's what will happen if you kill me."

"I'm not going to kill you, but I'm going to remind you of your place." Sheathing my blade, I send my inky ropes around his throat, letting them creep into his nostrils. "I want you to remember what you've done. Remember the girls you've hunted."

He gags as I press into his head, walking down his darkest hall of memories until I find what I'm looking for—girls with wide eyes and golden hair kneeling in the room where I'm standing.

I can't stay here too long, listening to them crying for their families. Begging the King not to feed them to the devouring trees.

The earliest scenes are tainted with guilt, but his remorse fades as I walk down the aisle of years. He becomes consumed with his mission, driven by his fear of what will happen if he can't find the missing daughter of the forest.

He's gotten good at stuffing those memories down deep, but I stir them up and force him to see them.

"Stop it," he says, dropping his sword to grab his head.

"Remember the ones you burned," I say, twisting deeper into his mind. It's filled with the shrill screams of people being taken to the pyre for his spectacle.

He resists me, blocking something he doesn't want to see. I push my way past that boundary, mining for that memory.

I see Queen Rina lifting her chin as she's tied to the pyre, trying not to scream as the flames rise higher.

When the heat becomes too much to bear, her shrill pleas torment the King.

I can feel how badly he wants to cut her ropes and carry her to a healer, but he stands firmly in place, steeling himself with bitterness.

"Don't look away, son." His voice pours out of my mouth, speaking above the atrocity. A child stands at my waist in this vision.

Prince Alex. His silky hair slides beneath my palm as if I'm really patting his head. "Love does not come before our legacy. This is what happens to anyone who stands against me."

He regrets what he did to his Queen. His self-loathing is all-consuming. I can feel it bleeding into my soul and sending me to a dark place. I draw myself back into my body, reeling from the agony he's caused himself.

"Rina," Stefan cries out, his elbows banging against the table as he falls forward. "I had to do it. You betrayed me, you—"

He looks around, his cheeks wet, seeming to remember where he is as Rosemary steps beside me.

She's absorbing my dark energy. Green threads ring her fingers and spread along her veins.

"Remember what you did to the witches," she says, her voice distorted. It's deep and filled with gravel. She doesn't sound like herself. "Remember how you stole them away to protect yourself from paying for the sins of your family."

The aura of her power doesn't glow like it usually does. It doesn't shine like a faerie's. Instead, it takes on the muted hue of a burial ground, deadly and infinitely scary.

"Remember that I've been chosen to set the forest free." Birds squawk past the windows, escaping the dark clusters of leaves quaking without any wind running through them. "They're coming for you, Stefan."

She looks to me with a silent request, her eyes rolling back and refocusing. I oblige, slipping back into his head.

I can see the view of the Hartwood from his window. He spends restless nights there, fearing the song of the forest. Nightmares of the ghostly maidens keep him awake. He dreams of them churning him into the soil, turning him into nothing.

I let those terrors play out behind his eyelids until he falls to his knees, plagued by his visions.

"It's not real," he seethes.

"But I am." Roberta slinks out from her hiding spot, grabbing the carving knife from the platter on the table. She shoots a look at me. "This is my kill."

The King crawls away, but I use my shadows to hold him on his knees as she tucks the blade beneath his chin, lifting his gaze.

"Remember a sheep farm outside of Heartshire and the kind couple who lived there with their four children," she says. "Your friend complained that their fleece prices were too high, so you had their property seized and sent the family to the pyre. All of them except for their eldest daughter." She screws up her face in a mocking imitation of the King. "*You're too beautiful to burn,* you told her. *I'll have you in my bed instead.* Do you remember that?"

"No." He rasps a defiant laugh. "There were so many of those peasant girls. How could I remember one out of a whole haystack?"

"Because this one hurt your feelings." Disgust coats Stefan's features as she brings her face closer to his. "Look at me. You remember her now, don't you? The young woman you sent to the whipping post because she humiliated you with her rejection. Those butchers nearly beat me to death before someone intervened. A princess."

Another maid steps out from the grate, holding the squabbling hatchlings. Marian. Sun bites her cap, pulling it off as she sets the pair down. She's nearly unrecognizable with her thick black curls spiraling over her shoulders.

The Queen hesitates, looking back at her handmaiden.

"Do it," Marian says, and the Queen moves the knife to the pulse point beneath Stefan's jaw.

"My real name is Marian Fitz. I'm a nobody. A poor shepherdess." She shoves the blade in and gives it a twist before removing it. Blood pours down the King's neck and sprays her dress. The cruelty in his stare is replaced by mortal horror as she says, "I protected the jewel of Heartshire by taking her place at your wedding. You've never touched *my* princess."

He flops around as he's dying, throwing his crown from his head. The Queen picks it up before the pooling blood reaches the golden circlet.

"You should've left me, princess," she says, carrying it to her handmaiden and placing it atop her unkempt curls.

"I couldn't do it." The handmaiden princess kisses her face. "I'm sorry."

I'd try to work out the details of their swapped identities, but I'm too concerned for Rosemary. The hatchlings scratch at her skirt and run circles around her ankles. She's standing in place, watching the crimson puddle spreading beneath the King.

"Rosemary."

She's lost control of her magic. The whites of her eyes shine as she gnashes her teeth.

A few words are interspersed with her snarling. *"Not enough. Rot. Rot. Rot. Crush the whole thing."*

I touch her waist, but she doesn't seem to notice me. "Rosemary, darling."

She throws her arms out and splays her fingers open, currents of energy running between them. Signal flares burst in the sky, lighting up the window.

The maid with the blow dart presses her face to the stained glass rendition of the trickster prince. "Get to the horses. The forest is creeping past the boundary. The Ivy Keep is falling."

"The boundary is broken," the Queen murmurs, her mouth tightening as Rosemary continues her strange incantation. "Did she do this?"

"She can answer your questions once she's safe," I snap back, shutting her down at the first hint of an accusation.

Rosemary is too stiff to throw over my shoulder. I tip her body until her knees soften and pick her up in my arms.

"Come on, love." I cradle her into a more comfortable position as the dragons run alongside me to keep up. "We've got to get going."

12

ROSEMARY

I'm an amalgamation of the Hartwood's fury. It shatters through me.

Some floodgate has broken after unleashing years of anger upon the King. I poured it out, and a dark desire rushed in, taking root inside of me. It branches out into my chest as the forest calls for revenge. It wants more.

It's not enough to spill the King's blood.

"Rot the city. Set the forest free."

The dining room tilts as I'm swept up and away from the castle, caged by warmth and a heartbeat pounding in my ears. I want to close my eyes and listen to it, but another wave of rage burns in my ribcage. It feels good.

I can't stop it.

Orange flames burst in the sky, leaving clouds of smoke that dim the starlight. I'm falling, but there's someone here to catch me.

"Rosemary." Two black opals stare down at me. "Come back, little witch."

I don't know how to. All of the voices of the forest are

inside my head. Claws scrape over my belly as two scaly creatures nuzzle my neck.

I tip my head back, overcome with the urge to crush everything. I lift my hand, tightening the vines around the Ivy Keep, digging in where the tower is cracking.

There is screaming in the background. So much screaming. Stones hit the ground like an explosion. Horns blast and warning bells ring incessantly, but even that noise can't compete with the chorus thrumming through my body.

"Are you ready, Zelladine? We've been waiting. Grab the three. Set the forest free."

A hand pushes against my cheek, turning my head to face the black hole yawning open in the Ivy Keep. Figures stream out of the leaning tower, racing to escape before it collapses. I wriggle around, trying to sever my tether to the Hartwood, but it won't let go of me.

"Not enough. Crush it all."

But it has to be enough.

I become aware of the lap I'm lying on, the dragons nestled close to my body, and the fingers stroking my hair as the fortress crumbles around me.

"You can do this," Carabosse says. "Pull back from the darkness."

The forest can't have its revenge tonight. Not at the expense of my family.

I focus on the strands wrapped around my heart, digging them out by the root. Nausea lurches through me.

Carabosse holds my hair back as I roll onto my side and vomit.

"Good work," she says, eyeing the forest. Its violent throes yield to the peaceful breeze shuddering through its leaves. "I think that did the trick."

I sit up, regaining control of my body.

The Queen's carefully organized plan has devolved into complete chaos. The top portion of the Ivy Keep has been busted open, and vines have overtaken the northern half of the castle's bailey. Brown spots mar the waxy leaves that curl and creep by slowly.

Moving to my feet, I pick Sun up, stopping them from sniffing my stomach contents. "Where is everybody?"

Carabosse points her chin toward the broken stones scattered around the Ivy Keep's foundation. "They're over there, fighting."

But my eyes settle on the green uniforms hanging on the wall above the ruckus, recognizing the olive dress in the middle.

Ruth. She didn't deserve this. None of the kitchen staff did.

I have to look away before I get sick again.

The Queen—*Marian*—has gained a bow from the open arsenal. She aims at one of the guards blocking the stables and launches an arrow, allowing Heartshire's true princess to mount a grey mare without any trouble. Her friend in the sheriff's uniform protects her with his sword as she waves to the witches staggering away from the Ivy Keep.

"Stay together," she calls, leading them to the gate. "Follow me."

"My godmothers must be with them." I search for three women in a sea of unfamiliar faces, my breath coming in short waves of anticipation. "They're free."

"Not quite." Carabosse draws her blade, holding an arm out in front of me as a man runs by, his armor clinking. This quick getaway is turning into a gory battle.

Some of the King's men have switched sides, gathering under Robin's banners. Others climb the wall, helping to raise the drawbridge, sealing us inside the bailey.

There's no way out until the King's men surrender. How

many lives will be lost to defeat them? "We have to do something."

"I'm working on it," Carabosse says as a cloud passes over us, darkening the sky. Snovida is circling overhead, dodging the sharp weapons being thrown at her wings. A stallion rears on his hind legs as she swoops past the stables, kicking up dust with her rough landing. She roars a warning that shakes the ground and clears the surrounding area.

"Unfortunately, there's no time for our normal safety precautions," Carabosse says, using her shadows to shield me from the arrows flying from the battlements as she helps me mount her dragon. She straddles my hips, her thighs holding me firmly in place.

Snovida bounds forward and leaps up, sending us soaring with one solid thrust from her wings. The hatchlings squeal from the sudden takeoff. I tighten my arms around both of them, tucking my chin until we level out into a smooth glide. Only then do I dare to peek past Snovida's dark wings.

The fighting seems even worse from this perspective.

Metal clashes as the yard breaks out into small skirmishes. It's hard to tell who's fighting who since so many of the King's men have joined the rebellion on the spot.

A chamberlain holds a poker over a fire. "In the name of King—"

"Fuck the King," a royal guard says, running his sword through him. He jogs to help a group of servants carrying a ladder to the wall.

The crowd at the gate is growing, leaving too many people exposed to the guards on the parapet. A woman collapses as she's struck by an arrow, and I scream at the sight of her lifeless eyes staring up into the sky.

She wasn't fighting. She was just trying to leave.

The rebels lean the ladder against the wall, climbing

despite the guards waiting at the top. A few of them make it, and a few are flung off. It's painful to watch them.

The rebels are taking too long to breach the castle's defenses. People are dying. My godmothers could be any one of them. The thought of them getting struck down when we're so close makes my throat constrict.

"I can't lose them like this."

"You won't." Carabosse bumps her hips forward as we fly over the gate towers. "Open the drawbridge!"

Snovida curves her neck downward, small embers falling from her maw.

The men in the towers crank their handles, and the chains fall slowly. A guard runs across the walkway, pointing his crossbow at us while a squad loosens arrows with a renewed fervor, taking aim at the people escaping below.

There's a desperate urgency in their movements. They're trying to take out as many rebels as they can.

Snovida's scales warm beneath me, and she unleashes fire on the guards as they launch their weapons.

Smoke hovers in the air above the crowd as the drawbridge hits the ground. The princess leads the charge out into the square. Witches, servants, and newly recruited soldiers form a loose formation behind her.

A stray guard bursts out of a tower, swinging a machete at the people waiting to get out. An arrow flies straight into his neck.

The Queen drops her bow after hitting her target and lifts the skirt of her stained silk gown to mount a chestnut horse, holding up the back of the line with Willow at her side.

Many of the escapees break away once they're past the gates, scattering to the shops in the castle square. They knock on lattice window frames to beg for protection. A guard maneuvers his horse around the crowd, ringing a brass bell as they march into the valley.

"The King is dead," he bellows. "It's time to meet the fearless leader of our rebellion."

Three riders trot behind him, sticking close together. My stomach does a somersault when the woman in the middle tilts her head. I know that gesture, the way she leans her ear to her shoulder, letting her blonde hair spill over it. Her spine curves to the side as if she's weary of sitting up straight.

I lean forward, nearly rocking out of my seat. *"Grace!"*

Carabosse slides a hand around my waist to prevent me from slipping as the woman squints at Snovida. The other two women follow her gaze, their mouths agape.

My heart raps a solid beat against my chest.

"They're here. They're alive," I crow, twisting my neck back to get another look, but we're already past them. The hatchlings wiggle in my arms, catching on to my excitement.

"Oh love, I'm so happy for you," Carabosse murmurs against my hair, then she digs her right heel into Snovida's side, pulling away from the city.

The wattle and daub buildings shrink below me. People look like miniature figures from this height as they exit their homes and businesses, rushing to steal a glimpse of the mysterious rebellion leader.

"Where are we going?" I ask.

"To the rebel territory."

"We can't leave them. Not yet."

"It will hurt the rebel cause if they allow me to fly my dragon straight into their city after that shitshow." She chuffs out a noise, sounding a bit like Snovida. "They're going to have a hard enough time recovering from that as it is."

I glance back at the destruction behind us. My view is

obstructed by Carabosse's shoulders, but I can see smoke swirling around the broken edges of the tower. "I caused that."

"Don't look. Don't think about it." She stiffens behind me, a solid wall of support. "The castle guards are outnumbered, and most of the royal soldiers have been sent to the southern border. It's over for now. Trust me?"

"I do." But there's a rotten pit of anxiety in my belly because this isn't a clearcut victory. There wasn't even supposed to be a battle this evening.

Jubilant cheers and screams of protest ring out from the streets. Men brawl in the alleys and tavern keeps open their doors, inviting people in for celebratory drinks.

An air of confusion seems to ripple through the city.

"I didn't mean to do it. I was so scared when we didn't leave like we were supposed to. And then I was angry. So angry when I remembered what the King had done. My gift overpowered me," I babble. "It's like it took control of my body."

"It's not your fault."

"What if it happens again?"

"It won't." Carabosse strokes her thumb below my ribs. "You'll be with your godmothers soon. They'll help you."

Even after seeing them, I'm having trouble imagining us all together again. I don't think I'll believe it until I get to hug them.

I lean into Carabosse until I can feel the scales of her armor against my back, their hard edges pressing through her tunic. It's been too long since we've gotten to be like this—together, out in the open. Her firm presence steadies me.

Everyone I love is alive and free.

We pass over the valley, veering west before we reach the place where my apothecary once stood. The song of the forest has quieted down to a soft chorus that whispers, *"Still waiting. Still waiting."*

Lollishire isn't the same place it used to be. So much has already changed the last May Day feast.

The King's City disappears into a blanket of trees as we pass over a range of rolling hills. They dip into another valley village. Flags flutter on the lamp posts below, marked with the birdcage emblem of the rebellion.

We've made it.

Snovida lands on a grassy bald near the outskirts of the village, and we dismount, the dragon's claws dropping twigs and dirt clods as she flies off again. The hatchlings bound away as soon as I set them on the ground. They chase each other across the crest of the slope. Sun catches Moon's tail, and they both tumble halfway down the hill.

Here, they have room to run and play. There's no more mausoleum caging them in. The castle has disappeared beyond the horizon.

Carabosse's eyes are locked on my profile when I glance her way. The look she gives me is bittersweet despite the curve of her half-smile. "We should get you set up with your new living arrangements."

We venture into the village, entering one of the tents set up in the town's market square. A man in a brown shirt pulls out a ledger, keeping an eye on the dragons as he goes over the details of my arrival.

"Here's what you'll need," he says, handing me a pile of clothes, a bread basket, and a key. "You'll be sharing a cabin with another family tonight, but you'll be traveling with the rest of the Merry Men to Heartshire tomorrow."

We thank him and find the cabin—a simple log structure separated from the one next to it by a thin line of trees. A crooked willow leans over its roof, its voluminous leaves hanging over its awning.

I stop at the door, clutching my clothes to my chest. I'm not ready to be cooped up inside again. "Should we go for a quick stroll and check out our surroundings?"

"It'll be safe for you in the cabin," Carabosse says, touching her knife handle. "I've got to head back to speak to your rebellion leaders."

The sound of laughter and conversation floats from the cabin's open windows, but I don't know the people inside, and I don't wish to join them.

"What? Already?" I sound screechy, but my body won't accept that I'm safe. My pulse is still racing like I'm crawling through a secret passageway. "You can't leave me here alone."

"I have to. I can't trust your foolish rebellion leaders to protect you after that disaster." She throws a hand toward the east. "I've never seen all underworld break loose like that before."

I attempt to explain what happened after she left. "The princess had to modify the plan. I hate that she did, but surely you can understand her motives."

She puckers her mouth, the v on her top lip deepening. "Not as a military leader, I can't. It's clear that Robin—Roberta, Marian, whoever the devil she is—cannot handle this. So I will."

"What do you mean?"

"I'm going to make sure the opposition can't gain a foothold in the capital."

"But you said it would look bad if the rebels allowed you to fly your dragon into the King's City."

"That's why I'm invading without permission. I'll take care of any lingering loyalty to the crown." Her irises bleed into the whites of her eyes. "No one will be around to hunt you down for your participation in this. You'll have a chance to be happy again, with your godmothers, in your own kingdom."

She strides down to the dirt path running back to town. I

follow her, and the dragons skip into the tree line, scrambling up low branches.

"Carabosse, wait. Don't do this."

"Robin blew it," she says, without turning back. "I can't return to my Queen knowing I've left your safety in the hands of someone so incompetent."

She passes beneath one of the willows, and I feel for the string connecting me to the tree. Its branches lean toward Carabosse, binding one of her wrists in a wispy cord of leaves. I understand my magic better now. It's easier to grasp it without any help.

"*Unff.*" She grunts as I call another branch down to trap her other arm and haul her upward.

Walking around the willow, I draw the tree's fronds toward me, pitching Carabosse onto her knees. I drop my newly-issued belongings. "From now on, my safety is in my own hands."

Her hair falls over her face as she laughs. "Let's not pit our gifts against each other, dearest."

"Why? Afraid I'll win again?" I taunt, fully aware that she could work her way out of these binds if she really wanted to. "It didn't work out so well for you last time, did it?"

"I'll admit you got me good, but I'm wearing armor now, and you don't have a knife." Her teeth flash in a tight grin. She bites down on it, her expression turning serious again. "I'm sorry, but I can't return to Sarteal without knowing you'll be perfectly safe and—"

I slip my fingers beneath her chin, cupping the perfect bottom point of her heart-shaped face. "You're never going to know that. You can't guarantee my safety, especially when you're not with me."

Her eyes glitter with dark defiance. "I'm still going to try my best."

"Me too. I've got to protect you from yourself." I stroke my hand back to feel the fluttering pulse on her neck. "*Pull back from the darkness.* That's what you said to me a few hours ago when I was ready to crush the King's City."

"Because that wasn't you," she says. "This *is* me. I'm the wraith of Sarteal. No one would be surprised if I decided to burn down a city. I'm a monster, Rosemary. So let me be one for you."

"No." I trace my fingers along one of her pointed ears, and she shivers. "If you're a monster, then I'm one too. I liked how powerful I felt when I lost control. I'm glad the King is dead and the witches are free."

"That's different."

"Is it? I don't understand what's going on with me, but I know you don't want to lose me to my power." Her biceps flex as she tugs against the leafy tendrils. She scowls as I wrench her arms back. "And I don't want to lose you when you carve all of the goodness from your heart just to protect me. Don't force me to love a shell of the woman you used to be. Our happiness can't come at the price of others' suffering."

"I don't care about—"

"Yes you do." I feather my fingers over her jawline. "I know you. If you really wanted me to let you do this, you would rip these vines away and leave, but I know you don't want to hurt me. You *love* me. The real me. And that means respecting my wishes as well as my safety."

Defiant tears well up over her bottom lashes. She hangs her head to blink them away and grouses, "That's it, then? I'm supposed to leave you with these fools and accept this is the best I can do for you?"

"Yes." I shrug. "Maybe this is all we get—a few meetings here and there when you can get away from your Queen. Visits in our dreams. So be it." I've never expected to get a sugary sweet ending like I'm some heroine in one of Grace's bedtime stories. "Don't fly back to the King's City. Stay with me tonight. Keep me company."

I brush my thumb across her bottom lip. Her mouth closes around the digit, warm and wet as I push it in.

"Stay," I repeat, working my thumb into her mouth a few times. I like how she feels and the way the depths of her eyes seem to swirl with sparks of light as her long lashes fan open. "Drive the darkness away with me."

Her eyelids drop heavy as she licks the underside of my thumb. She *is* a monster. She knows exactly what she's doing. "Then untie me."

"No." I turn my nose up, indulging in her mild irritation. There aren't a lot of ways to clear the gloom over her head, but annoying her is a tried and true method. "You're my captive now."

She gives me one hard suck, pulling back with a wet sound. "What do I have to do for you to let me out?"

"You have to be a good girl and promise you won't storm off to commit terrible deeds once you're free."

Her eyes narrow. "I'm only trying to protect you, but you make it sound as though my intentions are malevolent."

"Your intentions don't matter. Not when the impact would affect real people. Burning a city would make you evil." I know she's not herself right now. There's that oily dark magic clouding her thoughts, and I have to make her think clearly. "Promise me you won't leave."

She holds her palms up. "I promise."

"And you have to stay on your knees."

She groans. "Rosemary, please."

I kneel in the dirt, tapping my fingers together beneath my chin. "Or we could stay like this, and then you'd have to hang out with me until morning."

She side-eyes my wicked smirk. "Tell me you're joking."

"Maybe."

I release her and she grabs me beneath my thighs, wrestling me to the ground. We lie facing each other, our limbs tangled. Carabosse plies me with hot kisses down my neck, and I throw our tussling match, letting her nudge me onto my back. She moves on top of me, growling as I wrap my legs around her waist.

My body tingles where we're touching. I press into her, unable to get enough. I know I'm dirty and sweaty, but I need to feel her all over me.

Tonight has been a nightmare and a fever dream. I can't think about it yet. I want to lose myself for a few hours with her, seeking solace in the safety of her body.

She pins one of my wrists over my head and slides her hand up to twine our fingers together, her hips rocking down as mine rise in a blissful meeting that sends heat spreading over my low body.

"Carabosse," I breathe. "I need—"

Grawk.

"Damn it," Carabosse swears under her breath. She rolls off of me as Sun and Moon pounce from the bushes, tripping over knobby roots.

Rubbing her forehead, she sits up and says, "Hello, hatchlings."

We share a glance, tittering over the interruption from the tussling dragons. Carabosse unclasps her cloak and spreads it over the grass. We break our stale bread rations and watch the dragons burn off some energy until Moon prances to the corner of the cloak, yawning.

Carabosse lifts her crusty bread end toward the cabin. "Should we turn in?"

The shades are drawn, and the lantern has been put out. I

don't want to walk inside that small, dark house. "I'm fine right here unless you need a proper bed."

She seems to understand, scooching close to me as Sun and Moon curl up snout to tail and fall asleep.

Let this be enough, I wish as Carabosse and I cling to each other in the darkness, still together after everything.

Let this be all the light we need.

13

CARABOSSE

"There's still time to make it back to the King's City. Tear it all down while she's sleeping."

I conjure a glowflower in my hand, watching the sorrowgale land on the purple mountains, calling out for its mate.

I'm visiting the Starlight Court alone tonight, sparing Rosemary from the voice's badgering. It's been urging me to do its bidding since we fled, and she needs her rest.

"I promised her I wouldn't." I pick the flower's luminescent green petals, scattering them off the railing. "And I happen to like her a lot more than you."

A gust of wind hits my back and the palace doors swing open. Mal rips through the seams of my dream, stepping onto the balcony.

There's no time to shield myself. The back of her hand cracks across my face, forcing me to look at the black holes taking bites out of the mountain range.

It's a nightmare scene of the Fade, stolen from my memories—one I never thought I'd see again.

"What have you done?" She backs me up against the railing. "I ordered you to work with King Stefan, and you betrayed me."

"Turning on the King was necessary, my Queen. I found out Stefan has been working with our rivals. He had cigars sourced from Dardaran in his possession," I tell her. I recognized the symbol on the band when I smoked with him. "Lollishire's King would have turned on us eventually. It was better to catch him unaware."

"That's not why you did this," she says, taking the plucked flower from my hand.

"What other reason would I have had to attack his army?" I probe. "Perhaps it had something to do with the fact that you delivered my mate straight to him."

She picks the last petal and drops the flower's head over the railing. It falls into a black disc of emptiness, never landing. "I assumed you would've figured that out by now."

"How could you turn her over to that prick?" I spit. "Have you become that fucking heartless?"

She recoils from my harsh words. I've never confronted Mal, not like this. I was raised to serve and protect her, my Starlight princess.

"Years ago, I dug around in Stefan's head to see why he was so afraid that the devouring trees had started fruiting again. I knew he was looking for somebody, and what finding her could mean for Lollishire." She hoists herself up on the railing, reliving the day the Fade took our court. "Thea told me a few strange things about Rosemary, and I connected the dots."

"That's sick."

"Trust that what I did was in *our* best interest, nyxsisium. You don't really know what she is. I have a knack for seeing past glamours. You don't."

"What in the underworld is that supposed to mean?"

141

"It doesn't matter. I could've done worse, you know. At least I let her live. I didn't make you suffer what I felt when I lost Arryn," she says, hugging her arms around herself. The black holes jump toward us, wiping our childhood stomping grounds out of existence.

"Don't ever mess with her again," I warn. "Leave her alone, and I'll continue to serve you."

"It's not like you have much of a choice," she says. "Your life is tied to mine, not hers."

But I'm not afraid of the power she holds over me when it comes down to Rosemary's safety. I'll take her favorite toy away if I have to. "If you do anything to hurt her or interfere with her happiness, you *will* lose me. That's a promise."

I hold her gaze until that point becomes crystal fucking clear.

"I see where we stand now, Cara. She'll be safe as long as she doesn't come anywhere near Sarteal." She scratches her nail along the railing, green flames sparking threateningly. "Our lieutenants are anticipating an attack from Dardaran now that you've shifted our alliances. Fly to Claw Ridge and clean up this fucking mess." Her dress is like liquid starlight falling around her ankles as she slides down from the railing. "You have an hour to get your shit together. Consider that a kindness from me."

Her posture is unbowed, but I know she's in a rush to leave, shaken by the dreamscape she's chosen to mess with me.

"I'm not a fool, Mallory. This isn't about King Stefan's obsession with some prophecy," I call after her. "Why are you so afraid of anyone who gets too close to me?"

Her shoulders pinch together. "I don't know what you mean by that."

"Nova. Did you push her?" I ask, tense in the knight

uniform I would've worn if our court had survived the Fade. "Tell the truth. I'll know if you're lying."

Her hand flies to her heart. "I'm offended that you could think such a thing. Nova was my friend too."

Unexpected relief rushes through me. I've always denied my gut feeling on that subject. I've never wanted to believe that Mal could kill someone that she treated like family.

"That would have been a terrible ending for such an admirable rider," she says. "She thought her dragon was beneath her, thanks to my illusion. She wasn't afraid when she jumped to her death. I hope that comforts you."

There is no moon above me. All of the stars have been eaten. A black circle takes a piece of the railing I'm holding.

"What the fuck did Vellesse say to you in that cave that turned you into this?"

Her violet-painted lips turn down in a grimace. "Why don't you ask her yourself? Don't you think it's strange that she's never mentioned it when she lives inside *your* head?"

A cloud of stardust shimmers around her figure as she disappears, leaving one last warning rippling through the dream. "One hour."

The city is blank and dead below me. Scraps of the atmosphere hang in patches at the edge of the cursed court, torn pieces of the sky waving like flags.

"What do you want from me?" I shout into the void. There is no answering voice.

My question doesn't even echo back to me.

I'm swallowed by a sphere of emptiness, and I wake up in a cold sweat.

Real stars twinkle through the willow leaves, faint in the violet sky that's fading at the edges. Two baby dragons are fighting in their sleep beside my head, and my mate is snuggled up to me, her hair strewn over my neck.

The sight is better than any dream I could possibly create. It pulls me from the void and makes my heart swell achingly. I tidy a tangled lock away from Rosemary's face, careful not to disturb her.

Causing more mayhem in the King's City would have wrecked her peace. I'm glad she stopped me. I rub my face, accepting that I must respect her human needs. I'm constantly at war with my fae instincts.

She stirs, cracking her eyes open.

"Is something wrong?" she asks, her voice groggy.

"No." I bring my hand to her lower back. "I was just watching you sleep."

She smacks her lips. "That's creepy."

"I know."

"I kind of like it, though." Her eyes close, then open wide as she smiles, her toes curling against my shins. It feels like dawn, and the sunlight hasn't even touched the horizon yet.

We hold a conversation without speaking, our noses touching. The look we share says everything we're thinking.

It's unfair that fate keeps tearing us apart when we're meant to be together, but right now, we're here.

I want to condense years into the short time we have before I'm called back to Sarteal. She kisses me, working her fingers into my hair. I pick her up from the cloak, stomping into the thin patch of trees with her arms around my neck and her legs around my waist.

"What about the hatchlings?" she whispers.

"I'll be able to hear them from here if they wake up." My shadows swarm around us, darkening the spaces between the leaves until we're concealed.

She peels my tunic off and runs her hands over my dragon scale vest, picking at the clasps.

"I want to burn this damn thing," I say, pulling her maid's

uniform over her head. Her trousseau might've been the least important thing that was stolen from her, but it sets my blood to boil that my wife has been reduced to wearing rags. "I'll send you more of your pretty gowns when I can."

She undoes my belt, using the leather to pull my hips closer. "That's not important."

But I know she loves to twirl around in her blush skirts and corsets with floral embroidery. She's not concerned with status, but if I'd done things differently, she would be my—

I choke the thought off as she works my riding leathers down, my knives hitting the ground. "It's important to me."

"I wish that I'd be wearing them for you," she says, stepping out of her undergarments. We're both naked in the billowing darkness.

"Me too."

I close my mouth over hers, taking her in my arms. We touch lightly, skimming our fingertips over each other. She cups my small breast in the palm of her hand, and I suck a breath in, my nipple hardening. This feeling is more than the heat gathering between my legs; it's a swelling in my throat and a pressure beneath my skin.

I'll never get enough of her. Even if I'd gotten things right and could take her to bed each night, I'd spend the next day craving to touch her again.

I trail my mouth down between her breasts and over her belly, kneeling with my lips brushing against her damp curls. She pushes my forehead back.

"I don't know if we should do that. We've been running and riding," she says shyly, clamping her thighs together. But I'm a fae beast, enticed by her scent. I tip my head back, with a devilish grin.

She runs her fingers through my hair, considering. "Oh, fine."

Leaning back against a tree trunk, she widens her stance. I move right in, spreading her open to lick broad stripes up to her clit. I want all of her—her salt, and dirt, and grit. She holds on to the grooves in the tree as I absolutely devote myself to her sweet pussy, her nails scratching at the bark when she comes apart on my tongue.

I move back to admire the wet shine on her inner thighs, but she's not done with me. She moves to her knees, bringing me down to the grass with a sense of urgency. A root digs into my shoulder blades as she grinds against me, sliding her hips back along my thigh. I think I might pass out when she straddles my waist, sinking between my legs until we meet.

"Fuck," I breathe, reveling in the feeling of her wetness sliding over mine.

"I need to feel you before you leave," she says, her hips moving in a delicious circle that heightens the intensity. "Right here, under the open sky, you're not bound to anyone but me."

I feel her ribs and the curve of her waist, grabbing that soft bit of flesh on her hip. "You know I'm yours, Rosemary."

I try to take in every detail I can—the bead of sweat trickling down her neck, the scent of our sex, and the sound she makes as we reconfigure our legs, finding the right angle for our swollen buds to touch again.

There's something frantic, almost angry about the way we're trying to soak each other in. Rosemary's arms give out, and she falls into me, broken blades of grass sticking to our slick bodies. She pushes herself back up, and I support her hips as she comes down on me.

I dig my heels into the dirt, feeling the pulse of her throbbing pussy. My climax overtakes me, and we roll in the grass together, our hips still moving through each and every wave, pawing at each other until we're spent.

Early morning sun rays glisten on the leafy weeds as we lie back, holding hands.

"Maybe your Queen will forget to call you home and you can stay with me," Rosemary says, kissing my shoulder.

I close my eyes, humming. That's a sweet thought, but Mal's hourlong reprieve is over, and my scar is burning.

Rosemary dips her spoon into her bowl, blowing on the hot liquid dripping from a hunk of boiled cabbage.

"I think Roberta and Marian were feeding them fully cooked meals," she says as I hold out the handful of worms I've dug up for the dragons. Sun turns their snout away from the wriggling pink pile, and Moon gingerly takes one between their teeth before spitting it out. "Now they have a taste for castle delicacies."

I drop the worms and wipe my hands. "Spoiled rotten things."

"Perhaps they'll like rabbit better. I'll set up a snare when we arrive in Heartshire." She stares down the dirt path, anxiously awaiting news of the Merry Men's arrival. We've been waiting outside all day, only popping into the supply tent to grab our rations. She refuses to go inside the cabin when everyone we pass seems to be perturbed by my presence.

"You're resourceful," I commend her. Raising orphaned dragons comes with its own challenges, but if anyone can handle them, it's Rosemary. "I know you'll take good care of them."

Sun bats their tail against my bowl, splashing it near Moon's claws. They both lap the soup up from the grass.

We watch them wrestle with hopeful amusement, my

smile captured by a wince as a fresh wave of searing pain rolls beneath my skin.

"*Agh.*" I grab my scar, trying to put pressure on it. The heat is so intense, I can see green light sparkling behind my eyelids.

"Hey." Rosemary sets her spoon down and walks on her knees to me, her starchy wheat-colored dress hanging in stiff folds around her legs. "What's wrong?"

I grind my teeth. "Nothing."

"Your Queen knows, doesn't she?" she asks, pushing my sleeve back to look at the flesh bubbling along my scar. She touches the skin around it carefully. "Oh no, sweetpea."

I clench all of my muscles, trying to find some relief. "It's not that bad, really."

"Now I understand why you hate lying so much." She looks up at me, a full-fledged forest fire burning in her eyes. "You're terrible at it."

"Am I?"

"Yes, your nose and shoulders start twitching."

Damn. And here I thought I was getting good at it lately.

"How long have you been hiding this?" Turning my wrist over, she studies the flayed edges of the pink crescent. "She's been doing this all day, hasn't she? Why didn't you tell me?"

"Please don't worry." Shaking, I hold a straight face through the flaring pain. I've been suffering in silence, ignoring Mal's summoning. I won't leave until she's reunited with her godmothers. "The punishment won't last. She needs me in Claw Ridge."

"There has to be something that'll help." She pats her hip, her fist curling where her satchel should be as the town's church bells start ringing, announcing the rebellion leader's arrival.

I smile weakly. "It helps knowing that you'll be with your family when I leave."

"I told myself I wouldn't beg you not to go," she says. "But don't go. Please."

"I have to. I'm sorry." Fuck. I'm *so* sorry. "But if the distance is ever too much for you, I would understand—"

She scoffs. "Are you implying that I should move on with someone else?"

Vellesse's horns. That thought makes my envy burn hotter than the magic broiling my skin. But yes, I would understand. "I want you to be happy, Rosemary."

"Rude." She tears a fistful of white clover from the ground and chucks it at me. "I'm your wife, and I offer you no such privileges. As far as I see it, we have two options."

I brush the florets from my shirt and cock an eyebrow. "And what are those?"

"Find a way to be together. Or pine away for each other forever." She throws her arm over her forehead dramatically. "Tell me to be true to you. I know you want to."

I do. She speaks right to my possessive nature.

"Be true to me, little witch. And I'll love you faithfully." I stand as the pain recedes. Mal likes to give me breaks from the burning to ensure her next jolt is a shock to my system.

She hugs me. "I'm not ready."

"Me neither. But it's not goodbye," I say. "I'll see you in your dreams."

Her fingers trail on my cloak as I break away, walking up the hill toward the bald where Snovida is waiting. I pick up on the sound of footsteps approaching in the opposite direction. Rosemary and I look back at each other once before she hears them.

"Rosemary?"

Her chin wobbles, and she sprints down to the three women who appear around the bend in the dirt path. Her dragons leap near her heels, squealing and flapping their wings.

"Mothers," she shrieks, throwing herself at them.

They lock in a tight embrace, and all I can see is a cluster of hands, hair, and linen as the four of them bombard each other with questions.

"Are you hurt?"

"Where did you find these dragons?"

"Your *wife*?"

"Sarteal? What in the world? She's leaving already?"

Snovida bumps her head against my chest, and I stroke her scaly neck, hot tears brimming over my lashes. Rosemary has waited too long for this moment for me to taint it with a prolonged goodbye.

"I'm fine," I tell her, wiping my face. Since when the fuck do I cry like this?

"Sweet girl, you're still as pretty as a peach," one of Rosemary's godmothers says, sending her into a peal of tear-soaked laughter.

"She's going to be ok," I say, a sob slamming through my chest as Snovida spreads her wings.

14

ROSEMARY

Heartshire doesn't seem to be as hostile as it was a few months ago when Carabosse and I were attempting to reach the ferry. The city is still heavily guarded, but there aren't soldiers waiting in the trees with arrows or riding down the streets on horses, swinging swords indiscriminately.

I watch through the bars on the cart window as our coachman speaks to the women guarding the entry point. They let us through without any problems, and I loosen a breath, wedging myself between Diana and Candide.

Grace is curled up with the hatchlings. Diana was the one who suggested that she should tell them a story to distract herself from our less-than-ideal mode of transportation.

None of us are too pleased to be shut inside of a jailer's cart, but at least we're all together again.

"A silver disc poured its soft glow into the pitch black sky, and the Tree Mother knew her sister, the Moon Goddess, had finally broken free from the Lord of Night," Grace narrates as Sun rolls over, begging for chin scritches. "Then her coven joined her in the sky, thirteen stars orbiting her light. The Tree Mother watched with her feet planted in the soil she'd created, her eyes watering. She was happy for her sister, but she felt so lonely in her empty forest kingdom."

I've heard this one a thousand times before, but I lean back and soak her words in. It's just nice to hear to her voice again.

Grace has always been sensitive, but she seems so fragile now. Her pale blonde hair is threaded with white streaks, and Diana and Candide have been careful to steer our conversation away from anything too upsetting.

I have a thousand questions, but they can wait. There's no need to push them for information; we have plenty of time to discuss everything that's happened since they were taken.

I still can't believe my godmothers are here with me. I have to pinch myself a few times to make sure I'm not dreaming.

They're worse for the wear after their time in the Ivy Keep, but they're safe, and as far as I can tell, healthy. They have all their fingers and teeth, contrary to what I believed after all of the threats Robin sent me.

The cart rolls past the palace and the Woodland Temple. Grace presses her back against the boards as the horses come to a stop at the safe house.

"What if it's a trap?" she asks.

The coachman opens the door, and Diana jumps out, the sun highlighting the sallow undertones in her olive skin. Her wide-set green eyes crinkle as she squints against the light.

"It's not, sweetheart," she says with a gentleness I never knew she possessed. "Come see for yourself."

The safe house is situated on the banks of the Restless River. We're tucked away from the heart of the city, sheltered by great oaks and pale birch trees. Grace steps onto the carpet of green and gold leaves, spinning around to get a good look at her surroundings.

She pats the hatchlings' heads as if they're the ones in need of encouragement. "Come on, little ones. Let's go inside."

A portion of the Merry Men are already meeting in the cabin, crowding the kitchen. We walk in on the middle of a heated conversation.

"I can't marry Roberta," Prince Alex says, his chair angled away from a large round table. "She's my stepmother. That's disgusting."

The widowed queen tips her copper mug toward her handmaiden. "She's Roberta, and *I'm* Marian. You'll be marrying her, not me. "

"Pardon me. I've only been calling you the wrong name for the past five years," Alex says wryly. "It's a bit confusing. Which one of you is the bird lady anyway?"

The two women exchange a glance and Roberta says, "I like to think of us as two birds of a feather. *Robin* only exists when we're together."

They stare into each other's eyes as if they're alone in the kitchen.

Alex waves his mug side to side, drawing a line between them. "Why marry me when it's obvious that you two carry a torch for each other?"

"It's not meant to be a love match," Willow says, rolling a bit of dried herbs in parchment. She lights it over the wood stove and sucks in a breath. Leaning on the counter, she blows smoke out the open window and waves to me. "It's called a marriage of convenience. Fake it for appearances. People love that shit; they'll think your story is romantic."

The princess looks down at the untouched food on her plate. "Willow is right. Our personal feelings aren't important. The best way to unite our houses is through matrimony." Her breasts swell over her crimson corset as she doubles over with a coughing fit.

"See, you hate the idea," Alex says. "Your body's rejecting it."

Candide raises her hand. "May I suggest that your friend steps outside to smoke, princess?"

Willow's nostrils flare, two wisps of smoke steaming out of them. It gives me an idea.

"Actually, devil's trumpet is known to clear inflamed airways," I say, opening a cupboard lined with canned goods. There aren't any apothecary essentials on hand, only jars of jam and pickled onions. "Smoking the leaves might provide some relief."

Candide smiles approvingly. "You learned a lot in Sarteal."

I have Thea and Felix to thank for that.

I flinch at the memory of the fae healer coaching me through a hands-on experience with inflamed airways. She praised me with the same smile she was wearing when she pushed me toward the King.

Marian—the real Marian—pinches Roberta's arm. "Rose knows what she's doing. She'll have you on the mend before we ride out in the morning."

"Where are we going?" Alex asks. "I need to have my bags ready."

Marian points to Roberta, Willow, and the burly man with the thick beard standing quietly in the corner. "*We're* traveling to garner support near the border. And you're staying here, far away from the fighting."

"But I'm supposed to be the hero of the rebellion."

"That's why we need to keep you alive," Roberta says. "There'll be plenty of opportunities for you to ride out on your stallion for public events."

"Public events? That's a waste of my skills," he argues. "I'm an excellent swordsman."

"Your job is to show up and look pretty," Willow counters

"We do all the work, and you get most of the credit. Be thankful for it."

"But I want to be a part of it." He slaps his hands on the table, his long fingers smooth and uncallused. Roberta's hands look rough in comparison when she reaches out to touch him. There's no real warmth in the gesture. She doesn't look at him the way she looks at Marian.

"You will be, but this area will require your protection," she says. "The witches who trekked to Heartshire with us are taking shelter at the palace, and we have four very special people staying in this cabin." She looks to my godmothers. "You three are still confident you can break the curse that's taken the Hartwood forest?"

"Yes," Candide says.

"How do we break it?" I ask, nervous to broach the topic.

"It's simple. We recite the incantation we were given and make an offering," Diana answers. Grace makes a high-pitched noise, then drops down to rub the hatchlings' bellies.

"Then we'll bring you back to perform the ritual once we've reclaimed the King's City," Marian declares. "Stefan's advisors are holding the capital in the name of his young princes. We'll have to battle our way back in during the months ahead. Carabosse should have known better than to have swooped in on her dragon."

"Boss," I correct her, my skin prickling from the disrespect. Just because Marian knows her full name doesn't mean she gets to use it. "And she only *swooped in on her dragon* because she was lured back to the King's City to save me. I wasn't even the one who needed rescuing."

My godmothers go quiet, and so do the Merry Men. Willow taps her cigarette, the ashes falling in the tense silence as Marian's cold stare sends a chill through me.

"Be that as it may, the Commander's actions will paint her

as a war criminal," she says, emotionless. "Alliances will be shifting all over the realm, and we must plan accordingly if we're going to overhaul Lollishire's monarchy."

Her blunt delivery leaves me speechless and choked up on my worry. What kind of trouble has Carabosse gotten herself into for me? Her enemies will extend far beyond the borders of Sarteal.

"Come on, chicken," Candide says, rubbing my arm. "Why don't we go out and rustle up some of those devil's trumpet flowers?"

Marian is quick to dismiss us. "That would be helpful, thank you."

She turns her attention to the map being spread over the gingham tablecloth. I want to know their plans and what they mean for Carabosse, but I get the feeling that I'm being put in my place.

My role is to sit and wait.

I follow my godmothers out to the wooded area near the banks, slowly accepting everything. None of it seems so bad when Grace crawls out from beneath a bush with a handful of blackberries she shares with the hatchlings. Her face lights up as the fruit breaks between her teeth.

We head out again after I treat Roberta, foraging for any herbs that might come in handy. I think we're all looking for some purpose, a reason to keep our hands and minds busy.

"Marian says we can visit the old palace and help distribute supplies to the witches," Diana says, snipping chamomile.

Grace takes the bundle of flowers, wrapping twine around them. "It will be good to see some of our friends."

I open my mouth to ask them a question as I wander into a patch of blue mistflowers growing rampant by the riverbed, and a butterfly flits away from the cluster of fuzzy petals as they start whispering, *"Why did you leave, Zelladine? You were close enough to set the forest free."*

"Rosemary." Candide taps my shoulder to get my attention. "Why are you staring off? Is something wrong?"

I rub my temples, blocking the message. "I'm getting a little headache. I'll be fine."

"We should get some sleep." She places her cool hand on my forehead, wrinkles forming around her amber eyes. They weren't there the last time I saw her. "It's been a long couple of days. We're all weary."

Thankfully, the kitchen has cleared out when we turn in, and we're able to drink our mugs of mint tea in peace. We find our small room above the steps, and I feel the walls pressing in on us.

Diana marches over to the twin beds and strips the blankets. "Let's sleep under the stars tonight, for old times' sake."

Carrying our bedding outside, we set up a nest on the back deck that's stilted over the river. Across the way, the lush foliage of the Wildlands call to me sweetly.

My honeymoon days seem so far away now, but they still hold some of my best memories.

I lie beside my godmothers where they're snuggling beneath the tin roof awning. We're close enough that we can hear each other's breathing. It blends with the sound of water rushing over flat rocks and lulls me to sleep as I eagerly wait for Carabosse to find me in my dreams.

Autumn blows through northern Lollishire, stirring up the red and gold leaves that land on our porch each morning. The hatchlings prance through them as we head into the city, their scales changing along with the season. Sun's have deepened to a crimson hue, and Moon's have taken on a lavender sheen.

My godmothers and I arrive at the palace early, carrying hot thermoses and baskets filled with supplies. More people have fled to the ancient royal city, and many of them require healing.

"Has the latest shipment of barley come in from Gentrilly?" Diana asks the guard on the steps.

She shakes her head, her eyes sad around the nosepiece of her helmet. "I'm afraid not. King Morrow has been making it difficult for ships to reach the shores of Sarteal. The pirates have been held up for weeks."

Diana groans at Morrow's meddling. The Mermaid King has sided with Alex's siblings and the Dardaran royals, complicating trade routes on the open seas. "How about the crates of corn and wheat from the south?"

"No luck," the guard sighs. "An entire cartload was lost to the blight that's been spreading around the outskirts of the King's City."

"We'll have to make do for a while longer, then," Diana says, hurrying into the partially ruined building. She always rushes off when someone brings up the diseased crops in the southern half of the kingdom.

"What sort of blight is it?" I ask.

The guard raises her gauntlet in a salute to someone behind me before answering. "No one is sure. I've heard that putrid green vines are creeping past the Hartwood's boundary and rotting everything. The disease is apparently resistant to any of the standard treatments."

"Interesting."

I catch up with Grace, Diana, and Candide, my legs heavy with the sinking feeling that this has something to do with me. We walk the halls of the dilapidated palace, doling out remedies to the people who've taken shelter in its dusty chambers.

Guilt sneaks into the cracks of my busy day, rearing its ugly head when I'm measuring out cough syrup or placing poultices on bunions acquired from traveling. It twinges through me as I hold a man's elbow, studying the clean gash running across his hairy forearm.

"This looks brand new. What happened to you?"

"Part of the job," he says gruffly as I reach into my new satchel. Carabosse sent it to me last week. The leather hasn't been broken in; it's stiff as I feel around for my tiny bottle of carbolic acid. We're in short supply, so I use it sparingly, dabbing it onto a linen pad. I clean the cut, listening to Grace chirp away with a patient across the hall.

"In the Ivy Keep they allowed us one hour of sunlight daily. I clung to those precious minutes when they opened the slats in the tower," she says, willing to share details about her time in the tower with strangers, but never with me. "I know life feels dark right now, but you have to find a glimmer of light and hold on to it. The sun will shine again, I promise."

My patient grunts, and I turn my attention back to his wound.

"There. That should prevent any infections." I drop the pad in the dirty linen basket and cough to clear the thick feeling in my throat as I reach for the suture kit on the stone table's cleared surface. "I'll get you stitched up in time for lunch."

I've barely gotten the sentence out when his arm wraps around my neck, his muscles bulging and cutting off my breath. I claw at his forearms, but he's a large man, and I've been caught unaware. There's no way to pull him off of me.

"*Shh.* Stop fighting and I'll let you have a sip of air," he says as I reach for the new knife in my satchel. My fingers touch the resin handle, but he wrenches me back before I can get a grip.

"I've been sent by Prince Edward and Prince Richard to bring you back to the King's City."

Alarm bells ring through my head. I fling my arm out, knocking over glass tincture bottles and jars of calendula oil, desperate to make as much noise as I can.

"What are you doing to her?" Grace's shrill voice cuts through the haze as the room blurs around me. "Let go of my girl."

There's a release, and I'm thrown to the floor, sucking air through the raw pipe of my throat.

Warm liquid sprays my eyelids. My ears ring as I flit in and out of consciousness, but I hear the wet slide of a blade sinking into flesh and snap my eyes open.

The man is crawling on the floor, and Grace is moving after him. My fragile, sweet godmother grabs him by the hair and pulls his head back to stab him again.

Candide and Diana rush in, shouting. Diana holds Grace back as the man falls limp, and Candide drops to her hands and knees beside me. Her worried face is the only thing I see.

Her calls for help sound very faint and far away as I fall asleep.

15

CARABOSSE

"I spotted them a half a mile into the floodplains," Poppy says, her eyes trained on the pools of brackish water to the east. "I counted five soldiers, but there could be more hidden behind the trees."

"Weapons?" Nylah asks. Vencel throws his wings out, using the wind to hold himself back while the riders speak to each other.

"Harpoons and spears," she answers. "That's all I could see."

I run a hand down Snovida's ridges as she dives in front of Evzen. "Keep watch. Nylah and I will patrol the area on foot."

"Yes, Commander." Poppy flies off on her massive dragon to find a discreet lookout spot. If enemy parties are waiting below, it's better not to give them any warning that we're coming.

Nylah and I land near the marshy banks of the oxbow-shaped river curving around the city of Dardaran. We've been using the waterway to bring supplies in for the past few weeks.

It's risky to send rowboats down the river this close to

enemy territory, but it's easier for the pirate ships to reroute around King Morrow's strictly regulated areas and dock in a northeastern cove than it is for them to come ashore on the western beaches of Sarteal. The King of the Sea is still aggrieved that I refused to marry his daughter, and he's taking it out on our kingdom.

"Fucking merdick," I grumble as the loamy soil gives way to cold, mucky water that splashes around my hips. Nylah holds a grimace as she wades around a patch of cypress knees. I point the tip of my knife toward the chain of moss hanging over a small island of trees. "Let's split up."

She dips her chin, her strong jawline taut with tension. We reach the fork and move in different directions, looking for any hawks lying in wait to interfere with the supply boat we're expecting.

Nylah knows to take Dardaran's soldiers alive. We need to know who sent them and where they're getting their information.

I step carefully as I enter the swamp forest, using my knife to clear a path through the moss and vines. I swing my arm to hack at a thick green cord, and the inscription on my blade turns bright blue.

My breath seizes.

My head feels light as I wait for it to fade back to black again. It usually only takes a few moments, the enchantment flaring to life with Rosemary's anxieties. This time it stays aglow for a full minute.

Fuck. I twist the handle, wondering why I decided to take the knife back with me in the first place. I suppose I wanted reassurance of her safety, but it's torturous to see it light up when I can't do anything. It's not like I can fly back on a whim to check on her.

The distance between us is maddening.

Another minute ticks by, my distress growing with the passing seconds.

I jump into Snovida's mind to see how close she is. If this continues, we can get out of here and arrive in Heartshire in a matter of hours.

The blue light recedes, and my pulse decelerates.

I touch my chest, taking another step. Our bond is thrumming. And the brown water is rippling around the base of a tree several yards in front of me. I sheathe my father's blade, swapping it out for a sharp one near my thigh, flinging it out as I dodge a spear shooting through the scraggly branches.

The weapon grazes my arm. I grab the wound to slow the bleeding, approaching the man doubled over with my knife protruding from the flesh above his knee.

"Go ahead and finish me off, wraith," he says, his nose pink and peeling from a sunburn. I take him by the collar, the thin hair on his head thickening where it trails beneath the fabric.

"No, you're coming with me."

A shocked grunt sounds through the trees, followed by a tormented call for help. "Boss. *Shit.*"

The man notices my distraction and struggles against my hold, but I tighten my grip, dragging him as I stomp through the murk to find Nylah. "Lieutenant?"

She's perched on a stump, holding her palm to her calf. Blood flows between her fingers.

There's a splash as a woman surfaces beneath a layer of algae a few feet to my right. Still dripping, she trudges in the water for a few paces and drops to her belly, paddling back toward the royal city. The butt of her harpoon gun juts out behind her as she disappears between the trees.

I don't bother going after her. I already have one person to feed us information, and my friend needs me.

Nylah's tanned face is turning a pale shade of grey.

"Come on," I say. "Let's get you to the healer's tent." She slings an arm over my shoulder, leaning on me to support her weight. I'd worry about the swamp water causing an infection, but Thea can take care of that easily. I tug on the man's shirt. "Walk. Move your feet."

Snovida and Vencel have already landed when we arrive at the lake shore. Evzen comes swooping down behind them. I shove my captive toward him and shout to Poppy, "Interrogate this one for me."

The green dragon traps the man between his foreclaws, his red eyes narrowing and maw peeling back with a chuff of amusement. Vencel looks on as I haul Nylah onto Snovida. She's too weak to mount herself. Her human flesh is losing blood quickly.

"Stay awake," I order, rousing her as we fly back to Claw Ridge. Her limbs are limp by the time we land. Compact muscles are sculpted tightly into every inch of her body. Carrying her down the embankment to camp requires some effort.

When I reach the healer's tent, I throw her down on the nearest bed. "Thea, Nylah needs help."

Thea taps a nail against a glass bottle and glances back at us. "Queen Mal has instructed me not to use my gifts on the lieutenant."

"What?"

"My gifts require an immense amount of energy. They're not to be wasted on someone of questionable use and loyalty to my Queen. She's upset that the lieutenant chose to fly me here when I was supposed to accompany you on your last mission to Lollishire." She pulls the plunger back, filling a syringe. "Perhaps next time you'll think twice before involving your friends in your traitorous plans, Commander."

I see red. My blood boils beneath a soaking layer of bog water and sweat. "She'll die."

"Then one of the lower riders will be promoted to her position," she says, her violet braid hanging over her shoulder as she continues to organize her medicine tray. "They're all human. You're bound to lose them eventually."

It's a callous remark for anyone, let alone someone she's known for so long.

Nylah is still the same girl who climbed down into the pit with hope in her heart based on a whispered rumor, a shred of gossip. She's the same woman who helped us to build Mal's army. She's been flying beside us since nearly the beginning.

Felix jogs across the tent. "I don't know what the standards are for healers in Faerie, but I was required to take an oath to do everything in my power to sustain the length and quality of a patient's life." I've never heard him say a cross word in all the years I've known him, but he looks about ready to loosen a whole string of them. "You have a duty to heal her."

"My duty is to my Queen," she says, turning her back on us.

Felix grabs his bag of medical instruments and pulls out a brown bottle. "Roll up her breeches."

I listen to him, feeling helpless as he pours clear liquid down her calf. It fizzes with white foam when it hits the gash. Nylah groans in her sleep, and I hold her slack hand while Felix works to treat her.

"A sharp projectile injury," he says, talking himself through the procedure. "We need to cauterize the tissue."

"I'll be so pissed if you let that lucky shot kill you." I stroke Nylah's hair off her forehead as he holds the hot tool to her skin. "Don't you dare die on me, you doorknob."

I'll never forgive myself if she passes away from this. She'll be another ghost in my memory, a victim of her proximity to me.

Time moves like syrup, thickened by my guilt. It feels like I've been holding my breath for hours when Felix sets his tools down.

"She's stable now," he says, wiping his hands on a wet rag. He frowns at Thea as she changes the cot linens, humming a tune from Faerie. "I have some reading to do this evening. I'll keep an eye on her."

I've prepared a nasty speech for Thea, but I hold my tongue. She'll only run and tell Mal she successfully pissed me off. I bow my head to Felix and meet Poppy on one of the rock formations to discuss the information she gleaned from the captured assailant.

"As we guessed, they were sent there by one of the dukes of Dardaran," she says, still mounted on Evzen. The dragon curls his neck to sniff the blood on my uniform.

"Did he know which one?"

"No. That was all I could get out of him."

"Were we able to get the boat in safely?"

"Yes. The crew is flying our crates in as we speak."

That's one shred of decent news for the evening. I walk down to camp, looking for the golden-haired woman of my dreams. It's a habit I haven't broken yet. I don't know if I'll ever stop waiting for her to come running up that hill to meet me, held in my shadows as she should be.

The cool night air eases some of that warm longing and brings me back to my reality. Mal is trying to prove a point by picking off my friends. I fear what will happen if she can't bring me to heel. Rosemary is safer in her kingdom—kept out of Mal's reach.

It's better for everyone, even if it means being far away from me.

I turn on my right side in my narrow bed and pat the cold space beside me, closing my eyes to find her in my dreams.

~

I search for Rosemary in the honeysuckle forest of the Wildlands, pushing through bramble and checking every copse. It's late, but a considerable amount of time passes before I catch her scent on the breeze.

She appears in the soft blush skirt I sent her, the sage corset I had custom made for her laced over it. Butterflies hover near her shoulders and disappear into the trees.

"I've been worried about you," I say, stepping over a fallen log to get to her. "What happened today?"

"How did you know something happened?" She blushes, picking invisible lint from her dress. "Oh, your knife lit up again, didn't it?"

"It did."

"It was a rough day at the palace," she says. "A patient behaved poorly."

Her figure fades to a transparent shade and bounces back to its full beige coloring again. A few butterflies fall, their black markings blotting out their orange wings. Night terrors have followed Rosemary into the dream. I try to bolster the dreamscape's boundaries against the fear seeping in.

"What did your patient do?"

She laughs off the question and crooks a finger, bidding me to join her as she plays hopscotch over gnarled roots.

"Don't worry so much." She swings around a tree trunk, her loose hair spilling over her bust. "I've been waiting to see you. Come catch me."

She does this sometimes—skipping over the rough parts of

her day, preferring to keep things light and fun in our dream space.

"I've been waiting too. What took you so long fall asleep tonight?"

I find myself wanting to know everything, every detail of her life without me, but she usually insists that her stories would bore me, that her days are quite mundane.

That part of this arrangement kills me. We don't have time to talk about the hard times or the seemingly boring things.

We've turned this into a fantasy space.

Stepping on one of the thick roots, I give up on my questioning and play her game.

I lean in to kiss her, the v of my white blouse parting. "Caught you."

"Are you sure about that?" She smiles against my mouth, and the sun breaks through the fluffy white clouds. "Bet you can't do it again."

She runs off, her bare feet landing softly on the meadow grass. Echinacea flowers brush the hemline of my calf-length breeches as I chase after her around a tree and down a soft slope covered in clover. She rolls down, sprawling out in the private valley, laughing.

I move on top of her, caging her in with my body, and she slides her hands up to my shoulders.

"I ache for you," she says, a wistful look on her face as her lashes lower. "Physically."

My throat tightens, a sharp piece of reality cutting through our lush fantasy. More than anything, I long for this to be real. The voice hasn't bothered me in weeks, but I swear I hear the faint twinkling of laughter mocking me for the choices I've made.

Or maybe I'm imagining things.

Rosemary's fingers fly to her laces, sitting up to let her

corset fall as they come undone. She unbuttons my blouse and runs her hands over the stretchy band covering my breasts, kissing me roughly.

She drops her dress to her waist, inviting me to touch her. I trail my mouth over her neck and cup her breasts, pulling her nipple between my teeth. I let go abruptly as dark spots dance around us. Something squirms around my thighs, and I draw back, finding black vines slithering over her lap.

"What's going on?" I flick my wrist to banish them, and they retreat, worming back into the grass. "What was that?"

"Nothing. I want to feel you," she says, reaching for me, her touches edged with frantic energy, as if she's trying to anchor herself in the dream.

I push away from her and hold her wrists, stroking her skin down to her elbows. "Something's wrong. What is it?"

"It's nothing, really," she says, her arms fading even as I'm touching them.

"You're hurt," I state. "Show me."

I snap my fingers, removing the magical filter from the dream. A collar of bruises rings her neck. Her eyes are bloodshot as she looks at me, her hands moving to cover the sight from me. I move them away, touching the mottled skin gently.

"Who did this to you?"

"A patient."

"A murder attempt? That's what you meant by *behaving poorly*?" My fae instincts churn with agitation as she describes the attack to me. "How was it handled? Was he taken away?"

"My godmother Grace took care of it. He's dead." She bites her lower lip, unnerved by the memory. "It's fine."

It will never be *fine*. I refuse to accept that I can't do anything about it. "Something must be done if people are trying to take you back to the King's City."

My point is cut short by the darkening sky. Rabbits bound

out of the forest, scared off by an unseen predator. I glance at the place they're running from and see green light swirling through the deepening shadows between the trees.

No. Not now.

"Wake up, darling," I say, jumping to my feet to block her from what's coming. "Throw yourself from the dream."

"What is it?" she asks as Mal steps out of the forest, the halo of starlight circling above her head matching her silky dress. I've been too distracted. I didn't even feel her magic running down the walls of our dream.

"Isn't this sweet?" She smirks as a butterfly descends toward her finger. It transforms into a moth as it lands. "But I know you can do better than this, Cara."

Waves of violet grass spread from the train of her dress. The blue sky turns a deep shade of purple with sparkling pink clouds swirling in the distance. Starlight rains down and bounces back up to the sky again.

I look back at Rosemary. "Wake up."

She tries to move, but she's stuck in the vision, trapped here by her fear. I snap my fingers, putting her dress back in place and tying her laces over it.

"I'll meet with you in private if you give us a moment, Your Majesty." I bow to my Queen.

"And send her away before we get started?" she asks, making glowflowers bloom around us, emphasizing her control over our dream. My gifts might overpower hers physically, but she's always had a talent for illusions and dream walking. This is her domain. I can't compete. "It's only fair that she bears witness to your punishment, seeing as she's the reason you've been so distracted lately."

"What am I being punished for?"

"For getting us into a major conflict and not being able to win it yet," she says, waving a hand to swap my plain clothes for the Starlight Court's knight uniform as the first bolt of pain races through me. "For ignoring me when I tried to summon you for a meeting." Green light races across the sky and heat flares behind my eyes. "For getting caught frolicking with this creature in your dreams."

She splays her fingers out, hitting Rosemary with a burst of magic. I run to her as vines whip out around her shoulders like snakes. She lifts her hands, shocked by the green stains spreading from her fingertips and racing along her veins.

Mal claps her hands, and Rosemary appears normal again.

"Leave her out of this," I bark, forming the strongest shield I can around Rosemary "What we do in our dreams is none of your business."

She hooks her hands together in front of her diaphragm. "It is my business when you belong to me."

The burning starts at my scar and races up my forearm, scorching my shoulder. Rosemary shifts behind me. I fight to keep the shield up. Mal can't hurt her, but she can distort the dream and make her fear and anguish feel very real.

"Stop it," Rosemary pleads, holding my hips as I fold over.

"Don't," I croak as she tries to comfort me. "Just wake up."

"This is what happens when you demand my wraith's attention," Mal says, green smoke wisping through her fingers. "I have to remind her that she swore an oath to protect the Dragon Valley."

A flash of green fire flares beneath my skin, so strong that when Rosemary moves in front of me, her figure is limned with a viridescent sheen.

"Stay back," I warn her, but she's already running with all of the might it takes to get one's legs moving in a nightmare. Running to help *me*.

Bars close around her as she pounces toward the Queen, trapping her mid-air in a giant birdcage plucked straight from her memories. The structure comes crashing down as Mal continues toying with me.

"Let me out," Rosemary shouts, her voice muffled by the vines winding around the bars and filling the slats. I can't see between them, but I can hear her screaming. *"Carabosse."*

"Wake up Rosemary," I command, drawing on my last dregs of energy to force her from the dream. The cage and the vines disappear as the walls of the vision shudder around us.

There's only Mal and me.

She transforms the plane again. The moonlit meadow we played in when we were girls collapses beneath me. I fall through the sky, landing on opal tiles at her feet.

"No more distractions," she says, sitting in the Starlight Court's throne with her legs hanging over an armrest. "If I catch you fucking around with her when you have important matters to tend to, I won't hesitate to play around inside her head."

She leaves the dream, her threat ringing through the empty throne room.

I come to in my bed, shaking. Pulling on my leathers, I step past the guards outside my tent. "Tell Lieutenant Sampson I've left to take care of something. I should be back by tomorrow evening."

I cross the camp, and Snovida is already making her way toward me, her dark scales gleaming in the night as she shows her teeth, growling.

My emotions are all over the place. I know she's picking up on them and the images of Rosemary's face peering through the birdcage.

We ascend and she spins toward the west before I even give her my command.

"To the Dragon Valley."

16

CARABOSSE

Daylight touches the horizon as I approach the Vellessentian Palace, honing in on the flames flickering around the onyx dome below. Two blue dragons burst from the mist, their figures blurring in my periphery and blending into the sky as I make my descent.

I slide down the second Snovida's claws hit the platform of the landing room, and she flies through the arches, disembarking in one fluid movement. A cold wind sends the rope bridge swinging. I set my teeth against it, making my climb up the palace steps with one thought running through my head.

I reach the throne room, throw the doors open, and shrink back from the sight of the four people leaning over the throne's armrests.

Two men and two women are scantily clad in sheer silver robes with false wings attached to their backs. They suck on Mal's neck and run their mouths down her arms and legs, sliding their eyes toward me without stopping their kissing.

"Commander." The Queen's robe spills open around her

breasts as she tilts her head. "I don't remember giving you orders to leave Claw Ridge."

"I need to talk to you," I say, my cheeks flushing.

The ladies-in-waiting perched at her feet wave their feathered fans in front of their faces, appalled that I haven't addressed Mal formally or bent the knee. I'm sure it will be a scandalous topic later.

Mal pushes a man's face away from her neck and belts her robe as she descends her dais. Grabbing her scepter, she pads across the black velvet aisle runner to me.

"Leave us." She taps the rod on the floor, and her courtesans file out quietly. "To what do I owe this pleasure?" she asks.

Haughtily, she adjusts her horned crown as if she's won a challenge. It's the same look she'd give me when we were young. When she'd make silly demands and force me to obey them.

"They're just games, Cara," she'd say. *"I know you'll be one of the realm's greatest knights someday."*

I fold the years of history between us and shove them down deep.

"You know why I'm here," I say, flat out. "And I'm telling you not to do that again. If you have a problem with something I've done, then speak to me. Do *not* take it out on anybody else."

"Why shouldn't I?" She shimmies closer, the scent of her night-blooming jasmine perfume cloying. "You've been putting others before me." Her finger swirls on my forearm, tracing a slow, deliberate half-circle. "Don't you remember the promises we made to each other?"

I yank my arm back, revolted by the goosebumps on my skin. "Don't do that."

"Why? Because it would offend the woman you betrayed

me for?" The corners of her mouth sharpen into a smile as one of her ladies-in-waiting reenters the throne room and kneels beside me, her golden hair woven into a loose braid that falls over the back of her silver robe.

I glance down at the woman, and she lifts her eyes—mossy oak orbs that send my shadows rippling around her defensively.

It's Rosemary. An illusion of her, but Mal has crafted her with such precision that the resemblance is uncanny.

"What's wrong, darling?" she asks, her voice close to the real thing, but lacking the bubbly trill of her accent. "Aren't you happy to see me?"

Mal gloats over her creation. "Mate or not, she can't understand all that we've been through together, *nyxsisium*. She didn't experience the Fade, and she didn't have to compete in the Vellessentere, but we did."

Tiles break beneath Mal's throne, and black rocks roll out of the cracks spreading across the room. A skeletal hand reaches out of the gap. There is no skin or flesh, only bones. The tips of the stripped phalanges tap the tiles, finding solid ground. One of the undead from the tournament pulls itself out, its mandible broken from its mouth. Another skeleton pops out from beneath the clawed feet of the throne, its skull twisted in the wrong direction. Flames rise higher in the dais cauldrons, the green glow shining through the undead's ribs as it climbs down the steps, its body moving backward.

"Mal, what the fuck." My mind goes back to the last days of the tournament when the undead broke free from the ground, chasing the competitors in all directions. I thought we were going to die. I was sure of it after watching those bony hands drag several of the strongest players down into the underworld's pit.

"What would you have done if she'd been around back

then?" Mal asks. "Would you have left me—the one you *swore* to protect when we left Faerie—to face the horrors by myself?"

More of the undead thrash their way into the throne room until we're overrun by them, their joints creaking like unoiled wagon wheels. Bones clatter along the floor, the undead finding different ways to move when their toes crack off and their tibias fall from their knees.

I remind myself that I've already fought them off before. I could do it again.

My muscles are thicker now. I'm much stronger than I was back then.

But these illusions put me right back in that arena. My brain can't separate them from my reality. Especially not when there's a mimic of Rosemary's face contorting with panic at the sight of them. I step in front of her on instinct.

"I let my mate give his life for Vellesse's vision because I understood the importance of what we were doing, but you aren't willing to show the same loyalty to our cause." Mal's cry rings metallic in my ears as one of the undead breaks through the floor and arches its spine into an unnatural position, its open mouth yawning in Rosemary's face.

A quake warps the marble, lifting the floor in slanted slabs. An entire horde of reanimated skeletons creep out of the openings, clambering toward her.

She's not real, I try to convince myself, but I can't.

I wrap shadows around any bones I can grab, ripping off mandibles and smashing skulls into the walls. Disembodied hands reach for spare pieces, the broken bodies putting themselves back together again. I send wave after wave of shadows after them, exhausting my magic.

I can't hold them all back.

Rosemary's sobs echo through the throne room as the undead crowd around her, biting at her honey-spun hair.

Shards of broken bones dig into those rounded cheeks that are always so soft when I kiss them.

"Enough!"

My shadows whip around Mal's shoulders and neck, throwing her back. She drops her scepter, the glass orb empty as it rolls across the tiles. The flames in the cauldron burn orange, a shocked scream escaping her throat.

That sound shakes me from the violent illusion.

I release her from my magic, and she rubs her neck, coughing. The cauldrons light up green again, and the orb on her scepter refills with emerald flames.

She waves it around her, and the undead ones disappear.

So does the vision of Rosemary. Watching her vanish is painful, but it's nothing compared to seeing her in danger.

Mal could make Rosemary see those things. She could crawl inside her head and drive her mad with nightmare scenes.

I've been going about this the wrong way, thinking I could outsmart my Queen.

Deep down I know there's no way to work around my blood oath. I've known that since the beginning.

Threats won't work. Not when Mal knows my weakness lies in my friendships and marriage. No one else should have to suffer for my bad decision just because I want impossible things.

"I'm sorry." I grab Mal's hand and help her to get back on her feet. "I didn't come here to threaten you. You're right about everything. My oath is to you, and to the Dragon Valley."

I choke on my traitorous words as I step one foot back, bending my knee.

In the past few months, I've bargained with a jackass prince, made concessions to a conniving rebellion leader, and broken bread with a King who was holding my mate captive all to support her dream of setting her family free.

But this gesture is a final supplication for her safety. It's letting her go even if she'll hate me. In the end, all of my power is worthless if I can't use it to protect the ones closest to me.

I'll fight for my love until the day I die, but I can only do that by conceding to my Queen.

"I'm glad we finally agree," she says, rolling a shoulder forward to examine the mark my shadows left on her collarbone. The red splotch is healing already. She twirls her scepter and places it on my shoulder. "My faithful knight and beloved sister of Faerie."

She rolls the orb along my neck, using it to lift my chin. Water wells up in her eyes, bringing out the silver threads in the amethyst. I've only seen Mal cry once in my entire life—when we escaped Faerie and realized there was no going back. Even then she wiped those tears away quickly.

"I wish it wasn't too late," she says. "Now there's only one way to fix things."

I blanch as fire sears my brand, the pain erasing the thoughts in my head. There was a question I wanted to ask, but I can't remember it. I hear her shouting for her guards as she increases the heat. Crumpling on the floor, I feel the iron cuffs clamp around my wrists. Mal's guards wrench me onto my feet.

Big mistake.

I might be cut off from my magic, but I'm not defenseless. I swing my head against the side of a guard's face and round my knee into another's stomach.

"Mal, what are you doing?" I pant as two more guards rush in, pulling on the iron chain dangling between my cuffs.

"Stripping you of your rank, your position, and your duties," she says. "I know I'll never get you to truly submit to me, so I'm taking matters into my own hands to protect the Dragon Valley."

"Mal," I entreat her, resisting the two men trying to drag me toward the doors. There's no telling how long this mood of hers will last, and we're in the middle of a conflict that's about to explode into a full-blown war. No declaration can strip me of my responsibility to the dragons. "Listen. You need me."

Her mouth pinches, and she struts back to her throne, smoothing her robe over her knees. "I don't need anybody. Take her to the dungeon."

The cauldrons cast a ghastly green hue over her complexion as another bolt of pain shoots through me, allowing the guards to walk me to the back of the room.

"I've already arranged for Snovida to be brought down to the dragon burrows," she calls before the double doors slam shut.

"That's an unfair punishment," I yell, but there's no one listening.

It will kill Snovida to be placed in chains and locked away, separated from her mate. I can withstand the dungeons, but the dragon burrows are narrow prisons built into the mountain. They were designed by an ancient monarch to break wild dragons. They haven't been used since the beasts returned to this realm. Snovida won't even be able to spread her wings in them.

No.

I stop struggling against the men, tunneling into my mind instead as they lug me down into the bowels of the mountain. I see the world through Snovida's eyes—a muzzling net has been shot over her maw, and guards line the mountain ridge below her, pulling on ropes to keep her jaw closed. I feel the heat of embers burning in her throat as she swallows a roar, the mountain ridge rising as the guards pull her down, lower and lower.

Her confusion floods our bond.

She doesn't know what she's done to earn the Queen's fury. She doesn't want to attack the guards, but they're lashing whips at her claws.

Fight them. She senses me pushing into her mind, so I push even harder, willing her to channel her rage as they swing their swords at her wings, using her down strokes to aim for her phalanges. *Do not let them clip your wings.*

She can't understand my words, but we know each other inside and out. She knows what I mean.

I saturate my messages with everything I'm feeling.

Rage. Break. Crush. Kill.

Clouds and rocks flash through my mind as she flails against the ropes, knocking a few of the guards off balance. She spots the weakness in their line and swings her head abruptly, throwing them off the ledge. They scramble to climb up their ropes, but they can't hold on with the movement.

The world spins, and there's another net gun pointed at her. She bats her chained snout into the woman holding it and scrambles away from the ridge, climbing the slope to the top of the peak. It's a tiny cone beneath her claws, but she uses her speed to propel herself upward, away from the guards with their ropes, chains, and shields.

Rocks break, crashing down on the guards' helmets as she soars into the air. Two more dragons mounted by soldiers are quick to catch up to her. Her spine undulates as she bats her tail into a rider's face. She doesn't check to see if she's knocked her from her seat.

Fly. Fly. Fly.

Shake them off.

I envision the valley and all of the dangerous stunts we've

practiced over the years. Snovida doesn't have the strongest build or the swiftest wings, but she's clever and knows how to maneuver her body strategically. She runs rings around pinnacles, her pursuers lagging behind, unable to anticipate her moves. Strips of rocks and sky flip through the back of my mind as she aims for a tight space between two peaks and wheels around, diving beneath the other dragons to fit through a natural archway behind them.

They can't circle around to catch her before she sinks into the dark chasm where the Vellessentere was held.

She throws her neck violently to shake off her muzzle as she skates over the cairns of the dead, the canyon awash with pale green light. The metal chains fly from her snout, snapping and breaking. She darts upward, breaking free with a primal roar as I'm shoved into my dank cell, the bars slamming shut behind me.

17

ROSEMARY

I hold the base of the basket on my lap as I weave my silent wishes into the reeds, my day's work carrying into the evening hours.

"Why the long face, chicken?" Grace asks, bending a reed on the porch deck. She knots a ribbon to secure it to the large circle she's making. "Thinking about her again?"

"She's my wife. She's always on my mind."

It's been weeks since I've seen her in my dreams. She hasn't sent a package or written to me. But I see her face every night when I go to sleep, replaying the awful image of her burning.

Diana looks up from her needlework. "Sometimes I wonder why she hasn't come for you. If she's one of the most powerful women in the realm, shouldn't she be able to?"

"It's complicated." My reply comes out snippier than I want it to, my words barbed and defensive. Noting the concern on her face, I soften my voice. "If she could come back for me, she would. Believe me. I never would've gotten this far without her."

That damn woman. She's been so keen on protecting me,

but has she ever stopped to think about how concerned I might be for her well-being?

What kind of trouble has she gotten herself into with her Queen?

I create a pocket under a reed and pull another one through it, fuming. Am I supposed to sit on my hands when she's the one who needs saving?

I tug the reed too tightly, causing the side of the basket to buckle inward.

"Damn it," I hiss, misplaced anger mixing with my anxiety. I'm not really angry at Carabosse, but I'm growing restless here.

I have no way to reach my wife, and the rebellion wants me to stay in one place, waiting for Robin's message that it's safe to venture back into the Hartwood forest.

My godmothers and I haven't ridden into the city since my incident. A crow delivered a letter the day after it happened, instructing me to stay within earshot of the cabin, so we toil away in the woods, making tinctures to send to the healers at the palace.

We're technically under Prince Alex's protection, but it's Robin's guards who monitor all of our movements.

Alex spends his days throwing darts and drinking. When he's not hungover, he occasionally asks me to practice Sartealean with him, but it's rare to see him outside of his room before noon.

His partners are warming themselves near the bonfire down by the river, moving pieces on a board game between them. They were brought here to lighten the mood and provide entertainment, but even they've grown bored of his sulking.

"We're concerned about you," Diana says, setting her embroidery hoop down to rub her eyes. She still loves stitching intricate designs despite her farsightedness. "We want you to be happy."

It feels wrong to complain when I have everything I've been manifesting for the past few years. Diana, Grace, and Candide are all adjusting well to our new setting. We get to roam in the woods for hours and dip our toes in the chilly river water whenever we please.

But I can't ignore the piece of my soul that's been scooped out of me. I feel like one of the pumpkins we carved to scare off any malevolent spirits around the cabin—hollow and frightening.

Candles flicker inside the jack-o-lanterns' garish faces as they glower from the decks' railing.

"I'm content."

Grace runs down the side of the porch, dropping her hoop of reeds. "I have something that will cheer you up," she says, sticking her fingers in her mouth to give a wolf whistle. She takes the hoop and waves it over her head as Sun and Moon race down from a tree.

"That seems like a bad idea." I cover my eyes, peeking between my fingers as Sun sprints along the rocky bank, using a slick boulder to catapult themself into the air. Flying higher, they sweep their wings back in one quick movement, spiraling through the hoop.

Grace *whoops* loudly, and Diana rocks forward in her chair, watching intently as Moon follows suit, embellishing their spiral by cloaking their wings over their upturned belly and fanning them out for a dramatic landing.

I clap for them, and their pride swells through our bond along with the images of our smiling faces. Curiosity trickles through as Moon curves their neck around searching for something. I see an image of Candide accompanied by a question.

They want to know where she is.

"It's getting dark," I say, setting my weaving project aside for tomorrow. "I'm going to look for Candide."

"She said she was going out to gather some valerian root," Grace says, twirling her hoop for the hatchlings. "You know she likes her alone time in the evening."

Maybe that's what I need, some time by myself to ease my worries. I hug my shawl around myself as I stalk off into the woods, tracing spells in the dirt. Pressing an acorn into the soil, I mark the place where I've buried a rodent's spine as an offering. "Give Carabosse the strength she needs."

I dust my hands and find Candide leaning against an oak, whispering to herself. She sees me and sits up, startled.

"You snuck up on me," she says, pursing her lips to blow out a breath. "I didn't hear you coming."

"Sorry."

"Not on the stump," she yelps, swatting at me as I'm about to take a seat. "It's covered in poison ivy."

I roll my eyes but oblige her, sitting on the ground and leaning my head on her shoulder. "Were you talking to the trees like you used to when I was little?"

"I'm surprised you remember that. I hadn't done it in a while before we were taken..." She trails off, resting her chin on my head. "Anyways, I missed the woods while we were in the Ivy Keep. It's nice to share my troubles without placing a burden on the ones who love me." She pecks the top of my head. "You've had a lot weighing on you these past few years. I don't want you carrying it around forever. None of us do. Shrug it off when you need to."

"Are you suggesting I tell my troubles to the trees?" I muse.

"Don't knock it until you've tried it." She pulls away, pinching my cheek before patting it lovingly. Standing, she turns back to the cabin. "Try not to stay out here too late."

I press the crown of my head against the bark, and speak to

the autumn leaves above me, feeling quite silly. "What am I supposed to say to you?"

"*Zelladine. Zelladine.*"

"Never mind," I sigh. "Set the forest free, right? I'll get right on that once I get back to the King's City."

The humming cuts out, and tendrils of poison ivy unfurl from the stump, creeping toward me to coil around my fingers. "*Zelladine.*"

I let the wiry plant twist around my arm, knowing it won't irritate my skin. "I still don't feel like I'm the person you want me to be. I'm supposed to have these amazing gifts, so why am I sitting around waiting? Everything I do depends on someone either saving me or getting me to where I need to be. It's aggravating."

This isn't like any spell I've ever cast before. I'm not trying to manipulate energy or will the world to bend to my needs. I'm simply venting my troubles without any expectations.

It's easier to be honest like this, when I don't feel like I'm making an impossible request. "I know it's selfish to feel this restless when I have everything I've wanted for the past three years, but I still want more. I want my wife to be ok; I want her beside me." That's not even the worst of it. I recognize the privilege of having a safe place to stay, but deep in my bones, I know I was never meant to sit still. "I want so much more than I should ever hope for. I've been struck by wanderlust, and I can't shake it off."

I got my first taste of the open sky when a woman swept me away on her dragon, and now I yearn to see the whole world with her. We shouldn't be living like this, trapped in our positions.

A cluster of velvet shanks tip toward me, their orange caps singing softly.

I accept comfort from the forest and the strands of ivy

crawling up my back, blanketing my shoulders in a hug. A pulse quickens beneath the soil and thrums through the trees. It pumps inside of me, right beside my own heartbeat.

I stay curled up in nature's embrace until it's dark and the bonfire by the river is the only light I can see. My godmothers are clearing the porch when I arrive at the cabin.

"It might freeze tonight," Candide says. "We'll have to take all of this inside."

I help them get set up in the room over the stairs, pushing one of the beds right under the window so that Grace won't feel so closed in. Sun won't sit still. They burrow under my nest of blankets in the corner and toss them around, making a mess of everything.

"We were just outside." I stand with my hands on my hips, and they snort an ember, pouting. "Let's go downstairs and make some tea."

Prince Alex sits at the table, poring over a history text on famous knights as the hatchlings race back and forth beneath his chair.

"What's gotten into them tonight?" He slams the tome shut. "They're being little devils."

"I have no idea." The kettle whistles, and I pour a mug of mint tea, contemplating how much valerian root it would take to make the dragons relax and fall asleep.

A weight lands on the table, rattling the prince's dishes. I accidentally take a large mouthful of my hot drink.

"*Sun.*" I spin around to scold them and find Moon crouched on the tablecloth, ready to pounce. Their feathery eyebrows knit into a beastly frown as they lift a foreclaw and hold it over Alex's copper mug. Their tail swishes across the table, their vertical pupils constricting.

I gasp, surprised by their naughtiness. I rarely have to lecture Moon for anything. "Don't you dare."

They knock the mug off the edge of the table, jumping across the kitchen as the prince's ale spills all over the floor. He sits back laughing, watching the chaos.

I point to the door and look down at the dragons. "Fine. Outside. *Now.*"

They skip off into the woods, and I grab a lantern, my breath puffing out in a warm cloud in front of my face as I chase after them, following the tiny sparks flying from their mouths. I crunch over crisp, dead leaves, stomping any embers out. "You're going to start a fire."

Ugh. Little shits.

The thought pops into my head, unbidden. I shake it away, hoping they won't pick up on it.

Sun hops down to the river bank, jumping over the water onto a pointed rock. The current rushing around it is moving as rapidly as my fear-stricken blood is pumping through me.

"What are you doing? You'll drown." The dragons know they're not supposed to go down there. I stumble, slipping on wet leaves as I reach the muddy bank, the chilly mist spraying my face. "Get back here."

Moon paws at my leg, looking past the branches hanging overhead. I swing my lantern as a dark, winged creature flies in from the north, a black streak in the moonless sky.

Snovida. Carabosse has found a way to come back for me.

A guard whistles a warning as he makes his patrol rounds around the cabin. "Dragon approaching form the north!"

Sun leaps back to me, and I hold my arms out to catch them, dropping into a squat as another guard on safe house duty steps out onto the muddy bank. Both of them look in my direction.

"Rose, is that you?"

Shit.

I've already been spotted. They hold their heads together,

whispering, and the cadence of their stride shifts into a march. I don't say anything.

The taller guard cups his hands around his mouth and shouts, "Do you know why a dragon is crossing the border without permission?"

I have no idea what Carabosse is doing, but I need to come up with something. This will become a sticky situation if they pull weapons on Snovida.

"Yes, my wife is coming to meet me," I yell back.

"All dragons require Robin's authorization before breaching our boundaries," he says, his eyes glued to Snovida. "Send her back, or we'll be forced to use our weapons."

I come up with a response on the cuff. "We're only going to fly off for a while."

"We've been instructed not to let you leave either."

My mouth runs dry. I understand why the rebellion needs to keep me safe, but I never agreed to being held captive.

"Never again." I close my eyes, feeling strings of energy running beneath the world's surface.

Curling my fingers, I tug on the ones I need, drawing roots up through the soil to trap their feet. Snovida lands in the shallow portion of the Restless River, cold, foamy water swashing over the rocks as she lowers her neck, touching her snout to my chest in a greeting.

I rub her cheek, looking toward the rider's seat. It's empty. I slide my hand down to her neck and move around her shoulder, panic rising in me. "Where is she?"

She lets out a low, clicking whine, nudging her maw into my back. A soft *chuff* throws heat through the fabric of my shawl, and I turn back to see the large orb of her eye rolling up at me. "Can I do something?" Another *chuff*. "Can you take me to her?" She rears back slightly on her hind claws and throws out her wings. "I'll take that as a *yes*."

I reach behind the ridges on her neck, using them to keep my balance on the slippery rocks as I feel my way over her scales, looking for the hatchlings' harnesses. My fingers connect with the leather contraptions, and I picture Carabosse leaving them attached, just in case.

"I could kiss your face," I breathe, hoping I'll get the opportunity. *Please don't let me be too late.*

I pull the belt loops closer. Sun and Moon have grown so much since they last used these. I have to adjust the straps, my fingers numb from the cold as I fumble to undo them and slip the buckles a few slots back, fastening the prong to hug Sun's torso. I start working on Moon's belt, anxiety making my fingers clumsy.

The men break free from the roots. They run along the bank, pulling their bows off their backs.

I try to trip them up again, but I can't clear my head enough grasp my magic.

"I've got you, Rose." I turn my head toward the familiar voice, doing a double take as Prince Alex appears from the woods, pointing his sword at the guards.

They hesitate, stopping several paces away from his blade. "My prince."

"Get going," Alex says to me through the corner of his mouth. "Stay back," he says to Robin's men. He takes a swing at them. "I'm the future King of Lollishire, and I say she's allowed to leave."

"Why are you doing this?" I tighten the belt, getting Moon situated safely.

"There must be trouble in Sarteal if the Commander's dragon came without her," he says. "Go to her. "

I catch the scent of chimney smoke wafting from the cabin as I try to climb Snovida. "What about my godmothers?"

"I'll tell them where you've gone. No one will hurt them," he vows as the guards continue to bargain with him.

"Please step aside, my prince," says the guard with the arrow nocked in his bowstring. "We're only following Robin's orders."

"Back. Do not fire your weapons." He lunges into a defensive stance and flips his hair back toward me. "For what it's worth, I'm sorry about May Day. I'm sorry I stood by and did nothing."

A phantom pain cracks along my ribs as I grip the slack end of the harness strap, pulling as hard as I can with all of the strength I've built inside myself since that day. Carabosse makes mounting look much easier than it is. I've never had to do it by myself before.

My feet slip on Snovida's scales, and my body flattens against her side, the muscles in my upper body sorely lacking.

Chuffing, the dragon lifts a foreclaw and swats my ass, nudging me over the hump.

"Thank you," I say, straddling Snovida with the hatchlings curled against me. I settle into my uncomfortable seat, grabbing onto the dragon's ridges as I tamp down on my panic. Snovida bounds through the river, kicking up torrents of rushing water in her wake. I hang on tightly, crying out as air whooshes past my face.

Flying with Carabosse is one thing. Doing it on my own is downright terrifying. We cross the Restless River, my heart racing in my throat the whole time, but I don't even think about turning around.

I race to find Carabosse, knowing she'd do the same for me.

18

CARABOSSE

"Here wraithy, wraithy, wraithy. I want to tell you something." The man in the cell across from me whistles through the gap of his missing teeth. "You're not so bad looking without that cloak on."

I feel for the grooves in the stone wall, working a finger grip in the indents. Exhaling, I lift my body and lower back down again, making my muscles scream to block out the prisoner's nonsense. When I can't hang on any longer, I jump down, my grey tunic damp with sweat. I'll probably regret it when my body cools down, and I have to fall asleep shivering again, but working out until my calluses bleed is how I've survived these past few weeks. My shoulders complain when I lift the bottom of my tunic to wipe my face, but I don't mind the ache.

I promised Rosemary I wouldn't lose myself to the darkness, but it's smothering down here. The pain reminds me to breathe and think without letting the dread hook its claws into my head.

"Wait until I tell my friends I saw the wraith's bare

midriff," the man laughs, and I swing around to lean on the bars.

The sconces on the wall provide just enough light to be able to see his sunken, unshaved cheeks and the filthy poaching gear he's wearing.

"I don't think you'll get the chance to talk to them again if you're in here for poaching," I say flatly. "The man who was in your cell last week didn't."

He makes a vulgar face at me. "Ah, well. How about you, wraith? Will Queen Mal put her dog down now that she's fallen out of favor?"

Probably not. But if she has plans for me, she hasn't informed me of them.

"*Woof woof woof*," he barks and scratches his stringy brown hair.

"How original."

I retreat to the corner of my cell, unamused. Every prisoner who enters this wing of the dungeon insults me with some variation of the same line. *Lapdog. Bitch. Bark. Bark. Bark.*

I wish one of them would come up with something clever. If they're going to insult me, they could at least try to make it entertaining.

Closing my eyes, I tune out his obnoxious comments until he lies down and starts snoring. I roll my iron cuffs around my wrists, lifting them in segments to give my singed skin a break. A few of the newcomers dry heave from the stench of unwashed bodies and overflowing chamber pots, but at some point in the night, things quiet down and I can hear my own thoughts again.

There is no escape for me. Not even in sleep.

I ache to visit Rosemary in my dreams even though I've always known I might have to give that up eventually.

But I never would've severed our ties without a warning. And of course, I'd have to check in on her occasionally.

I bump the back of my head against the wall, smothering a sardonic laugh with my hand. Mal was wrong to lock me up, but she was right that I'd never submit to her again. Not in earnest. She knows my single-minded nature just as well as I know hers.

Nothing could break my fae obsession with my mate. I could write an oath in blood, promising to keep my distance, but I know deep down, I'd always be trying to get back to her again.

Even now, she's the thought that keeps me going.

We've only created a handful of memories together, so I try to imagine her where she is, strolling through the woods and creating tinctures with her godmothers. I hope she's finding some joy in being with them and isn't too pressed about my sudden disappearance from her dreams.

I hope no one else has threatened her safety or tried to drag her back to the King's City. Shadows hover over me, my magic inaccessible but always lurking, urging me to go inward and lose myself to it.

I return to imagining Rosemary instead, encircling a bonfire with her godmothers and reciting incantations. It's a peaceful thought that pushes the darkness away.

I relax slightly, a warm wave of drowsiness finally washing over my chilled and tense body.

It recedes at the sound of footsteps coming down the stone corridor. It's probably another wealthy trader trying to speak to one of the poachers they hired.

I know how it works down here. They bribe Mal's guards for a flight to the dungeons and promise their former employees to look after their families in exchange for any information regarding wild dragon eggs.

I turn my head toward the bars, glaring through the space so that they'll see my disdain as they pass by. But the visitor's steps stop short at my cell.

"I think you have the wrong person," I say, showing my teeth.

The cloaked figure shakes their head and throws their hood back. Firelight flickers over Rosemary's golden strands as she places a finger to her lips. I rock to my feet, my heart pounding.

"Go," I whisper, pressing my forehead to the bars, looking out for the guards. "You can't be down here."

She pulls a pin from her hair, a single forelock falling over her face as she picks at the lock and hisses, "I'm not going to leave you."

I finger my knife's handle, holding my breath. I thought Mal made a huge error by letting me keep my weapon, but I've come to realize she only meant to add to my torment.

It doesn't work to unlock my cuffs, and I can't use it against the guards who refuse to come near me, kicking my meals into my cell.

But it'll be a valuable tool once I'm out of here.

There's a glorious *click* as she hits the lock, and the bars slide open enough for her to meet me. She pulls a flask out from her cloak and unscrews the cap, holding it to my lips. "Have a sip. I know you're parched."

I am. It's been hours since I swallowed the last of my rations.

The liquid feels so good sliding down my throat. I can't help but gulp it down, keeping one arm around her.

She rises on her toes once I've swallowed, pressing her mouth to my chapped lips. I kiss her softly, taking in her scent —like starlight, metal, and a cool, moonlit river that I haven't seen in ages.

That's not right. Where is the sunshine and sweet nectar of her skin?

The honey?

I blink my eyes open as Rosemary kisses me more fiercely, running her tongue along my teeth. I grab her by the neck, shove her against the wall, and lift my blade to her throat.

"You're not Rosemary." I remove the blade for a second to wipe the taste of her from my lips. "Where is she?"

"What do you mean?" She bats her big eyes at me and presses her hands to my chest. "I came all this way for you. Don't you love me?"

"Cut it out, Mallory."

She drops the glamour, rising to her full height, her cloak shifting into a fae evening gown that shimmers around her curves like pale moonlight. "You're no fun anymore, Cara."

"This is supposed to be fun?" I ask, gesturing to the stinking cell. "Playing games with my head and trying to trick me into being unfaithful?"

"That's not what I was doing," she says, dropping her eyes to the knife and lifting them back to mine as the blade starts glowing.

"What's happened?" I ask. "Where is she?"

"On her way here, I think. On your dragon."

I haven't checked in with Snovida in weeks, trying to keep a barrier between us. I don't want her to come running back here for me when she runs the risk of being captured.

But I slip into her head to see if there's any truth to what Mal's saying.

The dark woods of the Wildlands pass beneath my dragon, and I detect a distinct weight on her back.

Mal is telling the truth. She's traveling with Rosemary and the hatchlings.

Turn around. I scream it through the bond, willing her to listen, but she throws me from the vision.

"I've sent a squad to hunt them down," Mal says. "They won't make it. One inexperienced young woman can't take on six riders by herself. I'm sorry, but I had to stop her."

Blood trickles down my blade as I nick her skin. "Call them back, or I'll end this."

"Oh, nyxsisium, can't you see?" Her face distorts, splitting in two. Twin teardrops leak from her silver lashes. "We're dead already."

My head is light. My muscles are weak.

I can taste it now—the sulfur and decay coating my mouth. It reminds me of a distinct, morbid odor coming from an underworld spring.

I glance at the empty flask on the ground and drop my blade, my hand too feeble to hold it.

"What have you done to us?" I murmur, falling to my knees. I crawl to the bars, desperate to reach Rosemary, to stop the squad from going after her.

My elbows and knees give out, and I fall on my belly, the floor gritty against my cheek. Mal drops down beside me, pushing my hair back. We speak quietly, our whispers traveling to our ears only.

"I'm sorry, but I have to fix what went wrong at the Vellessentere," she says. "I need to speak to Vellesse again."

I fight to keep my eyes open. "Please tell me what the Goddess said to you that day."

"She told me that I should give up on my dream of rebuilding our court in the human realm. She said I'd get close to achieving everything I wanted, but that one day your mate would come to Sarteal and ruin it all." She clutches my arm. "I couldn't give it up, though. Cara, this place is so awful. The fighting. The smells. The people. I hate it here. I'm afraid of the dragons, and they know it. They smell it on me." A childlike sob racks through her. "I miss our home."

"You never told me." I always thought we were in this together, the protectors of the Dragon Valley. "If you'd been honest with me, I might have done things differently."

"No. I would've lost you the second you caught your mate's scent in any scenario," she says. "I tried to keep her away by sending her to her King so that you wouldn't have to experience the pain of a broken bond like I do every day. I tried to give you the joy of seeing her face one more time."

"We can still fix things. Please don't do this," I beg, as if it will make any difference. I thrash my arms and legs in my mind, but they won't move for me.

"It's ok," she says, her words slurring. "It won't hurt. I've never wanted to hurt you. Not really. The other thing Vellesse said...she wanted...she... she wanted to use you to...it won't hurt...just go to sleep."

"Mal?"

Her eyes go blank. There's no spark of life behind them.

They're the last thing I see before I sink into an endless darkness.

19

ROSEMARY

I ache in parts of my body I've never even thought about before. Even my cheeks are tired from shivering against the wind. I'm tempted to adjust my shawl, but my hands won't unlock from Snovida's ridges at this dizzying height. I'm too afraid of falling.

The dragon pulls forward with a snort, and I slide back in my seat, her scales rubbing against the spots where I'm chafing. My thighs have never been this sore in my life. My skin is raw and my muscles are trembling. I scoot forward, the hatchlings nipping my skirt to offer support.

They stopped trying to glide beside Snovida hours ago, curling up on her back instead. I'd rest too if I could. Tension has crept into my neck and jaw. I'm not sure how much more flying I can take, but it's not as if I can tell Snovida I need a break.

If Carabosse was here, I'd lean back against her, warm from her body heat, tucked under her cloak. Her thighs would keep me in place, and I'd feel safe enough to sleep.

My chin nods to my chest, bobbing as Snovida speeds into

a dive. My eyes shutter open and thin white clouds streak past my face. Chancing a glance below, I note how much the terrain has changed—from woodlands to a boggy plain dotted with sparse trees. We're moving westward, but I'm not sure where we're going.

Centering my gaze, my eyes land on a golden dragon flying in our direction. There's a rider on their back, giving a command in Sartealean.

Perhaps they'll see I'm in distress and help me. I lift my stiff hand to wave for help, and a sharp object flies past it, missing its mark as Snovida veers to the left.

Perhaps not, then.

The golden dragon chases after us, hesitating to strike despite their rider's aggressive commands. The woman on the dragon's back grunts and swings her scythe at Snovida's wings anytime she gets near them.

"Faster," I say, my head pounding as my hands slip on her ridges. I can't think of any commands. "Breathe fire or something." A word pops into my head, a term Thea taught me. "Fjerto." Snovida screeches as the golden dragon cuts in front of us and circles around, making me a direct target. I lean forward, angle myself over her neck, and give the command again. "*Fjerto*, Snovida!"

She growls, heat rising beneath her scales.

Sun and Moon arch their backs and flatten their wings as she curves her neck to unleash her flames on the rider. The golden dragon throws their wings back, wailing. I close my eyes as Snovida flies past, not wanting to see the charred body. The oily smoke reminds me too much of May Day in the King's City. Nausea turns my stomach as I adjust my seat.

There's no time to process the attack before another dragon swoops in, their blood-red scales gleaming like garnets.

Again, the dragon mostly avoids Snovida, allowing their

rider to do the fighting. The twin braids in the man's brown beard kick about in the wind as he runs tight circles around Snovida, thrusting his lance in our direction. She dodges him with sharp, quick movements that jostle me on her back. The hatchlings sink their teeth into my dress again, as if they might be able to stop me from falling.

Snovida growls, spraying embers from her mouth, but she holds herself back from breathing flames in the red dragon's face, their amber eyes sliding toward the hatchlings. It seems neither of the creatures wants to bring fire into the equation when they're so close to baby dragons.

The rider goes for us on his own, stabbing at us without mercy. Snovida swipes her claws at him, and he hits the tough padding beneath.

A string of blood goes flying as she cuts away from him suddenly, her spine waving in a serpentine maneuver to put more distance between them.

My stomach flies to the ceiling of my chest as I catch air in my seat.

Only I'm not in my seat anymore. I'm falling. The world rushes up past me, tearing my skirt from the hatchlings' teeth.

I can't tell if my heart is beating. My life flashes before my eyes in a split second, and a claw rips through my skirt as Snovida catches me. I try not to flail in her grasp and risk tearing my dress completely, but it's impossible to hold still when I'm literally hanging by a damn thread over everything.

Another dragon flies toward us, a massive green beast with wickedly sharp teeth. I close my eyes. This time I know I'm dying.

"Attention, Surrey," the rider calls, her red hair flying behind her helmet as she aims her spear.

"Poppy?"

She grins fiercely and throws her weapon past my head,

inciting a string of curses from the male rider behind me. His dragon lets out a low whine and snakes down through the layer of clouds beneath me.

Goddess, I'm up so high. Bright spots sparkle in the corners of my eyes. I train them forward to keep myself from fainting.

"Jetta zutiens, surrey," Poppy calls, protecting Snovida's left flank. Her arrival feels like a miracle when I'm dangling helplessly in my undergarments.

I yelp as Snovida curves her claws through the air, tossing me up and catching me to clutch me tightly in them. This feels a little more secure, but I still don't like it.

Another red dragon approaches on my right, and Poppy crosses over Snovida to get to them, drawing her extra spear from the straps on her back. She swings it into the rider's head, incapacitating him. My relief from watching the dragon retreat is only temporary. I brace myself for another attack as a silver dragon slides into the position Poppy left open, loosening a breath when I see who their rider is.

"Nylah," I blurt, my relief accompanied by a bite of worry. Something serious must be happening if two of Carabosse's lieutenants have come looking for me. She slides her bandaged calf along Vencel's side and nods to me, her face serious. I tell myself not to fret about that. She always looks grumpy.

The lieutenants' dragons flank Snovida as the peaks of the Dragon Valley claw up through a heavy cloud covering in the distance. I think that's where we're going.

It takes forever for the dragons to make their descent into the mountains. The slopes are hard to see through the mist; the mountain range is much darker than it was the last time I flew over it. There's something off about the Vellessentian Palace. The sconces on its spiked spires have gone out. The surface of the landing room's dome is an unbroken ebony sheet.

None of the cauldrons are lit. No green fires are burning in the Dragon Valley.

Vellesse's flame has gone out.

Queen Mal is dead. I grab my chest, pain stabbing my heart before my brain can even process what that means. If their lives are bound together, then Carabosse is gone too.

How can she be dead?

The woman who would fight her way through a dozen men to get to me has been ripped from this world because of a few words she spoke to her Queen? No. I refuse to believe it. I've seen her brought low a few times, but never defeated.

We sink into a dark cloud, the scent of sulfur so thick I can taste it. Carabosse pointed this place out to me once. It's where the Vellessentere was held.

I'm already shivering from the cold, but now my teeth are chattering from the foreboding nature of the canyon stretching through two high black cliffs that curve inward toward each other, fusing together at the bottom.

Evzen and Vencel land in the field of dead flowers on the canyon floor. I kick my legs, hitting the ground running as Snovida lets go of me. I make it a few steps over the surface and face plant into its withered stalks.

Whispers run through the yellowed reeds. *Zelladine. Zelladine.*

I groan and roll onto my back, spitting straw from my mouth. I'm far too nauseous to deal with plants trying to talk to me. Snovida lands with a thud, and I crack my eyes open to someone standing over me. Nylah uncrosses her arms, shifting her weight away from her bandaged leg as she helps me to sit up.

I quell the urge to vomit, preparing myself for what they've brought me here to see. Will Carabosse be waiting in her funeral shroud? Will I have to kiss her cold lips goodbye?

"Rosemary," Nylah says, launching into a sentence in Sartealean. Evzen stalks around us, and Poppy sticks her head out from behind his neck to join the conversation.

"Wait." I hold up my hands, gesturing for them to slow down. "I don't understand what you're saying."

They look at each other and start acting out a scene. I do my best to interpret the meaning of their movements. Nylah cups her hands and pretends to drink, then leans her head on her shoulder as if she's asleep. Poppy holds up two fingers, uses them to draw a line across her neck, then puts one down.

"A drink?" I guess, trying to recall the Sartealean word for it. "Boss bevata?" I swallow, afraid of what they're implying with their charade. "Boss bevata...*poison?*"

Poppy shakes her head and folds her hands beneath her cheek.

"I'm sorry. I don't know what any of this means." My head pounds along with my growing frustration as I hold my hand to my brow like I'm searching for something. "Boss. Where is she?"

Nylah makes the sign of the horned Goddess with her thumb and pinky. Shaking her hand loose, she points to the narrow v-shaped crevice between the cliffs. "Vellesse."

She's lost to the underworld, then.

"This can't be it for us." I've accepted the thought of us circling each other for years to come—our paths never quite meeting outside of our dreams. But I'm not supposed to lose her completely.

I mourn in the patch of decay. My tears hit the withered plants, and green shoots along their stems. Thin stalks rise, their dead heads blooming with umbels of red petals. I touch the spindly stamens splaying out from their centers.

Red spider lilies.

"The wraith lies this way, Zelladine." A low voice shivers

through them, the flowers bowing toward the fissure in the canyon wall. *"There's still time to make a deal if you hurry... hurry...hurry."*

I take a step closer to where they're pointing, defying the instinctual dread in my belly. The scent of death rolls off the dark mist seeping through the crack. My body senses danger, but there must be a reason I'm here.

Nylah and Nova showing up isn't a coincidence. There's something I can do for Carabosse that these warrior women can't.

Sun and Moon snatch at my hair and bite at my hands as I kiss their foreheads and turn to Carabosse's lieutenants. "Look after them."

Nylah seems to understand the statement, limping to unbuckle the hatchlings. They squabble in her arms, earning a peeved smile.

Poppy looks grim. "Attention, surrey."

I heed her warning and grab my knife from my satchel as I find my footing on the slope of the canyon's base where the two cliffs meet. It looks like it's close to the ground compared to the height of the split, but it feels mighty steep while I'm climbing it. I lean forward, practically crawling to the bottom of the v.

Wedging myself into it, I look through the mist to an even larger canyon and climb down into the vast space. My shoes crunch over something, and I lift my foot, finding crushed finger bones. Cairns are stacked randomly around the canyon. I step around them and hop over misleading cracks in the ground. They're not wide, but they look deep. The skeletons hanging out of them look like they might fall endlessly if I kick them back in.

I shudder at the pair of hollow eye sockets staring back at me, trying to find a sign to tell me where to go as I wander around this grave. Ledges jut out of high bluffs in sharp layers, dark tunnels arching over them. Rotten ropes dangle from rusted hooks screwed into the rocks, and arm bones stick out of old traps in the ground.

I know we flew into the general vicinity of the Vellesentere's location, but I think this is the exact spot where it took place. I run my fingers over the rough pumice of the cliff walls, thinking of Carabosse surviving her trials. The horrors she saw when she was only sixteen. Dread still lingers in the air twenty years later.

She can't be gone after living through this.

A faint green light squiggles past my eyes. I rub them, trying to lift the black spots from my peripheral vision. They're worse when I open them. Another flash of green light swirls past my toe, and I look to my left.

There's a large cave at the bottom of the cliff. Soft green light moves in waves from its opening. I've seen this place before, in a dream.

"During the trials, a few of the competitors discovered a way to speak to Vellesse by entering a sort of Underworld lobby."

That's what Carabosse said to me. The red spider lilies were whispering an invitation to meet with the Goddess. My pretty little knife suddenly feels inadequate. I flip it around a few times, considering what she might want from me.

"Screw it," I whisper.

The soil of the Hartwood runs through my veins, and I have the Tree Mother's blessing. That has to give me some advantage when dealing with Vellesse.

I'm about to pass the entrance when my spine stiffens at the sound of crunchy footsteps. They stop abruptly. Whoever's in here with me doesn't want to be seen. Flipping the tip of my blade out, I turn around and find Thea slinking from a crevice in the wall.

"You can't go in there," she says, holding her hands behind her back. Her lavender hair is pulled into a tight bun, her features pinched and red from crying. "My Queen told me to stand guard and make sure that no one interferes."

"Interferes with what?"

"Her meeting with Boss and Vellesse."

"There's no need to speak in fae riddles," I say, trying to stop my teeth from chattering. "Tell me what I need to do to help them."

"You can't. Not with this. I told her not to do it, but she insisted." She swings a sword from behind her back, switching her grip on its ivory handle. "Either way, she is my Queen, and I'll handle it. It's nothing personal, so no hard feelings."

"That's hard to believe when you're the one who handed me over to my King." I step sideways to get away from her without exposing my back.

"That was Mal's decision. She would have never gotten the idea if you'd died nicely in your sleep like you were supposed to when I poisoned your tea."

I vaguely remember having a good night's sleep after drinking one of her migraine remedies, but she's moving too fast for me to stop and examine that memory. I jog backward as she takes her first swing.

"The moment I realized you were Cara's mate, I knew I couldn't let you live. But you were such a sweet thing and a brilliant healer, so I tried to make it gentle. The concoction of sedatives and poison I gave you would have sent anybody else into an eternal rest, but somehow you lived. I even tried to slip into your sleeping tent and finish the job by hand, but I couldn't bring myself to do it." She spins her handle and adjusts her stance. "I wasn't being cruel. I didn't want you to suffer once Mal realized you were a special girl from the Hartwood Forest."

Being a *special girl* doesn't seem very helpful right now. This place is a lifeless chasm, all rocks and death. I can't feel any plant energy flowing beneath its surface. I only have my knife to use against Thea.

Thrusting my forearm out, I spin into a crouch as she gets closer. "I never did anything to your Queen."

"Don't act like you're so innocent. You stole those eggs and used Cara's feelings to your advantage." She prowls toward me, her voice even-keeled and matter-of-fact. Not friendly, but not unkind either. "Not that I blame you for it. We all have to get our hands dirty to make it in this realm."

My back hits a cairn that towers above my head. I slide to my left, and Thea's blade hits the edge of the structure, forcing me to the center.

"You'll lie and steal to get what you need," she says. "And I'll kill to protect the child I've loved as my own since she was a babe in Faerie."

I know she means it. I can tell she loves Mal with every fiber of her being. She'd do anything to protect her, the same way my godmothers would for me.

I lunge to the right as she pulls her sword from the stones, striking a blow a few inches above my head. It hits so hard, the vibrations rattle through my teeth.

My body wasn't made for fighting. I can't get close enough to stab her without losing my head, but I can't evade her forever. I'm panting like a dog and she's not even out of breath.

Thea tugs on her sword again and raises it with a fae growl, her neck twisting toward the dragon plummeting through the black clouds above us. She swivels to face the great beast.

I take the smallest step to my right, eyeing the cave. Maybe if I make a run for it, I can make it.

The dragon's roar quakes through the canyon as they land, blocking my path. I lean my head back, the ground shaking as they stomp toward Thea. I've never seen a dragon with their coloring. Their scales are a pale pink that deepens into a darker shade around their eyes and along their phalanges.

"It can't be you," Thea says. "I thought you were dead."

The dragon sniffs the air around her, their crimson eyes narrowing as they rear their head back. Thea sprints forward, aiming for their heart, but they snap her up between their teeth, shaking her sword loose. The metal clanks across the hard ground, distracting me.

I think that's a good thing. I miss seeing them swallow her down. Goddess, she's gone.

She's gone, and I'm next.

I whimper and cover my mouth to stifle the sound.

It's too late. The beast's eyes are already on me. There's nowhere to run.

The dragon moves toward me, their red claws the same color as the barbs on their long tail. I stay still and square my shoulders, feigning bravery around them like Carabosse taught me.

Stay on your feet.

I force myself upright as they smell me, holding my body stiffly. Their rubbery lips pull back to reveal their long, pointed teeth, and they make a low clicking noise as they curve their scarred neck and chuff a burst of blood-tinged air over me, swinging their head toward the cave.

"Thank you." I keep my spine straight as I walk away, half-expecting to feel the heat of their flames against my back. I step over Thea's sword and block the image of her legs flailing in the air.

My head hurts too much to think about it. I'll come back to that thought tomorrow if I ever make it out of this canyon.

I move into the mouth of the cave, streams of green light washing over its walls like an aurora. Following the beams deeper, I let them lead me until everything is dark except for the light shining between two natural columns. Past them, the ground drops into a stone staircase. I take them, mildly surprised when they end at a rocky beach beside a glowing green stream and not another foe to defeat.

"I'm here," I call out to the Goddess, my voice echoing. "How can I speak to you?"

Fog rolls over the stream, layered voices stirring beneath.

"Bevato, Zelladine. Drink."

I trail my fingers through the water, then scoop it up. It's clear in my hands, the light in the stream only making it appear green.

"No poison has ended me yet," I say, knocking it back. I wait a few minutes. I don't feel any different. Maybe a little more tired, but that's it.

I lean over the stream, staring at my reflection. My mirror image cuts a sharp smile and presses her hands to the surface. I push away from the stream, but she reaches through the water and pulls me in.

20

ROSEMARY

I'm not swimming anymore.

My body is swaying through cool air, and my bare feet are shuffling over a carpet of red and gold leaves. The trees around the copse stand tall above me as my sisters tighten our dancing circle, then step backward, expanding it again. We unclasp our hands to wave them overhead, twirling our hips.

I peek at the other maidens. They're singing the song of the forest, their eyes closed as they swing along to it, entranced by the magic flowing through us.

It's the same thing we do every evening. How boring.

They pivot and skip across the circle, switching places. I use the transition to sneak away from them, snapping up morels as I run to my secret hiding place. Curling up in the hollow of a chestnut oak, I watch through clusters of leaves, waiting for humans to pass the edge of the forest.

They're never predictable. Some of them stroll on by, led by strange animals that walk on four legs with their noses pressed to the ground. Others murmur wishes and leave us strange offerings. I never know what I'm going to see.

A woman with hair like a glowing sunset steps in front of me.

"What are you doing here, little one?" Tree Mother sighs, pulling me from the hollow and slinging me over her shoulder. "You know you're not supposed to get this close to the forest's edge. Let's take you somewhere safe."

The world shifts as she sets me down, and I'm back in the cave again. Somehow, I crossed the bright green stream while I was dreaming; it's flowing behind me now. I press up on my forearms, careful not to move my head too quickly.

It doesn't hurt anymore. I don't feel ill at all, actually. I check my thighs. They're not sore or blistered.

The water I drank must have healed me. I set my skirt down and stare into the dark cavern, another thought running through my head.

Oh.

Oh no.

"Am I dead?"

"Yes." A voice rattles through the darkness. "But don't worry, Zelladine, I can send you back to the land of the living."

I move to my feet, searching for the voice from Carabosse's dream. The cavern expands into a domed room with stalactites hanging from the high ceiling. Glowing green water drips off their points, hitting the polished stone floor with loud *plinks*.

Tree roots claw up from the ground, twisting into each other to form a large throne. A horned black dragon is perched upon it, spitting emerald embers through their teeth as they speak straight into my mind.

"Kneel before me."

I do as I'm told, falling to my knees before the great beast. They shift, their scales peeling away and body shrinking until a woman is sitting on the throne instead. She's not fully human. Her fingertips end in sharp claws, and her black gown plunges down between her breasts, revealing her grey skin. The whites of her eyes stand out from the black stripe running across the bridge of her nose. Two horns protrude from the sides of her head and curl back above her straight, dark hair.

"Vellesse." I bow, nearly touching my nose to the floor. "Goddess."

"Rise. There's not much time," she says. "I'm assuming you know why you were called here."

"My wife. Something happened to her, and she's—" I glance back at the stream.

"Yes, she's in there with the other lost souls," Vellesse finishes for me. "So is her Queen. But only one of them will make it. That is the price of visiting with me. A life must be given for one to go free."

"But what about me?" I ask. "I came here alone."

"The blood of a deity runs through your veins. No sacrifice is needed for you to return to the mortal plane." She stretches her claws out to tap her armrests, the seat too wide for her present body. "Your wife on the other hand..."

"She needs a life to be released," I state.

"Yes, but I wouldn't count on her Queen to give hers up willingly." Her eyes drift to the stream. "Both of their souls are so heavy. I think they might drown in there before either of them ever make it to me. They'll forget who they are and the way back to their bodies."

"What price do I need to pay for her?"

"Let me explain," she says, and I fight back a groan. If our time is so limited, then why are we wasting it by talking? "By now, you know about your origins, and what happened in the Hartwood. When the Tree Mother planted the seed of her magic in your chest, I had to find a way to protect it, and I couldn't bring you down here with me. Instead, I gave you a human form and put you to sleep with a spell that could only be broken by someone worthy of raising you in your realm until it was time to set the forest free. If you want a chance to save Carabosse, it will cost you your human body. And if you're not willing, I'll send you back as you are. You must remain on your plane until you finish the task you were sent to do."

This is the only body I've ever known. I pat myself down, knowing I have watched these hands labor and love tirelessly. My legs have carried me through countless woods and acquired twice as many scrapes and bruises.

I'm afraid of what sort of forest creature I might become, but I've already made my decision. I know Carabosse will still love me. So will Grace, Diana, and Candide. "I accept your deal."

"Then search for her soul in the stream. If you lose yourself in there, I'll have to send you back alone," she says as I stoop at the water's edge. "We'll meet again soon, when you set the forest free."

I break the surface as she finishes her sentence, and I'm running through an autumn forest again, climbing a tree that tips a branch to the ground for me. I jump through the leaves and shimmy out on a limb to look at what lies beyond the forest. The world is big and wide, and I long to explore it.

I don't dare to tell the other maidens about my secret dream. I tried that once, and they called me silly.

We have all we need in the Hartwood.

But deep down, I know I'm different. I'm not where I'm meant to be.

There's someone out there in a far-off land, waiting for me.

"Carabosse," I whisper to the wind.

She needs me to find her. The branch snaps with that realization, and I fall, plunging down into the underworld's waters.

I can't see my hands in front of my face. I'm a formless soul. There's no vessel containing my energy.

Hundreds of spirits swim past me. Thousands.

How am I supposed to find one in the midst of so many?

I concentrate on that feeling I get whenever we're together, that tingle of magic. I know Carabosse by more than just her body.

Channeling myself outward, I wait for her, clinging to a ghost of energy brushing past me. At first, she resists, getting sucked into the stream's endless current, but I pull her back to me.

We become two beams of light when our souls meet, twisting into each other as we rise to the surface, only parting to find our separate ways back to our bodies.

21

CARABOSSE

I wake up in the cell, alive somehow.

"Mal?" I croak, only remembering fragments of what happened as I lie beside the Queen.

There's no answer. The Starlight Court is lost, and the last Starlight princess is gone with the rest of them.

I don't know why she's dead or how I made it out of the underworld alive. It feels like I went to sleep and can't recall the details of a bizarre dream.

"I'm sorry I couldn't save you from yourself," I say, closing Mal's eyes. It's a failure I'll have to live around, but there's no time to mourn right now. I have to get to Rosemary before the attack squad arrives. I hope I'm not too late already.

Our bond hums through my ribs. I tune into it, that feeling sparking a memory of floating down an endless sea. I was lost, but I felt Rosemary reaching for me. She was there, swimming through the stream of souls with me.

I rub my ribs. That can't be right. If she was there, then how did we both make it out alive?

I slip into Snovida's mind, and see the canyon outside of

the Vellessentere's grounds. She brought Rosemary there.

My wife saved me, but how? I open the unlocked cell, summoning Snovida to meet me at the dungeon exit.

"Hey, wraithy. Forget what I said before." The man in the cell across from me wakes up and reaches through the bars, trying to grab my ankle. "Let me out and I'll serve you. Whatever you need."

I stride away, and he shakes his bars violently, waking the other prisoners.

Their pleas fade away as I tunnel through the dungeon, my escape interrupted by a pair of crossed swords blocking the opening to the drop off. Two guards in heavily-decorated uniforms stand in my way. The ribbons on their lapels mark them as some of Mal's most trusted guardians. There's not a chance they would've allowed her to stay in a cell alone with me. She must have used her glamouring abilities to get past them.

"What have you done to Queen Mal?" asks the guard on the left—a stocky man with a short brown beard. "Vellesse's flame has gone out. You killed her, didn't you? How did you get free?"

I hold my fingers up, keeping my thumb wrapped over my knife handle with the tip pointing down. "It's not what you think."

"You're a wretched fae beast, guilty of murder and treason," he spits.

I bite the inside of my cheek, making it bleed. There's not enough time to deny his accusations. I'll have to clear the air eventually, but right now, I need to get to Rosemary. "The Queen is dead. All of your questions will be answered shortly, but you need to let me leave."

The guard steadies his grip on his sword, pointing it at me. "We can't let you go, Queenslayer."

His display of courage is commendable, but my patience is

dwindling. There are things I need to handle immediately. "I'm getting out of here one way or another, but I'd appreciate it if you would take the easy option."

The other guard pushes her partner's arm down. "We understand, Commander." Her ponytail swings through a hole in her helmet as she looks down her nose to convey a silent message to him. "Don't we, Tobin?"

He drops his sword to his hip. "Yes."

"Then unlock these, please." I hold out my wrists, rubbing the itchy skin once they're free. Neither of them tries to stop me from toeing my way over the ledge of the palace. I jump when I feel Snovida beneath me, and it's as if no time has passed at all, my heart swooping in my chest as we ascend. We fly over the Dragon Valley, the range looking as murky as it did when we first came to Sarteal.

We land in the small canyon outside of the arena, finding Poppy and Nylah on the ground with their dragons. "What are you two doing here?"

"There was a revolt at Claw Ridge a few days ago. A group of us called for Queen Mal to release you, and we were discharged from the Dragon Army. It didn't go over well. Many of the riders disbanded with us, refusing to keep their posts without hearing from you," Nylah explains, her eyes ringed with dark circles. Sun and Moon poke their heads around her bandaged leg. She should be on leave, resting after her injury. Not dealing with this chaos. "We figured something was wrong when Vencel saw Snovida flying with Rosemary, but we had no idea she'd bring her here. I'm sorry. We tried to explain—"

"It's ok. She's ok." She had better be. Poppy doesn't look like she believes it. But then again, she competed in the Vellessentere and lost a close friend in the underworld cave. She has every right to doubt me. "Fly the rounds and tell the people of Tresoran that there will be an announcement this evening."

I work my way into the crevice of the canyon, taking the hatchlings with me. I hold them in my arms to keep them from gnawing on random femurs as I make my way to Rosemary. There are so many macabre memories scattered throughout this place. I look up at a jagged cliff face and remember watching Poppy falling in slow motion. I step over a closed trap and see Mal go white as a sheet, her foot hovering over it.

I blink teary memories away, slipping into the cave. Rosemary is lying on the rock shore beside the stream, unclothed except for the green ropes wrapped around her body.

"What the devil?"

I see the ropes writhing and set the hatchlings down to draw my blade, ready to cut her free from a pit of snakes. They twist away from her body when I get close, slithering over my toes to wrap around my ankles.

They're vines, and they're attached to her.

Rosemary stretches on the cold ground, shivering as she curls her legs to her bare belly and tucks her green fingers beneath her chin. Green lines thread around her wrists, the way they usually do when she's using her gifts, but now they look inked into her skin as if they've been made permanent.

"Hello darling," I say, picking her up with caution. Vines protrude from slots along her spine and the curves of her shoulder wings. I don't want to hurt them.

"It worked. I brought you back to me." Her eyes flutter open. "I knew that was your ball of energy."

"Ball of energy?" I quirk an eyebrow, and she smiles to herself, a playful curving of her mouth.

"It's a long story. I bet you're wondering how I got these," she says, her vines twisting around my neck.

"I am." I want to know everything. Why she's here and how

219

we're both alive. But my need to hold her close overrides every-thing. "I'm going to show you something, and then we can have a proper conversation."

I carry her through the cave, only setting her on her feet when we need to move through tight spaces. The hatchlings scurry out behind us, running to Snovida the second she lands. We all get situated, Rosemary's vines covering her nakedness as we fly to another cave high on a bluff. The last time I was here, I had to climb my way to its thin ledge, my hands raw and bleeding as I pulled myself over it to escape the undead ones.

There's barely enough room for Snovida to glide into its opening, but she wriggles her way out once she lets us off. I glance down with a hand on Rosemary's lower back, wondering how I made it that day. It must have been the fear pumping through me.

Or maybe it was destiny.

An obsidian cauldron sits in the middle of the shallow recess. There are bronze words painted on the stone wall curving over it.

I sit cross-legged beside the dead cauldron, its surface still smooth and shiny after all these years. Rosemary ushers the hatchlings away from the ledge and sits down in my lap.

It takes me a full round of breath to comprehend her warmth and weight on my legs. Her softness. How real she is when she whispers against my neck, telling me about how Snovida came to the Restless River and brought her to Sarteal. My blood pressure spikes as she describes the dangers she faced to get here. I hold her through her story, rocking her slightly when she gets to the part about Thea, and the price she paid to save me.

"I hope you don't mind these," she says, her vines curling around my arms to twine us even closer together. "I must be quite strange looking."

I lean back, taking in her unchanged face and the pattern of her green veins—the way they swirl over her abdomen, branching outward over her collarbones like wings. "You're the most beautiful creature I've ever seen. Never in a thousand years could I find another woman as soft and fierce. I don't deserve all that you've—"

A vine snakes up to my chin, a leaf folding over my mouth. Rosemary bats her lashes as if she's not the one controlling it. "This is what we do. You save me, and I save you. We'll need to protect each other to get through this," she says, with a pointed look toward the dark canyon. "I don't know what happened with Mal, but I'm sorry. Even after everything, I know what she meant to you. I'd never begrudge you your grief."

I manage to force words out of my tight throat. "She shouldn't have tried to hurt you."

"No, but Vellesse and the Tree Mother could never coexist for very long in the same realm. Perhaps the same goes for their vessels," she says, reciting a line from the Old Texts. "It was always meant to be a tale of the dragon and the devouring tree."

That sentence has been on my mind since Prince Alex revealed the truth of Rosemary's origins.

I lift my hand over the cauldron and loosen my jaw, Mal's death releasing me from our blood oath, allowing me to speak freely. "No, it was always meant to be a tale of you and me."

She jumps back from the green flames that burst from the obsidian, highlighting the small script hidden beneath the words painted on the wall. "What is...how did you do that?"

I can finally tell her my story.

"Toward the end of the Vellessentere, after Mal told me that my mate had died, I poured all of my energy into keeping her alive. She'd been watching Poppy closely during the tournament and noticed she was climbing toward something when she fell. She thought if she followed in her footsteps, she might discover Vellesse's cauldron of flames. I had to fend off a group of reanimated skeletons to clear the way for her," I explain, remembering the heartbreak I felt and how close I was to letting the bones snatch me away from the mortal plane until I heard my father's words ringing in my ears.

Protect the princess. I decided right then and there to make that my mission. "I climbed this bluff to lead them away from her. They followed, but I could hear them dropping off, their bones breaking apart and falling away behind me. I made it to this cave and took shelter in it. The cauldron seemed to whisper to me, pulling me closer until I was staring down at my reflection in its black surface. When I held my hands above it, the flames erupted from its depths."

"*You* won the Vellessentere," she says, crawling off of my lap. The light flickers along the curves of her body as she studies the painted text on the wall and the luminescent script beneath it.

"Technically nobody did," I explain. "That paragraph states that Vellesse's chosen one must recite the incantation to accept their victory."

"And you didn't?"

"I hid in here for a full night after I read it, waiting for Mal to find me. I thought she'd kill me when she realized I'd been chosen, but she came up with a solution." She'd been scheming for days by then, and I didn't even notice. I just went along with it. "Using scraps of metal from her vest, she fashioned a brand to bind our lives together, in hopes that she could wield Vellesse's flames through me."

"What happened?"

"Nothing. She recited the incantation and nothing happened." I can still hear her frustrated screams as she repeated the spell for hours on end. "Vellesse's flames were contained within my body. She could only use them against me."

"But the flames were always lit at the palace," Rosemary says, waving Sun away from the cauldron.

"Mal made it seem that way. She has—*had*—a talent for creating powerful glamours and illusions. She could make people see things that weren't really there."

"Like you do in our dreams."

"Yes, but she could alter reality. With a flick of her wrist, she could turn orange flames green and make it seem as though my shadows were burning." She only used my gifts when she needed to prove she could call the flames to threaten somebody.

"It was all a farce," Rosemary says. "She really was a false Queen. That's why she wanted Sun and Moon so badly—to bolster her claim to the throne."

"I couldn't tell you," I say, feeling exposed. A fragile, naked truth I've hidden for so long has suddenly been thrust into the light. "Our oath was forged in blood and fire. The mark on my arm wouldn't allow me to talk about it."

"I believe you," she says. "But why would she want to break your bond through death? Wouldn't that leave her powerless?"

"Not if she managed to bind Vellesse herself."

She wanted another chance to take the Goddess' flame into her body when she realized she couldn't control me. I trace the scar over the fabric of my tunic and push my sleeve back. The raised skin has flattened.

My forearm is smooth and unscarred, as if Mal's brand was never there.

Every piece of her has been ripped from my soul.

Rosemary touches my marble skin. "Now she can't hurt you or force you to uphold her ruse."

"I took the mark willingly because I thought she'd make a great Queen," I say, needing her to know the truth. I'm not blameless in this. I still believe Mal could have been a good leader if things had been different. If she had healed from the Fade. If she hadn't lost Arryn. There were a hundred *ifs*, but she couldn't claw her way out from the trauma to see the potential. "I didn't start to question her until recently. It became obvious that she wasn't going to uphold our promise to work together to protect the Dragon Valley."

"What promise?"

"The one the incantation demands. Its speaker must pledge to wield Vellesse's flame to defend the dragons from mortal greed." I read the words again, making a rough translation. *I give my heart to the flame...* "Maybe that's why the spell didn't work for Mal. Perhaps the magic sensed she was lying."

"But you wouldn't be," Rosemary says, wrapping her hand around the clean slate of my forearm. "I know you share an affinity with the dragons. You'd defend them."

"Yes, but..." The hatchlings move from their spot to swat at my legs. "It's too late. The kingdom—the world—already sees me as a villain."

"It doesn't matter how anyone sees you. Because I know the truth. Your heart is good, and you have the power to change things."

"If I'm to lead them, will you stand beside me as my Queen?"

"Queen?" Her lips part, and a mauve blush creeps over her cheeks. "No. That's not me. As a ruler, you'll need to build a strong alliance, like the one between Prince Alex and Princess Roberta. "

"What happened to *find a way to be together* or *pine away after each other forever* being our only options?"

"It would only be for show, a means to strengthen your

claim and stop the conflict in your kingdom." She swallows as if she can't stand the taste of the words in her mouth. "We'd both know the truth, but this is what royals do."

"It's not what *I* do. I'd rather cut out my tongue than use it to break my vow to you." My fingers find their way to her waist. "Mal is gone. We might be torn apart by fate or circumstances, but never another person. Never again."

There's a slight lift of her chin as she echoes the sentiment. "Never again."

I step one foot back and drop my knee, kneeling before this nymph of a woman who'd fly across kingdoms and crawl through the underworld for me.

How could any royal ever be considered more worthy? No amount of gold-filled coffers or well-trained soldiers could ever compare to the value of her bravery. "You give me all the strength I need, so please, will you stand beside me?"

She runs her hand over my hair until my head tilts back. "Yes. I'll always stand beside you."

And she does stand beside me, her head at my shoulder and her fingers interlaced with mine as we stand at the cave's edge while I recite the incantation.

"Odais svoyascerze polminnovi i obicetsu chronich smoki."

Heat sparks within me. It's not the awful searing sensation I'm expecting, but a powerful warmth that resonates through my chest. Vellesse's flame isn't painful now that it's no longer contained within my body. A green light pours from the underworld cave, and we watch its glow fill the chasm and rise over its staggering stone walls.

Vellesse's voice reverberates through the space. *"It's about time you accepted your role."*

Soon the bells will ring and everyone will know we are the true rulers of Sarteal.

22

ROSEMARY

My vines wrap tightly around me as we take to the sky, leaving the warmth of the cave behind. Vencel pulls beside us, his wings throwing chilly wind. Nylah notices my transformed state and taps her chin but doesn't ask any questions.

She exchanges a few words with Carabosse and removes her cloak, tossing it in the air. Carabosse catches the thick, hooded fabric and drapes it over my shoulders. "That should keep you warm until we reach the palace."

My new leaves might protect my modesty, but they don't provide any heat. I tuck my nose beneath the cloak, peeping over its collar as the palace comes into view. "Are Mal's soldiers really going to let us in?"

"I'd never lead you into bloodshed," Carabosse says. "Look up."

Dragons are flocking in from the east. I count them as they circle over our heads. *Five. Six. Seven.*

They dive down to where Poppy and Nylah are already

flanking us, falling into formation around the Commander. Only that's not Carabosse's proper title anymore.

I turn my face and meet the taut jawline of the new ruler of Sarteal, still not believing she plans to make me her Queen.

She lowers her lashes. "Something wrong, darling?"

"No." I twist the bristles of the cloak's fur lining. "What if I misbehave and everyone dislikes me?"

"Oh, I count on you misbehaving," she says, low and throaty. "But I have a feeling you'll be adored by many."

"I think that's just because you like me."

She clutches my hip. "Maybe. Or I could be onto something."

I've been tossed about in a dragon's claws and had a sword come perilously close to my head today. Seeing the Vellessentian palace rise from the mist shouldn't be giving me this much anxiety. I breathe through my nerves as we glide into the domed landing room, my stomach jostling along with the swinging rope bridge. No one dares to bar our entrance.

The squadron from the Dragon Army arrives behind us. Several of them file in around us, keeping their weapons ready. Confused as the guards may be, it's clear who's in charge now. No one is taking up arms for a dead queen.

Carabosse leads me through a dark stone passageway and up a spiral staircase. The hatchlings hold the hem of Nylah's cloak in their teeth to prevent me from tripping. We reach a carpeted wing, and the maids posted outside a large bedchamber stop whispering, the group splitting to form a line down the hall, their wool skirts pressing against the tapestries hanging on the wall.

"We'll need supplies for a bath, a fresh uniform, and a dress for my lady," Carabosse tells them. "And something to eat, please."

A maid drops into a curtsy. "Yes, my—" She lifts her head, unsure of how to finish her sentence. "We'll have your things right up in a moment. We can run her bath in that chamber if you'd like to take the larger suite."

Carabosse looks between the rooms and realizes she means for us to bathe separately. "No, we can take care of the bath. Clothes and supplies are all we need. My wife will coming with me."

She closes the double doors behind us and walks me through the large chamber. The hatchlings scramble onto the big bed as she leads me to an attached room. An oval soaking tub paved with black tiles curves out from the corner.

"I'll get it ready," she says, turning a brass knob built into the wall. It creaks loudly, and I shrink back as water pours from a spigot hanging over the tub.

"Where is that coming from?"

"One of the many hot springs flowing beneath the continent. The ancient Sartealeans invented plumbing, but they abandoned their efforts to establish it throughout the kingdom at some point." She runs her hand under the water and adjusts another knob. "We planned to build upon the structures that were already in place in the Dragon Valley. But that was before we had to set up camp near Dardaran. It's hard to focus on progress without peace."

"Maybe someday."

She flicks water from her hands. "Yes. Maybe."

Cutting the water off, she leaves to answer a knock on the suite's door. I slip off Nylah's cloak and step into the tub while she takes the maid's delivery, holding my breath to let the warm water flow over my head.

My vines grip the lip of the tub, responding to my thoughts as naturally as any other part of my body. They don't feel as strange as I thought they would, moving from my back like long, flexible extensions of myself. I pop up, examining the gradient shading of my green fingertips.

Now, these might take some getting used to.

Carabosse carries a gold tray in, setting it down on the platformed ledge before using her teeth to uncork a pink bottle. Tipping it over the tub, she swirls the liquid in, creating a blanket of bubbles and filling the chamber with a powdery rose scent.

She strips her grimy tunic off, and I wiggle my toes through the foam, studying the muscles carved into her abdomen.

"Have you done anything besides exercise since we last saw each other?" I ask as she unlaces her breeches. She tugs them down past the ridges of her hips.

"Not really," she says, wiping a layer of grit from her skin. "There wasn't anything else to do in the dungeon."

My vines flail along with my hands. "Dungeon?"

She scratches the back of her head. "Yeah. That's where she kept me."

I have a few harsh words I'd like to say about the late Queen, but I think it would hurt Carabosse to hear them. I hold my tongue until my anger passes. "No wonder you smell like a horse's ass."

"More like a rat's ass." She sinks in up to her mouth, blowing bubbles across the surface. "That place is crawling with rodents."

"I know from experience."

The events since my last birthday seem to have passed in a whirlwind, but somehow we've survived all of them. We survive, make jokes, and keep going, always moving forward.

Her knees brush past mine, and she splashes the water between her legs, tilting her head. "Come sit with me."

I spin around, able to float with all of the water surrounding me as I settle backward between her knees. She pulls me against her chest in a tight hug. Minutes pass, and all we do is breathe, feeling our hearts beating.

She grabs a glass bottle and pours perfumed liquid into my hair. I lean back as she works the rose and vanilla scent through my strands. "Don't spoil me like this."

"You don't want to get too used to the royal treatment before we fly back to camp and have to wash ourselves with cold buckets of water again?" she asks, massaging her fingers into my scalp, the tension melting away.

"No, I can handle that," I say. "I'm afraid of getting used to this—us being together without any sneaking or secrecy. It would make it too painful to be pulled in opposite directions again."

"That won't happen." Her thumbs work down to the nape of my neck and slide around the bumpy inserts along my spine. "I'm having trouble believing it too, but one day it'll sink in."

She touches the base of a vine, and a shiver pulses through me. Goddess, that skin is sensitive. I place my hands on her thighs as she brings her mouth to my neck.

"I want to touch you so badly," she says, shuddering a breath. "But people are waiting for me to say something, and I know once I have you in my bed, it will be hours before I let you out of it."

"What are you going to do? Tie me up with your shadows so I can't leave?" I tease. Her hands cup my breasts, contradicting the words she's saying about needing to leave.

"I don't think that will be necessary, although I've spent plenty of nights imagining you wrapped up in my shadows and stretched out for me." Her index finger swirls lazily around my nipple. "I plan to keep you in place with my tongue and please you until you've made a soaking wet mess of the sheets. There's so much I want to do to your body."

I want her fingers to trail down even further, to delve into that space that's aching for her touch. But she removes her hands, and I spin around, grabbing the bottle of hair wash. "Then let's get this done so you can show me."

We take turns scrubbing each other and sticking our heads under the spigot. Toweling off, we change into the clothes on the bed—a standard black uniform for her and a stiff black dress for me.

It's too long, but at least it's not too tight. Even with the laces done, it hangs loose around my torso, leaving room for my new appendages.

Carabosse braids my hair tightly, and I part hers with a comb, letting her waves spill over her right eye.

Her shoulder twitches as she sheathes her blade in her belt.

"There." I adjust her cape, aware of her nervous fidgeting. "You look like a very queenly wraith."

"They'll call me Boss the Terrible," she says, her irises two cool black circles. "The Queenslayer."

"Stop it. You didn't slay Mal. The truth will come out," I assure her, upset that Mal's death will leave such a mark on her conscience. "And you're only mildly terrible sometimes. Boss the Slightly Unpleasant would be a more apt tile."

"I'll settle for Boss the Mediocre," she says, a green spark forming at her fingertip. "But I'll miss moving in the shadows, where my work remains unseen."

"Yes, but now we have a chance to show everyone you're capable of great things." I smooth my hands over her shoulders and kiss her cheek. "There's important work to do, and we've been given our gifts for a reason."

I don't think either of us fully understands what that reason is, but we can't sit around and dwell on it. That's not who we are. "This our chance to end the fighting in both of our kingdoms. You're the wraith of Sarteal—don't you forget it."

She bites her nail and gives me a cocky grin. *There she is.*

That's how I like her best, self-assured and arrogant.

We exit the landing room on Snovida with Sun and Moon strapped in and gliding at her sides. Courtiers, servants, and advisors flock to the palace's balconies as Carabosse shouts down from her seat, addressing them in Sartealean. I pick up on some of the words, piecing her statement together. It's an impassioned speech about fire, dragons, and the legendary history of the nightmare realm.

The horde flies in behind us as we ride over Tresoran. Bells ring on high steeples, and people drop to their knees in the streets, some of them crying at the sight of the dragons they regard as great deities. And I suppose a fraction of them are weeping because they're terrified of their new leader.

Their heads turn to follow us, two otherworldly creatures flying on the back of a fearsome dark beast. Carabosse makes the rounds for hours, her voice growing hoarse as she makes sure everyone is aware she holds Vellesse's gift, flicking green flames between her fingers to show them.

"Do you think enough of them have heard me?" she asks me softly in the common language.

"Yes, anyone who didn't will surely know by tomorrow morning." Shop doors swing open, and people shout through windows, spreading the news. "Word will spread quickly through the kingdoms."

"We'll need to fly out to Claw Ridge in the morning and reunify our forces before new alliances form against us," she says. "But I'm taking you home for one evening."

I'm looking forward to a night in bed, but I dread facing the looks we'll get as we walk through the palace again. The curiosity, uncertainty, and judgment.

We loop through two black towers bathed in green and dive down into the chasm surrounding the palace, bypassing it completely. "Where are we going?"

"You'll see," she says, a hint of excitement coming back to her voice. "Hang on."

23

ROSEMARY

The hatchlings jump back to my lap as Snovida flies so fast that the tunnels in the mountain blur into black lines. We round a dry basin and she thrusts up to land on a strip of a rock ledge angling out of a tunnel.

"There used to be a thriving city built into the slopes of the valley before the dragons left the realm. These tunnels were once dwellings for riders." Carabosse's boots hit the hard platform, and she slaps the tunnel's arched opening, admiring the worn stone serpent twisting around it. "I planned on calling this one home someday, but that was before my duties pulled me away."

"I wasn't expecting this," I say, glancing into the dark cave.

Carabosse looks back, her smile faltering. "Would you prefer the palace? We'll have a chamber there, of course, but I thought this would be a nice private spot for you and me."

"No, it's perfect." Stuffy castle corridors bring up too many bad memories. I'd rather stay somewhere open and free, where we can come and go as we please without guards posted at every corner. They could never make me feel as safe as my wife does. I know I'll sleep peacefully beside her, with our dragons nearby. "I love it."

Snovida butts her snout against the hatchlings and flies away as I usher them inside. Beams of light shine down through several slits carved high into the bluff, brightening the dwelling enough to see the details of the large, circular space. We explore while Carabosse kneels over the hearth to the left of the entrance and gets a fire going.

The side of a round tub bellies out from an angled stone slab. I step behind the half-wall, finding a lifted chamber pot with knobs above it, similar to the ones I saw in the palace. I push one, and a gurgling noise sounds beneath my feet.

"The plumbing will need work," Carabosse says, wiping soot from her hands. "The inventor in Corstylia who builds some of our equipment has sent us blueprints to get the system up and running, but that's a plan for the future. The distant future. Stabilizing our food supply and fending off attacks from Dardaran is sucking up all of our riders' energy, so there hasn't been much time for building."

"You've put a lot of thought into this," I remark, feeling like I've stumbled in on a piece of her life I was never meant to see. I can identify this woman down to her soul, but we've only spent time on the run together, and stolen a few hours here and there between. It will take years to learn her inside and out. What she does in her spare time. Her hopes and dreams.

"I thought this was what we'd be doing when we swore to protect the Dragon Valley. We never thought it would be so hard for Mal when we—" Grief passes fleetingly over her features. "Anyways, these are plans for another time." She pads over to the braided rug and opens a chest at the foot of the simple bed, pulling out two blankets. Spreading one over the mattress, she takes the other to the tunnel at the back of the cave, ducking beneath its low, arched opening to a narrow stairwell. "Sun and Moon will like this feature."

The winding steps lead to a small loft with a few slits in the rock to let light and fresh air in. Warm air rises from the fireplace, making it a cozy place for them to sleep. Carabosse wafts the blanket down on the ground, and the hatchlings cuddle up together. "I thought this was a storage space when I first claimed this dwelling, but now I'm almost positive it was used as a nest for orphaned dragons."

My heart could burst from watching them.

"It's like a part of you always knew we were coming," I say, turning down the steps, unable to bear the swelling in my chest. I have this fear that all the good things in my life will be ripped away if I indulge too much in my happiness.

"I like to think so too." Carabosse stands across from me in front of the hearth, her fists clenched at her sides. "Even though I'd lost all hope that I'd ever find you."

Is she nervous like I am?

Every time we've been together, there's been a deadline hanging over our heads. We've spoken vows knowing we'd have to keep them from a distance. Taking our clothes off has always come with a rushed sense of desperation. We've never touched each other with our intentions set on building something to last outside of a dream.

Carabosse undoes my laces, loosening my dress enough for her to lift it easily over my head. I take off her cape, and my vines trail over her biceps and shoulders, my elongated oval leaves touching her breasts.

"They're soft," she says, and I brush them over her abdomen, causing her muscles to tighten with a ticklish laugh.

"I wonder how they'll get along with your shadows." I step close enough for us to touch so that my green tendrils can play with her darkness. The whorls of night split into long ribbons, and my vines twine together with them as we kiss, Carabosse's thigh slipping between mine. It's a familiar syncing of our bodies.

Our magic twists and untwists as we dance toward the bed. For every pull, another press.

Back and forth until I have her at the edge of the mattress. One push and I'll be on top.

Her shadows untangle themselves from my vines and grip my wrists, tying them behind my back. She spins me around so that I'm the one closer to the bed.

"I thought you were going to hold me in place with your tongue," I say as she grazes her lips down my neck.

"I plan to. That's why I can't let you push me onto that bed too early." She tugs on her magic until I'm arching my back. Untying the ribbon holding my braid, she combs out my damp waves. "From this day forward, you're the only person I'll ever kneel for, and I think I need to spend some time on my knees." She plants slow, languorous kisses down my collarbones, trailing over the green lines that curve into my waist and round out over my thighs. Her knees sink to the rug, and she holds onto my hips, turning me side to side with my hands bound behind me. Spinning me into a quarter turn, she rubs my ass, letting its roundness fill her hand.

"Fuck. You're so beautiful," she says, erasing any doubt I have about my new appearance as she worships every inch of me with her lips and fingers. "I always miss the tiny details in our dreams."

Her hands slide around my thighs as she kisses my mound, her tongue washing over my clit in one hard, slow lick that leaves me craving more.

"That feels good. Please keep going."

"I will." She uses her fingers to part my damp curls, sending tingles all throughout my body as she brushes my clit.

"But I'm going to take my time." She continues her light teasing over my wet pussy, holding me open. "I love looking at you, feeling your little bud harden for me."

That *little bud* is tightening uncomfortably, desiring the pressure of her fingers. I wiggle my hips forward, and her shadows catch me around the thighs, coaxing my feet wider and holding me in place.

"No fair," I whimper as she drums her fingertips lightly over my pussy.

"Is there something you want from me, love?" There's a cheeky smirk tugging on her lips. "You should use your words to tell me."

"Your tongue. Use your tongue."

"Of course, darling." She traces the tip of her tongue along my folds and slowly licks around my clit. I groan and feel a puff of air as she laughs against me.

She's thoroughly enjoying my agony, and there's nothing I can do about it. I'm tied up in her shadows, sweat beading on my forehead as my core turns molten beneath her tongue.

I get one firm flick before she draws back. Shadows and firelight dance in the hard lines of her muscles as she breathes heavily, studying me.

She licks her fingers, and my head feels light, like I've had too much to drink as I see that blank stretch of smooth skin on her forearm. She's free to give herself to me.

I whine as her wet fingers skim over my tits.

"So needy, love," she says. "Let's get you taken care of."

Her tongue runs along the length of my pussy, focusing on my clit. She's worked me into such a frenzy that her warm, wet attention is almost enough to send me right over the edge.

Almost, but I hang on, taking in the sight of her knuckles going white and her black waves falling over her face as her head works back and forth between my legs.

I hold up a dam against the current of pleasure building in my lower belly, but that image destroys it, and my orgasm rushes in. She releases me from her shadows, catching me as I go weak in the knees, tossing me onto the mattress, letting my calves hang over the edge.

Leaning over me, she slides a finger into my wet entrance, an echo of my orgasm shuddering through me as she works another one in.

"We can stay like this all night if you'd like," she says, her eyes darkening as she works above me, her fingers thrusting in an unhurried rhythm. "Keeping you filled until the morning."

"I think I'd like that." A couple of my vines slither out from under me to rest on her shoulders, my body rocking gently with her movements. It feels so good to take her inside me, to keep her there.

She seems to know when to apply more pressure, circling her thumb over my clit whenever I need it, and when to back off, allowing me to recover.

I drop into a liminal space, where nothing outside of this moment exists. Our world consists of the heat and magic swirling between us, the sounds of our romp filling the room and blocking the noise from the chasm.

My leisurely orgasms build slowly and seem to roll over my entire body, Carabosse's breath hitching along with mine whenever one takes me.

Her touch on my cheek anchors me in the moment. I'm sprawled out beneath her, a puddle on the bed where she's been gradually nudging me to the center of the mattress.

Kissing me between my eyebrows, her lips linger on my skin as she rasps, "I need more."

Woozily, I grab her chin. "Then get in bed with me."

She pulls her fingers out, and I whine, my pussy clenching around nothing. The mattress sinks beneath her weight, and her hands appear at my hips, flipping me onto my belly. My limbs are so loose it's effortless.

I bite the blanket as she straddles my legs on her knees, coasting her hands down my lower back. New sensations tingle along my spine and spread to my ribs, my vines perking up at the roots as she pulls my hips back and slides a shaft of shadows into my slit.

We both moan as she sinks in, my tendrils curling around her wrists. I glance over my shoulder, turned on by the way she's watching me.

Goddess, she looks so good like that, with my vines wrapping over her biceps. She lifts her eyes, her gaze meeting mine as she bites her lower lip, a strip of her shadows breaking off from the opposite end of the shaft to swirl over her clit. She thrusts faster and deeper, and I can sense her climax approaching, the energy shifting in the shadows pushing inside of me.

Rocking forward on my hands and knees, I slide off of the shaft and drop onto my back, using my heels to walk myself lower on the bed until I'm right between her legs.

She lets the shaft dissolve into ribbons around her. "Is something wrong, little witch?"

"Only that I want to taste you before you finish." I reach for her thighs, but she stays high on her knees, always so aware of her strength and power when she's with me. "It's ok. You won't hurt me."

She lowers herself to my mouth, and I stick out my tongue, loving how she rolls herself gently over its surface. But she needs more than that, and I'm not made of glass.

Bracing her thighs, I get her to stop moving and thrust my tongue into her before licking her clit until her shadows are practically vibrating with energy. I close my eyes, humming as I suck and lick, eliciting unexpected noises from her. I relish the thought of being the only woman who makes the wraith whimper.

She pulses in my mouth, and I kiss her all the way down from her climax until she lies down beside me on the half-made bed.

We curl up, facing each other, pillowless.

"We're going to have to move some of our things in here eventually," she says, and I hold onto the fuzzy feeling that phrase gives me. *Our things.*

I stare at the bare cave walls, envisioning us hanging tapestries and placing knick-knacks on the mantel over the fireplace. I walk myself back from that, not quite ready to lose myself in a fantasy that was literally impossible two days ago.

But the hard stone around my heart is cracking open inside my chest, and there's a seedling of hope growing through the cracks as Carabosse's arm drapes over my body, a solid weight that grounds me.

24

CARABOSSE

Snovida's hollow screech rings through the chasm as we leave the palace, a single bolt of grief striking our bond. My feelings over Mal's death don't really make much sense. I'm not sure if I'm supposed to be more or less sad about it than I am.

I find Nylah flying rounds above the chasm, where I left Rosemary sleeping at the break of dawn.

"Poppy and the others have gone back to the camp," she says, flying down on Vencel. "Did you make the arrangements?"

"Yes. There'll be a private ceremony, and she'll be entombed by the priestesses." I left instructions for Mal's funeral with the palace advisors, forgoing the Sartealean tradition of having her body paraded down the streets of Tresoran. There's been too much animosity towards her to allow it. I'll fulfill my last duty to her by having her buried with dignity.

"Will you be attending?"

"No." I've already said goodbye to the broken princess of

Faerie who tried to break me. Her mark may have vanished from my skin, but I'll wear her scars on my soul for the rest of my life. "Rosemary and I will be leaving within the next hour."

I've been gone for too long from Claw Ridge. A few riders will stay here to protect the Dragon Valley, but the camp is still standing against our greatest threat.

"I'll be out here waiting," she says, and I compose myself on the dwelling's landing strip before I go in.

I find Rosemary sitting up in bed, a ray of sunshine wrapped in a blanket. I can only see her face when she turns to me, her smile breaking through the clouds of my depression.

"What is that?" she asks, her nose twitching in my direction as the hatchlings tussle on the mattress. "It smells delicious."

Sun and Moon quit squabbling and race toward me.

"No running so close to the entrance," I scold them, holding my leg out to stop them from sliding out over the ledge as I shift the boxes under my arm and drop my rucksack. "I have enough food for all of us."

Uncinching my bag, I lift the cloth covering the klobasniky and hand one to each of the dragons before sitting next to Rosemary. She pokes a vine out of the blanket to grab a roll, taking a big bite of the sweet dough.

"I didn't know these were filled," she says, covering a mouthful of hot sausage with the letter she's holding in her hand, the blanket slipping down her back. She takes a smaller bite and waves the parchment. "We received a message from Robin this morning."

I nibble my roll, tossing a crumb to the crow perched on my trunk. I've never encountered a magic text that explains how the birds sing their secrets to their mistress. "That was fast."

"Yes," she hums, reading over the letter. "She wants to

extend her congratulations to the new Queen of Sarteal and show her gratitude for your continued efforts to support the rebellion in the future. She expects to see us soon."

"*X-O-X-O, Robin,*" I say, reading her last line aloud. I know the rebels need our help. They have more support from the people of Lollishire, but they lack the funding for supplies and military equipment. It's hard to win any conflict when your coffers are dwindling. "What do you want to tell her? I'm sure she'll be expecting a response. "

"Me?"

"Yes, you, Rosemary the Sweet and Sour." I open the lid of my trunk, lifting a blank journal and crusted inkwell. "We'll be working together, so you should have a say in the message, especially when it concerns your home kingdom."

"Let's tell her that we haven't abandoned our promises to help the rebels take the King's City, and that I still intend to return with my godmothers to break the curse on the Hart-wood," she says as Sun jumps onto the bed to sniff her half-eaten roll. "I haven't forgotten that Lollishire is suffering from a crop shortage."

"That's not your fault," I remind her, noticing the way she's picking at her food.

"I know, but still..."

"It's not your fault. I know you feel guilty, but you have to eat to keep your strength. No one has told you what you're supposed to do as your Goddess' vessel." I shake out an ink blot and look up from the paper. "Did Vellesse mention anything?"

"Only that she'll see me when it's time to set the forest free. Has she ever told you what that means?"

"No." Mallory's final words come back to me. *The other thing Vellesse said...*

I'll never know what she was trying to tell me.

"Why does everyone have to be so damn elusive? My godmothers won't even tell me the details of the spell to break the curse until we enter the Harwood Forest. They insist on keeping it a secret." She reaches for the quill after I sign my name, sighing. "I should write to them myself, or they'll be worried."

"How are they?" I ask as she takes the journal from my lap.

"Fine. Adjusting." She jots a note, sticking her tongue out. "They treat me like I'm the one who spent three years in the Ivy Keep."

"I'm sure they realize you didn't have it easy while they were gone."

"No, but I didn't have it as hard as they did." She tears out her letter and rolls it up tightly with mine, feeding it into the crow's beak. "They'll be happy to hear we've found a way to be together finally."

"Will they?" I can't imagine I've made a good impression on them by leaving their precious girl behind.

"Yes, they've been overly concerned about my happiness." She rolls her eyes in mock annoyance. "They'll love you too, once they get to know you."

That's hard to believe, but I like that the thought seems to make her happy. I retrieve the pile of boxes I've dropped at the entrance, setting them on the bed. "Here, I got you something."

She unties the ribbon around the first one and pulls out a pink gown, holding it up by its pearl collar. "What an odd dress."

"It's backless. I bought a lined cape to keep you warm, but this should allow your vines to move freely beneath it."

She moves out from under the blanket, nude and shivering as she steps into the flowy fabric. I twist her hair away from her neck and fasten the pearl clasp.

"How does it look?" she asks.

She takes my breath away. The dress slinks down to the dimples of her lower back, showing the vines snaking out from her spine. They twist around her arms as she turns to me. "Well?"

"It's amazing. You look amazing." My tongue ties itself in knots. "I remembered seeing women in the Dragon's Den wearing those gowns, and I knew they would be perfect. I had to get you a few of them."

"The Dragon's Den?" She tilts her head. "Is that some meeting room in the palace?"

"No, it's a pleasure house in Tresoran. The owner is a friend of a friend. She has plenty of gowns on hand, so she was willing to sell them."

Her hands go still as she rubs her skirt. "You went to a pleasure house this morning?"

"Yes."

She raises her eyebrows, blinking slowly. "Without me?"

"I nudged you gently to tell you I was leaving," I say, watching the skin above her collar flush red. "I thought you wanted to sleep. Why are you so angry?"

"Because you can't go to places where beautiful women walk around with their tits out without me," she says, her tendrils untwisting from her arms. Tiny sharp thorns spike along the vines as they flick around her like cattails.

"Um, darling."

"What?" She taps her foot impatiently as I bite down on a knuckle, staring at them. "Why are you looking at me like that?"

I remove my finger from my mouth and point to the green strands. "I'm sorry, but it appears you've sprouted thorns."

She loops her vines over her shoulders, her mouth dropping open when she sees the thin red barbs. "*Ack.* They're hideous."

"No, they're lovely." I hold my palms open letting them dance over my hands, enticed by the sharp points grazing my skin. So alluring and dangerous. "You truly are a divine creature of the forest, a wild thing."

"How embarrassing for me, to sprout thorns when I'm only a teensy bit miffed," she says. Her thorns retract as I stroke my hand over her frizzy waves, and she presses her forehead into my chest. "I'm not usually this prone to jealousy."

"I am, so I understand. You don't have to gloss over your emotions with me or pretend you're ok with something." I kiss the top of her head, knowing what it means for her to be genuine with somebody, to not have to fake a smile for her survival. I want her to be real with me, to trust me with her prickly bits along with her honeyed sweetness. "I promise I won't go to a pleasure house without you again. There may have been a few tits out, but I wasn't there to gaze upon them."

"I know. I really like my dress." She swings her hips, swishing her hem over her feet as her vines curl around her arms, soft and pliable again. "These vines, though. I'm going to have to work on them."

I touch one of the fuzzy ends wiggling between her fingers. "We can have some fun practicing with them. Those thorns might come in handy."

She looks away, bashful. "I don't know if I can make them appear at will. They might only pop out when I'm irritated."

"I definitely know how to test that theory." I swirl a shadow beneath her chin and pull a cocky grin. "Want to meet me at our favorite rock ledge once we settle in at Claw Ridge?"

She rubs her temples. "I might need to sleep for a few days after everything. But I'm in."

"Let's leave before it gets too late, then." I wish we had an extra day or two to allow her body to adjust to everything it's been through, but there's already going to be a pile of shit waiting for me at Claw Ridge. "You can sleep on the way there."

I grab our things, meeting Snovida on the ledge. Once our supplies and the hatchlings are strapped in, we take off, Nylah and Vencel riding with us toward the sun as it climbs over the mountains. The green glow of the Dragon Valley fades behind us, and the sharp peaks soften into the flat, dead lands of the continent.

This flight seems longer than usual. Normally stamina isn't a problem for me, but the hours pass by, and my eyelids start drooping.

Rosemary's head lolls on my chest, and I try to stay alert, adjusting her every few minutes to stop her from slipping. She groans each time she wakes up, so I call my shadows around her, dimming the sunlight to ease her light sensitivity.

I catch a second wind as Snovida passes over the bog where two dragons are rolling in the mud, and I see Claw Ridge ahead —the camp clutched between the slanted rock formations.

"We're here," I say, rousing Rosemary. She dismounts drowsily, and I keep my hand on her lower back as the soldiers stand at attention, shifting uneasily as if they're unsure how to address me.

One of the riders must have informed them of my new position. The news has clearly spread around the camp already. A sergeant starts to bow, and I hold up my hand.

"Nothing changes," I announce. "We don't need to shift how we do things around here or waste time reconfiguring the chain of command. If you're unhappy with the recent changes to the monarchy, then you're free to request early discharge papers and leave without penalty. I want to work with soldiers who are committed to restoring the peace in Sarteal. For the people and for the dragons. That's my agenda."

I steer Rosemary away from the formation, giving the soldiers time to reflect on what I've said while I get her to our tent.

The soldiers posted outside salute me with mixed greetings. "Commander. My Queen."

"Commander's fine," I say, disappearing beneath the canvas flap with Rosemary and the hatchlings.

"Do you have to go already?" she asks, yawning in my bed.

"Yes, but I'll be back tonight, and I'll have someone fetch you something from the healer's tent for your head."

She winces. "Peppermint tea should help. I'm mostly nauseous from flying."

I kiss her forehead before I leave, running into Nylah at the food stations.

"I've been told the supply run squad was supposed to return two hours ago," she says, flicking her pocket watch open. "Are you ready to fly out with me to check on them?"

"I'll find someone else to fly the route with me. Stay here and keep an eye on Rosemary and the hatchlings."

She snaps the watch shut, balking at my order. "I'm not a nanny."

"No, but there's bound to be animosity toward me after what happened." I tighten the stiff straps on the new dragon scale vest I bought this morning, unable to get it to fit right. "Someone could hurt my family to get to me. I'll feel safer if you're here with them."

That's half of the truth. The other half involves her being seriously injured and too hard-headed to accept that she needs time to heal. She needs a job to do.

She attempts to disguise her limp as she moves forward in the soup line. "If you say so."

"I do." I turn on my heel, walking backward. "Oh, and she needs you to bring her some peppermint tea."

I catch the subtle middle finger she pulls from her pocket and laugh, thankful for this small opportunity to protect the loved ones I have left.

25

ROSEMARY

Carabosse's kisses are drying on my thighs as I pull the covers over my shoulders, soaking up the warmth from her side of the bed. I rub my legs together, repeating the same line of Sartealean for the third time, trying to concentrate on the open book on my pillow.

But my mind keeps wandering back to last night and all of the things Carabosse and I did when she finally returned to camp.

I met her on the ledge, testing the agility of my vines against her shadows. She pretended I could win for a minute, then whipped her silky dark ribbons out and wrapped me up in them.

It's only been a few minutes since she left to monitor the marshes, but I'm already wondering what kind of trouble we'll get up to this evening.

I roll on my back and drop the book on my face. All I do is daydream.

Dull days aren't something to complain about during troubled times, but it isn't like me to sit around in a tent, studying and waiting. Even if that's what I'm expected to do in my position.

Sun and Moon scratch at the curtain hanging around their nest and scramble to the tent's opening, abandoning the warmth of their blanket pile. They hear Nylah's arrival, springing out to meet her before she has a chance to announce herself.

Sitting up, I braid my vines down my spine and wrap them around my hips. I haven't perfected the technique, but it allows me to dress into a heavy wool gown with tight sleeves before pulling my fur-lined cape over my shoulders.

"Coming," I say in Sartealean, making an effort to practice with the lieutenant even though she gets impatient. Parting the tent flaps, I crunch over the frosted ground, and a snowball goes flying past my face.

Sun bats it with their tail, sending it right into a guard's back. He spins around with a scowl, and Nylah laughs behind her hand, tossing another snowball to the dragons. Moon spreads their wings and melts it with a burst of flame, surprising the lieutenant.

"Vellesse's horns," she says. *"Bo travaye."*

It takes me a moment to translate in my head. I think it means good job or something to that effect.

"Bo travaye," I repeat, clapping for them as the grumpy guard wipes snow from his uniform. His struggle seems to lift Nylah's spirits. She smiles begrudgingly, shifting her weight on the crutches Carabosse talked her into using at my suggestion while her splinted leg heals. She's almost pleasant as we walk down to the food stations, grabbing our breakfast.

We find a place to sit, eating our bowls of stew in silence. The broth has become thinner since we arrived. I sip the transparent liquid floating around potatoes and carrots, struggling to finish it.

It doesn't taste bad; the cooks have done their best to dress it up, flavoring it with available spices. But the crop shortages are getting worse. Many people will be having a bleak winter solstice this year.

Nylah taps me on the shoulder to see if I'm ready to leave. I take another bite of my crusty bread, forcing myself to finish it. I feel like I should be doing something.

A cook stumbles away from the station, barely making it to a trashcan before she starts retching. Nylah drops her soggy bread in her bowl as two riders stagger away from their breakfasts, their mouths tinted green around the edges.

"Well, that's not a good sign," I murmur to myself, watching them enter the healing tent.

It's the one place I've been purposefully avoiding during my daily walks with Nylah. Carabosse and I have both agreed that I shouldn't serve in the Dragon Army as a healer since my new status might make Felix and the others feel uncomfortable with giving me orders.

But that's not the only reason I skirt around that corner of camp.

I think about Thea often, and how important she was to the healers. Her absence must feel heavy there. I wonder if they blame me for it.

Another woman walks by, clutching her stomach as she ducks into the tent.

"I want to go there," I say, enunciating each word.

Nylah cocks her head. "No."

"No?" I'm sure she's been given specific orders to keep me safe, but I don't care. There are too many new patients flooding into the tent. The healers will be overwhelmed by all of them. "I'm going."

She follows me, her crutches slowing her down on the shoveled lawn. I make it into the tent, breathing through my mouth to adjust to the sick scent. Nearly all of the cots are taken, and all three healers on duty are rushing between them.

Nylah sticks her head into the tent, looks around, and points her chin over her shoulder at Sun and Moon. I understand she's telling me that she'll wait outside with them.

Ignoring my own feelings over Thea's death, I head to the back of the tent where Felix is rolling a rider onto her side. His brow is furrowed in concentration, but it smooths out, his eyes widening when he notices me.

"Surrey."

I brace myself for his reaction, acknowledging that he worked closely with the fae healer on a daily basis. But he spreads his arms out as if he means to hug me, then looks at his soiled shirt and shakes his head, thinking better of it. Lifting his hands in a question, he smiles at me.

"I want to help," I say, hoping I phrased it correctly.

He screws up his mouth, considering as he arranges antiemetic tinctures on his tray. Handing me a rag, he points me toward the prep station. I get right back into the swing of my duties, pushing my hair into a cap and pulling on clean gloves to deliver bedpans and place sick buckets where they're needed. Puke splashes into one of the containers while I'm still holding it.

"What the devil was in that stew?" I murmur, dreading an eventful night of tossing and turning from undercooked meat.

A healer named Marguerite tucks her nose into her elbow. "Fleeyeu."

I repeat the word to myself a few times to memorize it as I press a cool, damp cloth to my patient's forehead. I'll look up what it means later. Everyone is either indisposed or busy, including me.

I sprinkle sugar and salt into cups of water and move from cot to cot, trying to get the dehydrated soldiers to take a few sips. They moan and groan on the narrow beds, and I do my best to soothe them, but nothing turns a fierce rider into a sniveling pile of tears faster than food poisoning.

Felix swivels his stool away from the supply bench and wheels it over to me as I swipe a tray with an alcohol pad to clean the surface. "Surrey."

He points toward the tent opening, where I can see dusk falling behind Nylah. She's waiting for me.

"I'll be back tomorrow." I say it in the common language, but he nods, seeming to understand what I mean.

I scratch the hatchlings' necks, apologizing for taking so long. "I promise I won't stay for more than a couple hours tomorrow."

Their wingspan has been increasing rapidly lately. I purse my lips as they pull them back tightly to prevent scraping them on something.

If it weren't for the constant threats from Dardaran, they'd be able to practice flying with the other dragons. But for now, we have to keep them entertained on base.

They squawk as Snovida lands on a ledge, and I hold them back from running to meet Carabosse while she's talking to the squad that just came in. Nylah doesn't swing as quickly on her crutches as she usually does as we walk back to our tent.

I glance up, and she licks her lips, breathing through her mouth as if she's about to be sick. Reaching into the folds of my cloak, I hand her a tincture I pocketed earlier. She leans on a crutch and opens the lid, releasing its strong peppermint and ginger scent.

It should help if she gets queasy. I know she won't seek treatment in the healer's tent.

Heading inside, I strip my clothes into a pile and briskly scrub myself with some water from the washbasin. I'm freezing my tits off when Carabosse comes in.

Her eyes fall on my pebbled skin. "Nylah said you went to the healer's tent today. I thought we agreed you weren't going to do that?"

"We did." I hiss air between my teeth as I drag the cold cloth over my legs. "But I could tell they were hurting for help, and honestly, it was good for me. I need to keep busy."

She follows the path I make up to my thighs. "People will think it's improper behavior for a queen."

"Since when do you care about propriety?" I splash the cloth back into the water and wring it out, my teeth chattering as I wash my belly. "We share a bed each night, and you continue to perform your duties as the Commander. Will you stop doing those things because people frown upon them?"

Her gaze sweeps down to my breasts. "Goddess, no."

I take the long flannel nightgown folded on the crate beside our cot and drop it over my head. "Then know that fate matched us together for a reason. I don't give a hoot what anyone thinks either."

She wraps her arms around my waist from behind, sighing into the warm fabric. "I can't help worrying about you."

"I'll be twice as worrisome if you try to keep me cooped up like a houseplant."

I smile as she pulls my hair aside to kiss my neck. "That's right. You need sunlight, lots of space, and someone to water you." Her kisses turn into a fae growl, and she spins back to the cot, bringing me with her. I fall on top of her, giggling and kicking my feet until she lets me go.

I flip myself over, my stomach growling as I straddle her hips. "We worked straight through lunch, but I'm nervous to eat anything else until they find the source of the food poisoning."

"It's already been found. Fortunately the affected potato crate was only used in one batch of stew this morning." Her smile dips, edging out into a flat line. "We'll have to toss the rest of the shipment, but that should keep the illness contained."

"Potatoes caused this?" I recall the word that kept bouncing around the tent today. "Fleeyeu? What does that mean?"

She draws in a breath, reluctant to tell me. "Blight."

The word slips under my skin, making my belly turn even though I don't have any other symptoms. "It's spreading from Lollishire, isn't it?"

"Yes."

When my godmothers and I last ventured into Heartshire, rumors were circulating about the tainted harvest, but that was miles away from here. I slide off the bed, pulling my thick socks on. "I need to look at that crate."

"But it's so cold out there, and you're already dressed for bed."

She takes one look at my face and decides not to argue, handing me my cloak instead. She's learned it's better not to ask too many questions when I've got an itch to do something.

Night is overtaking the camp quickly on one of the shortest days of the year. The torches and bonfires are going early, but it's quieter than usual with so many soldiers holed up in the healer's tent.

Shadows spill from Carabosse's shoulders and swirl around me. I straighten, borrowing from her air of authority as we pass the riders. They treat us with the proper formalities even though I'm traipsing around in my nightie.

The cooks are cleaning up their stations and prepping breakfast for the morning, but they jump to attention when they see us.

Carabosse addresses the staff, motioning to the warped crates behind them. A gangly young man carries one over to me, setting it at my feet. He scratches at the sandy hair sticking out of his fur-lined cap as he looks at me.

"Thank you, Melvin," I say awkwardly. The last time I spoke to him, I was a common girl from Lollishire trying to find my way home again. He looks like he's trying to comprehend how I got to be here, standing next to the Queen. The Commander.

I want to tell him it's alright to wonder. I don't really understand it either.

Kneeling at the crate, I pick up a potato and wipe off some dirt. Its rough brown skin appears normal and healthy except for a couple eyes. Squinting, I notice the thin, dull green lines webbing out from the sprouts.

And then there's a death rattle, a quiet whispering. *"We're still waiting. Come back."*

Dormant roots awaken inside my chest, their branches twisting inside my ribs. Rotten strands run through my hand and beneath the ground where I'm standing, pulling my mind back to the Hartwood. The forest is growing impatient and angry.

"Zelladine. Zelladine."

"Rosemary." Carabosse lifts my chin, bringing me back to the cold makeshift kitchen. Everyone is staring, their eyes flitting between the soft touch of the Commander's hand to the vines slithering past my sleeve.

If serving in the healer's tent is considered improper, then I'm sure that sprouting vines and snarling will reflect poorly on me.

But I'm at the center of this, even if there are only a few people who know my secret. I have a responsibility to fix it.

Carabosse snaps her face toward the staff, and they all return to their tasks—stacking clean cups and mixing porridge.

"There's a way to tell if the food is affected." I drop the potato in the crate.

Carabosse's fingers slide over my jaw before falling away. "The cooks have told me it's hard to see the blight marks."

"Not for me." I run my thumb against the glowing point on my index finger, the origin of my gifts. "I can check the crates when they come in."

"Will you be able to manage it?"

Those invisible strings are always vibrating around me. I've grown so used to the noise that I can usually tune it out when I'm grounded. "I'll have to. We can't throw out entire shipments, and everyone needs to know their food is safe to eat."

"Right. This winter will be harsh enough as it is. We should use our gifts where they're needed," she says, pride glowing through her serious expression. "Nylah will accompany you, just in case."

"I'm sure she'll love that." I draw my hands inside my cloak and pull it around me. "Speaking of harsh winters, I'm ready to get back to bed."

I roll my eyes suggestively toward the other side of the camp, and she hurries out with me, ready to get warm again.

26

ROSEMARY

A streak of dragonfire highlights the silhouette of black wings beating against the dark sky.

I usher the hatchlings into our tent, slipping a bed warmer beneath their blankets as they settle into their nest.

"Sweet dreams." I nuzzle my forehead against theirs. Carabosse likes to tell me I'm spoiling them, but sometimes I catch her patting their backs when they get up in the middle of the night and need to be tucked back in.

They're taking up more room in our tent. They'll need more space soon, but I can't imagine letting them sleep out in the open with the other dragons. Not at Claw Ridge. Not until we stop this fighting and get them home to the Dragon Valley.

I place another sheet on top of them, hoping the day will come when I can let them fly freely without the fear that they'll be hunted. Smoothing the blankets over their curled tails, I leave them under the guards' protection, my satchel bouncing on my hip as I run across the camp. Nylah sits on a log beside a fire, drinking from a mug. The scent of mulling spices drifts from its steam as she lifts a finger from the handle in a greeting.

She doesn't try to stop me as I head to the western peak. She already knows where I'm going and who will be waiting for me.

My boots squish into the muddy hill as I climb to the rocky base. Spring is still weeks away, but winter is loosening its grasp on Sarteal, and I can sense the first signs of life stirring deep beneath the soil, ready to bloom again.

I'm riddled with seedlings of anxiety each time I think about the wheel of the year turning to the growing season. There's still a curse that needs to be broken, a seed of magic that needs to be planted.

I'm waiting for a crow from Robin, but her messages have been few and far between. The rebels are struggling to take the King's City. Stefan might be dead, but his army is still funded by Lollishire's noble families.

I tell myself their efforts won't last. No amount of money will keep Stefan's young sons on the throne when the forest is rotting the kingdom.

They lost their true power when they lost me.

I search around the peak for Carabosse, the damp cold penetrating my gown. She's usually here within minutes after she hits the ground.

Pressure bands around my waist and spirals along my torso, spinning me around to face a wall of shadows. Carabosse steps through them. "Looking for someone?"

"Yes, my estranged wife." I tie my vines around her shadows, wrestling them away while keeping a hold on them. "You're two days late."

A thread of real concern is stitched into my playful nagging.

"I'm sorry, but there was an explosion in the Midlands. We

had to make sure the territory was safe from another attack before we left," she explains.

"Were you hurt?"

"No, a few of Dardaran's mercenaries tried to capture me, but they didn't succeed." She touches the torn hole on her sleeve and grins. "Those sellswords won't be collecting a bonus anytime soon."

"I'm glad you find attempts on your life so entertaining," I say.

"I do." Her grin grows. "Especially when they try to cut me with plain old steel."

"Ugh, you are—" So frustrating. So sexy. So damn determined to drive me mad with the way she tilts her head and bites her lip, as if having a target on her back is no big deal.

"What?"

"A pain in the ass," I quip and twist a single vine around one of her shadows, testing my strength against it.

"But I know you missed me."

"Maybe."

"Have you kept busy?" she asks, resisting as I tug on her magic. I raise two more vines, trying to surprise her, but her shadows are ready for me. My tendrils are pushed down to my hips as she walks me backward. These are the games we play when we meet—practicing, training, and pushing each other like nobody else can.

"Yes, I've stayed busy," I drawl, thinking on my feet. I curl three vines around her thigh. "A shipment came in while you were gone, and a few of the riders needed treatments for their sore throats."

"Wonderful. I didn't want to leave my little witch pining away for me for four whole days."

She says it jokingly, but spending time apart is agonizing, even if it's only for a few days. Getting to do this permanently still feels surreal, like we're both waiting for the rug to be pulled out from underneath us and throw us from our dream.

It's good to stay busy.

I tug on my tendrils, causing her knee to bend. It trips her up and knocks her off balance.

"Your little witch has outmatched you this time," I say with a haughty smile. "I win."

I take another step back, hitting the base of the peak as Carabosse falls forward, bracing her hand on a rock beside my face.

Angling her mouth over mine she laughs, "Almost. Maybe next time."

We careen toward each other, several days of pent-up need exploding through me when our lips meet. My fists curl into her riding leathers, pulling her closer, needing to feel her and know that she's really here with me. I breathe her in, catching the hints of fae sweetness beneath the smoke and leather on her skin.

Breaking the seal of our mouths, she does the same to me —dragging her nose down the side of my neck to scent me. She flicks her dark gaze to my face and inhales deeply, her lashes lowering as she presses her thigh between my knees.

Supported by the rock wall behind me, I sink down, lifting my skirt up to spread my legs. The notch between my thighs makes contact with an uneven surface. I spring up, my pussy throbbing.

"What is that?" I pull my skirt up higher.

There's a new band strapped to Carabosse's thigh, but it's not holding weapons. It's equipped with a bumpy pad that spans a few inches over the space above her knee.

"It's for you," she says, hoarsely.

"For me?" I swirl a finger over the pad's rounded ridges. It's firm but soft to the touch.

"The captain of the pirate ship we work with has a strange sense of humor. They sent it as a wedding gift." I know she's blushing in the dark as she whispers softly to me. "I was going to toss it, but I know how much you like grinding."

Bringing my arms around her shoulders, I lower myself down again, the pad pressing against the curve of my mound. I pause, feeling my pulse beating there.

I rock back and forth, enjoying the strange pressure. Moving my hips, I discover different ways to send those sparks of pleasure rolling through me.

"Keep riding," Carabosse coaches me, bumping her knee up higher, pinning me to the peak with her body. "Get yourself off on me."

I widen my eyes, staring at her as I do what I'm told, riding her thigh until the tension is coiled so tight in my lower belly that I can't even think clearly. A curved ridge slips past my clit, and it all unspools, leaving me a mewling mess, clawing at her arms and chest.

Her vision is so much better than mine in the dark. Her eyes are on me as I come apart, and she can see everything. Pulling back, she leaves me leaning against the peak, breathless.

"Fuck. *Yes.*" She sticks her thumb between her teeth like I'm a meal she's desperate to eat. Growling softly, she clicks her thumbnail off her teeth. "I'm not finished with you yet, but I've got to get Lieutenant Sampson up to speed on everything that happened in the Midlands."

"Sounds fascinating." I shake my cloak out over my dress and head back to camp. "Try not to keep me waiting."

I swing my hips, loving how I don't even have to check to know her eyes are on me. I can feel them burning into my back the whole way down, her shadows wisping around my calves until I reach the warm glow of the lamplight coming from inside our tent.

264

I part the hatchlings' curtain. They're fast asleep, Sun's tongue lolling out and their back claw thumping near Moon's belly.

"I wonder what you're chasing in your dreams." I pull the curtain shut, the rings still clinking on the metal bar when a deafening *boom* sounds from the other side of the camp. The ground rumbles beneath my feet, sending the hatchlings skittering out of their nest. The ringing in my ears is too loud for me to hear their screeching.

"Come with me." They're getting too heavy for me to carry, but they nip their teeth into my skirts, following me outside the tents. The two soldiers posted on guard duty tonight motion for me to go inside, but I look past them to the smoke swirling in the east.

Nylah stands with her sword drawn, her stance permanently changed by her healed injury. She leads with the other leg as she prowls in the direction of the explosion.

That's where everyone is going. Riders pour out of the tents and run across the camp.

"Are we under attack?" I ask the guards, slipping into the common language.

They don't understand. They wave for me to move back.

I listen to them, my heart pounding as I walk back inside and see shadows moving along the canvas. There are three silhouettes slowly creeping around the tent. I call out to the guards, trying to warn them.

I hear them shouting and grab a decorative saber from one of Carabosse's chests. There are probably better weapons inside, but this one is the closest. I adjust my grip on the handle, not sure how to hold it.

There's a grunt and thump outside the tent. I spin around with the curved blade as an arc of blood sprays across the canvas.

A sharp knife tip sticks through the opening, sawing through the privacy ribbons. They're deliberately trying to get into the Commander's tent while everyone is distracted.

I'm not going to stand here and wait for them to break in.

I charge forward, my dragons snarling defensively beside me. The last ribbon falls away, and the tent flap is torn open as I swing my blade, hitting a man's armored shoulder.

He hulks over me, all muscle in his cream thermal tunic and olive breeches. Thick eyebrows and a full brown beard conceal his expression, but I can tell he's unintimidated by me.

I bring the blade back for another strike, but he lunges forward and catches my wrist, shoving me away from him. Sun and Moon dart forward, their maws opening at the same time.

"No," I cry.

The man shoves his boot into Moon's side before they can release a burst of flames. Sun lets out a roar and chomps down on his leg. The man swings Sun around, trying to shake them off, but their claws are dug into his calf.

I rush forward again, my blow blocked by his gauntlet as Sun goes flying. Knocking the weapon from my hand, he picks me up and throws me over his shoulder.

"Let me go, you big oaf." I beat my fists into his back and scream, but there's no one here to help me.

The guards are dead. Everyone has left to deal with the aftermath of the explosion. Two more men are waiting around the tent. One of them flashes a greasy smile, stalking toward something behind me.

I strain my neck to lift my head. The dragons are coming after me.

"Go!" I shout to Sun and Moon. I don't know who these men are, or what they want from me, but I don't think they're above poaching. "Get out of here."

They don't listen to the commands I'm channeling to them.

Instead, they claw at the ground, staring down the fool who's whistling with his hand out as if they'll come to him.

Anger courses through me, hot and rotten. A vine whips out from beneath my cloak, barbs sharpening along its tendrils as it whips across my captor's face.

He curses in Sartealean and drops me in the mud to lift a hand to his cheek. His lips curl back to show his yellow teeth when it comes away bloody. I scoot back in the muck, trying to get up before his boot strikes me, but his march is halted by a black cord lassoed around his neck.

I glance over my shoulder, sensing my wife's energy. A vortex of shadows is moving closer, sending clumps of broken ground blowing in the wind.

Carabosse steps out from the darkness, shadows fracturing into diagonal strips that orbit around her body. Her eyes have gone black all the way through, but I feel it when they lock on me.

"Nyxtrystia. On your feet."

Her words don't just slip into my ears; they echo across my mind as she lifts her hand and brings the man down to his knees. I stand on wobbly legs, the cold ground squelching.

He fights against her shadows, but she knocks his knees out from under him, forcing him to lie prostrate before me.

She throws her left hand toward the men attempting to flee, holding them in her magic without even looking at them. Green light sparkles along her fingertips and in her eyes, but her nostrils flare in concentration and the embers disappear into the darkness.

She strides to them, the hatchlings hiding their heads behind my skirt as she assigns death in a murderous dance. With a few graceful swipes of her knife, the men are dead.

Wiping the glowing blade clean with a handkerchief, she crouches down to the man lying at my feet. He chokes out obscenities as she fists his hair and holds her knife to his throat, interrogating him in Sartealean.

"Klayvis," he spits, her shadows pressing at his temples, turning his eyes black.

Her grip goes slack on his hair as she pushes deeper into his head, but he doesn't try to get back up again. His mouth falls open, blood trickling from his nose and ears.

"What's happening?" I ask. "I heard a noise, and these men ambushed your tent."

"I know." She wipes blood from her nose. "Someone set off an explosive to draw attention to the other side of the camp, but I ran this way because I had a feeling..."

Wind rushes past our faces as Vencel and Snovida land beside us. Carabosse sets her ire on Nylah, and the lieutenant fires back, gesturing to the dragons. She left to get help. She was coming back for me.

My wife's anger deflates as she rolls her neck. "Nylah is going to take you and the hatchlings somewhere safe until I can get this sorted."

"Zelladine." The Hartwood calls to me, a network of mycelium strands whispering through the torn-up thatches. *"Stay with the wraith."*

I step in front of her before she can reach Snovida. "Where are you going?"

"To find whoever sent those men to do this," she says. "I saw where they were planning to meet when I looked inside that one's head."

I fold my arms. "Take me with you."

"Rosemary." She kneads her temples. "I can't bring you straight to the people who paid them to steal you."

I glance at the dead bodies. "They weren't trying to lure you to me?"

"No. They planned this attack thinking I would still be in the Midlands. They want you—the klayvis, the *key*."

I can smell Stefan's dusty tomes in my nostrils and see the inked script in the back of my head. I'm the key to keeping so many noble families wealthy and powerful. They want me badly enough to hunt me down in Sarteal.

"Then you have to take me. I want to face them."

"It won't be safe for you or the hatchlings."

"I trust Nylah with Sun and Moon, but my magic is urging me to go with you," I say, listening to the inhuman song humming through the grass. "I won't ignore it."

These are my gifts. My magic. The goddesses might tell me where and when to use them, but I won't let them be taken and used by mortal men.

Never again.

Carabosse could refuse, but she doesn't. Her teeth click together as she fights her fae instinct and says, "Let's go, then."

27

CARABOSSE

Spineless. *Whoosh.*

Foolish. *Whoosh.*

Human behavior. *Whoosh.*

I berate myself for agreeing to take Rosemary with me as Snovida glides over the marsh. Each thrust of her wings brings us closer to Dardaran's border and the danger we're facing.

Why am I doing this? I should have hardened my heart and sent her away with Nylah.

"I can hear you grumbling back there," Rosemary says, her hand sliding over my knee. "I know you're worried about me, but I never feel safer than I do when I'm with you. Thanks for listening to me."

I've been working on that—considering her wants as well as her needs. Watching her become more sure of herself these past few months has been satisfying. Finding purpose pleases her, and therefore, it pleases me.

Her hair blows in the wind as she turns her head, stirring up her natural fragrance—a reminder that she's not from

Faerie. Sun-baked soil and honey-sweet ichor flow through her veins.

A nymph from a Goddess' wild forest should always be permitted to fly free.

This is what she wants. Who am I to clip her wings?

I wrap my cloak around her and sniff her hair discreetly. Her scent is a balm for my soul. It soothes my frayed nerves as I search the dark swamplands below for the image I saw in the man's head.

Careful not to circle too close to the ancient royal city, I peer through the pale tangled branches until I see a small boat rocking beside a dock. I guide Snovida down to a marshy bank nearby, the ground sinking beneath her claws.

I help Rosemary step onto a cypress knee to avoid the rising pool of brackish water, navigating more cautiously than I usually do. I test the firmness of the bank a few feet further inland and wave her down to start walking toward a shack at the edge of the swamp.

Staying alert, I listen out for any sounds of footsteps or talking, but we're the only ones here. The shack is abandoned, its foundation warped from water and years of neglect. I guide Rosemary over the missing planks on the dock to the pirogue beside it. "Watch your step."

It creaks as we step in, and I pull the pole from the shell, using it to push away from the dock. Floating down the stream, I push the pole into the swamp bed to keep us moving.

"How far do we have to go?" Rosemary asks, gripping the gunnels.

"I'm not sure." I dig the pole in, pushing forward. "I only know the men were planning to meet another boat that's supposed to be docked somewhere in this direction."

"Did the man know who sent him?"

"No. It seems they exchanged money anonymously." His

employers wouldn't have revealed themselves to him. I could tell he was a professional at this from being inside his head for a minute. His mind was saturated with memories of him doing jobs like this—capturing people for flesh traders or hurting them upon request.

He deserved to die. I don't feel any guilt over it.

"Do you think Claw Ridge will be safe tonight?" she asks.

"Yes." The boat catches on a thick clump of mud. I press down hard on the pole to dislodge the hull. "Lieutenant Sampson will bolster our defenses, but I don't think there was any intent to cause real damage."

She shrinks, hugging her muddy knees on the bench across from me. "They were only coming to get me."

"That's what I believe." I give a vigorous push, huffing. "But no one is taking you from me when you have the protection of my body."

"Do you want me to take a turn with that?" she offers half-heartedly.

"No, thank you." I like channeling my rage and nerves into the movement. The water deepens, allowing me to switch to using the paddle. It cuts through the water easily, sending us moving quickly down the stream.

The waterway narrows as the banks close in, lamplight flickering over the clusters of dead cattails on their shores.

"Rosemary, someone is up here." I pull the paddle back into the boat, slowing our glide. "Come sit with me."

The boat sways as she crosses the few feet between us and sits beside me on the bench. I pull my hood down and lower my head as we pass through the wilted vegetation, the stream widening into a bayou where another boat is waiting.

Five cloaked figures are seated on the larger vessel. One stands in the stern, lifting a lantern as we drift past their bow.

"Did you find her?" a woman asks, leaning over the gunnels. "Is she alright?"

"She's fine. She's with me." I throw my hood back, and the woman holds her hands up as I snake my shadows over the water.

"Wait, Commander. It's me." She removes her hood, her copper curls wisping past her golden brown forehead.

"Lady Myrren?" I stare at the noblewoman, trying to remember some sense of decorum. "What's the meaning of this? I was just in your territory, securing the Midlands from any outside threats."

She nods, and I put the pieces together. "It was a red herring, meant to distract me. Who put you up to this? What do you want with my wife?"

Green fire sparks in the palm of my hand. *"It feels so good, doesn't it? To know you could end them all."*

Everyone in the boat pulls their hoods back and holds up their hands. I dissolve the flames, surrounding myself in shadows to study the faces of the allies that betrayed me. Count Sylvester sits next to Lady Myrren, his blond hair styled with pomade and his face freshly shaven. His mother was Mal's predecessor, yet he prefers wine parties to politics. Seeing him in a boat with two of his cousins makes me sick.

The duke and duchess have never acknowledged Queen Lucinda's wishes to honor the decision of the Vellessentere. They've been funding the efforts against us since we took to the sky.

"So that's it?" I ask Count Sylvester, waving at his cousins. "You're working with these fucksticks now?" I cock my head at Lady Myrren. "And you'd blow shit up in your own territory to help them after they cut you off from the biggest food source on the continent?"

"No one got hurt," Lady Myrren says. "We set it off where it wouldn't harm anybody."

I throw up my hands. "Ah. Well, that makes all the difference."

Count Sylvester cuts in. "I have nothing against you, but things have changed. Queen Mal is dead, and everyone is unsure who's ruling."

"I am ruling," I declare, the words needing to be said, even though they don't sit right with me.

"I'm sorry," the duchess says, her silk gloves folded neatly in her lap. "I won't call you my Queen after you deceived us for twenty years."

"I don't give a shit what you call me."

The duke pushes his golden spectacles up the bridge of his nose. "Then surrender your crown to someone fit to rule."

"Do you think I care about a crown? I'd gladly give it to someone else if I didn't think they'd give into corruption the moment they placed that circlet on their head." I touch my scalp. I don't plan on ever wearing the horned crown. "But there aren't a lot of people I trust to protect the most vulnerable among us, so no, I won't be relinquishing it."

"Enough," Lady Myrren says. "This isn't a debate over our kingdom's leadership. That can be discussed once we stop this blight from spreading. Even the crops in Dardaran have been affected. Our people will starve if we don't do something. The heirs to Lollishire's throne have informed us that *she* is the witch who can undo this."

"Send her back to her kingdom and make her fix this," the duke says. "We should've never broken our treaty and gotten involved in Lollishire's business."

Rosemary leans past my shoulder. The most fragile web of events has brought us together. If I'd never broken the treaty on my Queen's orders, I never would've met her. She'd have made it through the Hartwood with no one to save her from the guards waiting on the other side. She'd have been taken back to Stefan, and I'd probably still be here, empty and ignoring my doubts to serve my Queen.

Our chance meeting changed the course of everything.

"Did they tell you what they'd do to her?"

"No." Count Sylvester shakes his head. "They told us it involves the magic that protects them from the forest."

"They intend to bind her and steal her magic instead of letting her fix it." I move over, letting them see her sweet face. "She is a person, and you're sending her off to be drugged and abused by her captors. We've been working with Robin's rebellion to find a better solution."

"I'm sorry. I didn't know." Lady Myrren's mouth trembles. "When's the last time you heard from the rebellion leader?"

I think back to the last crow we received. The rebels have been too busy to write lately. "Two weeks."

"Sadly, Princess Roberta has been captured, and I don't think Prince Alex will be riding out to save her," Count Sylvester says. "The rebellion's funds have dried up. We have no choice but to work with Stefan's heirs and let Lollishire handle their own business."

Rosemary covers her mouth with her hand to ask, "What did he say about Roberta and Alex?"

I whisper the information to her, and she holds her hand to her chest, my ears pricking at the sound of a metallic *click*.

"She's one person," the duke says, pointing a flintlock pistol at me, its barrel half-cocked. "One person who can save the lives of many by leaving. Hand her over."

Rosemary clacks her teeth together, humming as she curls her fingers. Sharp, strange roots curl out of the water, creaking and groaning as primeval trees hidden beneath the swamp bed rise up to surround them. Long, slick ropes of decayed vines and branches wrap together, forming a net between us.

The duke aims through the vines, visibly unnerved by the glowing green threads of light that show beneath Rosemary's collar.

"We already have enough monsters living in this kingdom," he says. "We'll all be better off without her."

Fire dances in my palm again. I visualize them burning through the duke and snap my fingers.

He lights up in a burst of green flames, his body disintegrating into ashes that scatter over the uprooted plants and the bayou's murky surface.

The duchess holds her face in her hands as she screams, moving to her feet so quickly that the guard in the stern has to catch her to stop her from going overboard.

"Threaten my wife again and see what happens." Power rolls over my body in tantalizing waves as the flames loop between my fingers. *"You could keep going…"*

"Pull back." Rosemary tugs my arm. "We have to get to Lollishire before they snuff out the rebellion. We can't let its light go out."

Extinguishing the flames, I close my eyes and call for Snovida.

"There's no need to go to war over this," Count Sylvester says.

"I think there is. We've been playing nice for years with people who think they should rule after blockading our citizens and ruthlessly hunting our dragons." I send my shadows through the maze of vines and dead things. "There'll be no more mercy. I'm calling a truce for two weeks. If there are any attacks from Dardaran during those two weeks, then we will rain fire on your territory and burn this ancient fucking city."

"And what happens after two weeks?" Lady Myrren asks, composed despite the chaos of her surroundings.

"We'll meet to discuss how we're going to move forward with the monarchy."

"The only discussion I'll be having is with your head on a pike," the duchess shrieks as Snovida crashes through the trees, sending waves rippling across the water.

"Two weeks, and you can try," I say, making sure Rosemary doesn't slip as she climbs my dragon.

Her chest vibrates with a hum as she responds to a song I can't hear, calling her back to her kingdom.

28

ROSEMARY

"We're here on friendly terms," Carabosse announces. "Do not shoot at my dragon."

My stomach drops as we descend over the Restless River. I can sense how much this pace has changed before we even land. The trees have lost their enchanted melody, buzzing like flies on meat. The blight is poisoning everything.

Lit torches guide Snovida to the rocky banks near the prince's cabin, and a couple of guards jog over the jagged boulders to wave us in. They allow us to dismount without any issues.

I thought I made enemies of Robin's men the night I left, but they seem relieved to see me.

"We heard about Princess Roberta," Carabosse says. "Are there any plans to retrieve her?"

"Yes," one of the guards answers, his tunic worn and stained beneath his red breastplate. "Marian and the rest of the Merry Men have left with the three witches from the Ivy Keep.

They're waiting for you to arrive before they attempt to sneak into the King's City."

"They're expecting us? We never received a crow." I didn't know they were waiting. I would have tried to come sooner otherwise.

The guard smiles tightly. "It's been difficult to communicate since Roberta was taken, but Marian said she knew you'd turn up once you heard the news."

"She was right," I say. "Where are they?"

"I'm not sure," he answers. "They were heading to the royal territory, trying to find somewhere to hide."

"How are we supposed to find them if Robin's birds aren't flying?" Carabosse asks.

The other guard rubs his stubbled chin. He looks like he hasn't slept in days. "Code words and symbols marking safe spots where you can gather information. The rebellion might not have enough coins to back it, but we've built a strong network with our friends. Travel southeast towards the capital. It shouldn't be hard to track them down if you pay attention."

Carabosse runs her hands through her hair, making her strands stand on end.

This isn't the quest we were expecting, but I know she'll agree to it. She understands how important it is. For me. For everybody.

"We'll have to move quietly," she says as Snovida dunks her maw into the water, washing herself in the river's current. "We'll need horses."

"I'll bring them around for you when you're ready to leave." He tips his helmet toward the cabin. "Feel free to take whatever supplies you need."

We take the steps to the deck, and I grab the hoop of reeds resting against the railing. "This is Grace's invention. The hatchlings loved it."

"They've grown so much," she says. "She's going to have to make a new one for them."

"She'll be surprised at how big they've gotten." The hatchlings miss her. I see her face through our bond sometimes when they're curled up in their nest. I can't wait for them to see each other again.

I light a lantern and lead her through the cabin, showing her tokens of the life I left behind. "Diana used to sell these along with our herbal remedies."

She takes the needlepoint hoop from me, tracing her fingers over the half-finished robin. "It's pretty."

"I know. I never had the knack for it," I tell her. "Or the patience."

She snickers, following me into the kitchen. Open ledgers and journals are laid out on the table.

A lonely feeling rolls through my stomach as I flip through them, skimming over the broken plans of the rebellion.

"If worse comes to worst, we could find your godmothers and fly you to the Hartwood," Carabosse says. "You could break the curse on your own."

"Yes, but it would kill the movement, and so many people have poured their hearts into it." I hold a page listing the names of citizens recruited into the rebellion, and what the King stole from them. "Countless lives have been lost and families shattered. They need this win. They need a princess who will fight for them."

"We'll help them get her back," she says, and I know her willingness is all for me as she presses her fingers into the creases of a map. "Look, they've circled safe taverns and inns along the way. That should give us some idea of where we're going."

"How far do you think we can make it by dawn?"

She looks up from the map. "Don't you want to rest for a few hours?"

I scratch at the dried mud on my ankle, itching to leave. "I'd rather change my clothes and get moving."

"If you're sure," she says, drawing a short line and jabbing an inked circle. "Then we can reach this tavern in time for breakfast. Hopefully someone there can give us more information."

I go to the room over the stairs, taking a few of my godmothers' things in a hurry. I slip into one of Candide's gowns, and Carabosse finds a pair of brown riding breeches in the prince's room.

She tucks a white blouse into her waistband. The fabric is tight around her shoulders when she stands, but the plain-clothes should help us to blend in during our trip.

My wife rides beside me as we return to the forest I once fled.

We spend our nights riding through the kingdom, safe in Carabosse's shadows. During the daytime, we slip into taverns and nap in tin-roofed inns, picking up secrets and tidbits of information where we can.

On the sixth day of our journey, it's hard to ignore the signs of the blight. My chestnut mare canters past putrid stumps, moss sliding from them in gooey chunks. Our path to the next village is a narrow grass strip between mold-streaked trees and toadstools, their creamy white spots tinted olive green.

A house is visible through the wilted leaves. Black ivy creeps over its white brick siding and wraps around the wooden sign hanging over its back door. Its worn letters read *Maude Lindsay's Bed & Breakfast.*

"This is where the innkeeper said they'd be," Carabosse says, speaking quietly now that we've entered royal-held territory. It took us an extra day to find our way around the checkpoints, but we made it past the guarded areas safely. "I'll knock and make sure it's not a trap before I wave you in."

She jumps off her horse and hands me the reins. An arrow whistles past her ear, and she whips around, her blade drawn in less than a second.

"I knew you two would show up eventually." Marian steps out from behind an oak, uninhibited by royal customs and rehearsed mannerisms. She might've made a beautiful queen, but she moves more naturally here, a huntress in her element. She's dressed in green trousers and a cream blouse with a scarlet underbust cinched around her waist. The outfit suits her better than the fine silks she wore at the castle.

"This isn't exactly the warm welcome we were expecting," Carabosse says, pulling the arrow from the bullseye painted on a tree.

"Rest assured, I'm happy to see you." Marian skips over a moss-covered rock, her long braid bouncing over her shoulder as she lowers her bow to her thigh. "Now the rebellion has a chance to pull through. Let's get inside. Everyone is waiting."

We tie the horses and catch up to her as she pushes into the bed and breakfast. The back door opens to a den sectioned off from the rest of the house. Several of the merry men are gathered around a table, sorting their weapons.

I recognize Little John—the large man with a crude tattoo on his neck sharpening a sword. Willow Scarlet is throwing knives at a target on the wall, much to the delight of the woman sitting on her lap.

"Maude. Willow. Knock it off, or take it to your room," Marian snaps, and Maude hops out of Willow's lap, her cheeks rosy as she fixes her cap over her light brown curls. "The princess is still waiting to be rescued."

Willow spins her knife on the table and lifts a finger toward me. "Don't fret, Marian. We'll be able to get her soon."

Marian's lids droop heavy over her tired blue eyes as she bundles a sheaf of arrows. "Yes, we'll head to the King's City after supper."

"Tonight?" Carabosse asks. "How well have you thought this plan through?"

"Everyone likes to question my ability to lead the Merry Men, but I promise we would have won this thing quickly if we had even half of our enemies' funding. We've lost momentum because of money. Not me." She slips her quiver down her shoulder and drops the arrows in. "I've been thinking about this day and night. I haven't slept since they took the princess."

She barely gets the last word out. Pressing her palm down on the table, she closes her eyes. "They bring her out in that birdcage to humiliate her on the castle square at the same time each night. Willow, Tuck, and I will infiltrate the castle to rescue her when they bring her back, and Rose can run to the Hartwood with Diana, Grace, and Candide. Make sure they get there no matter what happens to us."

"That doesn't sound too complicated," I say, trying to sound brave to lighten the dark expression on Carabosse's face.

"And you believe the war will be won, just like that?" she asks.

Marian straightens. "The princess will be safe, and Prince Alex will be waiting for a signal from the priory. Once the prioress rings the bell, he'll ride into the King's City to declare that the curse has been broken. I think it will be considered a victory. Our people are tired of fighting."

"A signal from the priory?" I ask, untrusting of their clergy. I always avoided them when they walked through the King's City, preaching the importance of the Ivy Keep and praising the goodness of the May Day burnings. Just thinking of their self-righteous sermons gives me the creeps. "Doesn't the priory serve the monarchy?"

"Yes, but the prioress is Roberta's first cousin," she explains. "She's been working with us this whole time."

Carabosse grunts, noticing how untrusting I am, but she waits to see if I'll agree without any extra commentary. I extend my pinky until it touches hers. We'll get to do this together.

At the very least, I know she'll protect me. "It sounds like the best option we have."

Some of the light in Marian's eyes comes back. "I'll gather everyone, then. Your godmothers are in the kitchen."

"I finally get to introduce you to them." I grab Carabosse's hand, leading her out of the den. Her steps are much heavier than mine, her shadows swarming around her limbs as we move through the pantry that hides the room from the rest of the bed and breakfast. "Don't be nervous."

They don't notice us at first. Diana is chucking raisins onto the slab counter for Candide to knead into her dough. Grace is sitting on a stool in the corner, making a corn husk doll of the Tree Mother.

Our days have gotten all mixed up lately. I nearly forgot about the celebration of the midway point between winter and spring—the welcoming of the growing season.

Grace hums as she ties indigo-dyed twine around her doll.

"Pretty," she murmurs to herself, placing it on a bed of trimmed rushes before she looks up and sees us. *"Rosemary!"*

Diana and Candide join her, trapping me in their embrace.

My vines find their way into the huddle, creeping over their shoulders.

"What is this?" Diana asks, her face pinched as she touches a leaf. The three of them glance at each other as I give them the tamest version of my story, cutting out the parts where I fell off a dragon and barely escaped being killed by a sword-wielding fae woman.

"But it's fine, see." I wiggle my vines. "It's not a big deal."

They don't say anything. They just throw their arms around me again. I manage to lift my mouth enough to gulp down some air and say, "My wife is here, mothers. Please say something."

They stand back, craning their necks to see her face as I introduce them to each other.

Diana's teeth show in a half-smile. "Wow. It's nice to meet you. You're so…"

"Tall," Candide says. "And…"

"Spooky," Grace offers.

We all turn to stare at her, and Carabosse laughs. "I've heard that before."

Candide spreads more flour on the counter, keeping her head down to hide her flustered appearance. I can tell she agrees with Grace's assessment, but she doesn't want to be rude about it. "I was going to say *lovely*, but you make our chicken happy and that's what matters."

"Cheers to that." Diana takes a swig of rum and pours some into her bowl of raisins. "I guess your arrival means we'll be riding into the King's City tonight."

"That's what Marian told me."

She knocks back the rum again and sets the bottle down. "Then let's cast a spell of protection as we prepare the feast for the growing season."

"I'll let you have your time together," Carabosse says.

"Oh no. You're not going anywhere." I pull her to the counter beside me and hand her a paring knife.

"Where are the hatchlings?" Grace asks, looking in the pantry.

"They're with a friend in Sarteal."

"I was hoping to see them," she says, disappointment crossing her features.

"Soon," I promise. "We'll be sure to visit once this is all over."

Candide leans over her shoulder, pressing her cheek to hers. "Sun and Moon will be safer in their kingdom."

Grace nods, forcing her pout into a weak smile as she helps to make the soda bread, singing a song to welcome the growing season. I sort their bags of onions, throwing the ones affected by the blight into the bin. The rest gets passed to Carabosse who cuts them up while I start the soup.

It's not much, but with the blight, it's the best we can do. We use the items we have on hand to invite abundance.

When we finish, Carabosse and I carry the tray outside where the rest of the merry men are waiting. We set it on the ground as Little John gets a bonfire going. Settling down on blankets around the fire, we break bread with our hands and sit in the heavy silence.

We all know we're standing on the brink of something monumental. This movement will end up being a tiny footnote in our kingdom's history books if we can't do this.

"Zelladine, Zelladine."

A chill runs down my spine as I hear the call of the forest. Diana elbows me, pulling me from a trance.

"Here, chicken." She hands me her soup. "I can't finish it."

"That's a cute nickname," Carabosse says, broth running off her spoon.

"We started calling her that when she was little," Grace says. "She used to peck the food right out of our hands."

Diana chews a mouthful of onion. "She had a terrible biting problem."

Carabosse's cheek dimples as she sips from her bowl. "I'm well aware. It resurfaces occasionally."

I bump my knee against hers. "Don't tell them that."

But my godmothers' laughter breaks some of the tension. Marian turns to Willow, starting a conversation, and soon everyone joins in.

For an hour, we talk and eat like we used to when we'd stop for the night in some unremarkable village. We can pretend we aren't queens or witches or members of a worn-down army preparing to sneak into the King's City. Right now, we're just a family sharing a meal.

But that illusion doesn't last. Reality sets back in as the sky deepens to violet.

The Merry Men are gathering their dishes and fastening weapons to their bodies.

"I've got to pee," I declare, wagging a finger at Carabosse. "No, don't follow me."

She leans on her elbow, stretching her long legs. "Be careful out there."

"Don't worry," I call back, mumbling under my breath as I hide behind a tree, "It's not like you won't be able to hear me."

I come out a minute later and find that my godmothers have packed themselves into my spot, whispering something to Carabosse. Her dark eyes move to me as Candide draws back and pets her hair.

"Every day in the Ivy Keep, we'd cast a spell," she says. "We always wished for Rosemary to be well and happy."

"We hoped that she'd meet someone who would be there for her in the good times and the bad. Someone who would stick with her after her heart had been broken and help her to put it back together again." Grace cups her hands around Carabosse's. "Do you promise you'll take care of her when it's time to take her home?"

Carabosse looks around helplessly. My godmothers are pouring their emotions all over my poor wraith, and she doesn't know what to do with them. "Um, yes. I promise."

"Sorry, we're not usually this sappy," Diana says. "But it's so hard to send our girl away, and we missed the wedding."

"Know that I meant every word of my vows." Carabosse's gaze burns through me, as hot as it was on the day of our dungeon ceremony.

I thought it was a matter of survival back then, but she didn't simply speak those promises to me.

She's kept them. She's proved how much she meant them.

"There wasn't much to miss. We were wed at a small, private venue. There weren't any guests. Just us and a priestess," I say, passing an inside joke to Carabosse because it's the only way I can cope with this uncomfortable tightness in my chest. Everyone is being too earnest.

Her mouth twitches. She just gets me.

"How romantic," Grace sighs dreamily. She's always been fond of love stories. "The three of us made a vow to stay together when we were nineteen."

"Because you grew up playing in the same woods, and none of you could remember a time before you knew each other," I say, reciting the tale they used to tell me. "It was always the three of you until you found me."

Candide picks at a wilted blade of grass. "Yes, but we also had a few best friends before then. The witches of the Devouring Tree Coven."

When I was younger, I never gave much thought to their

lives outside of their roles as my guardians. Everything they did seemed to orbit around me.

Now that I'm older, I see them differently.

They've been through so much, and I know so little of their stories. They were once young women just like me who faced something harrowing at the hands of the King.

Who were they before they fled into the Hartwood to escape the burnings? And how much did they have to give up to protect me?

"Rina used to bring her spell books into our secret clearing in the woods," Grace says, and it hits me that Queen Rina wasn't a mere legend to them. She was a dear friend, a witch from their coven. "Even after Stefan took a shine to her. She had so many plans for the kingdom. She was brilliant."

Marian comes around with a lantern. She twirls a torch through the bonfire, using it to light the flame inside the glass cage before handing it to Candide.

"It's time to finish what she started."

29

CARABOSSE

The main road to the King's City is guarded, so we spread out through the woods, our lanterns blinking like amber fireflies between the trees. Walking to the east, the lonely path leads us to the rolling hills where Rosemary's apothecary used to be. We're close enough to the Hartwood to hear its mournful melody.

The last time I was here, it struck me with a melancholy feeling, but its tune has shifted into something raw and angry.

"The forest is tired of waiting for me," Rosemary says, her eyes wide and staring as her vines peek beneath her collar. Their ends brush against soggy bark and recoil into an S-shape to avoid it. "I can sense its impatience."

She picks up her pace like she's being called to move faster. I take her hand to keep her from being drawn into danger. "The forest has waited for centuries. Another hour or two won't make or break anything."

We take the slope down to the valley in staggered pairings to avoid being noticed. Brownish-green vines writhe over the

290

cobblestone streets and crawl over the buildings. Most of the shops are boarded up.

I've heard that most people have already left the city to escape the worst of the blight. Thankfully the seediest taverns have kept their doors open. Lamps glow through their glazed windows, providing some light.

A man in a cap swings out of a building with a bottle of liquor in his hand. I keep my arm over Rosemary's body as he sways past us to throw a few coins down at a market stall. An old woman with deep wrinkles and grey hair working above a single tapered candle pushes a rotted squash forward.

"Doesn't he know that will make him sick?' Rosemary whispers. "It's obviously infected."

The old woman sees us walking by and rolls another rotted fruit along her table. "End times are coming. Take your troubles out on the princess who caused this."

I hear metal sliding along a sheath and see the man they call Little John wrap an arm around Marian to stop her from drawing her sword. He pulls her along, belting out a bar song.

It's easy to blend in like this, slinking through the shadows under the guise of drunkenness. Our small groups stay far enough apart that no one would guess that we're together, but I always know where we all are as we step between the vines that slither around our feet.

The broken fortress of the Ivy Keep is our lodestar, guiding us to the other side of the valley. The square opens up below the broken castle—a paved space traditionally reserved for the May Day burnings. Vines run between the buildings on each side of the square, stretching into a moving canopy above the people gathering to heckle the princess.

Up ahead, the castle lies in ruins. The drawbridge lies open and broken over the moat, and the bailey walls are crumbling. Only the rectangular structure housing the chambers has remained intact beneath the net of ivy. We'll have to move under the cover of my shadows to escape the guards' notice and split up once we've entered the bailey.

Marian, Tuck, and Willow will have to make their way around to the back to enter the mausoleum while Little John and I assist Rosemary and her godmothers into the forest.

We bob on the edge of the crowd gathered around the giant birdcage. Princess Roberta is inside of it, shivering in a white shift.

The structure is hanging from an iron stand atop a square podium, swinging in the breeze. Two young men are standing next to the torches on the outer corners, clapping as people pelt rotten fruit at the princess.

They look to be eighteen or nineteen at most, dressed in deep green coats with gold tassels that offset their auburn hair. Their cocky smiles are reminiscent of Prince Alex's.

"Prince Richard and Prince Edward," Marian says, moving around us, her cloak concealing her back quiver. "The royal advisors must have put them up to this." The shadows of her hood deepen her grim expression. "They're practically kids."

Willow takes a sip from the copper mug she swiped from a man in the valley and tosses it. "I'll try to keep them out of this."

Marian rises on her toes, taking one more look at the princess before dragging her eyes to the priory—a short tower on the opposite side of the square. "I'll tell Roberta's cousin we're here. She'll ring the bell to summon the prince after we've rescued the princess. They should be bringing her inside the castle soon, so don't go anywhere."

She heads off to meet with the prioress. Tuck and Willow guard her by staying a few paces ahead and behind her. Rosemary and I remain in the crowd with her godmothers, staying on the fringe of things as the spectacle around the birdcage grows raunchier by the minute.

An onion goes flying and splats against an iron bar. "The city is a rotten mess. Make the princess pay for this!"

I can't blame them for their desperation. They don't know what caused the blight, only that it began after Stefan's death. They have to hold someone accountable for their strife.

"We'll all starve to death!" shouts a woman in a stained tavern maid's dress. She slingshots half of a pumpkin, sending it through a slat on the birdcage.

Roberta covers her face, flinching as it hits her hands and breaks apart down the front of her dress.

The crowd jeers, and Rosemary looks at her feet, her eyelashes fluttering. Brown ivy lurches past the castle walls, lurching toward us. A few vines snap down from the canopy above, startling people as they curl and hiss.

I see Rosemary trying to slip away toward the Ivy Keep.

"Block out the song," I murmur, rubbing her back to keep her close. "We'll give her a few more minutes."

Marian's blue cloak appears, a swath of cornflower flowing beneath the white archway of the priory. It disappears between a throng of men, blending in with tattered jacket sleeves waving bets on scraps of paper.

Another woman steps down from the priory a few moments later, her hair covered by a gold mantilla flowing over her green dress.

The prioress.

The royal emblem swings on her necklace as she pushes to the front of the crowd where the royal advisors are standing below the birdcage's platform. By the time I realize what she's doing, it's too late to catch her with my shadows.

A man in a royal uniform leans his bald head toward her as she whispers something in his ear. Roberta's last shred of hope vanishes before my eyes. She drops her hands from her face, letting her guard down as her cousin betrays her secret.

She might be kin to the princess, but Marian and Roberta have made a grave error by putting so much faith in the loyalty of a blood relative.

There's nothing to do but watch it all play out as it happens.

The bald man gestures to Prince Edward, and he crouches down, his mouth jerking into an arrogant smirk as he listens. Then he stands and clears his throat, his voice cracking with the high-pitched twang of late adolescence. "Listen up, loyal citizens. The time has finally come for retribution."

It takes all of his advisors and guards to get the crowd to quiet down. The prince puffs his chest, posing in a more assertive stance. "I've been told the Merry Men are among us tonight." The woman in front of me cups her hands around her mouth and starts booing along with everyone else.

Prince Edward crosses the platform to speak to his brother. Prince Richard dusts off the shoulder pads designed to make him appear broader than he actually is. "Would the Merry Men like to reveal themselves to save their beloved Robin?"

Roberta grips the bars of her cage, her curls hanging in limp curtains around her gaunt face as she shakes her head.

Prince Richard grabs the torch from the iron stand in the corner. "No? We can smoke them out instead." I squint past peoples' heads, noticing the dried straw strewn about the platform floor for the first time as the prince touches his torch to it. He steps back from the small fire and calls, "Come out, come out wherever you are, while you still can."

I hear a small squeak beside me and see Grace from the corner of my eyes. "Goddess, no."

"It's alright," Diana says, holding her by the shoulders to

turn her away from the sight. She looks from me to the Ivy Keep and mouths, *"We have to leave."*

It's a shame to abandon the princess to such a brutal ending, but there's nothing I can do to save her without risking Rosemary being captured by the princes. She has to return to the forest. The curse must be broken. Tears stream down Little John's cheeks as the princes climb down from the platform to watch the flames spread around its edges.

"It's over, then," he says, wiping his face with a hand-kerchief.

The princess is uttering a quiet prayer as smoke curls in wisps, a dove in a cage accepting her fate. She looks as stoic as Queen Rina did in Stefan's vision.

A knife goes flying into the bald advisor's head, knocking him back. An arm wraps around another advisor's neck, and a fist drags a knife across his throat.

Willow Scarlet appears behind the slumped body as Marian sprints through the cleared space. She leaps to the plat-form, springing from its burning boards to fling herself onto the birdcage. Clinging to its bars, she sends the whole thing swinging on its stand.

"She'll die up there," I mutter.

I believe this is truly the demise of the rebellion.

"It doesn't have to be," Vellesse says. *"You could destroy them all with me."*

A green spark shimmers along my finger. There are too many people on the castle square. I can't slay all of them.

The Goddess' voice echoes eerily through my head. *"You can if you let me in."*

It would be beneficial for me to sever the alliance between Lollishire's monarchy and Dardaran. I roll the idea around inside my head, knowing how wrong it is. Most of these people are civilians.

"Are you coming?" Rosemary asks weakly, touching my wrist. I deepen the shadows around us as our group breaks from the crowd.

A horn sounds from the valley below the square. A second passes in silence, and then there's another blast that has me looking over my shoulder to see what's coming.

The crowd disperses in all directions as horses gallop over the hill. Prince Alex leads the cavalry on his white steed, charging ahead without a signal from the priory.

I can see the fiery rage in his eyes through the nosepiece of his helmet as he yells for his militia to save the princess. We start moving toward the forest while everyone is distracted, trying to find the closest entry point.

I hear hinges creak on the birdcage and see the hatch swing open. It slams shut when Marian climbs in. Roberta helps her to push on it from the inside, creating enough of a gap for one of them to jump out of it. The fire is growing closer to the bottom of the cage.

Only one of them will live.

Alex pulls away from his horsemen, riding through the crowd. He's heading for the pyre, but the flames have already licked their way across the platform, destroying any chance of using it as a springboard.

He dismounts his horse and sprints up the iron steps leading to the burning heap, leaping to the iron bars, grabbing onto them with his bare hands. With a primal yell, he draws his legs up from the fire, pulling himself to stand on the edge of the base.

"They're going to make it," Candide says.

The prince steadies himself and turns around, pressing his back against the bars as he helps to pry the door open. He holds it as Marian and Roberta clear the flames and race for one of the horses.

"They really did it," Diana exclaims. We watch Alex hold onto the door, using its momentum to launch his body past the fire.

"Go, go, go," he says to his soldiers. "Protect the princess."

"Unbelievable." Rosemary snorts her relief. "Jackass prince."

His boots pound the ground as he runs after his troops. He doesn't see his brother chasing after him. He doesn't notice his sword until it runs through his back. A coward's attack.

Alex watches the crimson stain spreading across his tunic as Prince Edward draws his sword back.

"Don't look, darling." I take Rosemary under my cloak as blood pours from Alex's mouth. "Let's get you to the forest."

She's shaking as we pass over the drawbridge. The five of us and Little John are concealed beneath my blanket of night, avoiding the holes where we can see the moat water running below.

The fortress has been reduced to rubble in some areas. We find a collapsed spot and step in as my ears pick up on footsteps approaching. Holding our group in my shadows, I wave them ahead. I'll catch up once I'm sure no one is following.

Two guards are patrolling the wall. I listen in on their quiet conversation.

"The prioress said the wraith would be here" a soft, feminine voice says. "It's best to be prepared."

"How does one prepare to face a monster?" a man responds.

"It's ok, if you see her you can run away," the woman taunts. "I won't tell anyone."

That's irritating, but something tells me these two aren't too keen on hunting this evening. I move back against the rubble and pace toward Rosemary, feeling a sharp prick in the back of my neck.

I touch the dart pierced through my skin.

"Fuck." It's iron.

Groaning, I pull it out, but I'm stunned by a loud blast that leaves me tangled in an iron net. I claw at the thin chains, cursing the guard peering over the broken piece of a battlement.

He's holding a net gun, similar to the ones used to muzzle dragons.

My shadows fall away from Rosemary and the others as I'm cut off from my magic, leaving them exposed in the middle of the ruined bailey.

"Run," I urge them.

They do run.

They come running for me.

I press on the iron burning my skin. "No. Please go, nyxtrystia."

The guards who were on patrol outside the wall come jogging in. The woman points to me, and then Rosemary. "The prioress was right. The wraith is here with her bride. Take her and the witches to the princes. We can fix this."

Little John draws his sword, taking on both of them at the same time. The man is strong, each one of his blows landing with a heavy impact, but the guards are much younger than he is.

Their bodies are agile, and they're quick to wear him down.

"Rosemary," I yell. "Get out of here."

An arrow flies from another broken fragment of the battlements, striking Little John in the arm. He takes a step to the side, and he's hit with another one.

This time it strikes him in the chest.

"Don't pull it out," Grace instructs, but he's in shock. He rips it from between his ribs and drops into a seat, watching the blood seep out of the wound.

Candide pulls Rosemary toward the Ivy Keep, the four of them running toward the furthest point of the fortress.

My wife stops and looks back at me.

"Do what you came to do," I tell her, straining and pulling on the iron because I can see the guards coming after them.

Run faster, I will them.

Let them make it, please.

"We can make sure they get there together," Vellesse says as the male guard catches Grace. *"My gifts are not limited by iron like yours are."*

"Your gifts can't help me when I'm trapped." I push at the netting with all of my might, but I can't get out of it.

"I can handle the iron, but you have to let me in."

Rosemary shoves the guard away from her godmother. He lets Grace go and reaches for her instead.

I lose it.

I will not fucking let her get handed off to those princes. She will never get carved up and used for someone else's gain like I did.

I curl my knees up and kick my legs out as hard as I can, trying to break the chains. "I've already let you in. Help me already."

"The invocation only allows you to use a small portion of my flame," she says. *"If you want all the power to save them, you'll have to dig yourself down deep into the darkness and let me all the way in."*

I do not wish for any more power than I already possess, but I want to get Rosemary out of this. Closing my eyes, I summon the shadows inside of me.

It's always there—the thick and heady grief and anger I keep locked deep within.

"Dive into it, let it draw you in."

I think of the ripped patches of the Starlight Court, and

how swirling voids ate up every one of the sights and sounds I knew when I was a kid.

I can never go back there. I'll never see it again.

An oily feeling washes over me. I reflect on the things that make my soul heavy, using them as an anchor that pulls me down beneath the surface of my memories.

There's Nova's death and Mallory's. There's a broken promise to my Queen and how fragile she looked when she tried to kill me.

All of those things tilt me closer to the edge of a bottomless pit, but hearing Rosemary calling out for help sucks me into it.

My father appears in the abyss. Over the years I've forgotten the fine details of his face—his long black lashes and pearlescent skin. Seeing him now that I'm grown is almost like looking at my reflection.

This is the last memory I have of him. I'm straddling the line between our realms, and he's fighting to keep the small tear in the seam open.

"Pull back, Carabosse," he says, his eyes pitch black. "Pull it back before it consumes you entirely."

This time I ignore his advice, letting the shadows swallow me whole, until I'm no longer *me*.

Green light sparks through the infinite darkness. There's only Vellesse.

I'm a blank space, a mere host for a Goddess.

30

ROSEMARY

I flop around in the guard's grip, watching Carabosse struggle against the net. She writhes on the ground, her shoulders convulsing as the metal hisses against her skin.

Goddess, she must be in so much pain.

Twisting my neck, I lift my arm to bite down on the hand holding onto me.

"Agh."

He lets go, muttering a violent string of curses as I rush toward the net, but I barely make it two feet before I'm pulled back.

"Zelladine. Join us." The forest calls to me with rasping breaths. *"We're waiting."*

Roots crunch through the soil, cracking the paved stones of the bailey even further. The woman holding Candide motions to someone hiding behind the battlement above us. "Take care of the wraith already. We have to leave."

Torchlight shines on the helmet that appears in the crenel as a royal soldier lifts a crossbow into the notch, aiming to kill my wife. The ground quakes beneath us, sending stones skipping off the edge of the broken castle wall.

I scream as the arrow is released, following its trajectory. Its sharp tip is merely an inch away from Carabosse's neck when its shaft bursts into green flames.

The weapon disintegrates before it can hit her.

"What the—" The man releases me, running to exit the bailey as the same green fire sparks along the iron chains.

Carabosse isn't shaking. She's *laughing*.

With a sharp cackle, she unfurls her body, the iron melting and rolling over her head and shoulders. The chains dissolve into nothing. Green flames trace her outline and congregate around her hands.

Standing tall, shadows wisp over her clothing, protecting them from the heat. They swirl around her head and curl back from her temples, forming two black horns.

Rocks fly back as the guard who held me breaks into a sprint, but Carabosse snaps her fingers and his body lights up with a green spark.

She incinerates him in less than a second.

My wife strides toward me, her unhinged grin striking terror into my heart. I've never been truly afraid of her before. Maybe when we first met, but even then she was so careful to treat me gently and give me time to come out of my shell.

"Carabosse," I whisper. The look on her face is dark and menacing.

Embers sparkle in her black eyes—green stars against the darkest night. "No, it's me."

The voice that leaves her mouth isn't her own. It belongs in a cave buried deep in the underworld.

My godmothers squeeze in around me, free from the guards fleeing the bailey. Carabosse's fist closes, and a string of green flames whips through them.

"Yes." A stray arrow flies across the courtyard, but she flicks a finger without even seeing it. Several explosions go off, green lights flashing in random spots along the battlements, killing everyone still hiding. "It is time to set the forest free."

"Goddess, please release my wife," I beseech her. "I want her here with me."

Her eyelids close and shadows curl from her fingers, elongating into claw-like strips. "I will release her once you plant the Tree Mother's seed."

"It's ok," Candide says, kissing my forehead.

"We're here with you." Grace grips my elbow, leaning into me as we move toward the ruins of the Ivy Keep.

Diana's hand rests on the crook of my neck as she walks behind me. "Always."

Carabosse trails behind us, holding Vellesse's flames in her hands. They cast an eerie glow on the tower's broken cream bricks and stucco. Its entrance is sealed off with rotten vines that squirm over the fallen cylinder lying across the courtyard.

"You did that, my girl," Diana says, her words laced with pride. I've carried so much guilt for the blight, but I can't bring myself to regret the destruction.

The Ivy Keep has been the ultimate symbol of persecution for us witches. I'm glad the forest crushed it.

"These are coming from the forest," Candide says, walking over the bundle of vines beside the tower's base. "We can follow them in."

We move alongside the thick cords until we reach the breached portion of the Hartwood's boundary. The forest's song kicks up to a roar as we stare into the opening. Vines pour through it, spreading out into a web over the ground behind us.

I catch Carabosse's gaze as I look back, but she doesn't seem to care or notice. "I've waited long enough."

"Come join us, Zelladine." Ghostly hands reach out from the trees beyond the boundary. *"We'll take you to where you need to be."*

"I can lead the way," I say to my godmothers, and they file into a line behind me, our hands linked. Holding my breath, I take the first step, walking over the vines to cross the broken boundary.

The thrashing trees fight against their own momentum, their limbs creaking as they slow their movements to let us in. The vines hanging from their branches make dizzying circles, still catching up to the lack of motion.

We crunch over rocks, bones, and twigs, and I follow the silvery streak of a nude woman as she slips behind a tree. Acorns knock together along with her laughter. *"Come play, Zelladine."*

Vellesse's light paints the ghosts of the forest maidens in an emerald sheen. Their translucent faces shine through the fluttering leaves as they whisper to each other. *"She's brought the three."*

"The three."

"The three."

A winged maiden twirls around a trunk, moving like mist over the ground, her feet never touching it. *"Soon we'll dance forever beneath the trees."*

Another maiden swings her legs from a branch, antennae protruding from her forehead. They sway as she crooks a finger, guiding me. *"This way, Zelladine."*

I veer to the right to move beneath her tree.

Candide squeezes my hand. "How do you know where you're going?"

"The forest maidens are showing me," I say, glancing back. "Can't you see them?"

She looks puzzled as a ghost runs her fingers through her hair. "No. I can only hear their humming from the trees."

"Only you and Vellesse can see our ghosts." A maiden with a sash of toadstools growing across her body walks backward as she speaks to me. She waves to the Goddess and spins around, skipping off with her long hair swishing around her thighs. *"I can't wait to feel the sun-warmed dirt on my skin again. Follow me."*

The specters brush welcoming kisses on my cheeks and dance beside me, leading me through the labyrinth of the forest until we reach an archway of tangled roots and move into the copse below it.

The Tree Mother's spinning wheel is sitting on the forest floor, its sparkling threads dripping down onto the grass. My index finger throbs when I see it, calling me to its magic.

"Now that you're here, the three can explain the spell," a maiden says, her black braids falling over her shoulder as she tilts her head. Carabosse lifts a ball of flames over the spinning wheel, filling the hollow with its light. The maiden's brown skin and moth wings glow fluorescent. *"Tell them it's time."*

"This is where we'll perform the ritual," I tell my godmothers. "You're free to share the spell with me now."

I wait for them to speak as they spread out, forming a loose circle. Grace looks at me, then tips her face up to the moon. Its gentle light filters into the clearing, gleaming on her pale strands as she rocks back on her heels.

"There are no set words for the spell," she says. "They must flow from the heart along with the offering."

"What does the offering entail?" I ask. We're all wearing satchels across our hips, equipped with stones, hair, and bones from our collections.

"Blood," Diana says. "That is the first step."

I grab my knife from my leather pouch and hand it to

Candide. We pass it around the circle, and it comes back to me. I hiss air between my teeth as the blade bites into my skin. Blood trickles over my palm and drips onto the forest floor.

We're all bleeding.

"It is done," Candide says. We fasten our hands and step in closer, tightening the circle. "There's something we need to tell you, Rosemary. It's about the second part of the offering."

"But first we must tell you what happened on that night over twenty years ago, when we escaped the May Day feast," Grace continues. "This is our story."

Diana's bloody palm slips against mine. "When we ran to the Hartwood and threw ourselves at our Goddess' feet, we were seeking a chance to serve her. Not mercy. We thought she would make us her vessels and channel the remnants of her magic through us, turning us into weapons of revenge."

Candide pulls on my hand until we make eye contact. "But we were led to a cage of tree roots instead. When they opened, we found a girl child nestled inside, sleeping sweetly and untouched by age, as if time had been frozen in the forest."

"The Tree Mother's vessel had already been chosen," Diana says.

"We didn't know what we were supposed to do." Grace lifts a shoulder. "But then a spirit possessed my body and spoke through me, giving us instructions on how to break the Hartwood's curse and set the forest free."

Sweat prickles along my skin, chilling in the cool air. I can almost remember a cocoon of roots surrounding my body and waking up to see three faces peering down at me. "What were the instructions?"

"To take the vessel and raise her as a human for twenty years." Diana seems ten years older than her actual age tonight. Her green eyes look impossibly tired. "Then we were supposed to bring you back here to return you to the soil from which you came."

My tongue sticks to the roof of my mouth as the ground churns beneath me. "What does that mean?" There's a pregnant pause, the silence swelling with dread. "Candide?"

She takes a short, sharp breath. "The spell demands an offering of your human memories, your human heart, and your human body. We were supposed to let you come here and be reborn again from the soil like the other forest maidens."

I open my mouth. Only an aching whimper comes out.

"My memories? That means I won't remember anything." I look to Carabosse who stares back coldly, her expression still possessed by the underworld's Goddess. "And I already gave up my human body. What will happen to me?"

More maidens have snuck into the clearing. They fill the spaces between the trees, sending vibrations running through my body as they whisper, *"We've been waiting for so long, Zelladine. You are the key."*

"The key."

"The key."

My time in the human world was always meant to be temporary. The forest maidens will continue to wander as ghosts if I don't surrender myself as an offering. The people I love will starve and suffer as the Goddess' gifts dry up completely.

"Rosemary," Grace starts.

"No, it's ok," I sniff, a tear rolling down my cheek. I look at my wife, but it's Vellesse who cocks an eyebrow back at me. "I know you're in there, nyxtrystia. I know you'll be angry. But one day, when your long fae years have dwindled away, come lay yourself down in my soil. I'll be here. I'll remember."

A soul cannot forget. I'll find a way to bloom again and sprout between her ribs.

"I'm fine now," I tell myself aloud, my fingers twining between Diana's and Candide's. "I'm ready to make my offering."

Candide squeezes my hand tightly. "We're not going to let you give yourself away."

I open one eye. "What?"

"We decided years ago we wouldn't," Diana says. "To the Goddesses, you might be a spellbreaker, a key."

Grace rolls her lips between her teeth. "But we are your mothers. To us, you are simply our beloved Rosemary."

"No, you don't have to do this," I argue, trying to hold on as tight as I can.

"We offered *ourselves* to be vessels. Not you. Never you," Diana says, with all of the firm sternness she raised me with. "When we're gone, plant the seed and free the forest, but most importantly, be happy." She nods to Grace and Candide, throwing her voice as she intones, "Tree Mother, we come to amend our offering. Spare our daughter and take these things from me." She lifts our clasped hands, watering the soil with our blood. "A mother's memories."

Candide raises our hands up next. "A mother's heart."

"A mother's body." Grace lifts both of her arms, and a breeze sweeps through the brush, swirling around our ankles and spiraling to encircle us. "Take our gifts and multiply them by three."

"By three," Diana repeats.

"By three." Candide's incantation rings through the clearing. "As we will it, so mote it be."

A gust of wind rushes around our necks. Our hair floats up toward our clasped hands. The Goddess' gift lives inside my heart, and now it flows through them. They repeat the chant, infusing it with all of their stubbornness, willing the forest to accept the offering.

"By three."
"By three."
"By three."

The soil rises over their ankles, but it stays firm beneath me. I try to hang on, to stop them from sinking, but they stare on, refusing to show a hint of fear.

"Mothers," I breathe. I was left here as a little one, alone until they came for me. They were the ones worthy of breaking my sleeping spell for a reason.

The ground is opening into pits around them, pulling them in. I have to crouch to hold their hands. *No. No. No.* I don't want to see them pulled beneath, to think of them smothering beneath the dirt, unable to breathe.

"Do something, please," I cry out to Carabosse. "Don't let it hurt them."

She lifts her chin, her shadowy horns billowing like smoke around her head. Her eyes sparkle as she makes a fist. Green light floods the clearing.

I tighten my grasp, digging my fingers into nothing.

My hands are empty.

I turn back to the circle. It's nonexistent. The women who raised me with the purest love in their hearts are gone. Taken in an instant.

"No." I clutch at my aching chest.

"The forest accepts their offering." Vellesse's voice booms from Carabosse's mouth. "Now you must plant the seed."

I want to rail against that demand and scream, but my defiance is shriveling. My godmothers made this offering. They did it for me, and in the end, it has to be worth something.

I kneel and press my hands to the ground, not allowing my tears to spill. I'll keep those for myself.

"Set us free, Zelladine," the maidens coo. *"Release us from our sleep."*

I tunnel my fingers into the soil, sensing worms crawling through the crust. I feel the forest's magic humming on thin strands, all of them running to a jewel tucked away deep inside me. Remembering Grace's words, I begin to speak, letting my spell flow naturally.

"Receive our offering and take the Goddess' beating heart back into the forest," I whisper, numb from the shock of sudden grief. It makes it hard to tap into the Goddess' energy.

I stop for a moment, swallowing.

This moment was made possible by so many people. Not just Diana, Grace, and Candide. I wouldn't be here if it weren't for all of those who came before me who wanted to see the forest freed.

I think of the quiet rebels and the families lost to the burnings. The witches who spent their lives in the Ivy Keep. Maids and guards who never had any choice but to serve a corrupt monarchy.

I remember the rancid smoke of the May Day feast, and a cook who handed me a pastry with hope in her eyes despite everything.

It's been a centuries-long effort, this rebellion. I won't let our sacrifices be in vain.

Warmth radiates behind my sternum and tingles through my limbs. I let it flow down to my fingertips, pouring twenty years of love and hope back into the forest. "Restore the fertile soil from which life begins."

My vines hug my arms as the Goddess' gift trickles through the ground, replenishing the roots and mycelium strands with the magic of growth, rebirth, and death. Behind my closed eyelids, I can see healthy bark patching itself over rotted tree trunks. Spoiled seedlings transform into green spirals, curled up and waiting to poke through the ground when it's time for spring. Toadstools drill out of the soil in a circle around me, singing joyfully.

"Zelladine. Zelladine."

I push further, feeling the Goddess' power spreading. There's a thundering roar as the forest pushes past the magical boundary, the bricks of the castle collapsing in the distance. Trees erupt from the ground, the forest blanketing the valley and overtaking the buildings.

It rushes out of me, bottoming out rapidly. With the last bit left, I make my own quiet wish, one that I'm too afraid to even acknowledge.

There's a crack inside my ribs, and 1 lie down as violets sprout from the frosty detritus, the first blooms of the growing season.

My hand is covered in blood and dirt, but I raise it to my brow and squint against the breaking dawn in the middle of the night.

A woman sits at the spinning wheel, her hair like sun rays stretching over a hill, her curves aglow.

I can't see her face. Her light is too radiant.

"Tree Mother?" I rasp.

"Yes." She stands, her brown skirt trailing over a carpet of decayed leaves. "You did it, Zelladine. You restored the heart of the forest and freed us from our cursed sleep."

"Mokosh." Carabosse walks past me, placing one hand on the Goddess' waist and another on her shoulder. "We've finally made our way back to each other."

"Wait, no," I protest. "You said you'd give my wife back to me after the offering."

She ignores me and continues, "None of my forms can last for more than a few hours in this realm, but this one will." She runs a hand over Carabosse's abdomen. "This one is made of darkness, and I can live inside it for centuries before I need to retreat to the underworld again."

It was always meant to be a tale of the dragon and the devouring tree... Those words come back to haunt me as the forest maidens dance around the hollow, their bodies opaque and their inhuman oddities vibrant.

They don't seem to notice my grief.

"Please give her back to me," I beg. "I've done everything that's been asked of me."

"All of my other maidens are so happy, but you are not." The Tree Mother's golden light shines on my face. "Why is that?"

"She took my mate's body," I accuse Vellesse. I hate that I sound like a toddler throwing a tantrum before two Goddesses, but I think I'm going to be sick. "She promised she'd let her go."

"Is that true, my love?" Tree Mother asks.

"It is. I would do anything to get back to you." Vellesse's smirk curls on my wife's beautiful lips. "You know that."

"I do." The Tree Mother's fingers hover near Carabosse's face, her rays mixing with her shadows, although they're not quite touching. "But you can't ask her to give up more than she already has."

"What are you saying?"

"She's not like the rest of the maidens. Her heart can be broken like a human's."

Carabosse goes rigid, her irises shrinking to the center of her eyes. "Rosemary. You will not break. I'll find my way back to you."

Her face distorts with an expression I've never seen her wear before, her eyes blacking out again. It's Vellesse's voice speaking when she says, "You've always taken too much pity on the humans who come to the edge of your forest, asking for blessings in exchange for their little gifts."

"It's hard to live on this plane and not take pity on them. Mortal life can be so cruel, but so beautiful in a way we'll never understand." She faces the west, where the humans dwell beyond her borders. "Let these two have their long centuries together. A demi-mortal and a creature of Faerie will not outlive our eternity."

The underworld's Goddess leans against a willow, unmoving in my wife's body. "You were torn from me. I cannot leave."

"If you love me, you will," the Tree Mother says. "I could never bear to crush a maiden's spirit."

"We will make it work like we used to, then." Carabosse's body casts a shadow of a giant dragon. "But when this world ends, I will twist you back into myself, never to be parted again."

The shadow dragon rears back on its hindclaws, its wings stretching across the clearing to rise above the treeline. Shooting a burst of green flames into the night, it breaks into wispy clouds, and Carabosse slumps to the ground.

"Rosemary." She crawls on her belly until she can get to her feet, taking me in her arms to crush me against her chest. "I saw everything that happened. I'm so sorry."

I scrunch my hands into her blouse. I can't talk about it yet.

The glare softens around the Tree Mother's face. Her full lips are the color of a rust-red leaf in autumn. "Are you sure you want to venture out into the human world again?"

"I'm sure." I don't know how long I can stay here. Pressure is building behind my left eye and pounding at my temple. "If you don't mind, I'd like to get going."

"Ah." The leaves shudder above us. "You're always

welcome to come home and dance. If you ever need us, just pluck your strands."

Magic crackles through my veins, that web of energy still present inside of me. I thought it would disappear when I cast the spell, but I can still hear the plants and what they're saying.

"That is *your* gift. You were made from the forest," she says, noting my confusion. "A piece of the Hartwood will always be inside of you, Zelladine. But you are free to leave."

She beams her light through the trees.

"Thank you, Tree Mother," I murmur, although I'm too exhausted to feel grateful for anything but my wife's arms around me. I want to get away from this place and the beings who call me Zelladine.

"One more thing," the Goddess calls as we're leaving the clearing. "I heard your wish. It's possible, as long as they want it."

"What wish?" Carabosse asks.

"I—" My throat is too tight. I can't get the words out.

"It's ok. We can talk later," she says, and we walk on through the forest with only the moon and the maidens to show us the way out.

"Follow us, Zelladine," a maiden sings, her feathered wings fluttering as she tosses violet petals in the air. Singing the song of the forest, the maidens guide us through a tunnel and over a fallen log.

They fête us with snowdrops and crowns of ivy, but I feel almost as though I'm merely trying to survive the night like I did the last time I was here. I keep looking for three faces that don't exist.

"I think you need a break," Carabosse says, dropping her rucksack to her hip.

"No, I have to keep going."

"I know." She holds her bag out by the strap, indicating for me to put it on. We didn't pack much, but my spine bows beneath the weight. She's right there to catch me, her knees bent to let me climb on her back.

She hoists my thighs higher around her waist. "You good back there?"

"Yeah. I'm good." I hang onto her shoulders, lulled by the steady rhythm of her marching. I give up on my search and listen to the sound of her breathing.

A forest maiden with a kaleidoscope of eyes on her forehead points to a cluster of bushes gathered between a line of oaks. "You're almost to the boundary."

I sigh against Carabosse's back. This is where I'll leave my godmothers. When I'm out of here, I'll grieve for them.

Twenty or so young women race by us in flowy white dresses, giggling as they play a game of hide and seek. All of them have dark eyes and golden hair like me.

"Are those the girls who—" Carabosse can't finish her question.

"Yes." Those are the girls Stefan sent to the Hartwood when he was searching for me. I wanted them all to have a chance to be happy and free.

"Excuse me."

I lift my head, and Carabosse stops in place. That maiden sounds exactly like Grace. Something rustles in the holly bushes, and a woman looks out from behind a tree, her long blonde hair swinging past its trunk.

"Grace?" I slip down from Carabosse's back and run to her.

She smiles at me. "Is that who I am? I just woke up here, but I feel like I know you from somewhere."

"You do seem familiar," Diana says, lying on a branch above me, her leg draped over the side. "I think I saw you in the most wonderful dream."

Candide pushes through a cluster of pine needles, the ever-greens covering most of her body. "Yes, I know you in my soul, just as I know those two. Are you going to stay awhile? It's almost time to dance and usher in the new day."

Tears sting behind my eyes threateningly. "Not now. I have to leave."

"Maybe another time?" Diana suggests.

"Yeah." I nod. "Another time."

Grace disappears behind the bushes and sticks her head back out again. "Here, I have a gift for you. It's for protection."

I take whatever she presses in my hand and leave without saying goodbye to them. They wouldn't understand. I wait until we're at the edge of the forest's boundary to uncurl my fingers, releasing a green sprig's pungent scent.

Carabosse pulls off one of its spiny leaves. "It's rosemary."

31

ROSEMARY

The forest spits us out where our story began. Its roots have broken through the black stone border, pushing the cursed rocks an inch further into a wood I know like the back of my hand. The sun is rising over a familiar line of stepping stones, and when I hop up on a stump, I can see the scorched remnants of the Briar Apothecary.

A horse cart is parked in front of the charred wood beams. Marian sits on the tailbed, kicking her feet in the dirt while Roberta pours alcohol over a gash in Willow's arm. The princess is tearing a strip of linen with her teeth when she sees us approaching. I hand her the shears from my satchel and find a jar of salve for the assassin's wound.

"You made it," she says. "I thought we might find you here."

"The forest took the valley and reclaimed its natural boundary, wiping out the King's City," Marian says, taking a drink from her canteen. She tips it toward me, and I catch the scent of whiskey pouring off her breath. "Congratulations. You broke the curse."

"What's next?" Carabosse asks.

Marian sets her canteen down. "Princess Roberta takes the crown. There's no one left to challenge her, so she can claim it on her own."

"Prince Richard and Prince Edward didn't make it?"

"No. They were crushed by the forest. It's a good thing most people had already left the city when you broke the curse. We had to ride like the devil to get out of there alive," Roberta says.

That means some people didn't. There was a whole mob gathered on the castle square. I told Carabosse not to burn the city, but I destroyed it.

Marian passes me her canteen. I gulp a mouthful of whiskey, letting it burn down my throat to numb the guilt and grief.

"Did your godmothers make it?" she asks.

I shake my head. They're alive in their own way, but not the way I remember them.

"Little John?"

Another gulp of whiskey. Another shake of my head. "Sorry."

"Yeah." She swings her legs back and forth over the side of the cart. "Tuck too. There aren't many Merry Men left."

Willow winces and flexes her fingers as Roberta wraps her arm. "But the Hartwood has taken its land back. We can officially end the burnings. It's what they would have wanted."

"Yes, all of them. Including Prince Alex," Roberta says. "He left a long will with his wishes for the kingdom in case he succumbed to an untimely death. It's almost as if he knew this would happen."

I take one look over the side of the cart where he's lying stiff and lifeless. They've folded his blistered hands over his chest.

"Maybe he did." Maybe he knew his bloodline had to end.

"You're not planning on staying in Lollishire, are you?" Marian asks. "It might raise some questions or draw attention away from the princess if anyone finds out what happened."

I don't care who gets the credit for healing the forest. I just want to get out of here.

"No. We're not staying." I bring my hands to Carabosse's waist. "Can we go home now?"

Home is anywhere with her. Anywhere but here.

"Of course, darling. I've already called on Snovida."

We sit on the stump and wait, away from the rest of them.

I go through the motions of mounting the dragon, not letting myself fall apart until we're flying away. But I do fall apart, hiccuping sobs racking through me as the night's events come rushing back in.

Carabosse's arm moves around my waist, locking my back against her body. "I know. I know," she says. "I promised them I'd help you to pick up the pieces of your broken heart," she whispers against my neck. "I don't care if it takes five, ten, twenty years. A lifetime, even. I'll hold you through the worst of it. I'll always be here to help you put yourself back together again."

32

CARABOSSE

"I'll be back in time for lunch tomorrow if you'd rather wait here with Poppy and Felix."

"Nice try," Rosemary says, pushing another pin through the coils of hair she's spent the past hour twisting and piling haphazardly atop her head.

The long bell sleeves of her black gown hang over her hands as she sticks her gifted gold stud earrings through her lobes, attaching a chained cuff to her left cartilage. Her dress is scooped out in the back, and her vines are on full display, crossed into a neatly corseted pattern along her spine. "But you're not getting rid of me that easily."

She turns to me, fierce and determined. A wild nymph in mourning.

She's only left the tent to take a few short walks with the hatchlings this week, preferring to stay hidden beneath our blankets. It's good to see her up and moving, even if it's to prepare for a flight to the Midlands.

I'd argue that it would be safer for her to stay here while I attend the Sartealean council meeting, but I know she'd never agree. "I'm glad you're coming with me."

"How do I look?" Her eyes roll upward, emphasizing the hollows beneath them. "Like death warmed over, I presume."

I pull her black velvet cape over her shoulders, fastening the dragon pins on each side. I kiss her throat above the two fine golden chains hanging between them, feeling her swallow. "Like a queen without a crown." I kiss her cheek. "The queen of my heart." I long to kiss her lips, but there's an air of sadness around her, something delicate. She responds better to soft touches, so I brush my thumb over her mouth instead. "The queen of everything."

Fidgeting with the pin on my uniform, she rises on her toes and presses a kiss to my lips. It's a quick peck—done and over with in two seconds, but that look in her eyes as she drops her heels is what makes it feel intimate.

I taste her as we take off for the Midlands, the hatchlings flying along Snovida in their harnesses, their wings getting stronger every day. Nylah rides Vencel behind us, providing backup even though this is supposed to be a diplomatic meeting. We're willing to fight dirty if they try to pull something with Sun, Moon, or Rosemary.

The dead plains of the Midlands stretch out below us, pale petrified trees twisting out of the cracked, grey ground. A castle sits on a mound of dirt ahead, its walls well-maintained despite the state of the field below it.

The Sartealean nobles are gathered in the patch of dead wheat instead of convening inside the building. Snovida lands in the wilted crops that grow stubbornly every year even though they never survive long enough to make it to the harvest season.

This was once a great farmland before Gentrilly's bombs

destroyed it during the Queen's War. Now everything dies as soon as it blooms.

"Commander," the duchess from Dardaran greets me as I dismount. A few of the council members murmur, "My Queen."

I check the sky and the parapets, looking and listening out for any threats. Nylah dismounts behind us, moving in to protect Rosemary.

Lady Myrren moves away from the rest of the council members, her hands clasped at the tight bodice of her traditional Sartealean dress. Her face is serious above the high collar buttoned all the way up to her neck.

"Is there a reason we're meeting outside today, Lady Myrren?"

"Yes. I want everyone present here today to understand the severity of the situation," she says, the fire in her voice making her speech sound genuine, impassioned even. I haven't forgiven her for her stunt in the swamp, but I understand her desperation. "This is what we're facing in the Midlands if we cannot come together to solve this problem. Scarcity. Starvation. There are reports that the Hartwood's curse has been lifted and that nature is healing. However, it's of little consequence when we're still being blockaded by Dardaran. It's been a hard winter. People are at their wits' end."

The nobles look out of place in their fine clothes among the withered stalks. Count Sylvester tugs on the lapels of his silk coat. His cousin, the duchess, scowls, looking down at her ruined slippers. "There is a solution," she says. "We will share our resources more freely with the kingdom, as long as you agree that *that* one should not be wearing the crown."

I glare at the finger she's pointing at me, and she drops it, her face paling. "As you can see, I'm not wearing a crown. I'm too busy working to defend the rest of Sarteal from your territory's actions."

"You admit that you ignore our customs," the duchess says. "Our traditions. You lied to us, and everyone is confused about who's ruling. There hasn't even been a coronation."

"I haven't had much time to throw a parade for myself," I say through my teeth.

"No, but you flew over Tresoran on your dragon to make your announcement."

At the time it seemed like an efficient way to do it, but I can see how it might have seemed frightening to the people on the ground.

"This isn't going anywhere," Lady Myrren interjects. "I don't want to submit to the royals of Dardaran after they've caused so much suffering, but I don't know how to trust you, or anyone else, for that matter, with so much power."

I rub my fingers together. Vellesse's flame still flickers inside of me, but I don't feel her constant urging anymore to use it and let it consume me. She's not trying to use me.

I've seen what the Goddess' gift can do, and it's scary. Even for me. "I understand that."

"What do you propose, Lady Myrren?" Count Sylvester asks, pulling a cigar from his jacket's pocket, even though there's nothing to light it with. "I'm assuming you've thought of something."

"I'd like for each of us to come up with terms for a new peace treaty within our kingdom," she says. "I propose our reigning monarch becomes a figurehead who acts in all of our best interests, only making deals with other kingdoms once we've all voted."

The duchess laughs. "I vote we get rid of the wraith as fast as we can. No one should be able to end someone with a flick of their hand."

"We can't stop Vellesse's flame, Winifred," Count Sylvester says, gnawing on the tip of his cigar. "There'd be another tournament, and it would go to someone else."

"That's right." Lady Myrren touches her dragon pendant. "The Goddess chose her to protect the Dragon Valley, and we must find a way to honor that."

The Goddess' reasons for choosing me aren't as pure as I hoped they would be, but I still plan on keeping my promise to wield her flame justly.

"I want peace in the kingdom as much as you do," I say. "I'm willing to work on a new treaty with everyone here."

There's a screech in the distance that sends the council members into a panic. They grab their skirts and stumble over each other, trying to get back to the fortress.

A lord from Trisikan looks up as three wild dragons fly in. "Is this an attack?"

"No. Wait," I call. It's rare for dragons to present themselves to people, especially in group settings. Having a triad show up like this is important.

They land at the same time—two pale blue beasts with golden wings, and a pink one I've met already.

I thought she died years ago.

She lowers her maw as I hold my hand out, and I watch Nylah's eyes widen. Rosemary comes up beside me. "This is the dragon who saved me when Thea tried to kill me. Do you know them?"

"Yes, this is Brona," I answer. "She was Nova's dragon."

Brona bumps her snout against my hand and turns, stalking toward Lady Myrren. Terror ripples beneath the noblewoman's brave face as the dragon bows her head.

"She wants you to claim her," I explain. "The dragons don't want to wreak havoc. They want to bond with their riders and fly freely through the Dragon Valley. We can rebuild and turn it back into a place of legends if we can ease their fear of being hunted."

Lady Myrren lets the dragon sniff her trembling hand. "That can be a part of our discussion."

"I can't believe this," Winifred says. "I will not agree to this plan. You can't convince me to look after the beasts just because you got a dragon all of a sudden. Three kingdoms support our family's claim to the throne. We have enough money and resources to make this last as long as we want to. How will you stop us? By snapping your fingers and burning us out of existence?"

I'd like to, if only to get her to stop talking.

But I know she's challenging me. I won't give her what she wants. Threatening to use the flame again will do more harm than good.

I massage my neck as the nobles squabble and make demands, anticipating the long months of fighting ahead. I can't see this conflict coming to an end.

The camp at Claw Ridge was supposed to be temporary, but we've been there for years.

Rosemary steps slightly in front of me and drops to her knees, placing her hands on the ground. Bushy green leaves sprout from the cracks in the dry soil, overtaking the dead wheat as they grow around the nobles' feet. Stalks shoot up from the leaves, flowers blooming from them, their petals curving inward before flaring out like white trumpets.

"This has to be some kind of trick," the duchess squeals.

I resist the itch to grab my blade just in case.

"It's for peace. We can heal it together," Rosemary says, in imperfect Sartealean. She must have practiced this line for this moment. "Life can still grow here."

She waves her hands over the non-arable soil as she stands, and I take a step forward, wanting to study her creation. She grips my hand and gives me a warning glance.

"Please, Winifred," Lady Myrren implores. "Consider cooperating. For our kingdom. For all Sartealeans."

"For all Sartealeans," the duchess echoes, picking a flower and holding it to her nose. "Maybe."

Everyone seems woozy, working in a daze as we deliberate over the terms of a new treaty. We agree to take down the camp in Claw Ridge, and I promise not to use Vellesse's flame if there's not a direct threat to the Dragon Valley or the kingdom itself. The blockade will come to an end, and we will convene quarterly to see how our plan is working.

At the end of our meeting, the nobles head back to the fortress to spend the night before traveling. Lady Myrren wanders off with Nylah, Vencel, and Brona, leaving Rosemary and me alone in her patch of white flowers.

"What kind of sorcery did you use this time, little witch?"

"What makes you think I did?" she asks coyly.

"That went smoothly after your flowers bloomed. Too smoothly."

"Datura doesn't grow in Sarteal, does it?" She picks a flower and twirls it between her fingers.

I study its flared edges. "I've never seen it."

"They release a chemical that can alter one's state of mind and leave them susceptible to manipulation. It can help to lower their defenses, making them easily influenced." She holds it over her mouth to hide her smile—a fleeting curve of her lips. I hold onto it, knowing there will be more ahead. We're wallowing through grief together, but the sun will shine again. "I hope you don't mind. I'm so tired of fighting."

So am I. I've been tired for a long, long time.

"I never mind your tricks," I say. "Let's go home."

Tonight we'll head back to Claw Ridge, and in the coming months, we'll fly back to the Dragon Valley to start our forever. Broken, but together.

ROSEMARY. THREE YEARS LATER.

"This dream again?" Carabosse steps into the Hartwood behind me, and the ground stops churning. She waves her hand, banishing the nightmare scene and replacing it with the sharp rock formations of Claw Ridge. We dangle our legs over the ledge of the highest one, looking at the peaceful grounds below.

We're far from the former military base now, but this is how it is. There are no more tents. The area isn't a battleground. A fragile peace was created by our new treaty, and it's lasted, growing stronger over the past few years.

We lean against each other, watching the sun come up together. The rays filter in from our reality, shining through the transparent sliding door we've fitted over the opening of our dwelling. It rouses us from our sleep.

I open my eyes slowly, finding Carabosse lying next to me. Her hair is a mess as she lifts her head from where she dozed off near my breasts.

"Good morning," she says, groggy after staying up too late last night, listening to me chatter about my day at the healing center in Tresoran. She kisses my nipple and gently tugs it between her teeth.

"Aren't you ever tired of me?" I ask, laughing as I roll onto my back. I sprawl out so she can climb on top of me.

She gives me a devilish grin. "You? Never."

Coasting warm kisses down my belly, she flicks her eyes upward, checking in. She's insatiable, but there've been times when I've closed myself off to grieve, and she's always been patient with me. In the months after my godmothers were taken by the Hartwood, I only wanted to be held. And she was there for me, her arms pulling me in close each time I crawled into bed.

When I finally turned to her in the middle of the night, she made it last for hours, pouring love back into me slowly, reminding me how good it could feel to be inside of my body.

I stroke her hair back from her face and arch my back to show her how eager I am for her to move between my legs. Our nightstand is filled with toys and lotions, but these moments are my favorite. The lazy mornings where we twist ourselves up in the sheets and use our tongues and fingers. I prop up on my pillow to watch her, biting my lip as I see her hips rolling on the mattress, her hand tucked beneath them.

She comes before I do, licking me as she moans against my pussy, the noise sending me over the edge. Kissing my thighs, she grazes her mouth over my body and crawls up beside me. An afterwave of my orgasm shivers through me as she trails a finger down my spine. One of my tendrils curls toward her, a peach swelling on the vine, perfectly ripe as it drops into her hand. She rubs her thumb over the fuzzy skin and takes a bite. Her mouth is sweet when we kiss.

"We have to finish getting our bags packed," I say, curling my toes along her shins.

"My bag is already packed." She places the peach pit on the

nightstand and pulls the blanket over her head. "I can stay in bed for another twenty minutes."

"Don't you think you need more than a pair of riding leathers to bring on our trip?" I ask, stepping into my dress. I open a dresser drawer, filling my bag with extra ribbons and undergarments. Our dwelling feels like a home now. It's decorated with Diana's needlepoint projects. Marian sent them to me, along with a couple paintings. A journal lies on the dresser, filled with the spells my godmothers wanted to pass down to me.

"We're only going to be in Corstylia for a few days," she says.

"But I'm not sure what's in style there." I hold up two dresses and throw them both in the bag. "We're meeting with two of the realm's greatest inventors. I don't want them to think I'm not taking them seriously."

"Don't worry. I don't think they'll mind what you're wearing." She lowers the blanket. "Bellamy and her father are quite...eccentric."

"What does that mean?"

She grins. "You'll see when we get there."

We've been working with the duo to improve the infrastructure of the Dragon Valley for a while, but this will be my first time meeting them. I cinch my bag and tear a few pages from my notebook where I've jotted down the questions I have for Bellamy about medical equipment so that I can share any new knowledge with Felix.

"I think that's it." I fold my notes into my satchel and wait for Sun and Moon to arrive. They outgrew their loft two years ago and took off into the Dragon Valley. I miss them being so close to me at all times, but they're never too far away. I roll the door back, thankful for the breeze and good flying conditions.

This will be their longest flight yet.

Carabosse groans and gets dressed. She's belting her riding breeches when a crow flies in and settles on the dresser. We both look at each other.

It's been some time since we've received one of these messages.

"I can read it if you want," she offers as I take the parchment roll from the bird's beak.

"It's ok." I open it, and another sealed roll falls onto the floor. I breathe to loosen the knot of anxiety in my belly as I read it aloud, "Dear R and C, thank you so much for our wedding gifts. I'm glad things are going well in Sarteal. Things in Lollishire have settled down too. People are starting to relax and accept that there'll be no more May Day feasts. I'm writing to you because we heard the strangest tale from a swarm of pixies when we went to return the missing pages of the *Grimoire of the Devouring Tree* back to the Woodland Temple. It reminded me of my favorite apothecary and her lover from Faerie. X-O-X-O. Your friend, Robin. R and M."

Carabosse takes the other parchment roll and opens the seal. An amethyst pendant slides into her hand. She holds it up for me. "Do you recognize this?"

My heart pinches for a second, remembering the day I received it and the day I lost it—two separate events that stand out in my memories. They're both important chapters in my story. "Yes, Candide gave it to me."

"Here, let me put it on you," she says, understanding its significance. I turn around and she fastens the clasp, brushing the baby hairs at the nape of my neck. I hold the pendant to my heart.

I still ache for what my godmothers gave, but I can feel the strings connecting me to the Hartwood, to them. They live peacefully now, dancing in the forest with each other and their friends. They don't feel any of the fear that constantly plagued them when they were raising me.

I remind myself to be happy for them. I know they wouldn't have done anything differently.

"Sun and Moon are here," Carabosse announces, and I step out to the ledge, ready for our adventure. My hatchlings are the size of horses now, excited to stretch their wings.

I jump off and land on Moon's back, gliding between Sun and Snovida. A soft summer mist rolls in as we head north, and the scent of petrichor rises from the ground below. Wildflowers pepper the soil, their petals opening to sing to me, calling for me to come home.

"Zelladine, Zelladine."

But I'm Rosemary, the little witch raised by Diana, Grace, and Candide. I have my wraith, my Sun, and my Moon beside me as we fly off to explore a new kingdom. I fling a vine out, and Carabosse cheers as I practice transferring to Sun's back.

I know I'm exactly where I'm meant to be.

ACKNOWLEDGMENTS

First of all, thank you so much for reading Carabosse and Rosemary's story! This was a story I dreamed of for so long, and I'm so grateful I got to tell it.

Thank you to my writer friends for your encouragement (Vicky and Amelia especially)

Also I owe my 2 am writing sessions to the Hadestown soundtrack and nerds gummy clusters. <3

I'm so excited to share more fairytales with you. Keep an eye out for Of Salt and Air—my Little Mermaid retelling coming soon!

Feel free to subscribe to my newsletter Hearts and Hauntings if you'd like to stay updated!

ALSO BY DARVA GREEN

Happily Ever After Dark

Of Tides and Snow

Of Dreams and Poison

Dreamers and Demons Series (All Sapphic)

She Came from the Swamp

She Came at Midnight

She Came for Blood